on

SOLWAY SAND

The Borderer Chronicles

(Other titles in the series by the same author)

Three Hills

Devotion and the Devil

MARK MONTGOMERY

on SOLWAY SAND

First published in Great Britain in 2014 by ruffthedog.com

Front cover; ruffthedog.com

ISBN-13: 978-1505612738

For the heart of West Cumbria; its people born;
its strength.

THE BORDERER CHRONICLES

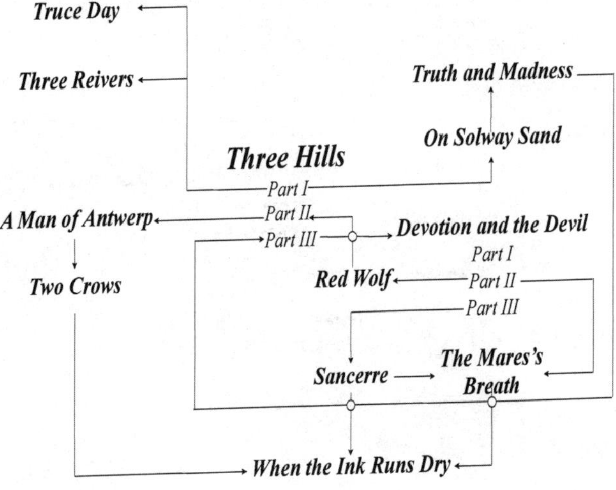

The Borders

The world of John Brownfield

Introduction

The year is 1554. Winter has come to its end. Mary Tudor, following the attempted coup and a brief 'reign' of nine days by Lady Jane Grey, has become queen and has sat on the throne of England and Ireland for nine months (with her claim to the French Crown still declared). Protestant rebellion still threatens her throne, and Princess Elizabeth, her half sister and the rebellion's figurehead, has been removed to the Tower. Plans of marriage between Queen Mary and Phillip of Spain threatens peace, as France, allied with Scotland, is already at war with Spain.

By the end of the year, England once more will be reconciled to Rome, and Mary will have re-established Roman Catholicism over a people already settled on a new Protestant Church, greatly advanced under her brother's reign. Scotland is already in the throws of Protestant Reformation, although a Catholic queen will rule through her French Mother, Marie of Guise.

Any relative peace that stood between Scotland and England is again threatened, and once again life in the Borders, that hard-lived strip of territory, split into six warden administered territories; the English and Scottish, West, Middle and East Marches, is prepared for conflict.

However, in a borderland already deformed by two hundred

and fifty years of repeated incursion by opposing English and Scottish monarchs, further conflict is but another day in a society already degraded by the misery of war. The need to survive, with honest industry almost impossible to maintain, has families and factions feeding off each other, by way of robbery, ransom and blackmail. Villainy knows no nation, as heinous crime is afflicted on cross-border neighbours and domestic neighbour alike.

The people are hard pressed in such a lawless land, more so the bringers of the law; the March Wardens, those with responsibility to administer the Borders; men of mettle, embattling to maintain order, whilst perversely sponsoring cross-border raiding to satisfy their monarchs' whims. In amongst the war they bring, they keep the peace and maintain the law, in a time of clans, gangs and reivers.

Amongst this uneasy political backdrop, continues the tales of lives led amongst the English and Scottish West Marches. *On Solway Sand* is the third volume of the *Borderer Chronicles*. It continues the story from the end of *Part 1* of *Three Hills*, and sees our man, John 'Jack' Brownfield, short-time married and re-established with his kin in the Scottish West March.

In fictionalising a life led from only a few scraps of history, allows a writer to be indulgent; to write our hero's story influenced not only by the histories of his own time, and nature of his world, but from a homage to the remembrances of the author's own past and sights and stories that are priceless for what they represent.

So it is my discovery of the Solway Coast that has formed the setting for this story, and a love grown by chance for this quiet area of Cumbria, and my earnest wish to point the way to a beauty often overlooked, because it lies in the shadows of the mountains of the Lake District National Park, or within the boundaries of

Galloway, little travelled by the tourist.

My second indulgence is the core of the story, taken in part from a screenplay; Akira Kurosawa's, *The Seven Samurai*, a tale of seven warriors who defend a village from a large band of brigands, and its subsequent reworking as a classic western movie, *The Magnificent Seven.*

These tales are not precious to me for what they tell, but as films that ignited a life-long passion for Japan's medieval history and a memory of Saturday afternoons sitting with my father; rare moments when a hard-working man had time to spend with his son and watch the greatest of all film-genres, the Western.

So I don't apologise for writing an historical tour guide to my beloved Solway Coast, or for borrowing the story of another. For the setting is worthy of a good story, and the story of good people overcoming an overwhelming evil, with the help of a few tarnished souls, is indeed a yarn worth the telling.

On Solway Sand

They said, on Solway, we once lived well,
with good abbey yonder, my ma would tell.
But now we live poor on Solway sand,
with faces to the sea, and backs to the land.

The men took all—hurt me too,
and left us nowt to see us through.
No pigs, no hens, no blanket, no pot.
It's easy to see what we've nae got.

But Ma says the land and sea are our blessin'.
But a meagre basket of berries and poor fishin',
does nae bring comfort to ma belly, only grumble.
My belly grows big now… I don't know how.

I had a pa. He was killed by the sea.
I had brothers, but fever killed them three.
Two sisters followed. They're earth's dust now,
buried in a wood somewhere, took from my sight for want of care.

I remember my ma tellin' me to work hard and I would prosper.
She worked hard and she did suffer.
We all do… in the Reivers' wake.
We all do, on Solway Sand.

Anon

Prologue

April 1554

The Solway Plain was always a better place to be when the sun shone. Winter or summer, spring or autumn, there was very little sense of the discord that filled the world of man. There was only a sense of God's good work in His placing of His green, and tree, and sea.

All was perfectly set down for sheep, and the shepherding man loved the land and the bounty it provided. There was always good grass, with trees surrounding—filtering the wind that blew from the Solway sea to the west, and from the Cumberland Hills to the east.

The shepherding man on the plain was free of his troubles—nettling mother and quarrelsome wife. He could sing without censure, curse without rebuke, and scratch his nether-places without scold. His sheep bleated a kindlier tune than his womenfolk. They caused him no pain, well not so much to cause him to cuss so bitter.

In all, the Plain held good things to quieten his mind, and to enrich the flavour of good bread made, and his beer to drink.

So with bread to scoff and beer to quaff, he lay on the grass to look at his world, and to think on how to make it even better. He looked to the trees, the grass and the sky, and all was perfect. Nothing he thought could make it finer. Then he looked to his shirt, patched and worn; his jerkin, cut and torn; and his hose, dirty, his codpiece stained; and then examined his poor brogues, rough and patched a dozen times more than his shirt. So he imagined himself in better boots, and then in hose of finer knit, a shirt of linen perhaps, and a doublet of better cut, and perhaps even a livery coat of fine colour—*a soldier's coat.* He thought some more on the soldier caste and the two-penny a week pay as a reward for wearing finer clothes and polished steel to better see him safe. And so into reverie he went, marching proudly through his new imagined world with strut and bluster.

Then perchance a horseman came into view. One carrying arms and wearing better clothes. He appeared from the trees. He stepped the narrow path that would see him join the road to the coast.

A soldier in steel, or a reiver set on stealing? the shepherd pondered, and he thought to hide in case ill fortune was about to spoil his fine sunny day. But the man thought, *no reiver would ride alone.* So he stood his ground to see the handsome show. Then a second appeared, and a third, and more. And the man counted to be sure of their number. So when those who had a concern asked him, the information he gave would be true. He counted in shepherd tongue—shepherd count, *'Yan, t'yan, tethera, methera, pimp, sethera...'* Then a woman appeared, and he thought to stop counting.

Six men bearing arms on the road to the coast. From Holm Cultram to the sea; to the Solway... Skinburness perhaps, Mawbray... or Allonby?

And as he thought, he studied the woman, old and grey. But

she rode in armour—reinforced jack and cuirass. Steel skullcap and mail collar. But she carried a broom not a spear. The man looked at her face, worn ragged with life. But in her countenance was a strength and purpose. So he counted the soldiers again… *'Yan, t'yan, tethera, methera, pimp, sethera... lethera—seven.'*

Dumfries
Annan
Kirkcudbright
Bowness
Carlisle
Skinburness
Holme Cultram
The Solway
Wigton
Allonby
Ellenborough
Workington
On Solway Sand

Chapter I

Cumbria's Solway Coast, February 1554

Behind closed eyes the priest said a prayer. He brought all his devotion and belief to bear on his words. Earnest words, softly spoken so that all around him could only see his lips move. Quiet words, so they could not hear his supplication to God. His request for God's will to be done… and perhaps spare His faithful servant for further works on Earth, rather than in Heaven.

He kept tight his eyes, so that he may be spared the sight of the old-grey reiver's blade cutting deep into his flesh, or so that he may be given a few moments more of life. He thought, even an executioner would not strike while a prayer was being offered by the condemned. But no shroud of darkness could hide the priest from the cruel sound of the reiver's words and his fell intent.

'I'm nae fer killin' a man o' God… but I'm not too feared o' the Almighty tae beat his man a little… or aplenty. Now betake yerself from harms way, or bleed. It's up tae ye, *Priest man.*'

The priest stood tall. He was afraid. It was plain for all to see. Yet he stood tall—a little taller than a moment past, because he knew death was no longer imminent. He opened his eyes and unclasped his hands. He maintained his place between the reiver and the two village men, kneeling in the dirt. The priest's hands shook, and he looked to them as if to tell them to hold steady, but they disobeyed, so instead he brought them back together to grip them hard and pull them into his chest… and again he pleaded.

'Leave this place. Leave these good honest folk. Stay your violence and go back to your homes and leave these people to their homes… in peace.'

The old-grey reiver stepped forward, within a sword's length from the priest, his torch held high, contorting his face into inhuman feature. He brought the point of his sword to rest under Thomas' chin, forcing the priest to raise his head away from the hurt of the blade.

'You deserve a better flock, Priest. I suspect ye're the only man here. But ye too are a sorry excuse fer a man… because ye piss yer pants at the end of my blade, Whit's the matter, *God Man,* are ye nae a pious man? Dae demons await ye in the after-life?'

The reiver felt the tension in the sword as it pressed up into the priest's chin. He thought on the pleasure of striking hard it home, to see a throat cut and the reward of deep red blood issuing onto his steel.

How best tae see my blade, but covered with a pious man's blood.

'No!'

The scream was loud and redirected many eyes off the reiver and the priest towards its source. A woman in finer clothes stood from the crowd in the darkness, bold and brave amongst the reiver men.

'No! You cannot do that… You cannot kill him. Your soul will be forever damned!'

The old-grey reiver looked at the woman, angered that his contemplation of murder be rudely interrupted. He spat his words.

'Lassie, shut yer gob.'

But the woman did not take heed of the reiver's rebuke, and

she shouted, 'You cannot kill him… *Thou shalt not kill!*'

The old-grey reiver broke his attention away from the priest. He removed his sword point, and marched over to face the woman. He intended his foul presence to quieten her, but she remained unmoved by his intimidation. Her eyes flashed defiance, cursing the man. The reiver was held for a moment by the power of the woman's gaze. But anger was about him, and he brought up his left hand to strike hard her cheek, with force enough to bring the woman to her knees; the pain, strong enough to bring her hand up to cup her cheek to soothe the hurt; the act, shocking enough to disarm her defiance.

She looked up, as a child would look up to a scolding parent.

'Ye're lucky, lass, I dinnae cut ye, or have my men here sully ye a little. But I know ye and yer family, and I would nae have yer menfolk seekin' retribution fer one of their womenfolk murdered or defiled.'

The woman nursed her hurt, but her face regained its condemnation of the old-grey reiver. And again she stood up, defiant.

'I am Mary Brownfield, and I need no family name to save my skirts. God and good justice will see you hang for what you do here this night.'

The old-grey reiver simply turned his face, and with a nod of his head signalled his men to open fire. Five matchlocks ignited and flashed, and as the priest threw his arms around his head in futile protection. The two village men next to him dropped like sacks. Both dead.

The reiver rubbed his grey beard, and thrust his sword into the ground, crouching down, disappointed not to have killed the two men himself. Another reiver came close and stood by his side. The old-grey reiver gestured with a finger pointed at Mary, and with brute force the other reiver dragged Mary back to the other women, standing under guard.

'Mind ye stay yer ardour, Richie,' he shouted to the reiver, and he rose up to look at the world around him.

He ordered five of his men to marshal the village women and young children into a pen, where stood a dozen sheep. Other reivers, with torches, directed the remaining village men, older boys and two young girls to pick from a pile; made of spelk basket, barrel, creel, bag and chest. And a line formed as they walked the quarter mile to the sea, across the mass expanse of Allonby sands, towards three boats resting at the limit, on waters edge, marked with torches bright.

The old-grey reiver stood and stretched as though he had been confined for a long while, and walked to a group of his men idle, whilst others were busy.

'Lads, dinnae just stand there scratchin' yer balls. Tide's comin' in.' He looked to the east and the outline of the Cumberland hills in the distance. 'Daylight comes too. So gather up the rest of our spoils. Load the boats. Time to go, afore the English Warden drinks enough courage tae come and face us… *eh?'*

The men dispersed. Not in obedience of their leader, but spurred on by the danger of a counter from an English force.

The old-grey reiver walked back to the kneeling priest, cradling one of the fallen villagers, giving the last rites to a man already dead; comfort as he could to a man past comforting.

The reiver growled at the priest, 'Father, I will have compliance from these rabbits, nae defiance.'

The sight of tears met the reiver—sobs from Thomas. 'You… you take their food… their pride… their… their… daughters.'

'English pig-pokers have nae pride, and their daughters will find mair pleasure with real men tae service, rather than these sorry boys.' The reiver sniffed the air above the dead men, then continued. 'I dinnae smell dead men, only pig shite.'

'It's the smell of honest toil, you *bastard.*'

'I toil too, Father… believe me. It's nae easy work, keepin' seventy fightin' boys happy, fed and content. I doubt whether I have the pickin's here tae see my men through the month, never mind the rest of winter's cost… I expect better pickin's on my return. Perhaps even the silver from yer church?'

The old-grey reiver then climbed a nearby barrel, left by the men on its transit to the reivers' boats. He looked around at the distress on the villagers' faces, none daring to catch his eye, lest the reiver took offence and meted out more cruelty. He studied the activity of his men, and took a longer look at the woman who defied him, now being comforted by another older woman. He then addressed all that stood around him. All that could hear.

'Ye all listen… Be grateful tae me… Be thankful for ma generosity, that I leave ye with yer lives and most yer daughters. Be grateful, I leave ye with some stores tae see ye through the winter. We'll be back again in spring tae collect mair spoils… So work hard, and make sure I'm in gud temper when I return. And be certain that ye show us better courtesy than ye did tonight… Fer it will nae be men we slaughter, but yer homes and farms we burn.'

It was a little while after the reivers had left, that the scream was heard. A louder distress than the cries of other villagers counting their cost, their losses. A woman's scream. Piercing. Chilling. Her loss was terrifying and all looked to its source.

It was Thomas and Mary, still nursing her hurt, the Blacksmith and his neighbour; the farmer and his wife, that ran to the house at the end of the village, to one of the fishermen's cottages that faced the beach and the sea.

At the front of the cottage, near the doorway, Meg kneeled in the dirt, face down, tears and snot dripping on the earth. Her world was taken, and she was left only grief, and undeniable pain and loss. The women showed no reserve in their comfort of Meg. She was inconsolable. The men stood around helpless in their action, awkward in their response.

It was Thomas and the Blacksmith that entered the cottage, stooping through the low head of the doorway, walking hesitantly the reed floor into the small room, shared by all that lived there; four generations of *Haytons*.

The fire was lit in the centre of the room, and the iron pot over the fire, hung by its long chain from the roof beam, bubbled and spat. It shared the beam with three generations of Meg's family. But unlike the cauldron pot, no life was in them. Her father, her husband, and her son hung from the roof truss. Their bodies hung limp. Their expressions distorted by fatal choking. Faces blackened and bloodied by beatings.

The horror quietened already sickened men, not finding words to convey thought to mouth. But more abomination met the men as they examined the room around them, their eyes desperate to leave the sight of death and find life. They looked for the crib, for baby Henry Hayton, three months old and fresh life for a growing village.

Even in poor light, the crib was easy to find in a small room sparsely furnished. Easier, as it was in the best of the room, close to the growing light of the window, shutters now open wide to the smell of the sea. Thomas walked over to the oak cradle, to open the folds of blanket that covered the infant… but he knew the worst of it before he uncovered the child.

His horror was absolute. Death total. And Thomas looked above him, at the Hayton men, and then back to the dead infant––to him who would be a Hayton man if he were allowed life.

All were dead in this house.

He lifted the infant in his arms to give it comfort. He uttered a low prayer and offered the rite of the dead. He cradled the babe like it was still alive, with a gentle hand held under its little head, holding him carefully so not to disturb him in his sleep.

Thomas closed his eyes to see the child in Heaven.

He took Henry Hayton out to reunite him with Meg, his grandmother, his own mother already in Heaven, waiting for him these past three months. She died giving him life, only for the cruelty of men to steal it. Perhaps she would be happy to see him, or perhaps be sad it was so soon.

Liddesdale

Chapter II

Liddesdale, Scotland, March 1554

'*Da*'s layin' out these hills wi' new woodland.'

Will sat, stretched tall in his saddle. He stroked away the irritation of his seven-day beard as he scanned the line of each rise in the land, imagining new tree lines to break the rounded summits, lying alternating dark and light under the shade of storm clouds that threatened the fell.

'*Da* says it's a time fer givin' tae the land, and nae takin' from it.'

He held his head back, hand running against the flow of new hair on his neck. He breathed in deeply, drawing the cool air through his teeth to taste it. He smiled, taking comfort from the rolling lands, and his smile grew broader as he thought of them as his one day.

'It's gud air we breathe, and there's nae better place tae be, *eh, Jack?*'

Will waited on Jack's response. But none came. Instead, Jack was caught in a moment of his own, lost in the grandness of the sky's canvas, and its notion of drama played out above the open lands of the Teviot Valley in the distance.

'*Da* says a hundred 'n' mair years o' timber felled in the low areas and nae replanted is poor policy fer oor family's fair issue. He says timber is wealth tae plant fer oor bairn's bairns… He thinks these hills and mosses are only fit fer trees and raggedy beasts. I think he's wise man tae think of it so… *eh, Jack?*'

Jack kept silent. He kept his mind's view on the sky, and his ear tuned to the water playing on the rocks as it broke free the hill to travel its course down the steep slope. He did not want to counter his brother. Nor did he did not want to question his father's notion of fair issue. But he could not help sighing, since no children ran the fields around his father's tower house.

He thought on his father with two sons and a third already lost before his full time; swallowed by the Moss eleven years ago. Three sons born; one dead and none with sons to call their own. No children at all to call out 'daddy' in the night, when bad dreams awaken the innocent. This was hardly fair issue. Will was twenty-eight and still without a wife, or even bastards to call him father. Jack was twenty, married to Mary and childless. No, this was not fair issue, when the hopes and dreams of an old man are not matched by the actuality of sons without progeny. And Jack sighed again with the thought of his father's aspiration ridiculed by the foolish boasting of his brother with self-serving bequest on his mind.

Jack looked at Will, fevered at the thought of the land, and the esteem it held for his name, but not his own, as Jack had long ago distanced himself from his clan name and all the meaning it held. He fashioned himself by another name, *John Brownfield*, an alias given to him in internment when he was a boy.

Jack knew the land upon his father's death would be given over to the eldest son, against legal expectation of a land divided between offspring. Jack would inherit only cold cash, a bequest without moral obligation to hold him place, which was as well, because his heart had left his father's realm long ago. He held his thought and bitterness, and instead smiled at his brother, glad the mantle of responsibility was not his, but the man who was shifting on his mount to see better the figures planting the saplings on the hillside in the distance.

'They will be finished plantin' by month's end. Aye, *Da* sees the need for new income, and our neighbours only clearing good woodland for better lowland pasture. He sees a shortage of timber and the potential for profit. He says these *fir* saplings will grow fast and provide fair timber tae fell. It's time tae put the land tae profit instead of stealin' from it.' Will winked at Jack. 'We'll concentrate on stealin' oor neighbours profit instead, *eh Jack?*'

But Jack had changed his view from his brother, because the power of the sky had brought him back to absorb him into a day's dream—thoughts of another land, under another sky. He neither looked to Will, nor to the labour on the hillside.

Will turned his view to Jack, to study him. He sighed. He drew in a breath that held both the envy he held for his brother's form, made stronger and better by time, and his sadness that his brother was a man different. He thought Jack was lost again, as he had been so many times this past year; a man with no head or heart for his place in the world, and sorry company because of it. So Will thought, jest at the expense of a father, may seek a better response from a brother, rather than praise of a father's prudence.

'What's the auld man thinkin', *eh Jack?* Mair wood tae keep his brittle auld bones warm this winter, or mair wood tae build a hundred miles o' palisade around oor lands tae keep the thievin' Elliots oot?'

Jack was not interested in hearing Will's poor attempt at wit and scoff. Will being favoured by a father, and in turn enamoured with him. Instead he dismounted and pulled a cup from his saddlebag, running his fingers around the inside to inspect the vessel for cleanliness. He then walked over to the stream's head, filling the horn beaker with the fresh cold water that tumbled over the rocks running a course from high hilltop to river's route along the bottom of the valley.

Will was caught, still amused at his own wit. 'At least the Armstrongs and the Elliots cannae steal whit's rooted in the ground.'

Jack then caught his brother's eye and he smiled, but not at his father's prudence, or a brother's wit, or even at a brother beloved, but at the irony of circumstance. 'True, they steal everything but the trees and the fields. So instead they'll just wait till we fell and mill the trees. Till our father sells the timber and claims his profit… Then they'll steal you, Will, instead of the trees, and ransom you for ten times your worth… and father will pay… and have the means to do so.'

'They might steal you instead, brother.'

Jack chewed on Will's words and shook his head. 'The second son is worth little.'

'Only while the first son lives,' replied Will.

'Whilst our father maintains his numbers of lances to call upon, and seventy more trained well, to daily walk the walls of his tower, he'll see his riches kept safe.' Jack looked hard at his brother. '*His riches, dear brother.*'

Will met Jack's self-pity with a grimace, and spat out his disdain on the ground, rich and fluid. '*Da* would pay twenty times mair tae see ye safe, and has already paid a hundred times dearer.'

'While I was interred?'

'Aye, while you were interned. Held in a soft gaol by the English, as a pledge while we carried out yer gaoler's biddin'. Fightin' fer the English against our own flag. Dinnae forget it, Jack… *Da* paid dear, and I paid the toll wi' him.'

'And what is our flag, Will? Is it the Saltire? I don't think so…

In the Borders it's only family that is the flag that calls the muster, and one's name is the fealty one fights for.'

'We are Scots, Jack, dinnae forget it.'

Jack grimaced. 'Call me a Scot when it suits, and a Borderer when it pleases. For it often pleases us to see us as separate from Scotland, so we may kiss the English backside.'

Will laughed. 'Aye, Mother Scotland daes breed practical men. We are nothing but a realistic race, *eh Jack*? And sometimes a kiss on the arse is far sweeter than one on the lips.'

Jack looked to the horizon, to the northeast, to where Edinburgh lay in his mind's eye. He was unmoved by the humour of Will, and said, 'Mother Scotland does nothing but abuse its borders. Holds us out like a shield to keep the miserly old woman safe in her bed.' Jacked sneered. He mocked, 'We are nothing but a faithless lover, treating the old woman with scorn, and climbing into the English bed, where the loving is sweetened with gold, kind words and promises… *For we are whoring race.*'

'…With a proud face,' added Will. 'Come brother, let's put our minds tae the task at hand. We've lost twa hundred beasts so far this winter. The Elliots and Grahams have already took us fer plenty. Let's put a stop tae these other foul raiders takin' their share.'

'Yes, brother. Let's remove a few more *reivers* from the land.'

'There's twa hours tae dusk. Still time fer them tae come-a-callin' in daylight tae steal our beasts. We'd better take turns. Put our heids down fer an hour or two. Nae heavy sleep now, best we both keep an ear tae the wind. It'll be another long night if our quarry disnae show their heads afore dark.'

'We should have more men to hand.'

'Where's the sport in that. We'll nae be able tae lift our heids high if we tackle the robbers with mair lances than we two. Best we subdue the vermin ourselves and earn all the glory. Besides mair men would likely scare the knaves off. Them been a cowardly breed… and I'm wanting knave blood on my lance by week's end.'

'You'll not be so bold if a dozen and more come trotting over the hill looking for beasts to take, and you in the way.'

'A dozen and a dozen mair, let them come on. Less tae worry our stock. Less tae bleed our profit, eh?'

'The odds are poor.'

Jack unlaced his leather jack, heavy with reinforcing plates, and free from its suffocation, the cool air lifted Jack's sweated shirt from his skin to bring relief and refreshment to a body that had been confined in its armour for four days.

Will shook his head. 'Ye'd best be leavin' that on… When they come, it'll be without warnin'. Ye'll have nae time tae don yer jack 'o' plate… and without yer waistcoat and doublet, yer skin will be all the mair easy tae prick.'

'Well then, when I'm knee deep in sheep stealers, with nothing but a blade between the killers and my sorry flesh, it'll make the *glory* all the sweeter. Will it not, *Brother*?'

Will smiled. No jibe from Jack's lips would make him sour, or provoke him to anger. His love for Jack was above all that. It always was.

'Then glorious brother, at least leave yer boots on.'

Jack smiled in return. 'I will, esteemed brother.'

ꙮ

He thought to wake Jack. The raiders were out there. Hidden. Waiting. Will knew it. He could feel the rush, the fluid coursing his body, telling him to ready the fight. But the night was too dark. And a torch lit would alarm his foe. Send them scattering for fear of the unknown numbers of men that waited. Men standing between them and their prize. And Will wanted as many pricked as his lance could find. As many bloodied as his skill could attest.

But Will did not know his foe were esurient creatures, with a long practiced knack of separating men from their herds. Sharp-witted and well rehearsed in ambush and diversion. They had lay in wait for three hours, watching Will sitting by Jack, without fire, without men to bolster a man's danger. They were bold, and their leader was without equal. A leader without fear. A leader with a well won reputation amongst his pack; comrades and family with a keen eye to their leader's directions.

Morning was coming. The shapes of the hilltops were clear against the dark sky. The deep shadows fading. Animation returning. A sense of the fells had returned to sight.

Then… a shift in the shadows. Stillness disturbed. A noise heard. Silence broken. A noise more. Animal sounds. Sheep bleating alarm. Horses screaming fear. Beasts on the move.

'Up, Jack!'

'What!' Jack was startled. But awake in a moment.

'Get up, get up, get off yer wet arse, brother. They're here.' Will jumped clear of cover. 'I'm changin' position tae get a shot wi' ma bow—higher on the valley sides. Bring the nags, and we'll run the bastards down. And ye're right…. There must be eight or mair.'

'Wait!' Jack's voice held fear for his brother's safety. Jack did not hesitate, or put on his jack, or retrieve his sword, or his bow wrapped in its cover against the damp, but ran to their horses saddled, kept safe within a gorse corral cut and formed four days past. Lances were affixed to the saddles, pistols already pre-loaded and also wrapped against the damp.

Jack cleared the crest on horseback, Will's horse tethered to his own. He stood the rise for a moment to see Will, not on the slope as he said, bow in hand, but running down the valley in the gloom, towards a natural deep hollow at the base of the hill, ringed high with dry stone and willow hurdles, forming a large pen. He ran towards a young tup, bleating fear. And within a dozen more strides he was amongst the raiders. Eight hungry for spoil, all with murder in their minds.

Wolves.

The beasts were startled by the appearance of Will, and suddenly their easy prey was more, rather than less, in the taking.

Jack steered his horse down towards Will, who had set himself between the young tup, a yearling ram, and the wolves, emboldened by their numbers. They were not for hesitating. The leader directed, and three advanced close on Will. They approached, lying low with furrowed brows, ears forward, and snarling with fixed intent on Will's threat. Two travelled a wide arc to come behind the lone fighter and two held back ready to snatch the tup, now straining against his tether.

But Jack came galloping from behind and scattered the pack's plan to the dawn.

He fired his pistols. Only one discharged and missed. But the impetuous of Jack riding into the circle and the pistol noise was enough to distract the wolves. It allowed Will to lunge at a faltering wolf, who had moved within Will's cutting arc. He lunged with his sword. The cries told all, and a wolf lay on the ground, bloodied, but not dead.

Jack's horse thought better of the fight and reared throwing Jack into the heather. A wolf and his lesser brother thought him an easy kill. One took his arm, and bit into felt wrappings Jack had placed beneath his shirt for protection. Jack felt the wolf's bite. Jaws clamping hard. His arm held firm. But he was able to bring his other hand and his dagger to puncture deep into the wolf's ear. It released Jack's arm to fall dead. The other wolf took Jack's leg and tore into his high-cut-leather riding boot, but the thick leather saved him from cut. Jack lashed out with his dagger. He punched hard the side of the wolf, but it would not release.

Will reached Jack, and descended on the wolf still tearing and shaking Jack's leg. He thrust his sword, two handed, into the wolf's back, killing it.

The other wolves retreated thinking better of the fight.

'Not a happy ambush, Will.' Jack examined his torn shirt and cut boot. 'Three should have been three more, at least.' Jack rubbed his arm, showing red and hurting from the wolf's bite. 'Four days, wet-arsed in the heather, for three mangy curs is poor reward.' And looking back to where the tup was tethered, Jack saw it dead on the ground. 'And we lost the tup. Where was your bow?'

'I wanted tae get ma blood stirin'. I've been spoilin' fer a gud scrap. It seemed a fairer fight tae get well amongst them.'

'*Brother*, you are lucky your blood isn't running all over the fell.'

'Nae, *Brother*, it would take a hundred wolves tae manage that.'

'I doubt there's a hundred wolves left in the Borders.'

'Well there are three less now.' Will examined one of the dead wolves. 'And this ones cubbin', so there'll be wee ones in her lair without their ma tae fend fer them, so perhaps three or four fewer still.'

'I doubt our father will count them in our tally,' replied Jack.

'I doubt da will even count the ones we kill,' added Will.

Chapter III

The stranger

Four hours off the fell, and an hour onto better-travelled roads, Will and Jack came upon two wagoners with their goods laden for *Hawick* market in the morning. Only one draught ox pulled their cart of kegs and bushel baskets; a beast worked harder since its pair was stolen Sunday past. The wagoners breathed easier to see the men pass by, and Will and Jack breathed better to be past the smell of fish too long out the water.

Will looked back to the cart as soon as its drivers were out of earshot. 'It's a poor beast tae pull that burden on its own. Better the idle sods be yoked, and let the ox eat grass. The beast be far more valuable than men in these parts.'

'Yes, Will, the beasts have value—shillings. A man's life—but a penny.'

'I wish a man's life *were* worth a penny piece, then I'd be five shillings richer, *eh Jack?*'

Jack smiled sweetly at his brother and his tally of men killed by an able man.

An hour further along the road, the two wagoners came upon three more men, travelling.

'Draw your knife, Tom. More men. But these smell like strangers. Prickly ones for sure, for their steel shines in the sun.'

Tom, the elder of the two men, looked ahead. He saw the three horsemen riding the path around the hillside, at a point where it skirted a stream. The sun glinted off their steel, but barely. He took a minute to study the strangers before replying.

'Aye, *Dickie Twa Names*, (*twa* or two names, because some called him Robert, some called him Dickie). They're armed reet enough, but one good nag between three doesn't shout robbers or reivers, for I doubt whether those plough nags could gallop a good raid.'

As the two parties approached each other, the two wagoners observed what they thought was steel was in fact iridescence shining in the sun, for the lead man wore a jacket and cloak of lustrous peacock hues, satin and silk. He was accompanied by two large men; servants; farmers or labourers by their clothes, but armed with as many pistols, cleavers and blades as a man could carry. But Tom, who was a man of forty, and twenty years of it warring overseas, could see the big men were dullards. Men who armed themselves as if the more tools he carried, a better craftsman would be made. But he could see these oxen were no craftsman, no soldier men, but brawlers, no doubt selected from the man's employ for their size, or pulled from a local inn for a few shillings to act as poor-picked escort for a gentleman not used to travelling dangerous lanes.

The peacock-dressed gentleman looked the wagoners up and down. 'Excuse me, good and gentle sirs, am I in fair Scotland? Am I where I desire to be?'

Tom looked to the man, and hearing what he thought was a southern brogue, he spat to the ground, wiping away any discharge that had clung to his lips. 'If ye had passed the marker on the road, ye would know where ye be, and not be a fool to wonder where he was.' Tom spat to the ground again. 'And if ye desire to be at yer final resting place… well ye be here, for many a loon would see ye cut to death for those silks and boots.'

The peacock-dressed gentleman looked at the shining discharge on the ground by the man's boots. He grimaced, bringing his hand to a mouth and nose already assaulted by the odour around him. 'Do you have a fever, sir?'

Tom formed his face sour as his reply. Then added words seeing the peacock-dressed gentleman unmoved by his warring face. 'I thought to polish the road beneath yer feet. Ye being a well-dressed gentleman.'

The gentleman laughed. 'Good, by your wit, I'm sure I've crossed the border. I'm glad to be in Scotland.'

'Glad tae be in Scotland!' exclaimed Tom. 'I've never heard that from an Englishman not intent on burning and stealin' from it.'

The peacock-dressed gentleman smiled. 'I assure you, my fine sirs, my intent is honest, and my purpose for the benefit of good Scottish gentlemen.'

'Gentlemen!' Tom's lips drew a faint smile. 'Then ye be travelling to *Edinburgh*, or *Sterling* perhaps, because ye'll find naught but thieves and loons in this province, *eh Dickie?'*

Dickie returned Tom's sly smile with a nod weakly offered, for he was a mouse in the company of gentlemen.

The peacock-dressed gentleman shifted on his mount, tiring of the wagoner-men's wit. 'Well, I am sure you are very mistaken.' And he poked a shrouded jibe. 'This place breeds fine gentlemen, for I've met two *gentleman* of quality already, so I must be in Scotland.' He smiled to hide his disdain.

Dickie smiled at the stranger's apparent fawning, but Tom

grimaced at the sound of sarcasm, for Tom knew the man's wit and scoff, a trait of gentlemen in fine clothes.

Tom thought to urge his partner on, and leave the peacock to his journey. He thought perhaps he be a *Courtesy Man*; a well dressed affable stranger, friendship his foil, theft his intent. And he looked to the two large ox-men behind him, one with a cudgel resting in his hand. But curiosity kept Tom's familiarity with the stranger, in order to see his game. His knife was at hand, fixed beneath his shirt, and Dickie was no slouch in a brawl. If fell intent be the gentleman's game, the peacock would be the first to suffer.

Tom looked around him. 'Scotland?' Tom smiled, 'If ye stand in Scotland and can still smell England on yer boots, ye are nae in Scotland, ye're in the Borders. And standin' here, ye're so close tae England ye could spit at it.'

'Surely Scotland is Scotland and England is England?' asked the gentleman.

'Nah, Lad. Ye're in the Borders, the Marches. Say other and ye'll only find first-felt hospitality tainted wi' ridicule. The Scot has no land here. On this spot ye're either in clan Armstrong, or clan Elliot… and if ye're not them, ye not even borderers, but sheep tae feed the first.'

'So are you Armstrong or Elliot men?' asked the peacock-dressed gentleman.

'Nah, we are the sheep… but sheep that bite and butt. That is if ye wish to test us with yer sword and yer oxen guard.'

The peacock-dressed gentlemen simply doffed his feathered cap and walked on his horse. He shook his head. Wiped the smell from his nose. Regretted his wasted words on such lowly men. But they were wagoners, and as such carried news across the kingdom. Men to know '*the know*' and all the gossip about.

His guard followed on, one spiting to the ground where the wagoners stood. And both wagoners raised their hands in mock salute to the mounted party.

The thought of 'the know' made the peacock-dressed gentleman reach into his pocket. He searched the space, once filled by a small, red-velvet letter packet, and he pulled out a gold filigrane, kept there to scent his letters. He drew it under his nose to replace fish's foul scent. He smiled, pleased with himself and his act, his show before the wagoners, his feigned patois, for he knew very well his location in the Marches and his own true nationality. His polite acquaintances were made with lowly men only for the intelligences he could glean.

Nothing learned—wasted words.

Chapter IV

Tower, house and hall

Tower…

Within the barmkin walls, standing in the presence of tower and hall, after a week away, and a full day on foot, both brothers were glad to be close to the comfort of a better meal and softer bed. But before them were a father and a wife; two not best met when fatigue was their mantle and wits found wanting. Because for all their fellowship, better shared on moor and moss, their accounts were lacking. Will saw his kill as poor payment for a week away from duties better served on his father's estates, and Jack saw his time away poor in terms of absence, because before him stood responsibility better avoided.

'We'll talk on this matter nae mair, lass.'

'But...'

'Nae buts, lassie... There's nae mair tae be said.'

Jack was concerned, not for his wife, but what topic had nettled his father so.

Mary had not seen Jack approach. She had hoped her request

to her father-in-law could be made without his involvement, for she knew she would not have her husband's support.

She turned, and was shocked to see Jack standing. She hoped he had not heard his father's rebuttal, and she retreated with only a nod of greeting to her husband—indifference to a man not seen for thirty days.

Jack's father turned his attention to his two sons approaching the hall, three wolves tied about their horses. Horses unhappy to have dead meat about their flanks.

'Why dae ye fetch their stinkin' carcasses into my tower? Seekin' praise, boys? Expecting bonus from yer *pa*? A coin or two perhaps? Bring me half the dozen mair, and ye shall have it!'

He walked past his sons to inspect his sons' kill; one large dog, one smaller dog and a small young bitch. 'Seven days away and only three tae show me.' He ran his hands over the larger dog's carcass, his eyes holding a sadness from his two sons, for a bold beast killed. 'Better ye hung them from the trees, or traded their carcasses fer bounty… Better ye come tae my table wi' tall tales of a score killed fer all yer efforts.' He feigned a sniff of a poor smell found. 'In sooth, I'm nae so sure they're even fresh. Did ye buy them already killed, from an auld tinker on the road, perhaps?' He stared at Will, then at Jack. 'Well did ye?'

Both sons wanted to lower their eyes to the ground, but both men held their father's stare.

'Go!' A father looked away, his hands gesturing; pushing away his two sons. 'Go! Go see yer ma. Have her wipe yer noses!' Then he turned again, to look upon two sons, loved, but not regarded. 'I suspect even yer ma will not be too fond… Boys… Boys who shy away… Boys who forget their responsibilities.'

Jack just looked at Will, and Will said all to Jack with his eyes—*say nothing.*

'We've a guest. A guest from Edinburgh, wi' greetin's from the

Earl of Arran.' Their father turned again and walked away, still barking. 'Supper is within the hour. Go clean the stink from ye. Yer ma will nae thank thee for bringing the smell o' death intae her hall, and mud onto her floors.'

'Fret not, Jack,' said Will, looking to make sure his father was out of earshot. 'If we'd brought twenty back, he'd expect twenty mair.'

Will beckoned one of the young boys, moving fodder from the last haystack standing, to take the horses. 'Archie, see tae the nags, and take the wolves tae the sheriff. Take a couple of yer boys wi' ye. Claim any bounty, and share it amongst yerselves.'

Archie smiled, eager to see more coin in his pocket, and broader with the thought of trip into Langholm, with coin to spend and friends around to see it spent.

'Mind ye wrap them,' shouted Will, '…and mind they're nae takin' from ye by bigger boys on the road. We've mair thieves than wolves in this shire.'

Archie grabbed the horses' reigns and at the trot he ran them to the stabling, hearing Will's words ringing in his ears as he ran.

Will walked up to the remainder of the haystack, about ten barrow fills. 'We'll need two haystacks mair this next winter season… Eight is nae enough tae see our beasts through the winter, especially with raidin' lasting longer into spring. We'll be needin' tae keep our own beasts longer behind walls, fer protection.'

'And what about our tenants? They've no stone walls to see them safe.' Jack was mindful it was a long winter for many, and a hard winter for more, with so many mouths to feed. It often meant as many oats went into the mouths of beasts than their keepers, and whereas the young saw food, it was often at the expense of the old, who made the sacrifice to see children fed and stock well fattened. Also, increasingly, animals were being overwintered longer within people's homes. In bastle houses and barns if they had the provision, in their cottages if they had not. It was the only way to ensure their meagre holdings of cows, pigs and sheep were kept safe. But this only meant raids took a greater toll on life, as beasts were pulled from their shelter, and people lost their lives in their protection. More and more the reiver brought anger and flame to their task. And as their work was made harder, as people clung to their possessions, it only fuelled the suffering they left as payment in kind.

Will was deaf to his comment, so instead Jack surveyed the stone built and thatched outbuildings; stables, storehouses, and the few dwellings that housed family, followers and servants. He looked to his own home amongst the cluster of buildings, modest in size in comparison to the Hall with its kitchen block attached. He looked to the rectangular pele tower, four stories tall, with a four-story wing attached. And then he looked to Will walking away to his bed in the tower.

Jack shouted, 'Wait up, Will, lets share a jug, I'm thirsty.'

Jack followed Will, and Will followed his desire, via a timber fore-stair to the first floor, to enter by a stout door protected by a yett; a metal door. A turnpike stair led to the upper floors, and all the while Jack watched his brother's hand caress the stone and plaster as he travelled, his eyes flowing over wall and window, partition and beam.

The Tower, once upon a time, only had three tall stories, with a flat top and a parapet for defence. Living accommodation was on the top floor, with stores and stabling on the ground, and a kitchen on the first; with space for armour and more stores stored in a room, which doubled as the tower's great hall. But with aspirations for a growing household, an addition of a gabled roof and a new wing was made to contain more chambers, and a chapel (planned but never created), and the second floor had been converted into a grander hall and office, more fitting a man with status to show.

Will's room was on the top floor, barrel vaulted, partitioned off from his parents sleeping quarters. It was filled with bed, with barely enough room to fit a chair, coffer and a cabinet from which he brought a jug and two cups. He filled his cup and half-filled Jack's.

'Half a cup?' asked Jack.

'It'll dae ye.'

Jack held his cup out to Will. 'Fill it, Brother.'

Will shook his head. 'Nah, take yer drink and get ye home. I'll see ye at supper.' Will sank his drink, refilled his cup and put the jug on a large pewter platter resting on the coffer. He looked back to the cupboard, its door ajar, and seeing a portion of lace wrapped in ribbon, he closed the door in shame.

'Be kind, Jack.'

'Sorry?' said Jack.

'Sweeter words tae yer wife may help ye find better concord wi' a woman worth the while.'

Jack looked to his boots. He understood Will's words. Will had seen through Jack's reluctance to return to his own quarters—his wife was waiting.

'Come on, Will, another drink.'

'Nae, brother. If I had Mary waiting after weeks missin', I'd be mair keen fer a sweet reunion, than a cup of stale ale.' Will sank his drink in one gulp—*bitter compensation.* 'She's nae hard tae look at, and she stands taller above all the slow-wit lassies in this land. Get yerself home and spend what time ye have afore supper, takin' the benefits o' marriage.'

'But...'

'Nae buts, leave me tae my own sorry lady, let me finish *my* jug.'

'But…'

'*Go!*' growled Will. 'Ye cannae hide in here, *brother*, there's nae room.'

The days Mary, my wife, spent away on God's errand, were the days of my relief in months of my veiled antipathy and closeted disenchantment. A good husband would forbid her visits to the English March. To the villages outside my father's dominion, to the villages she once called her father's estates.

With her away, I can spend my evenings in quiet contemplation without the unease of obliged discourse, or feigned interest in her musings. Yes, I find comfort in the days and nights she is away. I find my bed a welcome place without her in it, for I no longer find pleasure in her by my side.

To be fair to the record of my life, and to counter poorer thought, it had been a better making than I anticipated. Marriage to a girl, attractive, articulate and amiable. She was perhaps better bred than I deserved, but she was not of my choosing. And there again, I am reminded that marriage is rarely a choice of the heart, but one of necessity to bind unrelated families, create new allegiances, and provide mutual care. It is clear to all sane men, no man should be without a woman to see him fed and his house well kept.

To my credit, I had good intention. My design was to be a good husband, and for years I have endeavoured and worked hard to be that. Generous I was, attentive and kind words only offered. I meted out no punishment or restriction. I encouraged all that made her happy, including dedication to the Church.

She has been with child, but now twice failed to bring them to see the world. The last had proper form, and was a boy… a son. But he will never raise a smile to my lips, only a sad remembrance in my heart.

Perhaps children would mean all the difference. All the cause a man and woman need to stand together as one in common reason and mutual intention. But now, we do not couple, neither to procure new life, or in love, or even to quell a base lust. No, we lie to sleep, and in truth I sleep badly. It has been eight months now since we had union, longer still since my body, heart and soul had given affection in the name of marriage… yet…

John Brownfield, MDLIV (1554)

...house

'Boil water, Moira. The Master has several days of country dirt, blood coloured from his sport.'

'My back's fair ragin', *Mary*, d'ya want it tae break fillin' pans fer the bath?'

'No, fill the washing bowl, Moira, there's no time for a bath.'

Mary watched Moira walk from the bedroom, hand cradling her back to demonstrate her suffering. But Mary had little sympathy for such a shiftless spirit, full of subterfuge and spite.

'Moira, set the bowl up in the kitchen, and make sure the Master's clothes are washed before they are brought into my bedroom.'

'*Mair work!*' she cried.

'No, Moira, less time for you to think on your pains.'

Mary watched Moira, through the door, bring down the washing pan from its hook on the ceiling beam, without a thought or sign of a troubled back, and Mary wished she ordered the bath, if only to see Moira labour the more in its filling. A bath was a rule of Mary's, learned from a household where a mother maintained a code of cleansing and regular washing, *'to purge the demons of infection and plague'*.

Finally, Mary closed the bedroom door and stood before an oak coffer, richly carved with flowers of spring bloom. She looked at the iron lock upon it. She took it in her hands. She matched it with a key taken from her pocket.

The lid was heavy.

She carefully drew back a sheet of linen scattered with herbs. She smiled with affection at the contents.

She grasped the neck and shoulder line of each dress in turn and pulled them free of the coffer, to hold them up to meagre window light. Each dress prompting a past memory of childhood, each dress smaller until the bottom layers were reached, space enough for two dresses to lie, unfolded, side by side.

She formed three piles. The first, made with dresses to wear in honour of her father-in-law, who was in receipt of a guest of means. The second, made with dresses still fit to wear, with alteration or adjustment. And finally, those of child's wear, too small for alteration—dresses kept for her daughters, when they reached an age to fit them.

Her mother and her sisters had filled two coffers with such dresses. A wardrobe to do her honour in another land, to shine over Scottish ladies at a Scottish Court, to dress her daughters so they shone like jewels in the mud of the Borders. But Mary had never seen the Scottish Court. She only kept court at her mother-in-law's table, where guests of better breeding were few and far between. And daughters to dress were dreams yet unfulfilled, and her hope-shaped aspirations had slowly become sad acceptance.

One coffer remained. The other and its contents already sold to provide funds to help those she visited. Those who suffered privation at the mercy of cross-border raiding.

Mary thought on the state of life in the borders. There were only two conditions—loss and gain. The women bore the loss and the men fought to gain, only to bring loss to bear. If Mary had taken some comfort in her arranged marriage in an alien land, it was the affection she had for her husband—*had*, but no longer had. Even the kindness shown by Jack's father and mother had grown poorer with the years, with no children born, and their own son kept in sadness.

Ruff, Mary's little black and white dog, turned his head to the door, his ears back, tail's wag abated, low growl pre-announcing a bark that was stayed by Mary's finger held against him. Mary sensed the foul presence too.

'The Tutor tae see ye.'

Mary, at first, ignored the malapert at the door, choosing to ignore the curt announcement given by a discourteous servant. But then she thought on her welcome guest.

'Send him in, Moira.'

'It's nae proper tae have an unwed man in yer bedroom.'

'Wed or unwedded, men are men, Moira. Rarely do wedding vows change improper behaviour.' Mary feigned a wistful look. 'And I suppose… women will be women.' She kicked out a leg to tread an irreverent step with her ankle exposed. 'Ah yes, Moira, lust lives on and needs to be fed, for in marriage, with familiarity, it often sleeps.' Mary caught Moira's stare and laughed at her own wit. 'Or hides within a *proper* show, eh Moira?'

Moira, displeased to hear such wanton words, waited at the door for Mary to come out from the bedroom. She stood still, her body shouting at her charge to do as her servant required and preserve decency in her domain.

Mary sneered at the sight of Moira's stolid stance and irksome face, full of her own twisted sense of propriety. And Moira, in turn, returned scorn ten fold through her eyes, but as she thought of Mary's shame, she also thought on opportunity, because with Mary gone from the bedroom, she had opportunity to examine Mary's clothes on the bed, as Mary's coffer was always kept locked to her.

'Well, Moira, do you expect him to ravish me outside the privacy of my bedroom?' Mary looked at the mean faced girl. 'Well, do you?'

The Tutor appeared at the door, putting his hands around Moira's waist, to which she recoiled and retreated from the scene, muttering her disapprovals of both a brazen Englishman and a disfavoured English woman.

'I'm afraid the game is up, Mary.'

'Who lost, Master Tutor?'

'We did, Mary.' The Tutor walked to a chair and sat down. 'I have had instruction not to encourage your travels, or accompany you south any more.'

'And will you obey?' asked Mary.

'My wage is paid by your father, Walter Traquere. My instructions come from your mother, Anne Traqucre. I am yours to command. But my presence here is subject to your father-in-law's permissions… I'm afraid he seeks to send me away.'

'Will you go?'

'It is hard to justify my presence here to your father-in-law. And, in fact, salary from your own father is in arrears. And, in truth, I grow weary of this land.'

Mary's shoulders fell with the weight of her dismay. 'This Scot's air suffocates us, Master Tutor.'

'It is not the air, but the altitude.'

'But we are not high, Master Tutor. The mountains are well to the north.'

'Whenever you occupy a house that governs other houses, the elevation causes discomfort. Jack's father is a lord in his kingdom. A poor kingdom it may be, but he keeps it well, and suffers its burdens. You cannot expect kindness and soft words. The weight of his world keeps them suppressed.' The Tutor stood up to walk to Mary's bed. He ran his hand over one of Mary's little dresses. 'He fears for your safety, and expresses it badly.' The Tutor picked up the little dress and held it to the light. 'I remember this, so long ago you wore this… Jack was only a boy interned into your father's charge, and you were a little girl peeking through windows and around trees to see him.'

'I was third in line for his affections. Eleanor was his choice and Edith, although he never knew it, would have gladly seen our sister fall from his eye.'

'And you, Mary?'

'I was too young to know the truth of a girl's fancy. I simply played a game, and joined in with my sisters to want what they wanted… It is the way with peers, is it not?'

'Perhaps so, but perverse is the nature of fate that sees you both married against all odds and probability.'

Mary looked hard at the dress held high by the Tutor, and fearing reverie, turned her thoughts to more pressing matters. 'Jack's father will not intercede with Lord Maxwell to curtail the raiding across the Solway. I grieve for Meg, losing all; her father, her husband, her son, and her grandchild.'

'Yes, poor Meg.'

The Tutor remembered the Traquere's flinty housekeeper with some affection. For all her manner was brusque, she had a care for the Traquere's household that was to be praised. She had spent twenty years looking after Mary's mother, father, and her sisters, to finally find work's rest, when her charge left their northern home to relocate to their Hampshire estates in the South, leaving her to spend her remaining days in selfish watch over her own family. Now it seems fate had taken that from her too.

'Jack's father is right, you should stop your visits to Cumberland. Your home is here now, and not the one you and your parents left behind.'

Mary smiled at the Tutor's kind intentions, but Mary could never call this place home. Mary was an outlander, kept from the business of household. Kept as a guest, served politeness but never inclusion. Involvement in family affairs absent, she took comfort in the Tutor's kind attention. Her tutor, placed with her by her mother to keep her safe in a hostile land. Hostile, because it was outside her mother's realm; a polite society of women tutored to do service to men of good breeding and of position of value within noble society.

The Tutor nurtured Mary's education beyond that of a lady's expected measure. Her measure increased because she willed it, and because the Tutor offered it in lieu of her exclusion from duties within the Tower's household.

In the absence of letters of candour from a daughter in distress, the Tutor maintained regular reports to Mary's mother, so the truth was told of her condition (without defamation to his good friend, John Brownfield). In turn Anne Traquere maintained regular letters to Mary.

But often letters from her mother brought Mary such sadness, that days would come when she was taken ill without apparent cause. News of sisters finding themselves, by way of marriage, into the households of propertied men, provoked jealousy into indisposition. And it was news of her sisters' pregnancies, and the greater care they received because of their position, that provoked indisposition into malady. Her malady bringing her to her bed to lie for days, full of anguished thought that their care would see their babies thrive and not wither in their bellies.

Such was the sadness the letters brought.

ജ്ജ

For all that Will had directed him to return home with some haste, Jack hesitated to travel to his house. He thought of reasons to keep him from it. He looked about for work to do, for people to direct into supervised task. But he stood alone. He stood and stared at the building before him. He viewed it as a man might look to his gaol set before him, or a gatehouse set in his way, preventing him from his journey.

It had two storeys; ground floor store, living on first floor, accessed by a stone stair and entered by a stout door, protected by a yett. The house was once the home of Jack's eldest brother, Thomas. He and his wife both died ten and more years ago. Little had changed to the house, because little love had been offered to it by its new mistress, saddened by its occupation, and by a master indifferent to its placing.

He dared not call it home, but he needed fresh clothes, so he entered the house.

The light within was poor. Candles were forever lit to bring light to the darkened corners, even when the sun shone brightly. Disregarding the gloom, the dwelling was well furnished; wall linings of oak to soften stone, tapestry and velvets to warm the oak. The fire was burning and Moira was about.

Seeing Jack enter, Moira quickly removed the kettle

from the fire and poured the contents into a bowl set upon the table. All was done deftly.

'Freshly boiled, and a jug of cold sits aside it. I thought ye would be needin' a wash after yer adventures.'

'Thank you, Moira.'

'No thanks needed, Master Jack. I'm always thinkin' of yer care.'

'Thank you, Moira.'

'I wanted to fill yer bath, but the mistress stopped me.'

'Where is the mistress?'

'She's sortin' herself out in the bedroom. The Tutor's been wi' her. Awfully long they were together. And he was carryin' nae books or pamphlets fer learnin'. Havin' a *chatter* I suppose.'

'Thank you, *Moira*.'

Mary was in her bedroom. Hers, because it was filled with her things, the only room furnished anew with what she had bought from merchants in Edinburgh, with monies generously gifted by her mother on her wedding day. Bought when second-days of marriage promised so much, and entente was well seeded between a new wife and a new husband.

When wolves reunite after separation, bonding is affectionate; it is the way of most beasts in the world. It is the natural consequence of pair bonding. Why would it be anything else? And as Jack finally joined his wife, there was a need within him to embrace her; relieved he was to see her safe. But Mary's stance was not an inviting one. Her indifference to him was still apparent. If only he could read the words in her head. Her head; a learned book bound by a stout cover and brass lock fashioned by her pride.

'It is cold today. I feel cold,' announced Mary to the

room. For her eyes were on the walls and not her husband.

'Spring is nearly here. The weather will warm.'

'You say that each year, *my husband*. Each year from the year we arrived. Four have since past. Only in the first year did I feel warm.'

'The Northern Marches are cold, but we are fortunate in the West, for the weather hits harder in the East, and the snows linger longer.'

'I think the Western Marches linger in winter longer than you think, *my husband*.'

'The sun shines in summer to warm, clouds to cool, wind to dry, rain to wet. There is nothing more to add to weather. Winter is winter, summer comes and summer goes. The only thing I observe is; for a *lass* of eighteen years, you feel the cold too easily.'

'And for a man of twenty, your wits have still not formed, *my husband*.'

'I have wits enough to ignore your weather report, *my wife*.'

Mary had pricked her husband's temper, and so her own hurt was eased a little.

'Did the wolves die easily?' she asked.

'Nothing in the Marches dies easily. They, like all, fight well to stay alive. But my brother fought better.'

'Will is the better man perhaps?'

'Perhaps.' Even though agreement was given, Jack was irked by his wife's accord given to his brother, and therefore it pleased him that he did not offer affection as his opening play to a wife not seen for weeks.

'Am I to face a scolding from my father?'

'What do you mean… *a scolding*? For killing wolves?'

'No, another reprimand that I cannot control a wife. A

wife who feels she can journey south of the border as she pleases. A wife who finds no issue with riding through lands filled with threat. A wife who takes no servants for her company. A wife who would be better employed on her chores. Is this the case to answer, Mary?' Jack waited on a reply, but Mary was silent. He softened his tone, lest answer came more easily from a reticent wife. 'Where have you been?'

'To my old home. To visit our forest. To see Missy, Meg's daughter-in-law. To see her newly born babe.' Tears came to Mary's eyes. 'But she died giving birth.' Mary's tears ran down her face, her words broken. 'Meg… saw her husband murdered. Her son. Her aged father too… Her grandson dead… Scottish Reivers killed her life. Men like you... I was there. I saw it all.'

Jack was alarmed to think of Mary in the middle of a raid. Bloody and unkind they are. But his concern was delivered as rebuke from an angry man. 'Never call me, *reiver*.'

'Why not? Your family have stolen cattle. Burned people's farms. Murdered women's husbands.'

'I have not done these things. And do not insult the family hand that gives you bread, *wife*.'

Mary stared hard at Jack. 'Stolen bread.' She turned away to show her disdain. 'You do what your family tell you. You are part of their clan. A clan built on murder and strife.'

'I am nae my family, and ye'll dae whit I tell ye!'

'Seems your rude voice returns, *my husband*... The crude sound of the Borders taints your sound once more.' Mary's next words were delivered musically, as a rhyme chanted between children. '*Here returns the stripling Scot, with snot on his face, and dung in his hair.'*

Jack's face twitched at the insult. His eyes full of hate. Composure returned to his talk. 'You will do as I tell. You will do as my father says. You will do as my mother instructs you. You will act the wife and not the petulant child… *Mary Traquere.*'

'Who are you to talk to me like that? *Who are you?* It is very proper you use my birth name, because you have no honest name to give a wife, *Mr Brownfield.* But even your birth name is no prize for a girl of breeding, imprisoned…' Mary looked around her, more tears filling her eyes and fogging her view, '…imprisoned in this foul cage!'

Jack grimaced, his own pain shared. 'Just go, Mary. I do not hold you to our marriage bond. I never have. For it was always a shackle and not a silken cord that tied us. Please go, and do as it pleases you, for it pleases me that you do not return.' Jack looked away to hide his hurt from her, and thus weaken his angered show. '…I do not know why you keep coming back.'

A terrible rage grabbed Mary. Teeth clenched hard, holding back vile words. Frustration filling her whole body with angered power. Her furious spirit required release. She grabbed a missile, and pitched the pewter candlestick true. No man could have thrown it better. And it hit Jack hard on the shoulder, causing him to recoil with shock and pain. She felt no discomfort at Jack's suffering. No fear that her action had caused dire wound. No regrets with her terrible show, or that an inch better may have landed a fatal blow. Kill or hurt, she cared not.

Jack, his left hand covering his pain, marched up to Mary, right hand held against her, ready to cuff her cheek for the harm she caused. She did not flinch or withdraw, her wetted eyes shouting defiance.

'Hit me, *husband.* It will be good measure of the affection I get from you.'

Jack held his breath and his hand. He placed humour in front of his anger. 'You throw well, Mary. I count myself fortunate the cook's knife was not at hand.'

'I am sorry it was not, *husband.*'

Jack turned away to leave the room. Retreat a better policy to save more harm. And as he walked to the door, he hid from her a smile that was founded in respect. For as much as he resented her petulance, and hurt by her words, he admired her mettle. And as he left the room, he caught Moira where he would always find her—at the door, close to the keyhole, ear to the oak.

'Moira, collect up your mistress' riding clothes and burn them all.' A glance behind confirmed his words had struck their blow well on Mary. 'She'll no longer be needing them.'

Moira nodded courteously and smiled mischievously.

There are angers born from hate, from betrayal, and from injustice. These are wounds upon our spirit that rob fair reason and fester to poison the soul. There is also hate born from melancholia; rancour, which is applied without good reason, born from bitterness and envy caused by the twisted spirit. And there is anger born of frustration, which is but a moment's rage, born from love sorely tested.

John Brownfield, MDLXXV (1575)

...and hall

The last appreciable building within the barmkin wall was the Hall. A simple structure, built onto the wall that surrounded the Tower. It had two storeys of stout stone, stores below, reception hall above, and was covered by a stout roof of tile and not thatch of the lesser buildings around. All seemed plain, it built for dour purpose and not for show. It was without ornamentation, except the windows were larger and more numerous. Protected by wooden shutters, the casements were illuminated by both plain and blue-coloured glass, caught fixed between their lead cames; glass of such colour that the sky was a perfect blue even the cloudiest day.

The Hall was connected to the kitchen block at the first storey by a short, covered, timber walkway and the stairs to the first floor from the courtyard were kind to those who entered by its stout main door, with shallow risers and broad steps that allowed people in pairs to climb without exertion.

Overall, little provision was made for its defence, outside the shutters that flanked each window and the stout oak door that filled its portal.

Inside the Hall was a world given over to Jack's mother. A world that saw the stone walls plastered and not warmed with wood. Painted intricately with depictions of life and nature at its very best, by an artist well worth his fee.

Along the top, between ceiling and wall, was intricately carved cornicing of alternating heads of young and old women, and children with scrolls playing with cherubs. Designed to be painted and gilded, it ran its course around the walls plain, holding up a frieze of painted flowers.

In the centre of the room was a long artisan-made oak table, not the kind to find in a kitchen or even a Border tower of standing, but one that could grace any palace without shame. It sat on fan-shaped supports, and was decorated around its stretcher and ornamental end pieces with carved decorations to match the cornicing. All in all, a fine table appropriate for stately dining, business or conversation with guests to impress. Around it sat eleven stools and eleven chairs, one chair at each end of the table. The eleven chairs, far grander than the stools, each rested on lion's feet and wore lion masks on their arms. The seats were grand thrones, but four of the seats were larger still, of the same design, but taller and fatter. Four chairs for four senior men, four chairs for four wives and three chairs for three first-born grandsons.

Six chairs had cushions upon them.

Oh how a mother must weep, embroidering six cushions for chairs without seats upon them, three in black for those never to be filled.

All the furniture was imported from Venice, a gift from a loving husband to a wife with aims for a family to fill her palace. Indeed the Hall was constructed when she had her three sons, and expected a large family to follow. Margaret made the Hall her place, and it was kept for only for her, and used only by her permission.

ᘏ

That night the Hall was busy—an important guest to entertain, and the table was well laid with dishes of meat and meal, fish and fruits, wine and watered spirit of local design. Jack's mother supervised all, and all was as perfect as it could be in a poor hall, richly decorated and better furnished than the halls and towers of their neighbours.

'Jack, I wish ye tae travel tae Carlisle, Monday next. Slack 'o' Jack is up afore the Quarter Justice, having kicked his heels in the town's gaol fer three months.'

'Whit are Slack 'o' Jack's crimes of concern fer us, Da?' asked Will.

'He is of my concern, and Jack is a man gud wi' words tae see tae his comfort. A bag of coin should see his fines paid, and let us hope his crimes dae not see him presented at Carlisle assizes fer crimes too expensive fer gold.'

'Aye, Daddy…'

Jack heard Will's peevish reply, and felt uncomfortable to have his father's preference, yet proud to have his acknowledgement of his better learning.

Jack announced, 'I'll take Robert Hardie and Tom Kemp with me.'

'Ye'll tak' neither. I'm needin' gud men fer my own escort. Instead ye can take yer man-beast tae wipe yer nose, and your niggardly little man tae ensure his complaint rings in yer ears and nae my own.'

His father's reference was to Bendback Bob and Francis Bell. Bendback being a hunchback, six-foot-and-more tall, even with his bent and twisted back. Fearsome to see, Bendback had been Jack's bodyguard since he was placed in his care at nine years old. Francis too, was part of the Watch that was assigned to Jack when he was interned by the English Warden of the West March, as a pledge to ensure good favour from Jack's father in relation to border affairs. And just as Bendback's love and loyalty for Jack was immeasurable, Francis' kindness was measured in his inches, and he had precious few to call his height. He was small, mean, spiteful and curt. But no one was better with bow or bolt, musket or pistol, except perhaps another of Jack's Watch—Finn McCuul, an Irishman, forever assigned by his father to patrol the borders of his land.

'He's faster, he's feared, and he fights as four.'

These three, along with Robert Hardie and Tom Kemp, were Jack's men—tried and tested. Jack's friends—tried and true.

Jack watched Mary, pushing her food on the plate with her spoon. 'Not hungry, Mary?'

Mary glanced at Jack and to spite his conversational punt she turned her attention to her father-in-law's guest, sitting across from her. 'Do you read, Mister Ramsey?'

'Aye,' replied Ramsey, putting down his spoon, a sign the others seated had recently learned heralded a long oration. '*Ahem*… M-My library boasts over forty books. I have read at length and consider myself well read. I recently acquired an English translation of Thomas More's *Golden Little Book*. A fiction and a foretelling of his fate, methinks. Aye, I consider myself literate and therefore lettered.'

Jack shot a telling glance to the Tutor. To boast of forty books owned in front of the Tutor would be like saying to have forty farthings would make a man moneyed, when indeed he would barely have a shilling. For the Tutor's collection was a wall of books.

Jack, who himself was well read, could not resist but test the guest, to ascertain his intellect, and in turn expose him as not only a liar, but a dullard in front of Mary, who herself had read More's, Golden Work… *the New Island Utopia,* in its original Latin text.

'Mr Ramsey, do you find Thomas More a palatable read?' asked Jack.

'*Ahem*… A-Anything from the once great chancellor of England is worthy of one's time. Of course, I had the pleasure tae have fair acquaintance of Sir Thomas More in better times for England, when I was guest at length in his home.'

Jack, still nettled by the visitor and his likely boasted words, hid his anger behind his smile. 'You pluck a name far gone... A name lost in a score and more years, and half the dozen chancellors… Dead men can rarely confirm their aquaintences.'

But Ramsay ignored the jibe, and thought to draw Jack in to belittle him with fine-picked words. His spoon was placed on his platter. '*Ahem*… I mis-speak myself, for More was no great chancellor, for I suspect he was the only honest man in an altogether dishonest realm.'

Jack prodded Ramsey. 'And you think dishonesty is the mark of a fine chancellor?'

'*Ahem*… W-When one serves monarchs, one serves souls corrupted by their own vanity. *Princes of Pride* serviced and coddled by men of avarice. They have their bellies filled with plenty, whilst the poor starve. What honest man can truly serve such beings and do it well. For to do it well means one must be untrue to oneself, and thus not be the man he is to be.' Ramsey picked up his spoon and Will sighed relief. But the spoon was put down once more. 'Men grow strong and grow in mind when they have suffered the trials of life; the hungry belly, hard toil, and the loss of those they love by the wilful act of war and the wanton act of nature. Kings and queens have none of this... *yet*…' Ramsey retrieved his spoon and stirred the air.

'*Yet... yet... ahem...*' Ramsey thought on his misplaced words poked at sovereigns. Words to bite him back if they found their way to higher places. '*Ahem*... B-But princes and nine-day queens have other trials that test their souls' mettle.'

'Do you mean poor Lady Grey, who lost her head?' asked Mary.

'Aye, it is particularly nettlesome for English high-born women. For to be born into that Tudor cage they call a court is to gift one's head for its pleasure. And I say caged—for caged-birds are all they all are. To sing for men's pleasure when they desire a sweet song, and to lay eggs as they will it. Birds to be traded for politics. But a caged bird rarely lays an egg.' Ramsey picked up Mary's hand from the table and kissed it gently. 'It seems, madam, they make sport of lopping off ladies' heads... I have, myself, seen women that indeed would be far more pleasing without their powdered pate, but as a rule I have always found a lady's head most pleasing while it is attached to the body... Yours is particularly well placed.'

Mary, indifferent to Ramsey's flattery, drew him back to the subject of Lady Grey. 'Did you ever meet the Lady Grey?'

'*Ahem*... Of course, Lady Jane was a towering woman, hair of earth, noble yet plain.'

Jack challenged, 'Strange, I heard she was very petite, childlike, graceful, hair of claret, and eyes to match.'

Ramsey countered nervously. '*Erm...ahem*.... Aye, of course, I must declare I saw her only briefly, and a lady's shoes can belie one's true height, and she was wearing a fur-trimed hood when we met.'

Mary, nettled with Jack's goading, interrupted to show

her support for Ramsey. 'Do you think it fair they lopped her head off?' She looked at Jack. 'I can think of other heads best removed far closer to this table.'

Ramsay grinned at Mary's taunt. '*Ahem*… Fair or foul, I am afraid Queen Mary will lop off her sister Elizabeth's head too in lieu of a failed political… *ahem*… sorry… protestant uprising.' Ramsey picked up his spoon once more to hold it to the broth. '*Ahem*… it is better to be here in Scotland, I think.'

Jack's father was not unsympathetic to Jack's mood. Him thinking, Mary a little too comfortable in Ramsey's presence, and he offered, 'With Scotland favorin' the French by marriage of oor own Queen Mary tae the King o' France, and the English by marriage of their Spanish begotten Queen Mary tae the King o' Spain. What else can become of this whole isle, but a Catholic isle of convenience… a place fer the French and Spanish tae bring their ladies tae peer at each other over the *March Dyke* as their husbands throw stones at each other.'

'*Ahem*… How goes the Dyke,' Ramsey enquired, 'I was secretary to the French Ambassador when he arbitrated a solution to the line of partition between England and Scotland in the debated lands.'

'*Of course you were*,' replied Jack, his sigh heavy on his lips.

'A bank 'o' earth will nae keep the Grahams from stealin' oot tae slit the English throat,' announced Will, 'They've a fancy fer English linen, chattels and their women.'

'*Ahem*… I assure you it is simply a judicial line, not a wall to keep the peace,' replied Ramsey.

Jack's father announced to all, 'Better tae fill the ditch wi' Grahams and Elliots and use the dyke tae cover their graves.'

Mary shook her head at her father-in-law's reasoning. 'Murder will never bring peace to the Marches.'

Jack's father was none too pleased at Mary's dissent, and threw Jack a stinging look.

Ramsey who had seen the exchange sought to make worse the fracture in a family. '*Ahem*... You have a wife who challenges men's minds, *Mr Brownfield.*'

Jack rolled his eyes and gritted his teeth, mindful he sat at his father's table and Ramsey was his guest, and more so, his mother's eye was upon him in order to keep good grace at her table. But the sight of Mary's face, thought alight with pleasure of her discourse with the coxcomb, provoked Jack and his pride. His silence was hard fought.

Mary's delight was clear. 'Well said, Master Ramsey.'

'Please do not maintain unfamiliarity... *ahem*... call me *Hugh*, or better still *Ursus*, as my mother and sisters call me, out of their great love and affection.'

Mary nodded her head and closed her eyes. 'Ursus.'

'*Ahem*... Mr Brownfield, can I question how you are here at this great man's table?'

'He is my son,' answered Jack's father in his stead.

'Curious, a son who does not carry his father's name... *ahem*... What strangeness is this?'

Jack's father looked to his son, and Jack looked away. 'He denies his name as protest.'

Ramsey hid his pleasure; splintering Jack from a wife's favour and now his father's. 'And... *ahem*... is it imprudent of me to enquire what manner of issue requires such protest?'

'It *would be* imprudent of you to enquire so,' replied Jack sharply.

Jack's mother only saw conflict at her fine table, and

dishonour brought to the memory of those in tribute by its standing, so she interrupted. 'So what, Master Ramsey, brings you to my hall?'

'*Ahem*… I am sent by way of message from James Hamilton, the Earl of Arran, *Regent of Scotland*, to invite you and your husband to attend a month's celebrations he plans. As I have told your husband, the Earl expects attendance.'

Margaret looked to her husband with telling eyes—*alarm*.

But Jack's father was not concerned. 'Fear not Margaret, the Regent seeks only tae understand his support in adversity. He has a thorn stuck in his arse, which is the Queen's mother, Marie 'o' Guise. She seeks the regency in the wake of the Earl's risin' unpopularity. His celebrations, I think, are designed tae again make him popular. But it'll take a sea o' spirit and a goodly forest o' fine cheer tae warm the Scottish gentlemen tae that spineless cuckold, who the French name *Chatelot… a fine name fer a jester.*'

Margaret was still alarmed. 'But… but to leave our home and hall for the disquiet of Edinburgh.'

'Fear not Margaret. We'll take a good strong guard with us.' Jack's father looked to his sons in turn. Oldest first. 'Will tae remain with an eye tae watch oor property. Jack tae lend his better men tae oor own watch, see tae Slack 'o' Jack's comfort, and remain as Will's right hand.'

'Slack 'o' Jack… that feckless sot!' declared Margaret, to which Will nodded in agreement.

After the table was cleared with women retired, and Will and his father sat out the night with two jugs of spirit, a fire, and a hundred stories of war and recollections of friends lost and enemies cut, Jack found himself outside, alone with Ramsey on the steps of the Hall. Both men had elected to leave the other men to their drinking and to take cool air to calm their heads.

'You are well favoured, John Brownfield.'

Jack listened.

'You are well placed here. With a fine wife who cares for the losses of your neighbours.'

'She cares, yes,' replied Jack.

'*Ahem*... Do you not think to fight her cause? She has told me of the hardships inflicted on her former homeland.'

'What are the peoples of a paltry fishing village in England to me?'

'Nothing,' said Ramsey counting the stars. '*Ahem*... Except they mean much to your wife. But as they mean nothing to you, I don't hesitate to come between a husband and a wife's pairing.'

Jack looked on Ramsey. He thought Ramsey had given him opportunity to prick past complaint and wounded honour. He thought to force Ramsey to draw a blade and so offer Jack a chance to cut away the insult brought against him. Punish him for his woo on his wife. Perhaps cut the coxcomb's tender parts. Jack thought Ramsey would best be bled for his sins, and a duel would be a good service to Jack's cause.

But instead, Jack's interest was pricked by Ramsey's next words, delivered different than those at the table. Delivered sober by a different man—a man serious and earnest.

'Marie of Guise's agents are picking out some of her noble dissenters and commissioning their kith and kin into

French battalions, overseas. I suspect her plan is to lessen the numbers of gentlemen her critics can draw on if they feel the need to argue with her regency. It is a subtle policy, but a sensible one. And there is room for any able young man who would bolster the numbers going overseas. Indeed, the *Humes* and *Kerrs* dispatched some months ago already have distinguished themselves as able Border Horse. Although I must say, they were sent under different circumstances, by Arran.' Ramsey smiled with a thought of an old enemy to be removed. 'I should say*, to be former regent Arran…* He saw those sorry souls free from harm after they murdered the Warden Buccleuch… *ahem…* I suspect the poor Buccleuch thought himself safe on the streets of Edinburgh.

Ahem… B-But I digress… Border Horse are now much sought after for France's fight. Fighting for fees worth half again more than other mounted men. I can see you in more noble attire, young Brownfield. A better match for that noble sword you carry. A gift I understand from a voguish Frenchman of our mutual admiration and acquaintance.

Jack pricked an ear and said, *'Per astra ad astra.'*

Ramsey looked puzzled.

'Family motto?'

Jack looked away. '*Ahem*, yes… of sorts.'

'Our Frenchman has a commission for you; a fight in France. A fight against the Huguenots.'

'As a mercenary?'

'What are Border Horse if not mercenary cavalry? And you will need a good troop to satisfy conditions of the commission. And…*ahem…* I suspect the commission will not receive the blessing of either father or wife.'

Ramsey reached into his jacket and produced a small red-velvet letter packet and handed it to Jack.

Jack took the packet and stroked the fine velvet cloth between his fingers. It still held the owner's perfume and he looked closely at the wax seal fixing the gold cords that tied it closed.

A gift from a Frenchman, he thought.

I've travelled some. It's a soldier's life. I'm no garrison man, no lord to serve. No gentleman and his estates to protect. I fight for those who pay, and it's the greater purse that fuels my footwork.

But with age I grow weary, pain my close companion, and I wonder how much of my life has gone in travel, for I have marched as many miles as I have rode, and a hundred saddle miles are no more comfortable than a hundred miles on foot, for sores and aches are simply felt in more tender places.

The bondsman who applies his tools in the earth, or on wood's grain, or works leather, or beats iron; he sits in his domain, his travel is confined unless he is called to pilgrimage or his sovereign's war. His world is defined by the boundaries of his calling, so his shoe leather lasts a hundred days more than the skin of a soldier's boot. And with that thought, I wish for the life that will see me in a workshop, or market, or in a field, my feet no more to march, but only to apply a boot to my servant's arse.

But then I laugh, for the tilt is worth the toil, the fight that boils the blood and quickens the breath, the need to raise a banner and call men to arms, to bloody an enemy, to cut his flesh.

I know the silver in my soldiers' scrip is not the draw, but the rush that comes with war. It is the blood of my life and without it my soul would perish. My heart runs on the fight, but it cannot be love, that would be too perverse, so it can only be another hunger of the heart, that fevered desire that fills the mind—the lust for war.

Anon, MDLIV (1554)

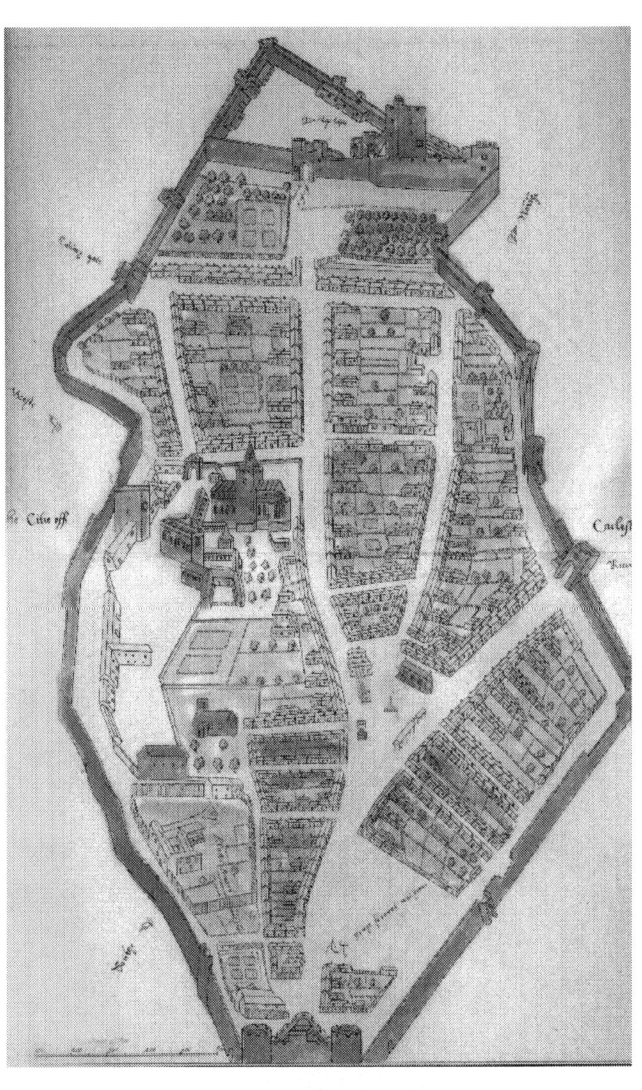

Carlisle

Chapter V

The visitor

Carlisle received many travellers that day; pedlars with goods to trade, men with goods to buy, travellers taking rest on route to and from Scotland, drovers, soldiers, clergy, and those with business best done in Carlisle and not in the parishes about. Men of all castes too, including those in rags, those in steel, and a gentleman in parrot-coloured leathers. They came in by English Gate and Rickard Gate. Some to the fish market, some to St Cuthbert's and St Mary's. Some noisily, riding with friends through drovers, sheep and cattle, announcing the need for men for a commission in France. Some quietly riding in, but with show, through the Caldew gate, as an important guest of an important merchant in Annetwell lane…

'*Per aspera ad astra.*'

The merchant, a small man with a hooked face, longer for the beard he wore, wearing clothes of serious nature, plain and functional, nodded his head. He wore a thick felt mantle to keep out the cold, for flesh he had none. He did not smile. The greeting was formal, guarded.

His visitor's arrival was unexpected. His home was not ready to receive. He spent little on comfort in a house that stood proud of the other dwellings lining the street. Proud, because of the stone courses that formed its first storey, taller for the extra storeys it carried, and better for the slate that topped the storeys when all the rest had thatch.

Both good and bad news came with this parrot-coloured visitor. Good news for the merchant's purse, as he was always richer with his visits. Bad news, as the favours the visitor required were often at the cost of his own serious endeavours, and the forfeit of many of his own favours held over great men, because of the credit he allowed them.

The merchant bowed and replied, '*Semper paratus, semper fidelis*.'

The visitor smiled. 'It is good to see you, *mon ami*.'

The merchant relaxed his stance. He took his visitor's arm and embraced it warmly. 'It is good to see you too. Kind you are to visit a humble merchant. Are you here with more wine to trade, or are iron and slaves your business… or is it Guild affairs that presses you to visit this poor city?'

'Kindness only, *mon ami*.'

'Then your kindness and my coin should get together over a drink.'

'I hope you have some of that excellent brandy left. The memory of it stays on my tongue.'

'I do, although I have lost large consignments of it; through raid, through requisition and through gifts to great men for the courtesies they give.'

'*Ah oui*, bribery… Bribery and war are expensive overheads for merchants… War works in our favour only if we supply the warring, and not when warring reaves the suppliers.'

The merchant sent his servants for refreshments, and three young boys went running from the room. Chairs were found, and both men sat.

The merchant sighed. 'It is good to drink with a man of the world and not of the Marches, for only feud fuels their conversation. Retribution and the honour of their names.'

The visitor leaned forward in his chair so he could reach the older man, and clamped both his hands on the merchant's right hand. '*Mon ami*, business is a far better reason to drink than feud… profit shouts louder than pride.'

The merchant smiled, and seeing the servants return with trays of drink and food, asked, 'And the business to accompany our drink is?'

The visitor sat back and smiled at the merchant now directing his servants to where the trays should be placed. A pause followed until the visitor was sure he had all the merchant's attention.

'A man will travel through Carlisle with men to his back, and a commission in his pocket.'

'And?' replied the merchant.

'I need you to watch. I need you to apply favours in high places for this man—for his benefit, *if need be*.'

'For his benefit?'

'He has my commission, so he is me, and I wish him well. I want him where I want him, whichever road he chooses. His road will be his choice. His destination my design. See it happens so.'

'What if the road he chooses is outside my influence?'

'Come, come, *mon ami*, I know your influence holds well on both sides of the border, throughout the Western Marches. Favours from lords and louts alike. Apply them where they are needed… *and know it is for my benefit too, Master Merchant*.'

Chapter VI

The Baker's house had ale and beer. It was a meeting place for those in the know. It was a place for wicked folk to come and play, sell and buy, to game and plot. A place the constable visited for his own reasons, to mix with malefactor and miscreant, to share a jug of stolen beer and meat from 'borrowed' beasts. He left his virtue at the door and placed his blind eye to the fore, for the Baker was well in with the Justice and the Warden's office for the favours he gave and the monies he paid them.

Its patrons affectionately knew the Baker's house as the *Bell and Spoon*, even though it was neither registered inn, nor alehouse. It suited those who had goods to sell out of the view of honest folk and authority. The Justice knew of the place, so did the Warden, his deputy, his sergeants, his slaves and scullions. All used it, even if they turned their eyes from it as they passed by, and feigned their knowledge of it in conversation.

But at night there was often an honest man, or his agent, bidding on wares and goods obtained dishonestly; loot from raids carried out by the English borderer wanting to move his booty on for coin. But, in truth, as much came from Scottish Borderers. Spoils taken from the English, and even their own neighbours.

At times, when goods came in quantity, the Baker held a *roup*–
–an auction. A practice started in earnest when the monasteries and religious houses were in threat, and needed to dispose of wealth quickly and quietly before the Crown could lay their hands on it.

The Baker held the roup this night, an auction of goods that were not legally owned, therefore not legally sold. The goods were held and sold by the Baker. No buyer knew the seller, and no seller was told the buyer. Thus the Baker held his favour well with most, for he kept their secrets.

The room was busy and still filling up, and Jack sat with Francis and Bendback, scanning the room. There were all sorts; good suits, poor suits, farmers, lawyers, ladies even. At the back of the room were private booths, with curtains drawn against the crowd, where people could remain unseen.

Jack cast his eyes to the curtained booths.

'No doubt that's where the clergy sit in confession,' Jack swept the room, 'with all the sinners of Carlisle seated in one place.'

Francis leered at the crowd about him. 'Aye, the Bishop be better conducting services here than in St Mary's. There be far more souls to be saved. The rich too mean to pay a proper price for honest goods.'

But Jack and Francis both knew the private rooms were for better men and ladies to bid in private without the lower orders of Carlisle seeing them in such poor surroundings.

Jack wondered who sat behind the tattered brocade, but only for a moment.

However, from behind the curtains, through a lace panel sewn into them, a moment more was spent by a man watching Jack. He sat back and smiled, and brushed down his brightly coloured leather jacket of peacock hues, wishing he brought his velvet one, for he thought its texture showed better in poor light.

With the auction about to start, Jack's attention was brought to the auctioneer, the Baker. He wore good clothes, testament to the success of his commerce. Clothes for a gentleman. Collar in fine cambric. But he was at odds with the suit. And Jack thought a dirty face with an unkempt beard and hair above good clothes, does not make a gentleman, only a pig in silk.

Bidding was melodic and energetic, frantic for the goods of greater value and rarity, slower for things that made poor sense to a gathering that had little use for books and fancies, unless they could be sold on easily, at a profit.

Jack read down his *menu*, a list of goods to be auctioned; armour, linen and lace, beasts, barrels of lime, brandy, and an item caught his eye, more so because it was announced by the Baker.

'Here we have a coffer of clothes… Fine dresses from a fine household… I wonder what the lady now wears? Eh boys!' His joke was shared by the room, enjoyed by a few, and only appreciated by a few more.

The Baker lit a candle on a table to his side and reached deep into a bag at his feet. He produced a baby rat by the tail and trapped it, with the candle, beneath a glass bell.

'Silks and damasks, linens and lace… How do we start? Five shillings get yer interest?'

Bidding was brisk at first, and Jack was distracted by the noise of the Baker's song.

'Six 'n' seven, 'n' seven 'n' half… eight 'n' nine… come on boys… ten… the lot's worth a pound or two… thank thee, eleven.'

There was the flash of a silver spoon raised, then another and two more, as clothiers, market men, and ladies agents all bid on the coffer.

Bendback grinned. 'You'd have to be careful where your lady

wore'em, lest the lady who lost 'em, squeals theft!'

The candle in the bell showed bright, and the rat ran its glass gaol, young eyes in its head and a great long tail. It sucked the air. The bell was large, but poisoned air was its charge.

Seasoned bidders had learned the sight and sign of the flame's life, and could judge the time bidding had before the flame spluttered its last refrain. But the Baker had a trick. Within his sack of rats, and rats he had aplenty, was an airtight box, crammed with rats, half-suffocated. With a half dead rat placed in the bell, the flame would live longer, and so spur the bidders on to reach a proper price before the light was lost. He figured the chest of clothes had legs to run on and on, to fetch a pound or two more in a bidding war, finding the spendthrifts amongst the misers.

Jack looked at the dresses the boy held up in turn. All were fine, but one was magnificent, better than any he had seen on Mary's mother, or his own. It was a show, even without a lady's curves to fill it. Lucent greens and blues, and much golden thread. It sparkled in the candle's light. This was no costume for a Border lady, robbed, but a lady of the Court, of places and palaces Jack had never seen.

'One 'n' three.... Come on, boys let's make it two.... and four...'

Bidding slowed, and the candle grew dim as the bell slowly suffocated the flame.

'Come on boys... Come on, gentlemen... clothes to make your lady happy, to keep you in with your wife, to please your mistress, or your fancy.... Hard for your sweetheart to keep chaste with a pretty present such as this to offer...' A spoon was raised and the Baker nodded. 'Thank thee, 'n' five.'

Jack, without warning, picked up and held his spoon high.

'And a new bidder.... Good man... that's one and six.... Gentleman, one pound and six... who will give me seven shillings? Another spoon was shown. 'Thank you. One pound and seven shillings.' The Baker looked to the candle. The rat lay still.

Bendback shot a glance at the bidder; a man directed by a woman, dressed as a lady's maid.

Jack looked at the bell, the flame too dim to discern, and raised his spoon with two fingers held high.

The Baker smiled, holding two fingers to the sky. 'Two!'

Bidding hesitated, and Bendback watched the man and the lady's maid squabble.

The flame went out.

'Sold!'

Two pounds spent. Two months wages gone. Jack's eyes lowered to the table.

The auction was over in another hour and the room was filled with drinkers and drunkards, and Jack studied the tables and the groups of men about.

'Bendback, if we are to look for soldiers without employ, then this is the place.' Jack nodded towards another table. 'Like him, seated over there.'

Bendback looked to Jack's signposting.

There were three men at the table, but only one wore riding boots, the others wore shoes. The horseman at the table was about thirty. Thick set around the face. A flat nose, broken. Chin with beard growth, but no fashioned beard. A week, perhaps two, of growth on a clean face. His beard the consequence of a man not able to shave, rather than the growth of purposed hair. His red hair was receding, tied back tightly behind his head. He wore a scarf around his crown, and Bendback looked for a steel bonnet about. It sat at his feet. *Soldier caste.*

'He carries good weapons,' announced Jack. His bundle looks heavy—armour. He dresses well enough—quality, but his shirt is long passed replacing… his boots too. His friends have paid for all the drinks he quaffs. He is here to sell, not to buy, because he was absent during bidding. A soldier out of funds, selling, and open to a new commission perhaps?'

Jack encouraged Bendback's scrutiny of the man. And both witnessed another approaching their man's table.

'Are ye named Geordie?'

The seated man did not turn to acknowledge the voice, he kept his eyes on his drinking companions. 'I'm called many things; Mister by my tailor, Graspin' Geordie, by those who think on me bitter. Mercenary, by those who employ me. Those who sit with me call me, friend.'

The standing man grinned. 'Aye, and some call ye a back-stabbin' bastard.'

'Some do,' replied the seated man, eyes still on his comrades.

'Some call ye a defiler of women.'

The seated man grinned at his companions. 'I'm afraid a willing lass in the evening, can see the act different when I don't come a callin' in the morning. And some wenches will get sore when I find their wares not worth the price they charge.'

The standing man continued. 'Some call ye coward, who'll kill his comrade for his share of loot.'

The seated man turned on his stool to look at the voice in his ears. The voice had a big man at its root, very big indeed, now standing directly behind him.

'It seems by your provocative words, you wish to fight, big man.'

'Aye. Ye murdered my kin… stole his purse, and so I want it back, and I dinnae back stab, *Graspin' Man!*'

'I'm glad to hear it… so I take it you'll not be sinkin' a blade in my back as I stand. It's good to know you fight for gold and no for poor justice for your kin.' Geordie made to stand, but changed his mind and rested again on his stool. 'And so I know who disturbs my drink, can I know who your kin be?'

'Davie Johnson.'

'A common name in these parts, I believe.'

'Davie Johnson of Armathwaite.'

'Ah…Then by the sight of you, you'll be his big brother, Lang Tam.'

'Aye… Tam Johnson… It'll be the last name on yer lips. Now outside! There's cuttin' to be done.'

Jack did not see the cudgel. No one saw the cudgel. It came rushing round to meet the man's leg and struck hard his knee. The big man groaned. He clutched the pain, and sank to the floor.

The seated man's knife came up to meet his quarry's throat.

'You're a little too big for a fair fight… Now you're a little more my size.'

The big man growled through gritted teeth. *'Bastard!'*

'I'll be outside if ye want to draw blood… But be quick, afore the crowd draws interest from the constable.'

The seated man, rose, picked up his bundle and walked from the room.

The big man did not follow.

'A bonny box of dresses you bought. Your *ma* in need, or is your mistress in want?'

Jack looked up to see the Baker, smiling, standing at his table.

'They are for my wife.'

'Dresses for yer wife? Money wasted on a woman already bought. What need of you to impress a wife? She is yours already.'

Jack did not reply, but thought on Mary, his by marriage, her own by nature.

The Baker hearing no reply, said, 'I have put the word around about you needing men for commission.'

'Good, *Master Baker*. Do you know the man, just left?'

'The one who runs from a fight?'

'Surely he withdrew?'

The Baker held his smile to hide a thought. 'He is a *Reed* of Redesdale, born Otterburn I believe, although he is no clan man. And whereas borderers are mercenaries all, loyal only to the name they carry, he fights with glee against even his own name for any coin he can make. His coat has carried many a badge.'

'Do you know him well?'

'Geordie?'

'Yes.'

'Geordie…' The Baker rubbed his chin. 'All I can say of Geordie is, if he were offered a gold piece, he would take two, want three, and never be satisfied with four, for he wants all the gold in the world, and all the silver too. Yes, Geordie, take that I owe from Geordie and you will see his sin.'

'I don't understand?' said Jack.

The Baker's ceaseless smile waned a little. 'Think on it, *young recruiter.* In these parts a man's namc is the sin he carries...and believe me only sinners live here.'

The Baker walked away.

Jack turned to Francis. 'Go tell Mr Reed of our commission in France and the pay and spoils on offer.'

Francis stood up and grabbed his sword. 'Will there be a time when a man can take a drink in company without either a fight breaking out, or errands to run?'

'And Francis,' said Jack, 'There are times for exaggeration. Times to overstate the prize… *This is one of those times.*'

Francis had not even left the room when another voice distracted Jack.

'I hear you are looking for men for a commission in France.'

Jack turned around on his bench to see a man, dark and

unknown. His hood was deep, and its shadow covered his face, and his cloaked form filled Jack's view.

'Yes, men of fighting creed,' replied Jack. He looked about for any other men that may be standing in the man's shadow.

He was alone.

The shadow looked about the inn—to each table and each face that sat in revelry or in solemn discussion. Only after he considered the nature of each man in his mind, did he speak, his deep voice spitting its contempt. 'Is there any other type of man in this quarrelsome land?'

Jack smiled. 'There are scrappers aplenty. And scrappers more with every jug of strong ale taken. I can them get easy enough for silver coin. Carlisle is filled with them. But it is soldiers for gold I'm needing, for fighting work in France. Sign-on for a gold mark, thereafter a shilling per day, a shilling bounty per warrior-kill, doubled for a gentleman warrior, and of course there will be loot to be had—*the spoils of war.*'

'Expenses.'

'All powder, lead, damages, food and lodging at your own cost.'

The shadow nodded. 'When would we travel? My purse is low.'

'In a few months. We rest awhile. We've more recruiting to do, ale to drink and perhaps seek an inn fight or three to test the mettle of the men who take my coin.'

The shadow said nothing for a while. Then with a long sigh taken, he announced, 'As I said, my purse is low. My fighting is restless. It's been six months too long since I drew my sword in fray. It does not suit me to sit around whilst you fill your ranks with boys and butchers, with only the *perhaps* of inn-fighting.'

Jack heard the troubled edge in his words. He looked into the shadow of the man's hood and smiled to hide his thoughts.

A man too desperate for the fight—and therefore not a fitting choice.

'It seems you travel a poor path, stranger. A road through strife. Perhaps you are needing a new road? A one more green and less… red?'

'Is there such a road?' His voice now still, deep and unforgiving.

'There is…' Jack laughed at the irony of it all. '…Except for the strife in its travelling.'

The stranger's voice softened with a laugh. 'Then there is no such road.'

'There can be with the removal of the wolves that haunt it.'

The stranger laughed again, and raised his hands to remove his hood. 'There are always wolves, thank God.' The stranger's face, revealed, was still hidden under thick greying beard and hooded brow, ingrained dirt, long hair with a low fringe that almost covered his eyes. His face wore menace, but his eyes wore hurt. They were tired, dull in the dim light. His skin was burnt, or perhaps coloured amber by the mix of parentage of different race. Jack could not discern.

'The question is…' The stranger paused to swallow, '…how many wolves and how well is the huntsman paid?'

'As I have said, coin enough.'

'Then coin too poor, for I have earned one hundred times more, and spent it in a day… How many fighters do you have, my well dressed wolf killer? And how will go the odds?'

Jack looked at Bendback. 'Only two so far.' He looked towards Francis' travel. 'Perhaps three, with a troop to bolster our numbers coming from Liddesdale within three months.' Jack poured himself a drink. 'We are commissioned as Border Horse, so we will always be first-pushed into the fray… to skirmish, raid and prick hard enemies of greater number. You will certainly earn your pay, and be always in shot's way.'

'First in the fray.' He thought. 'Hmmm, poor odds for survival when you are placed as the army's spear point. But well placed for plunder, though.' The stranger rubbed his beard and stroked his side. 'No, wolf killer, you have more.' He looked at Bendback. 'Your man here fills two men's boots, sitting down. Standing up, it may be three. But four or forty against the world, the odds will always be against you.'

The stranger's face was earnest, and Jack nodded. He took the man's disinclination to join Jack's cause with understanding. Jack looked away to hide his disappointment. His judgement told him this would have been a good man to have in his troop.

'And the higher the odds, the better it sounds, for the rewards are always greater when odds are stacked against victory.' The stranger's words drew Jack's attention again. 'And a few months rest from the road seems a good purse. I am tired of travelling, but in need of fighting. Can you guarantee a good fight, wolf killer, and a bed filled with feathers and not mud and heather?'

'I will send word to the innkeepers to pluck their geese for the softest bed. And if fight doesn't come-a-calling, I think we might call on fight ourselves.'

'Good words,' said the shadow, 'Then you have one more.'

'Then take an ale from the jug… and find a stool to rest with us.'

'I'll thank you for the ale, but I will maintain my own company until you are ready to travel on.'

Bendback, who had been silent, broke his quiet. 'How do we know this stranger is worth our purse?'

The stranger looked on Bendback and pulled open his cloak. He was dressed as a *demi-lancer*, and wore his half-armour well, like it was a part of him. He filled his steel cuirass, and attached was a further reinforcing steel breastplate, fitted against bullet. His sword was of princely quality, with a dagger to match, and he carried a second knife of foreign form. He carried two large Dutch wheel lock pistols of fine quality in a leather harness about his person. His hands were calloused, his stance confident. All was well-worn with him, and well-used with dent and scar; signs of a embattled life. This man was a soldier. His presence before them declared it. Even warrior Bendback could see it.

'Seems your *troll* questions my worth,' said the shadow.

Bendback stood up, face of fury.

'Sit down, Bob,' ordered Jack.

As soon as Jack was assured Bendback was seated and settled, he addressed the shadow. 'Time will learn you to give Bob here some respect.'

The shadow smiled at Bendback. 'I ask forgiveness, *Bob the Troll*, but you looked worthy of a fight.'

Jack asked, 'What's your name?'

'Call me, *Brother Soldier*, for my birth name has been lost in a hundred fights and a dozen wars in the morass of the rank 'n' file.'

Chapter VII

Jack stood, for the benches were full. The court lists were full too, and the Justice and his Clerks dispensed their justice over the lists of misdemeanour, disorder and dispute curtly.

Only one Justice of the Peace sat; Richard Musgrave, High Sherriff of Cumberland. He had no chairman overseeing the process, and no one recorded the evidences presented. He sat in his oak throne, while the rest sat on stool or bench. He sat and conferred with his Justice Clerk, a man much older than Musgrave. And the Justice Clerk in turn addressed all to the court, to the plaintiff, and to the accused. But the Justice Clerk's wisdom was born of a buffoon and not of King Solomon, for his legal advisors forever whispered in his ear their good advice and legal propriety, only for him to apply his own brand of border justice in service of those he favoured over those he despised; poor men and men of a name not supporting his patron; First Baron Wharton.

With the crowd came flies and flying creatures abound, and Jack found himself swatting away the nuisance with regularity. He was irritated to be in the confines of the Court and the closeness of the bodies around him, and more than once had to shove hard the man and woman next to him to remind them he did not tolerate his space being taken about him.

He was irked too that he was not allowed to speak as advocate on Slack 'o' Jack's behalf, as was his father's wish. Jack worried, as the name of the plaintiff in the case against Slack 'o' Jack was Curwen. The Sherriff was born of a Curwen mother, so Jack feared dire outcome for Slack 'o' Jack, as he had seen the harshness of the Court and he knew the nature of the defendant, and so he knew the truth of his crimes made.

A clerk quietened the Court, and the Clerk Justice spoke at Slack 'o' Jack.

'Is your name Robert Black, also known as Builder Jack, Peddlar Jack, Prigger Jack and Slack 'o' Jack?'

'Aye, sir. I've bin called all them names and mair.'

'Were you born Annandale, captured as a palliard within this burgh and are presently of Carlisle?'

'Presently of Carlisle only cos o' the locked door in the gaol prevents me movin' on, sir.'

A wave of titters ran over the courtroom.

'Silence!'

'Are you a builder by trade?'

'Aye, sir.'

'I will ask you again, Mr Black, and the truth will be a better utterance in this court. Are you a builder—*by trade*.'

'Nay, sir, I took tae the building last year when…'

'Aye, or nay will suffice,' ordered the Justice of the Peace.

The Clerk Justice nodded thanks to Sir Richard Musgrave, before re-addressing Slack 'o' Jack. 'Were you employed by George Curwen, gentlemen, on the third of November in this past year of our Queen Mary's reign, to rebuild roof and that part of said gentleman's house that was brought down by its collapsing?'

'Aye… well me and another three lads… I couldn't dae all of it myself… I'd cause ma'self a mischief!'

Titters again were heard in the courtroom. Louder than before.

The Justice of the Peace, rang a hand bell and shouted, 'The prisoner will only answer aye, or nay.'

'Well, Mr Black?' asked the Clerk Justice.

'Well what?'

'Aye or nay to the question put,' repeated the Clerk Justice, irritation ringing in his words.

'Aye, sir.'

'Did you procure all the materials for its rebuilding. And also commit to building, on commission by George Curwen, gentleman, a separate extension to his property?'

'Aye, sir. He wanted tae put his wife under a different roof. And seeing her, I'm nae surprised. A frightful sight she is.'

The Court erupted into laughter.

'Silence!' shouted the Justice of the Peace, again ringing his bell.

Quiet fell on the Court again. Fear dictated it so, when one man, still laughing, was roughly grabbed by the collar of his jacket and marched out by a Court guardian.

'There are charges from another gentleman, Christopher Chambers, that you did enter his roof space within the aforesaid month of the commission, with lighted candle and live coal, with intent to wilfully burn said gentleman's property. It is surmised that the fire, which consumed the whole property belonging Christopher Chambers, gentleman, was a result of your malicious actions.'

'I was in lookin' fer my chisel. I'd been in his house a month previous tae dae some repair work tae roof timbers. I needed a light tae see ma way in the dark… I didnae light his roof and burn his home.'

'The prisoner will remain silent,' ordered the Justice of the

Peace.

'Did Christopher Chambers, gentleman, give you leave to enter his home?'

Slack 'o' Jack looked to the floor and kicked his heels. 'Nay, sir.'

'It is reported that much burned timber, tile, lead and stone that fell from the aforementioned gentleman's property was then carried away in the night. It is also reported by several witnesses, including Abbot Hardon, and Sir Edward Adcock, that you were leading the men who did carry away the good stone, tile and lead fallen in distress. And this very material is the same used to fulfil your commission with George Curwen, gentleman.'

'It's a lie, sir.'

'Is this the bill,' the Clerk Justice waved a piece of paper, 'that you submitted to George Curwen for stone, tile and lead that you claim to have purchased?'

'Nay, sir.'

'It is written in your hand, sir.'

'Er… I mean aye, sir.'

'Were you in funds aplenty to purchase such materials required for the building as required by George Curwen, gentleman?'

'I got them on credit.'

'From whom?'

'A man I know in Penrith.'

'And his name?'

'Er…. William… I think.'

'Come, *Builder* Black, there is no William of Penrith to supply you with honest goods. The material you used was instead most untruly and maliciously procured?'

'Nay, sir.'

'Aye, Black.' The Clerk Justice looked to Sir Richard Musgrave, who nodded in return. 'I also have petition from George Curwen, gentleman, that your building work was carried out, and within the fortnight part of the roof, which you had built at his requesting, did collapse, killing his favourite dog and frightening, into malady, his lady wife.'

'Aye, I heard he was sore about the hound and disappointed about the roof missin' his wife.'

The Court was again in laughter, and the Justice smiled too.

'I understand you have a Mr Brownfield sitting in court with monies to pay your fines.'

'Aye, sir.'

'Is he such a rich man to have gold enough to pay for all your crimes, Mr Black? Enough to offer full restitution of all properties lost, including a dog valued at three pounds and physician's fees at two pounds?'

'I hope so, sir.'

'I am also informed that you have appeared fourteen times before the Manorial Court, as a sorry record of your dispute with your neighbours and your misdemeanours as a husband to three widows of the same manor.'

Slack 'o' Jack looked to his toes, as he waved his hands at a bee, buzzing around his head, and smiled.

The Justice of the Peace stood up from his throne. 'I am in a mind to accept all the Court brings to me in evidence against you, Mr Black. I will even allow this Court to accept Mr Brownfield's gold in lieu of your crimes against the plaintiff's property. But I feel your crimes against men are beyond the gold Mr Brownfield may have. And I am of a mind to do Mr Brownfield justice by saving his purse from emptying completely, as he makes good your ill. You therefore will be held for the further pleasure of the Assize Court. For I have you recorded previously as a soldier with a Scottish army, fighting the English Crown. And so this Court will treat you more than a miscreant, but as an agent of the Scottish Crown, seeking ill on English lands, and as such I will apply the laws said of the Marches.'

Slack 'o' Jack seemed to swat the bee that bothered him so, as the Justice made his address.

'I find you with ill purpose, and think you did seek to cheat a member of our knight Curwen's family, and also you have other foul purpose, in that you intended to cause greater malady to this town and a greater fire within it… as is the nature of a Scot's born man to do hurt amongst good English folk. Trial will be heard within twelve months from this date, before a judge appointed by the Crown, at the assizes.'

Slack 'o' Jack put his hand to his mouth, seemingly in distress.

'Sergeant-at-arms, take him away.'

The sergeant and another guard, took Slack 'o' Jack by the arms. Slack 'o' Jack backed away, resisting, but they held firm.

They began to drag him from the Court, but as they did he convulsed violently. His guards held on, as Slack 'o' Jack jerked and writhed. He went deathly pail. Then he frothed at the mouth, as seizure gripped him.

The men let go their grip, and Slack 'o' Jack fell to the floor, shaking and sweating profusely.

'*Plague!*' came a shout, then another, and another. '*Plague!*'

Sir Richard barked his command to the sound of his hand bell. 'Take him quickly from this Court, before we all succumb.'

Only one guard was brave enough to bend down to pick up Slack 'o' Jack, as he kicked around on the floor, as the Court emptied at the stampede. Confusion was all around, and Jack thought to tackle Slack 'o' Jack's guard to free him, but he was swept along with the throng.

People ran, and amongst it, the guard dragged poor Slack 'o' Jack along the floor.

At the door, and being jostled by the fleeing crowd, the guard's grip on Slack 'o' Jack's feet loosened, enough for Slack 'o' Jack to kick free the guard, get up and bolt for the door.

Outside the Court, Slack 'o' Jack thought he could lose himself into the retreating crowd, but all around him seeing who it was; a fevered cove, a plague bearer, scattered to the four ends of Carlisle, and he found himself alone in the street, exposed, a musket shot from the walls and towers of the Citadel, the city's southern defensive gate. He was an easy target. So he ran the length of English Street to put on a distance.

Still exposed, he ran to the lesser lanes and avenues, those not paved and seldom trod for they were green with grass, and in places almost entirely covered with weeds and underwood. Although the route hard to run in the wet, he thought it a safer route to escape. But the lanes opened up back onto English Street, and fresh with rain, the gutters were so deep with mud and filth, he found himself running the stones in front of the houses, to cross the road where stone bridges were laid to span the street to the high stone causeway that ran the entire road length.

With no cover and garrison men behind with their latches and firearms primed for firing, Slack 'o' Jack turned into another lane and the first open door he reached. Inside was an ancient woman at the fire-hearth, bent-double, adjusting the position of a heavy iron fire-dog. She hardly had time to look up to see the intruder, as Slack 'o' Jack raced to the door at the rear of the room. Once through the portal, the door closed behind him, swinging closed on its hinges, and Slack 'o' Jack found himself trying to recognise shapes in the dimly lit room. The light was poor, but there was no other door, and Slack 'o' Jack had to retrace his steps in the low light to the door he had just entered. Shadows stood the corner. Shadows he nearly touched as he groped his way back to the door. He could make out an old man standing still, bent-double, hose around his ankles, applying his lust to the rounded buttocks of a girl, *or perhaps a boy*, he thought. The light was poor. Slack 'o' Jack's eyes had not time to determine the truth of it, with escape heavy on his mind. The old man was lost to his lust, and his grunting did not abate or lose its want, as Slack 'o' Jack noisily retraced his steps back through the house.

And so he found himself back outside, in the lane, and the garrison men were near. They raised their matchlocks to take a shot, and so he ducked into another open door. He ran to the back of the single storey daub and thatch house, hoping this house had another exit and escape. There was a door, and it was weak against his strength and it gave way easily to his shoulder—too easily, as he crashed through it onto the ground beyond.

A high wattle fence was all around. No escape. He was not alone. He turned, his thoughts to retreat back the way he came, to choose a route back into the pursuing garrison men, the lessor evil. For his present company was one to face in fear—*a hundred deadly warriors*. And all those fighters came at him, in royal white livery and armed with canny weapons of harm—*a hundred angry geese*. The gaggle had only one design, to peck and snap at poor Slack 'o' Jack's arse and arms and legs and feet, to bleed him for his sins.

He could feel the violent stabs of pain as geese reached him, and his pace picked up a new and urgent tempo. Slack 'o' Jack reached the front porch of the house, with a goose or two still in pursuit.

The porch linked all the other houses on the lane to create a gallery. And two men stood at each side of the doorway. Leaving the only free route straight into the quag that was the gutter—a filthy trap for sure. The four garrison men faced down Slack 'o' Jack, and he stood in his tracks fearing the lead the men would fire into his flesh, for they all held matchlocks pointed against him.

Then a shot rang out. The retort dampened by the air of the enclosed lane, thick now with a new mist forming. Slack 'o' Jack recoiled. A garrison man fell to the floor to slide into the gutter, face down. He did not to resist the mire slowly swallowing him, so he had to be dead. The other three span around to let loose their shots into the mist, to the point of danger.

Slack 'o' Jack saw his chance, and ran past the single man standing in his way, the shot his rescuer, the mist his ally.

ꕥ

Jack had thought Slack 'o' Jack was well gone, and hoped he had found his way back over the border, back into Scotland, or better still into the Debatable Lands, where criminals and woebegone souls could lose themselves from the law.

So it was no wonder Jack was startled by Slack 'o' Jack's appearance in front of him. It was a surprise to see him standing in the shadows of his room, neither breathless, nor furtive from his escape. Not pale from his seizure, but drunk from five hours spent in the back room of an ale house, where the ale was ten times the price than front of house, but the ale servers' tongues were quiet and questions absent.

'It's good to see you Slack 'o' Jack.'

'It's gud tae see ye, Jack m'boy.'

'Are you well? Have you a fever or sickness?'

Slack 'o' Jack look puzzled at Jack's question, and it took a moment to search out its meaning.

'Oh…. The frothin' at the mouth.'

'Yes, what ails you?'

'I held a bee in my mouth. He took his time a stingin'. I had tae chew him a little tae make him mad.'

'You were stung?'

'Aye. I knew a bee-sting would bring foam tae my mouth and swellin' tae my handsome face… a frightful sight, indeed.'

'How did you know a bee-sting would contort you?'

'I'd eaten bees afore.'

Jack did not need to ask Slack 'o' Jack more. He was not surprised.

'Slack 'o' Jack, you best be going. The best place for you is across the border.'

'I'm nae wantin' tae go back tae Liddesdale.'

'It matters not where you go in Scotland. It matters that you get out of the Sherriff's reach.'

'I'm runnin' out of friends both sides o' the border.'

'My father still favours you, otherwise he wouldn't have sent me down with a purse for your fine.'

'Aye, yer da was always gud tae me. But this time I'm needin' tae lose myself gud 'n' proper. Over the water, perhaps. Ireland, or Wales.'

'Wales is not over the water.'

'Well ye know whit I mean.'

'No, go and see my father.'

'I'm afraid I've well wore out my welcome at his table. Yer uncle's too.'

'What's my uncle to do with it?'

'He's ma brother.'

Jack was stunned. 'That means…'

'Aye, nephew, I'm yer uncle. Black is nae my true christenin', but an alias adopted after I shamed good the family name. I wore it out till I was told tae find another. I was considered a badger amongst good lambs. My da thought I stole into his nest, I was such woe tae him. So like ye, I wear another's family badge… But unlike ye, mine was taken because I shamed my good name, I did not become ashamed tae wear it.'

Jack thought on his newfound kin. How best to save him. 'Shave your head. Shave your beard. No one will recognise you. Come with me. Lay low. Travel to France, and we shall be kin without a clan.'

'We shall be all the clan we need, young Jack.'

Jack smiled at Slack 'o' Jack, an uncle found. Jack was not disappointed. An indolent man he may be, but Jack could only recall a childhood memory of the man. And he could not recall a man with a wicked heart.

'And Jack…'

'Yes, *Uncle*.'

'Thank ye fer the well-aimed shot tae see off my pursuers.'

'I'm sorry, Uncle, it was not me that put a shot to your defence. The Sheriff's men had me held for five hours whilst they searched for you.'

Chapter VIII

The next day, with Slack 'o' Jack hidden, Jack and Francis quietly toured Carlisle to see if they could further bolster their numbers. But with Jack's commission to fight for Frenchmen, his levy fell on deaf English ears, and with increasing danger of challenge by the city's authority, he retired to prepare homeward travel with his few men, in the knowledge that Scotsmen would be easier to muster. They were fonder of fight, French gold and French keeping.

Jack thought a tardy return, be better than prompt. Better to coincide with Robert and Tom's return from Edinburgh. Better not to see Mary.

So he spent the rest of the night and two hours into the following day, writing a letter to his wife. Although he tried, he could not explain why he wished to travel to France.; to fight another's war, or why even he was going to war, only that he was.

All the words he used, none felt like the truth. His mind fought with his heart, and neither knew the truth. He could not claim he was leaving because of a marriage poor, or even because he longed for fight, or travel, or to see France, or for gold, or even because his father's realm was uncomfortable.

So a night spent writing was thrown into the fire the next day.

Jack knew it would be weeks before Robert, his second, could muster enough men for the journey to France, and weeks more before Slack o' Jack could travel without the constable's breath on his back.

And so came into his mind his thought of Allonby, and time to sit out a month or two free of the constable's watch on the roads. It would give Jack the opportunity to gather men in need of gold, or vocation for the fight in France. He thought of the opportunity to train country men above and beyond the *March Day* muster (the parishes commitment to militia service), to cross their swords in real fight against reivers, to draw blood, to test their mettle. True, they would not be border horse, born in the saddle, but with a long way to travel to the fight in France, horse craft could be taught, and horses 'found' on the way.

With such an opportunity he could take better-seasoned men, instead of fodder for the blades of better soldiers. Better still, he could train them at the expense of the parish for the aim of defence of that parish. Jack knew there would be men and boys who once their first kill was made, more want would follow, such is the evil spirit of men who grow to like the power of death over their fellow man. These men would leave their farms and wives not just for gold, but also for the fight and the adventure of it. More so, more pleasing to Jack's reasoning, was that his actions towards defending Allonby would sit well with Mary. Why he should care what Mary thought of him, he did not know, for his actions were born in deceit, his true purpose hidden from Mary, yet still he cared what she thought of him.

And so he wrote letters to Mary of his intentions to support Allonby against the fight against the reivers, and that she should remain in his father's keep until he returned. But Jack was in no mind to return to Mary, but that he left from the letter.

A second letter he wrote to Robert Hardie, his sergeant at arms, instructing him to keep his intentions on France and the muster quiet from all, and to meet him in three months, perhaps time enough for the reivers to strike Allonby and men to be gathered. With the letters he sent the coffer of dresses he purchased at the auction—guilt offering, parting gift, or a present of affection?

He did not know.

Holm Cultram

Chapter IX

Armed men walking the path to the rectory door was not a welcome sight for the servants and bystanders looking on. Neither was it for Thomas, who stood at the window as he weighed up their intent and origin.

He waited for their knock. Would it be politely sounded, via the serpents head, or hammered home with a fist on the oak?

The cast iron knocker sounded, and Thomas breathed easier once more.

'Not the Warden's men, Meg, nor bad men come-a-stealing. Their step is too polite for thieves. Their knock too quiet for the Warden's men come to do the Crown's foul bidding.'

'They are familiar to me, *Father*, friends I think, not foes.'

'Friends, Meg?'

'Aye, from my old life, tending the family Traquere. I washed the lad's pyntle when he was a boy, and oft chased the hunchback out of my kitchen, his hands filled with my pies.'

'Mary's man, Meg?'

'Aye, shall I open the door, Father?'

'No, I will attend to it.'

Thomas opened the door and studied the men at his door; a

young man, a short man, a large man, and three mounted men at his gate in steel and brown woollen cloaks.

'I come to speak to the rector of Holm Cultram,' announced Jack.

'And you, sir?' replied Thomas.

'John Brownfield, husband of Mary who is a friend to this parish, and so I expect this parish to be a friend to me and my friends here, Francis Bell and Bob Bendback Musgrave,' Jack pointed to the horsemen at the gate, 'And my men; my uncle, Robert Black, Geordie Reed, and he who wishes to be called, Brother Soldier.'

Thomas nodded to all in turn. 'I welcome you all in the name of the rector of this parish, Gawyn Borrowdale, who is indisposed and takes to his bed.'

'And so who are you?' asked Jack.

'Thomas Smith. I was placed here by the Diocese of Carlisle, *ad interim*, for matters of Church.' Thomas hesitated as he thought on his circumstance forced upon him by a change in sovereign power. A beneficent Protestant King replaced by a divesting Catholic Queen.

'And those matters are?' asked Jack.

'Matters of Church and not of men, Master Brownfield.'

'I apologise if I pry, but I am here by way of a wife who cares for this parish.'

Thomas stood in sorrow, and brought into his mind his own wife, absent, and then Mary and the affair at Allonby a few weeks back. 'Forgive my terseness, Master Brownfield, I am Thomas, friend to your wife, so I am friend to you…' Thomas looked again to Jack's motley men. '…and yours.'

Jack knew the name, Priest Thomas, for Mary had spoke of it, but he also knew the name of Thomas Smith and his rank and purpose in the land. 'You boast the same name as the Dean of

Carlisle.'

Thomas looked away. 'I am, and I am not the Dean of Carlisle.'

'Forgive my blunt wit, for I do not understand,' said Jack.

'I am Sir Thomas Smith, *Legum Doctor*, Priest and now to become former Dean of Carlisle, but I am Thomas Smith, a married priest and so under renewed Catholic edict I cannot hold the office of the Church.' Thomas stepped back from the door. 'Come into the hall, but I'm afraid there is little room for all your men.' Thomas looked at Bendback. 'My ceilings are a little low for such a mountain in my parlour.' Thomas then looked at Francis. 'It is as well you travel with small men as well as large.'

Francis grimaced, his eyes replying his disdain.

Thomas then clapped his hands. 'Meg, food for these boys, and get Melissa to see to the men's horses.'

Meg stepped forward from the shadows. 'Melissa is not about.'

Thomas shook his head.

'Melissa?' asked Jack.

'Yes, a girl named for the mountain nymph who cared for Zeus. A girl only in form, for she is as busy as a bee.'

'Hence Melissa,' added Jack.

'Yes, Master Brownfield, you know your Greek mythology… Melissa, who fed men honey, thus transformed them from eating man-flesh.'

'And whom Zeus transformed into a bee,' continued Jack.

Then both men, in unison, said, 'After Cronus, Zeus' father transferred her into an earthworm for thwarting his plan to devour his son.'

Both men laughed at their recital and comparable knowledge of the work of *Mnasea*, the ancient Greek historian.

Francis looked on, irked by the men's knowledge.

Meg interrupted. 'The Rector sees her employed. She's meant

to serve, but I'm afraid he lets her roam like a dog without a home.'

'Food, Meg,' said Thomas, curtly.

Meg led Thomas and Jack into the kitchen and on the table between a stack of wooden platters and bowls, and bundles of greens and picked herbs, was a pile of neatly wrapped packets. Jack counted at least twelve that he could see, but reckoned there were easily more hidden beneath the towering, pyramid of parcels. Each bundle was wrapped in linen or cloth of colour, and all most perfectly tied with dried grass, or cord, or leather strips, and even some with ribbon.

'Presents, Sir Thomas?'

Thomas looked to the direction of Jack's gaze. 'Oh, those.' Thomas grinned and then his face flushed with red, not from glee, but from embarrassment. 'Cheeses, and I even think there is a packet or two of *whitemeat*, in honour of your presence, *perhaps*.'

Jack was well aware of whitemeat, a field-ration amongst the Border raider; hilltop ewe-milk cheese, unyielding, long lasting and often tasteless. Many a good knife was blunted sawing off a piece to chew. Many a soldier lost a tooth to it, and many more complained bitterly as it rested heavy in their bellies for days at a time, rendering their stools fixed within, and painful to remove.

But there again, Jack thought, *many a strange fellow preferred it.*

There were many an occasion that Jack's days were fuelled on rations of whitemeat and oatcakes, especially on long-range forays to retrieve stolen beasts, or retribution raids to exact an eye for an eye, or a beast for a beast, which usually resulted in beasts acquired being more the number of beasts lost—*there was always profit to be had in revenge.*

'Whitemeat is not a favourite of mine,' announced Jack, 'but it is very fine to see you so well liked and receive so many gifts.'

'I would like to take pleasure in gifts given out of love, but alas these gifts are given at a cost. Once I made the error, at Sunday service, of praising a gift of cheese from a wife of *Mawbray*, only to receive another gift of cheese a day later from a wife of *West Newton*, and within a week a dozen gifts of cheese entered my life from a dozen wives of a dozen homes. Each feels her cheese is best, each wishes her cheese blessed. I'm afraid all the cheese is a pleasure too great, and I have grown fond of it in every hour, from waking to sleep, which I'm afraid often eludes me through dreams too strange to maintain the closed eye, or through pains from the cheese that, in a good wife's eagerness to present, was too green to eat. I am afraid the good wives see it as their pride to create the cheese that I would bless, which in turn is the root of my newfound gluttony. I have to say, the drunkard is ruled by his drink, and I am now ruled by the cheese that comes through my door. I am Thomas, the glutton, for although I would offer my guests food aplenty, I would always eat the last piece of cheese.'

Jack smiled, *what could he say?*

After the food and drink was selected by Thomas. After he overlooked the pile of cheese and filled the trays with bread, pastries and meats. The trays collected by Meg and taken to Jack's men. After the men consumed all and drank all down, Thomas directed Meg to escort Jack's men to their billet at part-ruined Wolsty Castle. He asked her to stay with them and make good their comfort, while Jack would stay within the benefit of Borrowdale's home.

Wolsty had space enough to house the men and their horses, and tenanted by one who would not fall short in his hospitality to the men, because he owed Gawyn Borrowdale and the Church plenty. A gross sinner repented, by the intercession of a priest, always owes his priest more than his life. He owes him his life everlasting.

Thomas, meanwhile, showed Jack around Borrowdale's home and then the Abbey Church.

Jack was impressed. The size of the church rivalled Carlisle's Church of St Mary's, and provided a far greater spectacle as it stood tall and dominant in its position on the Plain, not crowded in by a city's spread, but at the same time Jack was sorrowed by the destruction around it. For the Crown, worn badly by Henry Tudor, had dictated much of the prominence of the Abbey should be wiped away; its cloisters, dormitories, infirmary and kitchens removed or ruined, its gardens and orchards untended, and its greatness well bruised.

The Abbey Church was largely intact, and Thomas explained it was allowed to stand, because its nave was used for the parish and the people's devotions for some considerable time before the great surrender of the monasteries.

'The people about, petitioned the great architect of the Dissolution, Sir Thomas Cromwell.'

'He may have dealt his blow to the Abbey,' said Jack, 'But God, through his King's axe, put the blow on him.'

'True, sin directed his ambition, virtue removed his head… it is the way of things.' Thomas looked high to the tower from their vantage fifty yards away, in what was once a kitchen garden, now overgrown with weed and fruit bushes turned feral. 'Alas, this is now one of only a few Cistercian churches to remain, but it too will fall back into the earth, for the good parish here, for all their charity, are too poor to see to its care.'

Jack looked at the signs of neglect on the church, for the ruination of the cloisters had been carried out without careful regard to the standing building. Cracks had appeared on the walls of the church, and stone had been removed from foundations close to the walls without reconsolidating the earth. There was no shoring of the ruined structures left behind, which now pulled at their ties to the church building, forming fractures.

'The roof leaks,' announced Thomas, 'The glass is broken.'

Thomas led Jack on, to walk the outline of the cloister. The grand scale of the complex still showed with much foundation and the lower part of the walls still showing; red stone, itself reclaimed from ancient Roman structures now reclaimed by the Crown to improve and build new edifices of defence and stately power in the region.

'For a quiet price, stone was removed to set to improvements of Carlisle's defence and to gentlemen's houses about.' Thomas picked up a stone that had fallen from a ruined wall, once hall, and placed it best he could from where it had become dislodged. 'The Stewards of the Crown care little for four hundred years of Godly care. The monks here brought industry and wealth to the realm; wool and salt, good husbandry and fruits from the sea. It saw to the protection of its peoples about and the construction and care of many a village.'

As they walked on, down well trodden paths cut into the green, evidence of Thomas' habitual walks, Thomas' love for the church was evident, as he tired Jack with his tour, leaving no room unseen, no broken stone unturned.

'The Abbey has been the resting place for Robert de Brus, Sixth Lord of Annandale for a quarter of a millennia,' announced Thomas, 'Robert de Brus, father of the Robert the Bruce, King of Scotland, hero of Bannockburn. Such a noble man, yet the Scots would trample over his grave for a moment's pleasure.'

Jack sighed. 'Yes, I'm afraid the Scot is a fickle man when it comes to his heroes. History will see him sing his country's champions only as an excuse to raise a jug.'

'You talk badly of your kinsman, Master Brownfield?'

'I'm a Borderer at best.' Jack twisted his face. 'To call me Scot is to pluck my eye, for I do not think myself subject to any Crown.'

Jack quickly changed the subject for he wished to avoid any conversation regarding himself. 'So are you made rector here, deprived of your higher office?'

'No, I am placed here to keep me from view, but at hand, for the new dean, who is the old dean restored by a re-born Catholic administration, is not liked. Gawyn Borrowdale is rector here. He was the last abbot, allowed to stay after the dissolution of the Cistercian house. It is in his house in which you stay. His by way of a pension. Him fallen from the tree in a Protestant wind and picked back up from the earth by a new Catholic Queen.'

'And you, *Father*, do you sing Catholic and pray Protestant, or do you shout Protestant and suffer for it?'

'I am a man, learned, plucked from Queen's College by good King Henry as this realm's eyes on the World about. I am not seen as an enemy of my sovereign or this realm's faith.'

Jack smiled at Thomas' clear devotion to the Crown. 'Who benefits from the wealth of this land?'

'Our new queen has, by charter this very month, given the rectory and all its tithes and profits to the University of Oxford for its pleasure.' Thomas turned to Jack. 'Why do you ask?'

'I wondered who has the most to lose from the reivers' visits.'

'Only the people, for the Manor's fines, fees and rents are to be paid regardless. True, the reiver hurts the Crown's pride and may bloody the gentlefolk around, for the reivers are nothing but fair-minded. They see not the difference between prince and pauper, but it is still the pauper who has less, but pays more.'

'Does this *Abbot* Borrowdale have a voice to ask for better protection for the Parish… Do you not?'

Thomas' face was earnest. He thought carefully on his reply. 'I think Gawyn Borrowdale is no crusader, and I am ordered to remain quiet while I sit in the shadow of the new Dean. Besides, the Warden has more concerns on his doorstep than in his garden.' Thomas sat on a ruined wall to face the church, the earth beneath his feet well trampled. This was his repose. 'I am told Gawyn Borrowdale was not with the fifteen thousand pilgrims that had marched on Carlisle in protest at the Crown's continued suppression of the Abbey Houses, but I am told he did visit those peoples forced to camp at Cockermouth, as many pilgrims from this Manor were there to stand against the Crown. Some called it rebellion.' Thomas looked at Jack. 'Many were hung when the pilgrimage failed. Some were hung in a village near to your wife's home—*Torpenhow*. I think you know it.'

'I was interned there as a youth,' replied Jack, 'I heard the stories. Some peoples saw kin dragged by chains and hung by rope.' A bitter memory filled Jack's mind and so he diverted Thomas' discourse away from talk of his wife and his youth. 'What happened to the monks here?'

'Twenty and more monks found themselves with pensions and no home. Seven monks took to farming… took the tenants' fine. Some returned to positions within a new church order, for some were only in the abbey by way of sufferance, castrated for their crime of simony; their temporal gain for spiritual offering. Those men had been placed in the Cistercian order, a life of manual work and earnest prayer, simply as penance, to heal their souls of their greed.'

'Were they healed?' scoffed Jack

Thomas smiled, and shrugged his shoulders. 'Who knows how deep their sins run?'

'Nuns?' asked Jack.

'There were no nuns, but four were placed within the Abbey as their own Cistercian houses closed. I was told the Abbot was against it. With the monks seeing their monastic life ending and a secular one beginning, temptation for pairing was abound.

During the suppression of the monasteries, and following the inspections, there were terrible reports made of scandalous behaviour—*much exaggerated I think*, but unfortunately a nun in the Abbot's charge fell pregnant, and he was forced to cover up best he could, the shame of a child born in ignominy.'

'Sadness is always carried by a bastard born.'

'And what is the sadness you carry, my son?'

'Sorry, Father, I did not mean to show a troubled mind.'

'Do not be sorry. It is God who reveals your troubled soul to me. And it is my calling to tend it.' Thomas looked up to the Heavens, bringing hands together in supplication. 'He keeps me very busy.'

Jack grinned at his confessor's silent plea for respite. 'Save yourself for your flock, *Father*.'

'But while you stand in my parish, you are in my flock.'

Jack sighed, and yielded. 'They are petty burdens, Father, a mere drop amongst the sea of regret and woe that surrounds our lives. I am sorrowed, that I even consider them. More so if I show them on my face.'

'It would please me if you call me, Thomas. I accept my calling is priest and knight, but my name is Thomas, given by my earthly father, sustained by my Heavenly father. Now my son… *what are your burdens?*'

'Married to an absent wife, wedded to a wanting life.'

'Absent?'

'Her heart is with me to a degree, I suspect, but her nature is a poor match.'

'Our natures are different, and different by degree… One is truly blessed if we are married to our perfect partner, truly blessed, as perfection is God's dominion only. Otherwise we would be sorely disappointed come the Rapture. I suspect it is marriage and its hold that suits you badly… Not your wife.'

'Perhaps.'

'I suspect too, your union has not been blessed with living children?'

'No…but you will be aware of that.'

'Children are a marriage's blessing. Without them love can wane. But proper accord needs to be reached. Respect for God's sponsored union, first. Your love for God displayed in the strength of your earthly union, regardless of its trials.'

Thomas studied the discomfort on Jack's face, and it was clear Jack was uncomfortable to be on the end of Thomas' admonition.

ജ്ഞ

That night, Jack's men sat in the shadow of their billet, Wolsty Castle, or what remained of it. A castle built at some distance to defend the abbey of Holm Cultram seemed at odds with its purpose. And with the abbey gone, and the western coast sparse of raid, its walls only protected those who lived within it, those tenants paying fines and fees.

Francis shook his head and poked the embers of the campfire into flame. 'It feels foul to be sitting back in Cumberland.'

Slack 'o' Jack joined Francis and shook his head too, but he shook out thoughts of the perversity of a man who would think foul of being back in his birth-shire. 'Francis, dae ye ken this coast from yer days under commission fer Jack's gaoler, Captain Traquere?'

'As a member of the Captain's Watch, I had reason to travel to the harbours at *Parton* and *Dewentfoot Haven*, but I never ran up the coast for my own pleasure.' Francis glared at Slack 'o' Jack. 'And if I did… it would only be to spit at my kin across the water. Those bastard Scot, who turned their backs on family across the border. Bells born, to be shunned by Bells, simply because my bastard Scot forefather shagged a Cumbrian lass.' Francis spat into the campfire. 'He would see him bring his name to Cumberland, and then be shunned for it.'

'Bitter is the past for some,' replied Slack 'o' Jack, and he moved his head to rest his eyes on a shadow in the corner.

Soldier sat; a cloaked man; a statue outside the fire's glow. Hood drawn over his head to place a deep shadow over his eyes.

He sat. Still. Silent.

Not only Slack 'o' Jack studied the shadow, but also disdain viewed the show, and its spittle hit the earth. Geordie approached the men and asked, 'What's his story?' Slack 'o' Jack just shrugged his shoulders. 'Another lost soul? Another transient without a name, or a place to be?'

Francis simply poked the fire, ignoring Geordie's question. But Geordie waited for Francis' reply, thinking he should answer, but Francis showed his contempt and raised his eyes to Geordie to acknowledge him, only to return them to stare at the fire's blaze.

Geordie scowled at Francis' disinterest, and he walked up to stand over the cloaked man, a footstep away.

'I'll give you a shilling for your sword.'

He sat. Still. Silent.

'Mine's a little battered… It's seen some use…'

He sat. Still. Silent.

'Two shillings, then?'

With Geordie standing between Soldier and the campfire, Soldier's hood covered all his face. He was a shadow. He sat. Still. Silent.

Geordie cast a glance back at Francis, and seeing him look up from the fire, finding interest in the taunt, he grinned at him, meeting the mischief now on Francis' face. Geordie turned back to look at the cloaked man, and filled the gap, a footstep closer, to have the toe of his boot make contact with the shadow's cloak.

'I'd give you three… but a shilling I'll need to put an edge on the blade and clean off the rust.'

Soldier sat. Still. Silent.

Geordie's tone changed, his taunt turning into a testy temper. 'Lost your tongue, *Soldierman*?'

Soldier sat. Still. 'It's been six years since I saw you stripping the dead at Inveresk. You wore the English badge then. But it was not the battlefield you walked for spoil, after your sword had cleared it of Scot, but it was English dead, caught in our own lines by Scottish cannon, you were stripping. I suspect Scots armour was poor pickings for a picky man like you. Yes, I remember you, stripping our own English dead, slain on the fallow fields of Inveresk. Did you get a fair price for their armour, Mr Reed? And the purses, Mr Reed? Dead men's purses. Those best given to their bereaved families. Did your own purse feel all the better for their fill?' Soldier sat. He pulled back his hood. 'I was with Luttrell. With the vanguard. We wanted to cut all you carrion from the earth, but we had Scotchmen to kill.'

Geordie's taunt had been badly poked, now his hand fell on his sword, for fight was as evident, as it was that all the good humour was absent.

Soldier stood up, and let his cloak fall to the floor. An armoured warrior stood before Geordie, and Geordie fretted. Toe to toe the men stood. Soldier four inches taller and ten years meaner and harder by the toil of life than Geordie.

Geordie could not retreat, his hand was in play, a poor hand it was, so bluff was his game. 'Gads, you are an ugly man,' said Geordie, smiling, 'Looks like I'll be having your sword for no fee.'

'In a moment, it'll be the closest thing to your heart,' replied Soldier.

'First cut… or to the death?'

'Death. It will do the World a great service.'

Meg, seeing dogs at war, stepped in with a jug of spirit, freshly brought from Holm Manor. Spirit to heat the blood perhaps, but she knew shared drinking amongst men could the cool temper.

She ensured their cups were large and full.

Slack 'o' Jack appeared with a stout wood box, pulled from Geordie's pack.

'Play.'

Geordie accepted the box from Slack 'o' Jack. He opened it and removed his alto-crumhorn. He backed away from Soldier and put his horn to his lips.

Geordie entertained the men throughout the night. All enjoyed his skill. Even Soldier was impressed with the sounds he made, as he never heard a single crumhorn played outside a consort of such—*soprano, alto, tenor and bass.*

Meg stepped a dance, and Geordie refined his tune into a jig of his own design, such was his skill. Slack 'o' Jack kept the beat with an upturned pot as a drum, and Soldier stepped in to provide Meg with a partner. Even Francis was lost to Geordie's tune.

The Pied Piper had arrived in Cumberland and all fell under his spell.

After the music abated, all rested around the campfire. Francis found his eyes lost on Bendback, gruesome in flame's disfiguring light. He watched the mountain eating a loaf and quaffing the group's ale. He spat into the fire.

'There best be beer where we going to,' mumbled Bendback, spitting food from a mouth smaller than the bread it contained.

'I'm sure we will find comfort,' replied Francis. 'Dying is thirsty work.'

'What is landed at the port at Skinburness?' asked Geordie.

Francis replied, 'Goods for Carlisle.'

'And loaded?'

Francis sighed. *A question too many.* 'All I know is that boats are bound for Ireland, Scotland, Liverpool and the like. I presume they take what Cumberland provides; sea-salt, wool, metal and stone from the earth, beach-cobbles even… whatever needs to be shipped from Carlisle under the watch of the Warden.'

'Gold?' asked Geordie.

'Perhaps.' Francis narrowed his eyes, as his curiosity grew taller than his impatience.

Geordie rubbed his hands over the fire and took the ale from Bendback who, now drunk, had let his grasp loose on the jug. 'Comfort indeed,' he muttered to himself.

Soldier's ears were pricked by the conversation, and asked, 'At Allonby, will there be a warm welcome or cold comfort?'

'*Captain* Jack says, the priest will meet us at Skinburness. *Captain* Jack says, he'll take us along the coast to Allonby. He has business at the port, apparently.' Francis paused while he scratched his balls. 'Apparently, he will speak our purpose… and procure all support for this venture.' He sniffed his fingers to ascertain the cleanliness of his hose. 'Perhaps he speaks our purpose to the Almighty too… for I suspect a miracle is needed.'

'I'll take his place,' interrupted Meg.

'Sorry, Meg?' replied Francis.

'I will speak on yer behalf.' Meg put a log on the campfire. Her broth was cooling. 'To ease ma neighbours' fears.' She stood before Francis, and Francis shivered with remembrances of the washerwoman's severity. *A far bitterer wight than he.*

'I know them sorry folk, all, more than Sir Thomas. I know the sorry recreants who would talk succour, but whisper protest. I will speak. All trust this auld woman, and the ones who don't, fear ma scold.'

Francis nodded. He did not doubt Meg's boast.

'I will take up arms… I will take up arms to see the feckless raider killed,' added Meg.

Francis' eyes showed mild alarm, and hidden beneath a scowl, a smile appeared at the thought of this washer's courage. 'Meg, you are a woman of pluck, and one to put the fright on any warrior, but you are only a woman, and an old woman with no weapons. Keep to the care of the men who fight.'

'I'll get a weapon, there's plenty about.'

Francis was still impressed by Meg's mettle. 'Old lass, you've no skill in killing. You'll be cut down on the first pass.'

'A sword's a tool just like ma carving knife, and a reiver just another piece of meat to be chopped.'

Francis' hidden smile broke through his scowl, and he said, 'If we were firing words, Meg, you would cut down a dozen reivers, I've no doubt. But the meat on your cook's table does not come at you, screaming with a blade. You'll find cutting a reiver's throat a little more challenging than butchering a side of pork.'

'We'll see, lad. We'll see.'

Back in her own kitchen, Meg thought on Francis' chide and dismissed it. She picked up her cook's knife, big and sharp, raised it into the air, then brought it down in feint. She smiled at the thought of the blade sinking into reiver flesh. Then she grew unsure as she studied the blade in her hand, and her mouth formed a frown as she revisited Francis' words, and an agreement formed in her mind regarding her competence with regards to killing a living beast with bigger blades and better fight.

So she visited Gawyn Borrowdale's collection of arms and armour. Kept in a store. Kept from view and the knowledge of others. Much was older than she. Weapons of antiquity, ancient swords and shields, mail corsets and collars, steel caps and plate from two hundred years past. Borrowdale collected, but his collection was secret, for what man of God should take pleasure in weapons of war? She selected items to wear and a sword. The sword felt heavy in her hands. She tried an axe, a mace, a spear. All felt alien in her grasp.

Back in her kitchen, anger was in her work. She pounded the dough. She beat the laundry. She stabbed the pork on the spit to see it bleed fat on the hearth. And in all her dozen chores, she saw the men who had cruelly taken her family. She thought of them in her grip, in her burdens, and she choked, and beat the life out of them all.

She picked up her cooks' knife again. It felt comfortable in her hands. Her skill with this blade was well trained. *But the blade has no reach*, she thought to herself. Then her eyes fell on a broom standing against a doorjamb, and a memory pricked at her brain. A memory of a feckless, but fair husband, three children and countless sluggards coerced into compliance by a beleaguered wife and mother wielding her broom. She smiled a warm smile at the particular remembrances of a husband now deceased and three children departed, and set about her work. She cut thin leather strips from a hide hanging in the kitchen, and soaked the thongs in water, tying the handle of her knife securely to the end of the broom with the wet cords. This she thought would give her knife security on her broom, and then she set about her work brushing the floor, before preparing the men's rations for the days ahead.

Chapter X

On Solway Sand, April 1554, day 1

Seven took to the road from Holm Cultram, horses in single file, walking the rut that was the road to the sea. Jack led, as was his place; Francis followed, never content to be more than horse behind the leader, resentful he was not leading; Soldier, a dour cove for lack of fight; Bendback, tall on his horse, Meg's pies in each fist; Slack 'o' Jack, slumped in his saddle, in the dwam afore asleep; Geordie, counting his imagined gold in his head; and Meg to the rear, scowl worn on her face, brush-spear carried in her hand.

Along the green lane, Jack looked to the lie of the land and its long flat journey to the sea. It was more than a league over the Solway waters to Scotland, and to land rising high with the hills of Dumfriesshire.

He glanced back to his retinue and thought it a poor start for a troop to take to France, and hoped Robert, back in Scotland, would muster many more men to his commission. Jack hoped that he could persuade a dozen men and more from the peoples of the Solway coast to stick to his company, perhaps disadvantaged farmers in their prime, with glaives, or lads of age with a lust for a life outside their own bourn—men to train as troopers. With a musket unit more, or halberdiers perhaps, or even pikemen, his commission would command greater fee and see him in greater authority within a foreign army. The thought of it raised his head and hoisted his pride.

As he rode on, he worried his plans were perhaps too ambitious and badly thought out. Especially as Francis and Geordie carried complaint about the change in their purpose. Fighting a parlous reiver action was not in their interest; the pay was poor. Only Bendback, ever loyal, and Soldier, keen for a fight against all odds was behind his decision.

But as he fretted and chewed over his concerns, he looked to the coast, to the sight before him, and a sudden calm overwhelmed him.

Geordie dropped back, to separate Meg from the column. He looked to the woman and studied her face. Then he turned away and grimaced. Then he returned his head to look upon her again and smiled. He pushed his steel cap to the back of his head and looked to the path ahead. He raised his voice, so Meg could hear, and hid his face to hide the deceit drawn upon it.

'What's the wealth in this land, lass?'

'Its good folks,' replied Meg, sternly.

'Is there gold in the earth… copper perhaps?'

'Copper is in the hills to the east, lead too.' Meg looked sourly at Geordie.

'Gold?'

'Gold only sits in the coffers of the landowner, not in the earth for good folk to find.'

Geordie cast his line again, with better bait for a better catch. 'I suppose there are rich gentlemen aplenty?' He winked at Meg. 'Men to take a fancy to a handsome widow?' He smiled at Meg to dress his point.

Meg scowled at Geordie's sham flattery, she knowing the truth of her own poor looks. But replied to his question nevertheless. 'Aye there's a number about. Curwen's Hall sits pretty at Workington, on the mouth of the Derwent. It's good for salmon. A gentleman, Senhouse, has a hall nearby, at Ellenbourgh. He collects artefacts from the earth.'

Geordie grew excited with the thought of buried treasure. 'A horde of ancient gold and silver, perhaps?'

Meg grew disinterested in Geordie questions, but answer again she did, with a scowl on her face. 'What I have seen is stone and clay… great slabs of stone from the ground.'

Geordie grimaced, threw away his sham smile and looked again to the path ahead. He dismissed his questioning of Meg as a waste, and he stared hard into the back of Jack's head as if to read his mind and see the aim of his quest in such a poor place, and wondered where the riches lay.

As the seven rode on a mile longer, each man and the woman saw a shepherd sitting in a field, drinking his ale and chewing his bread. They had little thought for him, he being a shepherd. The shepherd however studied the seven most carefully. He counted them. He noted their progress, the time of day, their direction and demeanour. All in case he had cause to be questioned.

Not only did the shepherd study the riders as they filed down the lane that led from Holm Cultram, but a pair of eyes, most blue, studied the riders too. Eyes, shining at the sight of the riders in armour bright. Eyes, hidden atop a grassy bank, peering through bush and fern. Eyes, that had followed the riders from their sanctum. Eyes, carried atop legs that would run a wide arc to keep the riders in their sight, but out of theirs. They counted the horsemen as was their way, staying with the first rider to the count of seven, which was time enough for them to study the rider most meticulously, then they considered the second and the third… until they counted fifty-six, the last rider demanding a double count, because they had a sight of a face familiar above an unfamiliar sight. An unfamiliar sight because it was atop a horse, and most peculiarly it was riding well as if the rider knew how. The eyes smiled at the sight of it, and widened at a secret they thought to tell only their dearest friends; a story of Meg, riding like a knight. But the eyes drew back to the fourth rider—one most broad, with a lance long, in steel aplenty, on a horse most tall. The eyes lingered, until a dream pulled them away to face the sky so to complete the dream that could only be formed mind's eye.

ꟹ

At Skinburness, Jack met up with Thomas, who had explained away armed strangers in plain view of the March Warden's watchmen, as a tale of armed escort sponsored by the Church for protection of his own travel whilst on lesser byways inhabited by thieves.

'Allonby is over a league along the coast.' Thomas' words were loud enough for the Watch to hear, and listen they did as they leaned on their staves. Helmets pushed back on their crowns and questions rattling around their heads.

'These are not the Warden's men,' shouted one of the Watch, rubbing his beard, picking out the crumbs from a lunch started at the eleventh hour and still in the eating at three of the clock.

Thomas replied, 'The Church cannot afford the Warden's men, just as the Warden cannot afford his men to delay Church business.'

The Watch let their questions go and the party turned their horses to walk the coast path.

'I think you still might attract the Warden's attention,'

announced Thomas. He looked back towards the Watch on the road. 'Let us hope stories of armed men at Allonby are brushed away by his Watch, thinking they are under Church commision.'

'Then let us hope God delivers the Warden's attention when the reivers come to call,' replied Jack.

'You call on God to bring a miracle to bear?'

'We have God's man, why not expect God's hand in our good work too.'

The day was fine, the afternoon warm and the sight before them the lure, hazed by the sun. The coast path led them to sights of the sea and the reflection of post-noon's light on the silk-smooth sand. Wild geese in flocks stood the tide and waders of all kinds picked on the rocks that stood in pools waiting for the sea to return.

Ahead, the men had view of a saltpan and men working a *sleech* pit, laying straw, while others led an ox dragging the beach for wetted sand.

Thomas noticed Jack studying the work, and said, 'They let it dry to evaporate the water, to leave salt caked sand behind. They'll fill the pit with the sand, or sleech, let it wash with seawater and soak out the brine. They will recycle the brine several times until the liquor is strong enough to boil and extract the salt—winter work. The farmers need it to preserve their winter cull of over-stock and to sell on for profit. It is hard work.'

Jack was less interested in the industry, more so in the task he had to hand, and asked, 'Yet the reivers attack in spring to steal the salt, surely a winter raid would see a bigger haul?'

'Yes, it is strange. I suppose a winter crossing of the Solway is more perilous.'

Jack thought more on the season of the raid, and answers to its timing. 'More so perhaps the reivers are busy in the months after

Lammas and before Candlemas; months to see them reiving beasts on the hoof in the darkening days and longer nights. Taking winter grain stores and cattle strong from summer feed. Their own horses running fast and strong from cheap bought oats.' Jack thought on. 'Is the spring store of salt, large at Allonby?'

'Truth is, the farmers are canny, and their output is far greater than is ever recorded. The Manor ledger is a lie, more profit for the farmers. They stagger production from each saltern as the farmers about seek to maintain supply at the best price...so there is always a good stock of salt held back.'

'And it finds its hidden store in Allonby?'

'Probably... I would not know.'

Jack surveyed Thomas to detect any lie on his lips, but Thomas' face was an unwritten page, as clergymen often are.

Thomas continued, 'Skinburness once held all salt stock for distribution. Once an easy target for Scottish raiders from across the Solway, but it too was an easy count for Wardens and the Crown. I suspect Skinburness sees only that the tenant farmers, those with licence to operate the salterns, wish to be seen.'

Thomas looked to Jack to check his understanding. He saw only a man in conundrum, but still he delivered his history lesson, because he enjoyed history so.

'It was the priories and abbeys, established by the Norman that brought salt production to a scale better than the Roman who sat in governance of this shore in antiquity.

'How many priories?' asked Jack.

'There were seven Abbey Houses before the Dissolution,' replied Thomas breathing in deep the sea air. 'Seven built strong on the fertile plains of Cumberland; Lanercost, Carlisle, Wetheral, St Bees, Calder, Furness and Holm Cultram. Seven that stood for both the spiritual welfare of the peoples, their protection and their wealth, for it was the priories and the abbeys that worked

Cumberland for its bounty; wool, minerals, salt, fish and farm. Protected by river and marsh, these good Christian centres harvested both land and sea, and it was they who established the saltpans on the coast, and most productive of all was Holm Cultram. It built the first pans around Moricombe Bay, backed by good peat plains cutting good peat and turf to fuel the fires...sea-coal too, when it is found.'

'Did the industry suffer with the end of the Abbey?' asked Jack.

'Since the dissolution of Holm Abbey, salt production has been carried out without proper direction of the manor tenants. It was thought the revenues would be lost when the Abbey closed. But *Abbot* Borrowdale did not want to see the tenants lose their livelihood with new masters of the Manor, so he encouraged the saltpans to be maintained. He even brought new ideas to better make the salt.'

'The reivers know the secret of salt on this coast?'

'They do.'

'How so?'

'The Blacksmith's wife and step-daughter were taken by a raid on the border three years ago. Raids started two years past... It is thought they may have been the ones to tell the secrets, God save their souls. But who knows how the secrets were revealed?'

Jack had learned on his ride to Allonby that industry was the nature of the English Solway coast, just as strife and feud was business on the Scottish side. If it was not the road ahead filled with stock on the move, or ox-wagons carrying baskets of beach cobblestone to supply paving for the better houses and streets of Cumberland, it was the barrels of salt and fish loaded be shipped south to Liverpool.

Just as the land supplied food and peat for fire, the beach was the source of much of the industry, with coal collected, and old ship and boat dismantled for timber for the sea walls, dykes and building about. Shrimp and herrings landed and shipped.

So for all the loneliness of the villages, and the scarcity of the peoples about, work found all men and women, and all worked willingly. But the beauty of the plain and the beach that ran with it was not in its industry, but in its endless sight, and the sight of it made Jack give a thought to Mary.

He understood why she had a care for this place.

There is a place, ethereal, where the elements of rock and sand slowly melt into the sea. A place to find in the morning, when the wind is stilled and tide receded. When God's breath sits over the water and clouds the distant hills of Dumfriesshire in blues of unnatural hue. When he colours it all so perfectly with subtle brush.

He paints a canvas greater than any devotional artist. No fresco painted by man could be greater. Nothing could be painted so well. God's creation, wondrous is his imagination, greater than any thought in the minds of great men.

The remembrance of it overwhelms me. It humbles me to the earth. It brings me to my knees to pray:

Help me, God, settle my mind and heal my heart, for this thought of a place so perfect, is too good for such a lowly man. Forgive me for petty thought and selfish action, for to share them in a mind that remembers that sand, and sea, and sight of it, is grave injustice. For that place on Solway shore is your gift in a world of gifts for men. You gift beauty to the eyes, your wind to brush the skin, your sea to perfume the shore.

Thank you for Solway Coast. Thank you for Solway Sand.

John Brownfield, MDLXX (1570)

Annandale

Chapter XI

Moira was not shy in entering Will's room. Nor did she knock loud enough for him to hear. It was two hours before dawn, so he should be sleeping.

She hoped.

She crept so as not to wake him. He was not naked on the bed as she expected, but well covered under sheet and blanket.

Still, she hoped.

'Master Will,' she whispered.

Will slept soundly, undisturbed by the mouse's voice squeaking in his ear.

'Master Will… Master Will.'

Will slept on through murmur.

Moira gingerly tugged back the bedclothes to see his condition. Although a maid, Moira was not lost to the knowledge that a man would often stand proud in the morning. She was not disappointed.

She hoped… and dreamed.

Will had poked her before, when he was drunk and wanting, so she hoped he might do so again, when lust in the morning takes a man's fancy. She had not forgotten his ardour. She objected of course, it was her way, virtue her show, chastity her badge, and lust her hidden thought. She hoped to chastise Will again—*she hoped.*

Will stirred, and Moira quickly returned the covers. Will woke.

'Ahhhh…' Will was always a bear when sleep was left. His wits remained in dream. His temper to the fore. His eyes in discomfort, as he tried to see world.

'Whit dae ye want ye feckless drudge?'

'It's a letter, Master Will.'

'Can it nae wait?' Will turned his back, and closed his eyes. He sought to re-join his wits again, left in paradise, where he always won at cards, his estates were endless, and all the women were of easy virtue, with sweetened tongues and temper.

'She's gone. I found this letter.' Moira shook Will's shoulder.

Will swatted Moira's hand away and brought his blanket tight around him. 'Leave me be… ye scold… leave me be!'

Moira pulled hard on Will's blanket, but he held it fast.

'She's gone, gone… *A letter,*' she cried.

'She?' Will sat up, rubbed the sleep from his eyes and took the candle from Moira's hand to shine it on her face. 'Moira… where's your mistress gone now?'

'I dinnae ken?'

'Gi' me the letter.'

Moira handed Will the letter.

He read it knowing Moira, *the pry,* had already read the contents.

'I should ask ye what it says. Save ma poor weary eyes,' said Will, as he struggled to read the letter by the candle's light.

Moira hid her deceit behind a simpering smile. 'I don't know where she's gone.'

Will glanced at Moira, better served by the dim half-light that colours a sour face kinder. 'It says she goes tae petition Lord Maxwell, the Warden o' the West March,' he gave Moira a stern look, 'But ye ken this.'

Will threw back his covers. 'Pass me the pot, *ye scold*.'

Moira passed Will the chamber's pot, and he relieved himself without modesty.

Moira looked away, still simpering. 'I knew ye should have the letter urgent.' She turned her head to glimpse Will naked, standing tall, finely built, broad shouldered, strong buttocks and good long legs.

She hoped.

'I hope ye don't mind me entering yer room while ye were sleepin' 'n' dreamin'.'

'Should I thank thee? If ye'd been at work when ye were meant tae be, ye would have found the letter and alerted me sooner... Ye shiftless piece o' shite.'

Will had no time to raise more than four men for the chase. And chase he did. He rode his nag as if he were chased by a thousand *bodaich*—a thousand spectres. His men could not keep his pace, and with his torch forever fading in the distance of the half-gloom, they kicked hard their nags, praying for the sun to rise behind them to shine better the road ahead.

Mary was not caught till late morn.

Will was breathless, and he feared his sweated-nag was showing poorly for its exertion. But with Mary caught, his pursuit was complete and he hoped a deserved rest could be made before return.

But Mary was not for resting, and Will's entreaty was made atop an unsteady horse.

'Lord Maxwell holds nae fond feelings for this family. He's a poor route tae savin' yer village, lass... Forget woes ye cannae sweep away and look tae yer own house... Come back wi' me.'

Mary rode on, clutching her little dog, Ruff, close to her chest, shouting her response to Will, his own nag now halted in its pain and exhaustion. 'I must do what I must do. If my husband fights my cause, then I must do all I can to fight my cause in my own name.'

'Stop, lass!' shouted Will, kicking his nag. But it had finished its race and rest was its new master. 'Jack is able. Mair able than most. He's been born wi' mettle and he applies it well.' As Mary moved on, Will shouted louder. 'If any man can teach yer village tae protect itself, he can. It will gi' him small comfort tae ken ye here, takin' on the reivers yerself.'

Mary halted her horse and turned to look at Will, just as his escort caught him up.

Will kicked his nag hard to press on, but it would not move. His entreat became desperate. 'End yer march, lass. *I order it!*'

Mary turned her horse away.

Will seeing his poor strategy, shouted more words, more forgiving in their form and delivery. 'Mary, good lass, at least let us escort ye, tae keep ye safe in yer quest.'

Mary halted. She stood a while. She turned back to Will, and seeing his horse badly sweated, red nostrils flaring, head down and in stagger, she thought to stop her ride to save Will's horse the kicking. 'I will not be changing my mind, Will. My mind is my own, and my will, *will be done*.'

'As ye wish it… Just give my nag a little comfort and walk a while.'

Mary dismounted, and waited on Will, as he handed his nag to one of his men to lead to nearby water.

'Ye dae nae favours. *Da* will nae think on ye kindly fer this deviltry. Neither will yer frettin' husband.'

'*Deviltry!* Is it the Devil's mischief to intercede when men think it plain and proper to steal and kill?' Mary wore green and her face wore red. 'And as for my *husband*, for all he takes on the mantle of defender, I suspect he cares less where I am and who I am, for his demonstration, plain and proper, as a husband is a poor one.'

'When the seeds 'o' pride are sown, it raises yer head so high ye cannae see what's in front of ye.' Will looked to Mary, but she seemed deaf to his words. But his entreaty was still delivered earnestly. 'Jack's a hurt man who has lost his sense of place, and therefore wishes tae seek a better place. He sees ye as part of the walls that hold him, but have patience, lass. He will see sense of a gud woman, and the gud land he lives in.'

Mary cast Will a doubtful eye, and Will too, in the end, doubted his words.

Horses rested, Mary and Will, with their guard, took to the road again—the road to Annan, for the road to Maxwell and Caerlaverock Castle.

Will and Mary talked.

Will's discourse with Mary had been thinly scattered over the five years since they met. He had little reason to talk to women. His women served his will and whim, and gentle discourse was never his pleasure. He lived his life in conflict with his neighbour, safeguarding his name, his kin and when he could, his country's honour. Borderer born he was. A patriot to his country's Crown in his heart, and thus he stood separate from border kind, those who thought themselves a nation of their own, neither Scottish nor English.

But today he took his pleasure to be riding alongside Mary, a woman handsome and of wit. She seemed different to him, and whereas five years had took the smile from Mary's face, it had matured a girl into a handsome woman. He recalled his brother's wedding day to mind—Jack and Mary's wedding day, held in an English church, in an English village sitting within her father's realm. Since then words were rare between them, although mutual care and respect was always held, and where words were offered, they were always fond words.

'Aye, Mary, pride is whit a man wears as his badge in this land. Pride mair than honour. I lost ma pride in seven years fightin' for the English against Scotland. The price tae pay for keepin' Jack safe whilst he was interred with ye father as a pledge.' Will shifted on his mount and changed his tone to sombre. 'Mary, boys are moulded by their youth. It was hard fer Jack. His growin' years were marred by his uprootin' from his home. He was in love wi' yer sister, true, and offered tae ye as a groom in spite of that. But despite a poor start fer ye both, Jack will come tae terms.'

Mary countered, 'I suspect my husband is still in love with my sister and does not care to be wedded to me.' Mary looked kindly towards Will. 'Your brother is ungrateful for your sacrifice, Will. Yet you still speak well on his behalf. I think you be the better man.'

Mary's smile stirred Will. Her words of praise pleased him. Will shook his head to remove the thoughts growing in his mind, and instead thought to counter Mary's poor opinion of his brother. But another sense took him. He studied Mary. He thought on a good woman wasted. So he buried his praise of his brother for a while—the while she thought better of Will and worse of Jack.

As they rode on, Will did not think to force Mary to return home. He knew to parry her will would be wasted. Wasted too that day was Will's good sense, as days more in her company became more appealing—more appealing than his sworn duty to kin, now forgotten.

Ruff always took the lead. For him it was his place. Mary would call him back, but with only one ear compliant to his mistress' voice, his will was his own, and his place was at the front. He would run high on the ridges, climbing rocks and high places. He would watch the way, keeping his pack safe, keeping his mistress from harm. He knew best. But from time to frequent time, he would return to check on his mistress. And with always a smile to greet him, he knew the harshness in her pleas for him to stay close were kindly meant, and not chide for him to suffer. So his tail would tell her, and the sparkle in his eye would tell her, his devotion was for her, and his disobedience wasn't badly meant, it was just that he knew best.

The danger of her journey did not concern Mary. A fine dressed lady would always attract attention in a wicked land. So, for travelling, local ladies would wear plainer clothes, with colour careful not to shout its expense. For a flag of riches and a meagre retinue would invite the road-thief to come-a-calling. But Mary was not concerned. She aimed to impress the Warden. She wanted favour, and she thought finer attire might effect a kinder reception. Plus, she hoped the March Warden's wife, Lady Herries of Terregles, may provide better discourse, as well as being a lady of the West March worth the know.

Mary was in need of good company. She missed her sisters. She missed her mother. Her letters to them, were a poor replacement for heart-felt discourse between women bound by blood. Her letters were read by mother and sisters with disharmony, because knowing their sister, knowing her daughter, they could read the words felt, but not written. They could read beyond the gracious rhetoric that disguised her sadness.

They had been riding without proper respite since dawn. Bread was past and shared between riders, apples too. Will concerned himself with their horses, needing rest and water, but Mary pressed them on. Rest was delay, and delay was more time to add to the Devil's pleasure and his reiver children, out for mischief and mayhem.

Even if Mary was unhappy with her surroundings, she also found it beautiful. For as much as the nature of her new realm and family caused her discomfort, the land's nature; fell, hill and expanse, found tremendous favour in her eyes, especially when she found herself on a high place looking south towards the Solway Firth and the massive expanse of sand that spread wide and long from the green land at low tide.

However, the beauty of the route was marred, because on the road was a sight to take eyes off the splendour of the green, and onto the wretchedness of man. For walking the path was a group of men and women, children too, all naked, all walking towards them, blackened with soot, bruised and bloodied.

'We've been burned oot… told tae leave oor homes… they've killed fourteen of us, and three of the bairns are near tae death.'

Mary set about immediately, stripping the blankets from the men's packs and blankets off their horses. She ordered the cloaks from the men's backs, and even though protest was given, Will ensured all complied.

'Who would do such a thing?' cried Mary, running from naked soul to naked soul, putting a hand of reassurance on those she passed.

'Where d'ya come from?' asked Will.

'We farmed land ootside Annan.'

'And ye be?'

'All Johnstones, a few Littles and Hendersons.' The man looked back into his group and sighed. 'Although it's only baby Davy Henderson, he's just lost his da, and his ma was killed last harvest, so he's orphaned now.'

'And was it Armstrongs, or Maxwell's that stripped ye bare?' enquired Will, as if he already knew the answer.

'Armstrongs,' came the sad reply.

Will sat back on his horse and addressed Mary, looking to him for support. 'There ye have it, Mary. *Thou shalt love thy neighbour as thy self, the Book of Mark.*'

'What do you mean, Will?' asked Mary.

'The Armstrongs left them alive… that's an Armstrong's only notion of love, of charity, tae leave them with their life.'

'*Foul they are… Wretched they are!*' screamed Mary, her blood boiling with injustice.

'Dinnae be too hard on the Armstrongs, lass. I like them less than a turd on my boot, but nae doubt they had cause, and cause long outstandin'. Naked and bruised their victims may be, but I've nae doubt their families are nae angels.'

'Children, women… *What have they done!*'

'They are born and begettin' mair. Reason enough tae see them harmed.'

Mary's rage turned to tears. 'Is there justice in this land? Is there *charity?*'

Will shook his head. 'Have ye learned nothin' in yer time here?'

'Yes, Will. I've learned that the men do the razing and the women do the mending.'

Will nodded in agreement. 'Aye, I've heard my *ma* say it a dozen times.'

'Will.'

'Yes, Mary.'

'Give over your purse and make sure two of our men lead them safely to the nearest town or village. Make sure they find proper food and shelter.'

Will smiled. He did not counter Mary. He did not protest her order to half their own guard, or even to relinquish his own purse in the name of Mary's charity. He complied without complaint, his admiration of Mary's spirit evident. He simply shook his head, thinking himself unlucky not to be matched with her, and resented a brother ungrateful for such a splendid match.

Will dismounted and walked over to see to their nags. He fretted over the horses with their blankets removed and saddles replaced. They'd be walking more to Caerlaverock Castle now, to save the horses' backs. He gave the instructions to the men to escort the people to Dumfries, by way of the nearest settlement; clear orders of care for their charge, and warnings to the men to avoid trouble. He felt the weight of his purse, and halved its fill, passing the coin to the men.

'Make sure ye get good grace fer the price of my charity. Fer the good peoples of Dumfries will know the cost of their care and add a penny piece mair tae it fer their greed. I'll expect nae profit tae be made at my expense.' The men grunted their understanding. 'And boys, see tae it my charity disnae end up wettin' yer lips, or my wrath will be seein' me wettin yer skin with ma whip.'

The men understood very well.

Chapter XII

The March Warden's castle was reached late afternoon, and Mary and Will were the only ones allowed to enter across its timbered bridge and drawbridge. There was a third. Mary carried Ruff, hidden in her cloak, for he would not be parted from Mary or Will.

Caerlaverock was a castle strange. Moated, but that was not peculiar. Its gatehouse stood tall, twin towered, impressive. But it was its form that stood it different from other border towers and castles, for it was a castle of three sides, not four, and that stood it dissimilar from any fortress Will had ever seen.

Whilst crossing, all eyes scanned the lofty stone. Eyes drawn upwards by the height of the twin round towers flanking the gate, topped by projecting parapets with slotted defenses; machicolations, built so castle defenders could throw missiles at those below. Then to a tower built high upon the gatehouse top, so the gatehouse became greater than any city portal. Will felt the eyes upon him from above, and he was not happy.

Will had been standing for an hour, waiting in the triangle courtyard of Maxwell's castle. He felt uneasy that Mary was out of his sight, even though she had been taken indoors politely, to await an audience with Lord Maxwell, with all the courtesy of a lady of rank.

His concern had blinded him to the slowly gathering group of men, studying Will, mocking his dog companion, and looking for sport to while away a day spent idle.

The growing threat however had not been lost on Ruff, whose tail had dropped and whose hackles had risen. More so, because three hounds, tall, were brought into the sorry mix around them.

Ruff stood his ground, resolve his shield, bravery his badge. The Lord's slew hounds stood around him, heads low, mean-growling their discord with the intruder into their domain. Three hounds far bigger than Ruff; veterans of a hundred fights; killers of men; ruthless defenders of their Lord's tower. But behind Ruff stood Will, alert now to the threat, contempt worn on his face against the beasts. No fear shown. No fear felt. He had faced down wolves; these mealy pups caused him no fright.

But Ruff's purpose was his own. He stood in defence of Will and any who he called his pack. These hounds would not have the best of his friend, or his mistress, or his noble stand.

The numbers were against him, but Ruff, with eyes about him, singled out the leader for first bite. Head low and snarling, he knew the rest were cowards, and Ruff knew to strike first and tear the throat of the leader was an able strategy to see him win his fight.

About were the Lord's men; high born and low born, but scoundrels all, betting to see how quick the little dog would be torn. They laughed at the little dog's plight and thought to restrain one of their hounds to make it a fairer fight. But with their hounds standing twice as tall, with weight again to subdue the little dog, it would not take the Lord's poorest hound long to shake out the puppy's life.

But the lead hound caught Will's stare, and saw his teeth bared, his intent clear. It smelled the wolf on him; its blood, and it knew he faced the wrong foe… *The bigger dog behind the smaller one was the one to fear.*

Those who watched the encounter with anticipation of a little dog torn, never knew if the three dogs yielded to the little dog or the man behind him, but yield they did. And Ruff, seeing victory, cantered off. His tail held high in happy wag. His head higher than his tail. A leg cocked in disdain, urination to mark his place, followed by two front paws scratching the ground to throw his scent back up to the hounds' noses.

The little dog caught the eye of Will, and came to him to sit for reward. But Will only had words, kindly given, and Ruff took it as praise.

'Ruff, ye'd be better pickin' on dogs yer own size.'

Ruff threw a sideways glance at Will's words. His brown, shining eyes underlined by their whites, said his reply.

Will smiled and nodded in agreement with what he saw in the little dog's eyes. 'Aye perhaps yc're right… Where would be the sport in that?'

As the men chained their dogs, Will walked up to the man who seemed to direct the others. He stood before him. 'Ye're lucky. Nearly lost three valuable hounds ye did. If yer master is a hunter, I suspect he values the hounds mair than the houndsmen. Keep them in check, or see them slaughtered, for if ye goad them again against my Lady's pet again, it'll be my teeth at yer throat, and I have nae tasted man-flesh fer quite a while. I miss its sweetness and other men's blood is my favoured liquor.'

The Lord's houndsman stood staring, Will's words settling in his ears, his spittle wetting his eyes. He did not know if Will's threat was boasted or real, if Will's bark was worse than his bite. But his growl sounded crueller than his own dog's, his gaze sharper than his own sword. So he nodded his compliance—*prudence better than pride,* he thought.

The noise outside roused Lord Maxwell briefly from his study of the vellum in his hand. He thought to go to the window to see what had roused his hounds into aggression, but instead returned his eyes back to the script to be read.

'Nae wonder the English think we're a canny larder tae raid fer beef 'n' mutton. Wi' claims fer loss as grand as these, the English must think oor hills swarm wi beasts.'

Lord Maxwell picked up the stack of paper from his clerk's desk, reading the top sheet, peeling it off, and thrusting it before his clerk's eyes. '*Look at this, look at this!* Beany Bell 'o' Palnackie, who obviously overswears his claim fer loss. He reports he lost twenty cattle within the week. Within the month he claims a further thirty stolen, which I know is ten times mair than he ever owned at any time, him being a feckless tenant who sells what mangy beasts he has tae pay his gamblin' debts.' Maxwell cursed beneath his breath. 'I have seen the man sittin' in my church, at mass, wi' a face o' an angel, whilst his family starves.' Maxwell read the second sheet. 'And look at this, Angus. A claim fer thirty sheep 'lost to the English'. Whit daes the fool expect when he drives his animals tae graze over the border…' Maxwell peeled of another sheet, another, and another, letting them fall to the ground one by one—all for Angus to collect. 'All these feckless cuddys expect others tae pay their bills with spurious claims. It is time we educated them all, so they can count tae ten without it addin' tae a hundred mair in their favour.'

His rant abated at the last page, which read, '*Disbursements*', and he read down the page, the list of his charge; the land and water sergeants who policed the March; clerks to keep his courts; stewards to keep his households; the watch on the fords and crossing points; his own company of guard, and the sundry payments to the keepers; Scottish gentlemen of the Western

March who provided watch within their own lands—*names* that included Jack's father.

When he reached the bottom of the page he thrust that paper too in front of Angus, just re-seated after collecting the fallen paper. The paper was so close to his eyes that he had to lean back to see the print, so much so, that he nearly toppled in his chair.

'Is this figure at the bottom of the page correct, Angus?' Maxwell's finger underlined the gross amount.

'Aye, sir… it is.'

'Rarely does the Warden's purse see two thousand pounds for the upkeep of security in this territory, yet the cost is always five times mair. Gad, a garrison the size of Berwick's would cost nae mair than twenty thousand. Tell me, Angus, dae we have five thousand troops tae call?'

'No, my Laird.'

'*Well, where are they, Angus?* Dae ye hide them under a rock, or in a cave. For our bill here lists a pretty price. Surely two thousand pounds pays fer mair than the petty shite we have wi' a sword in this land. Fer shite is all I have.'

'The bill is the new Warden's. Shall I pass it on?'

'The bill is my brother's, unpaid. God rest his sorry soul. The debt is mine tae find.' Maxwell looked to the ceiling, as if he could see his deceased brother looking at him from the rafters. As if he could see an old face drawn with the worry that had seen him into death with the burden of stewardship. His brother, Robert—the former Lord Maxwell, last Warden of the Western March, who had died the year previous. 'Oh, Almighty God, who surely stands now wi' ma past kin gone tae serve, gi' me an army so I can bloody every sorry soul that sees my family poor. I'd gladly flush out those rats that scurry about our Queen's Court… Shite that seeks power and privilege only fer themselves.'

Angus bowed his head in a show of agreement, even if his eyes tagged his new master, *hypocrite.*

Maxwell marched over to the window, to open a transom, to breathe in fresh air to quell his anger and frustration. Below were men of his company; his guards, family members keen to distinguish themselves in the ranks of the Maxwell clan by acts of renown, disguised as violence and notoriety through raid.

All were grouped around a man and a small 'fancy' dog of black and white.

'Seems my company have new swords tae carry, new jacks tae wear, and new bonnets tae keep dry their tresses. Men wi' time tae spare playin' wi' ma hounds and tellin' stories, nae doubt, how they've shagged my kitchen girls.' Maxwell chewed over a fitting penalty for men laughing whilst he was grieving. 'We pay them too much, Angus. Cut their wages by a third, and raise their bounty payments by a half… Let's make them work fer their finery. Coin less in their purses will see mair raidin' and less restin' fer these boys. It will see them keener wi' the blade, and hungrier fer pay. And we'll be needin' keen men tae watch our backs, Angus… Wi' our gud Queen's French mother tae the fore, tae be rulin' Scotland, and the English Queen insistin' on a marriage tae the King of Spain, we'll be at war wi' England again afore ye know it. And me sittin' on the border wi' only a thousand men tae call.' He looked to his clerk, a half smile trying to battle through grimace. 'And I'm preferin' tae see you, Angus, with a quill behind yer ear, and nae a pike over yer shoulder.'

'I applaud your sentiment, my Laird.'

Maxwell looked back through the window, spying Will. 'Angus, who's the man wi' the black 'n' white pup?'

'Oh, that'll be Mary Brownfield's escort; the lady who has an appointment with you, this afternoon.'

'Isn't she the daughter-in-law of James, the Laird of…'

'Aye, sir.'

'An Englishman gentleman's daughter married off by Lord Scrope to a Scottish gentlemen intent on peace in the borders… I hear she is a well-mannered woman and well educated.'

'She seems so, my Laird.'

'She is here?'

'She waits in the Hall for your meeting. Lady Agnes keeps her company.'

'Then, Angus, this is information I should have been given afore yer bills and entreaties. Now yer badly chosen priorities will send me tae join my good lady wife and her better company wi' a hot and fractious temper. Gud sense is nae yer callin', Angus.' Maxwell took a deep breath. 'Still the ladies will cool my blood.'

Maxwell took three steps towards the door and spied two large crates in the corner of the clerk's room. 'Whit's those, Angus? Mair bills, or new quill-pens and paper fer yer pleasure?'

'They're Lady Agnes' new dresses.'

Lord Maxwell thought on his sorry purse. 'There again, perhaps it's better my blood boil over tae scold my heart. Fer a quick death in this realm is God's blessin', fer if the cost of keepin' this realm daes nae bankrupt me, my gud lady will, fer all the land my marriage tae her has brought me, the cost of havin' the land, costs mair than the land itself.'

When the door closed and the latch clicked, and Lord Maxwell was five-steps gone, Angus let out a deep sigh. The other two clerks lifted their eyes from work already long completed, and returned to their chatter.

'He's in fine mood today,' announced one of the clerks, raising his eyebrow.

'I suspect he's fearin' the outcome of the change of Scotland's Regent, fer I think Marie of Guise is none too fond o' the Maxwells,' answered his desk mate, pushing his quill behind his ear and admiring his cartoon of his master kicking Angus up the arse.

'Aye, that'll gi' him somethin' real tae complain aboot. A wish I were a penny behind him, fer I'd be the second richest in this realm. I'd have my wifie sent tae the Americas, and I'd buy myself a couple of slaves from Edinburgh tae dae my biddin'.'

Angus barked, 'Shut yer gabblin' gobs, and find some work worth yer wit. If the rule of this realm was left to you, timorous beasties, we'd be all with English masters by now.'

Maxwell muttered to himself all the way to the Hall. He cursed the air about him and the hundred pricking thoughts that blinded him to scullions standing idly when work would be better done, and to the men standing waiting for another opportunity to better fill their hungry purses. He thought to cover his snarl with a smile, so that a lady visitor, new to his eyes and reported fair, would find him to her liking. The smile became a smirk, because a woman without her husband to hand was, in his prurient thought, a woman in want. Such was the arrogance of this man of power, whose pride was so boundless that he thought his lust could only be welcome.

But in the Hall, only Lady Agnes, his wife, was waiting, and his disappointment was clear.

'Whar's my visitor?'

'She's by the fire in my rooms, *Husband*. I've reunited her with her escort and her cur. Your rowdy boys make poor the need tae treat guests and their escorts with noble courtesy.'

Maxwell recalled the scene from his clerk's window and nodded his agreement. 'Then you better send fer her, Agnes. So I can conclude our business.'

'There is little need fer ye tae see her, *Husband*, because I know why she is here. She has told me of her entreaty. She comes tae plea the case fer the peoples from her previous charge, on the English coast. She comes tae ask ye tae intercede over the raids on that coast by reivers… Pirates sailing out of Dumfriesshire.'

'Then, *Wife*, she has wasted her horses making the trip, fer I have enough problems wi' ma own realm tae start doin' the English favours.'

'Are ye not afraid the English Warden will counter raid, John? Is it not best we turn the reivers' attentions off the English coast fer the sake of peace?'

'While Johnstones, Armstrongs, Halls and Elliots ply their reavin' trade outside my charge, I am a happier man. For my kinsmen, clansmen and tenants get to keep their cattle, and keep their sons and daughters safe at home.'

'You will dae nothing tae help this girl?'

Maxwell shook his head. 'I will do nothing tae help the English, but leave her tae me, I will send her home happy.'

Lady Agnes, shook her head too, because her husband's answer was expected, and his action poor. 'I will not allow ye tae send her home with the thought that the matter is in hand. No, John. It is the way with men in this land tae throw deceit around as easy as a child throws mud.' Agnes stood before her husband. 'You have forty-two years on this earth, John. How big will be the reckonin' when its time to meet the Lord… Deceit is poor coin tae pay the gateman of heaven.'

Maxwell did not take heed of the kindness in the lady's eyes, only the scold on her lips. He bore the marriage well, for it came with a title of the great *Herries*. He had her respect as his wife, her loyalty too, but it came with a price—*another voice about him to prick at his conscience.* 'I paid a rare price for yer hand, Agnes. It may suit ye tae be happy aboot it, or smile graciously t' hide yer sadness. But I dinnae expect ye tae involve yerself in men's affairs, or seek tae flay me every time my actions dinnae suit ye.'

Agnes held her head low, remembering Johns' suit of her, seven years past. How she had thought a bold knight fought for her hand. How, Sir John Maxwell, Master of the Maxwell as he was known, stood against her own protector, the Earl of Arran, Regent of Scotland. She was promised to Arran's own son, a match not distressing to her, but the spirit of the affair with Sir John wooed her. Two thousand warriors he brought to bear in support of his courtship. *What woman would not be wooed?*

It was little comfort to her, to learn via public commendation, that her guardian gave her in marriage to Sir John Maxwell, on the grounds that; *'through his manifold labours he had not only drawn a great part of the inhabitants of the West Borders from the assurance of the English, the old enemies of Scotland, to the obedience of the Scottish Queen, but had also expelled the English from that realm.'*

But the truth was a sorry affair. For Sir John, in order to coerce the Earl into accepting his suit of Agnes, had formed an alliance with the English, with Lord Wharton, only to abandon it as it suited him. He also abandoned the good young Scottish gentlemen he had left in captivity as assurance of his fidelity to the English cause. They were hung in Carlisle for his deceit. The flower of Scotland left to rot on the rope to pay for her husband's pride and greed, his lust and his envy… For the title of Lord of Herries, that came with marriage, was a prize more than heart's want for a woman.

She tried not to put fancy in her mind. For it does a young girl's fancy good to think a man fights for her hand for reasons of love, but an older head knows the truth that love is never the virtue of marriage wanted by a man of power, but simply to hold his pride in a good match made. Perhaps it was lust for a woman seen, or anger that his suit was denied, envy for the grand title she brought, greed for the estates she inherits.

Love or lust; love or pride; love or anger; love or greed; Agnes never really knew the true nature of her husband's heart, but the murder of so many good men, was a price too heavy for her heart to hold—*sin to see her damned.*

Mary would hear the truth. Lady Agnes would make sure of it. But she hoped Mary would return home, and put her thought of deliverance for the poor Solway souls in her heart, out of her mind. She did not know Mary.

Maxwell rubbed his beard and scratched his head, for he had seen that look in Lady Agnes before, and for all his self-service, he thought not to have the lady sad. But even in an act of contrition towards his wife, there was profit to be made for his own cause. So he took a sheet of vellum from his desk and put pen to paper. Words written and wet ink blowed, he melted the wax and sealed it with his ring—his fathers ring, taken from his dead brother's finger.

'It is a perverse country we live in. If I see a Johnstone, an Armstrong, an Elliot or a Hall, I would likely kill him fer his sorry name, but I would give him courtesy with it, fer we are all Scottish gentlemen of sorts. James Hall is the man with an interest in Port Kirkcudbright. This letter will give oor visitor some safety in his keep, and see him parley with her as both an acknowledgement of my station and my deference tae his. But for the sake of good sense, I suggest ye tell oor visitor tae return, immediately, tae her father-in-law's tower and forget her childish quest.'

'With respect, Lord Maxwell, it has been many a year since my behaviour has been called childish. And forgetfulness is a reward I give myself for things not worth the remembering. Men murdered before my eyes. Men hanging at an other man's whim, are not easily forgotten.'

Lord Maxwell, startled, turned quickly to see Mary at the door.

'Ah, oor guest comes tae see us. Does my wife's quarters nae suit ye?'

'I saw you from the window, enter the Hall. I thought I should introduce myself.'

Maxwell was peeved to have his opinions overheard. 'Strangers should nae walk another man's home without escort or invite.'

Mary smiled and bowed graciously. 'I have my escort. My brother-in-law waits on me outside. Your good wife, already invited me into your private apartments.'

Maxwell smiled at Mary's counter. 'I do not know what these hanging men are tae ye? Were they kin?'

'Not family, Lord Maxwell, but they are my brothers and sisters. Mankind, Lord Maxwell, is begat from a single issue from God. One family, Lord Maxwell. He foresaw no opposing tribes and clans from his union of Adam and Eve… The wrath of man against another's name is the Devil's doing.'

'A noble thought, lass, but these are not generous lands. Neighbourly love is a price too dear tae pay, fer while ye embrace yer neighbour, his kin will be likely reivin' yer livelihood, and the man I send ye tae is the master reiver himself…' Maxwell paused. 'There again, he was, for he is a crippled man now, but there again to call him a cripple would be tae call him false, fer he is a cripple's cripple, a half-man's half, fer he is as helpless as a new born babe, wi' nurses tae wipe his arse and feed him food.'

That night, Lord Maxwell hosted Mary and her party, giving them bed, supper, and rest and care for their horses. Ruff was allowed to wander Maxwell's Hall, while his beloved hounds kicked their heels in the kitchens, dislodged from their beds close to Lord Maxwell and his wife.

Before morning came, Lord Maxwell requested Mary six times more not to continue with her quest, and each time Mary politely thanked Lord Maxwell for his concern. Each time, Mary reinforced her case, and seeing her resolve was strong and not wishing to send her on without some better care, he provided four more guards to see Mary safely to Kirkcudbright. He knew if harm befell her even within fifty miles of his charge, her father-in-law would hold him responsible, and another feud was not a gift to be taken.

And for Will, Maxwell gave him new blankets for their horses (for which he charged him five shillings). Blankets they were, new they were not, and he was forever carping on that road to Kirkcudbright that his horses, 'had expensive bought rags, for the cash spent, could clothe him nicely.'

Chapter XIII

Betty's smile was playful. Her cheeks flushed red and her fingers plied her lust on Richie's chest, tugging at his shirt lacings. Her thought in want, her voice in melody, she rhymed, 'My husband keeps me *tight*, but ye have me heart each *night*, Richie Hall.' She looked up into his eyes. Her smile telling him she craved him. She continued, her fingers reaching up to caress his lips. 'Ye could have it each *day*, if me husband went *away*.' Her smile dropped into a lickerish grin.

Richie feigned amusement at Betty's verse. He grabbed her hard, and replied, 'Aye, ye wanton trollop, now why would I want tae send yer man away? He owes me four shillings at cards.' He winked. 'Besides, he's too gud a fighter tae lose, too gud a swordsman tae duel, to big a man tae thump.' He took a kiss from Betty, long, lusty and hard.

His kiss released, a breathless Betty, asked, 'Will ye be vistin' ma wantin' at midnight? To dip your pole, perhaps?'

'Nah, I'll nae be humpin'. Ma daddy has guests, and I've been told tae stay well away.'

'Then later at dawn, visit me in my bed, I'm always eager in the mornin's.'

'Nah, I might be visitin' yer mother instead. She keeps a cleaner bed, and a better skillet o' porridge by the fire. Nae burnt like yers.'

Betty raised her hand to slap Richie. '*Ye bastard!*'

But Richie caught her wrist. 'D'ya nae like me teasing ye, Betty?'

'No, I never knows when ye're teasin', and I knows ye like my mother.'

'I like both of ye. There's somethin' comfortin' aboot English lassies. They seem far keener.'

'I'm keen on ye, Richie Hall. My bed gets cold without a man to keep me warm.'

'Then be a good wife and warm it well—*fer yer husband.*'

'*You pig…*' Betty raised her hand again, but Richie was waiting and he grabbed it. '*You Scots are all pigs, and my husband's the worst!*'

'Well ye married him.'

'It was a poor choice. My ma and me kidnapped, and set up to slave or whore… Marriage was the only way to see me and my ma safe from humiliation.'

'Aye, ye both kidnapped, and likin' yer kidnappers mair than yer own kind. What wanton women ye are.'

'*Pig!*'

'Nah, Betty, nae pig, I'm a hound with mair than one bitch tae shag. But a moment tae spare and a need tae loose ma lust in a willin' wench.'

'Then let go yer passion and ride inside me… I like it.'

Richie smiled. He took his eye off his sentinel watch. No light could he see across the Solway. He tugged up Betty's skirts.

'Er, have ye a shilling, Richie?'

'I have, and five mair besides, with a fondness fer each other's company.'

Betty's eyes were bright, thinking on Richie's coin, and not thinking of his clumsy fumbling beneath her skirts. She did not even feel him enter.

'Ye're a decent poke, Betty.'

'Ye're a generous man, Richie.'

Richie smiled at Betty's apparent compliment, and Betty smiled at the thought of Richie's gratuity. Both misunderstood the other; both were lost to each other's meanings.

ꕥ

By mid-afternoon, Kirkcudbright's town walls had swallowed up Will's group, and Will was a man disturbed. It had been a comfort to have Maxwell's men at his back, for not only did six make a better guard than two, but also, with Maxwell's own badge on the men's livery, courtesy was given more than refused. But with Maxwell's men turning for home and Maxwell's letter placed (and lost) within the hands of Maxwell's man on the burgh council, the Kirkmaster of Kirkcudbright, Will was ill at ease to be contained within a walled town of hostile intent. Hostile, because he had past cause to reive the good Kirkcudbright folks of goods and cattle, and the Halls of this parish were no friend to his own family.

Will's disquiet had been further poked into anxiety, when two prominent members of Royal Kirkcudbright's Council (Royal because, Scottish King James, the second of that name, had made it so) had come to see to their comfort, and tell them of the arranged audience with James Hall, burgess of Kirkcudbright, the Master of the Halls in that burgh, and *'celebrated for the generosity of his gold in matters of civic pride.'*

Will had disliked these fawning Scottish gentlemen, for their words hailed fair Kirkcudbright as perhaps James Hall's, bought and paid for, and so he only saw internment for himself and Mary, if James Hall had a mind to do so.

What else would a rogue do?

Will only knew James Hall as a once renowned rogue, a thief of every kind. He had stolen goods, gold and beasts, men's lives, their family's bread, their livelihoods. His ships had stripped bare English trading vessels on the Solway. But all had been done in the name of the King. All for Mother Scotland's will. He had been quiet these past years, but with any complaint against him 'handled' by the burgh council, and with Kirkcudbright's own wall and ditch to hide behind.

What was the truth of it?

The townsmen had explained to Will and Mary, with much bluster, that James Hall's able contribution to the defence of Kirkcudbright against an English raid, led by Sir Thomas Carleton, seven years past, had won him honours within the town's council.

Sir Thomas Carleton had raided South-West Scotland; Teviotdale, Canonby and Dumfries, looting and burning as he went, coercing all to demonstrate allegiance to England's king. But Kirkcudbright shut its gates to Carleton and his siege was beaten off, with only one good townsman killed by an arrow, and another taken as hostage for ransom. Relief came; The Laird of Bombie sponsored a company of local-raised men to see off the siege, yet still Carleton won the day, losing only one man, against three killed and prisoners taken. The good folk lost two thousand sheep, fifty horses and twenty cows and oxen. And all was done under the direction of the English Warden of the West March, Lord Wharton. James Hall's bravery and direction had saved much more, and the action earned him good standing within the town. It also earned him a broken back, falling from his horse. Now crippled in arm and leg, he directs all from his bed, even the town council.

Some say via bribes and favours.

ജ്ജ

The Kirkmaster escorted Will and Mary to meet James Hall, and Will ensured his blades were sharp, hidden blades carried, his pistols primed and his men sober.

The Kirkmaster counselled caution, and he related his own complaints made to the burgesses of Kirkcudbright about miscreant behaviour of its citizens marring the town's good standing as a port of good worth. But his fears fell on deaf ears at Council meetings, plugged by the gold paid into civic coffers and distributed amongst Council members.

The Kirkmaster held his torch high to direct them from the market cross to the road ahead, away from the way to the quays and off the high street. They were soon heading on a quiet lane that would eventually lead to the town gate and towards the *Boreland farms*, the town's wealth outside its port.

'Lass, what will ye dae, when ye see James Hall? Perhaps ye in yer pretty blue dress will mak them thar Devil's breed see decency?' He waved his torch like a sword. 'Perhaps persuade them let go their stealin' ways? Take tae the plough? Or take a pilgrims path tae find oor Lord's way?' The Kirkmaster turned to Will. 'I can understand yer lass petitionin' the Warden against the attacks against yer lass' village, she been English bred, but a good Scottish man should have more sense aboot him, for just as ye met cold comfort at the Warden's fireside, likewise ye'll find nae greater comfort at the reivers' door… only worse awaits there.'

'Hall still reiving?' asked Will.

'Whit man with rowdy-men in his charge is not a reiver in this realm?'

Will nodded his agreement with the vociferous man. 'Listen to the good man, Mary. He knows the fruits of this endeavour will see rot before they see ripe.'

'I can only try, Will,' replied Mary.

Will shook his head. 'And I admire ye fer that, Mary. But I'm fretin' over ye being in mortal danger.' His head flinched at the sound of a dog suddenly aroused to bark. 'These are bad lands fer any soul, mair so fer an English woman. And mair and mair, I'm fearin' foul deeds are sponsored within these town's walls.'

Mary put her face to a new wind that came onto the night. 'I have you, William, and you are enough to see me safe.'

Ahead, torches were seen, two then three. Laughing was heard. Then jeers, and then animal cries.

Mary was alarmed, and Will thought to hurry her on to their destination, but she took the path to see what animal would issue such torment, and within the grounds of a field, bordered by a shallow dyke, a woman, not a creature, was being stoned by a group of men and boys.

'It's oor archery field. We play ball there too,' offered the Kirkmaster.

'That poor woman!' declared Mary.

'Pay her nae heed,' said the Kirkmaster, 'The local peoples call her *Sister Maoilíosa*, although she's nae longer a nun, nor a man… but Irish she is.'

'Does she nae belong tae the Franciscan monastery?' asked Will.

'Nah, she is an itinerant, suffered by some, mocked by most,' replied the Kirkmaster.

The woman was doubled and struggling with bundles fixed by ropes about her back, cutting deep into her shoulders. Her load made worse, as her free arms clutched a small bundle as if she swaddled a baby to her breast. She brought tight in the bundle to protect it, and endured the striking-stones without thought of raising an arm in her own defence. A pitiable sight it was.

Mary, with charity forever in her heart, directed Will and his men to her assistance. Will stepped forward and drew his sword, his men followed.

'Desist, ye mice!' ordered Will, 'or it'll be yer stones I'm feedin' ye instead o' cheese!'

The group turned to face Will and hesitated a moment. They thought to turn their stones on Will, but seeing three with swords and the Kirkmaster to their backs, they turned tail and ran.

Mary hurried to the woman to see to her wounds. None showed on her face, blackened from an age without wash. Her clothes were in rags and in the form of a habit—nuns' garb. She seemed to have the frame of a portly woman, but the layers of garments beneath her habit belied the truth of a woman half-starved. Mary reasoned her to be a woman once lodged in safety of an abbey, now destitute without kin to see her safe.

The woman pushed aside Mary's searching hands and looked to the ground. A coin she found—a penny. She raised her head to Mary. She smiled, and raised the muddy coin to each and every face about her. 'God provides. A penny fer the poor. I shall buy bread. Food to see the hungry fed.' And she carefully tucked the coin within a fold of her clothes. 'Strangers to these parts are ye? Ye look like strangers.'

'We are,' replied Mary, 'You from the monastery?'

'Aye, I am,' said the woman, her eyes searching the ground for other pennies that may have fallen from careless pockets.

'Do you wish us to escort you there?' asked Mary.

The old woman looked to the stars. 'Where?'

'The Franciscan monastery?'

'Aye, I know it well. As I do all the homes and fields. All the hills and rivers.'

Will came close to Mary, and put his hand on her arm. 'Come Mary. The woman has lost her wits. The Kirkmaster says she is nae from this burgh. Come Mary, we've an appointment tae keep.'

But Mary resisted Will's strong hand. 'Have you a bed?' she asked the woman.

'Kind lady, my bed is always the last shelter I find, before dark finds me. I am never without food, nor shelter. Never without a kind thought, nor a fond remembrance.'

Mary looked on the woman tenderly, cupping her dirty face. She smiled at her as if she were dearly regarded kin of her own. 'Then permit us carry your bundles for a while.' Mary turned to Will. 'Let strong men give you respite.'

'Please, Mistress, I am strong enough. I carry clothes for the poor.' She hesitated. 'My love is coming for me. Don't ye fret. He told me so.' She pushed her finger to her nose, a sign of a secret to keep. Her voice dropped to a whisper. 'I have my white linen kept safe. I do not give that away. I keep that for myself and for my… my *blackened man*.'

'What do you carry there?' asked Mary, pointing to her small bundle clutched tightly.

'My baby of course.'

Mary wanted to look into the swaddling, for the bundle was lifeless. She moved towards the woman. The woman recoiled, pulling the bundle deep into her chest. Mary feared the worse, but still she approached.

Will stepped forward and put a firmer hand on Mary. 'No lass, best leave well alone.'

Then the woman, eyes bright, retreated. She pointed at Mary and shouted, 'Seven sinners stand against seventy, yer husband amongst them… He's in good company, but the Devil stalks him.'

'What do you mean?' pleaded Mary.

'Good sisters; Faith, Hope and Charity walk with your man, and your man's men… but they'll not be able to save him for you, my dear.' She looked to the black sky, searching for more stars to see, but cloud covered all. She turned. She scurried across the field to disappear into the night.

Chapter XIV

The ill-given supper

Mary had always the benefit of a good table. All her life it had been so. Food of varied nature; well prepared and finely flavoured. Her table company too, was always polite and well mannered. Even after she left the well-provisioned table of her parents' home to sit at the table of Jack's mother (for it was always the senior lady of that family who kept table), it was maintained in a goodly fashion, with good manners, gracious hosting, and careful service. However at that table, at first, thanksgiving was errant, although it was not by the wishes of Jack's mother, but by an impatient husband and father-in-law who thought thanks to the good Lord was better maintained by eating the food hot, and thanking the Lord after it was consumed. Especially as many a supper was interrupted before first mouthful was taken, when the call-to-arms was raised and reivers were afoot. But opportunity was taken to make a new daughter-in-law comfortable, and it encouraged proper thanksgiving at the table once more, much to the ladies' joy.

But the presentation of James Hall's table was a sight of primitive display.

Mary was worried. Will was not with her. Her own escort had been removed; prevented from accompanying her to the Hall's victualing chamber; a refectory by its design; a room with ecclesiastical origins.

Arrival in the Hall's complex was without incidence, until that is, a crowd of Hall men separated her from Will and his men, under duress. With ten times Will's number, he had little chance to offer objection. Five times, and no doubt Will would have drawn swords and made his point better heard, and sharper felt.

The Hall's refectory was large and filled with tables; all filled with men eating and gaming. The jugs of ale outnumbered the men, at least three to one, and Mary counted six tables with eight and more men per table. Each table had large platters, not pots, piled with porridge into which the men worked their spoons, slopping the wet oatmeal directly into their mouths, bypassing their own bowls which some used as drinking vessels, cups being in short supply. Men played cards while they ate, joked and cursed. There was no sign of civility or courtesy shown for a lady. The men were the worse kind of dregs.

But worse than the sight of fifty and more ruffian man crammed into the refectory, was the sight of half of them with prurient eyes debasing her, for she was the only lady present—the only woman.

'Ye're a lucky lass, nae competition fer a man's attention here,' announced Davy *'twa tartes'* Hall, wiping the remnants of his ale from his beard, his ale pot emptied, its full content sunk in a single swig. 'We used tae have servin' lassies, but the men got a little rough, so now boys serve, and the lassies hide in the kitchen. That is…' Davy belched loud and clear, Mary reeling from the fetid odour. '…till the men are too drunk tae care.'

'Where are the men's wives?' asked Mary, seeking womankind to bolster her defence against a room full of surly men.

'They eat in the kitchen, or in their own homes.'

'But surely the presence of your wives would ensure better behaviour from your men?' said Mary, pulling her head back as a piece of bread flew past.

'Nah, the men come here tae eat, drink and play, free from their scolds and skirts.' Davy Hall leaned forward to breathe stale ale into Mary's ear, and spit porridge onto her cheek. 'Dinnae worry lass, whilst ye are a guest at oor table, only the Hall man that takes yer fancy will be allowed tae sully ye.'

Mary recoiled at his words, at the very thought of it, and replied, 'Is this your idea of Border hospitality, Mr Hall? To insult your guests so?'

A tall man stepped close, and ushered Davy Hall away from his seat. Easily he did so, as he was a foot taller and an ale jug lighter in consumption.

'Forgive ma ample brother, Davy, he does not ken good manners from bad. It's the sad price for losing our ma twenty years gone, and having nae gentle womenfolk tae see us right. May I introduce myself, I am Jock Hall, first son of James Hall, your host.'

Mary felt relieved at Jock Hall's words and his manner.

'I'm afraid the men here are unschooled when it comes tae proper behaviour around ladies. But they're all canny fighters and worth three apiece of Maxwell men, and five of any Englishman. You must understand this is a hard land, and every night could be any man's last, for tomorrow some will be risking life tae keep our revenues healthy enough tae keep our followers and their families. Our victuals are always in want.'

Mary thought on Jock's words. She realised he talked of reiving. 'So you sponsor stealing?'

'We do, it is the only way for a clan tae survive in this cruel land. Rob or be robbed, cut or be killed. Does your family not do the same?'

Mary dropped her eyes, and sighed. 'My husband's family does, although they are quiet about it.'

'Your father-in-law has some standing in the Scottish Court, it serves him better tae be canny about the truth, especially as he is a friend of the English Warden.'

'Only by coercion.'

'Friends are friends, it matters not the nature of their contract.'

Mary thought to refute Jock Hall's statement, but as she opened her mouth to speak, he pointed to the ceiling.

In the centre of the ceiling there was a hatch, a yard square, which had opened revealing the floor above. A young voice was heard through the hole; a loud call, *'Mind the floor, the Master of the Hall comes yer way.'*

From the ceiling, a platform came down, lowered by ropes. A pulley's squeal could be heard from the floor above, and soon enough Mary could see a man seated on an oak throne. Both were lowered carefully to the floor. Four men came forward and slotted two long wooden beams through two iron rings attached about each side of the chair, and carried man and throne to the head of the largest table.

Mary watched the man being carried. Leather straps tied him into the chair and his head into a metal cradle fixed to the top of the seat back. The leather strap running across his forehead seemed to restrict his head as he tried to look at Mary, as he passed. The man's sallow face was clean-shaven, and his limbs were unnatural in their lie.

As they placed the throne at the table and removed the carry-beams, a tall man came to his side—Jock Hall, and Mary looked to her side to see him gone from her, leaving her without newfound kinder escort and exposed, once more, to the fat man, his brother Davy.

Jock raised a jug. 'A cheer for James Hall. A cheer for the man, for he be the head of this fighting clan.'

All raised their cups and bowls, some even jugs to their lips. All took a long drink, and the moment's silence unnerved Mary more than the foul cacophony, before it.

After a further two hours were spent in discomfort, with Mary closing her ears and eyes to the lewdness of the men around her, James Hall retired. The men's drinking was continual, and their revelry broke into isolated fighting. Mary had to endure crude upon crude remark directed at her virtue, her breasts and haunches. She was relieved when Jock Hall returned to her table, for a poor friend is the best of friends in a friendless world.

'Da, will see you now,' announced Jock.

'I will not be sorry to leave this room,' replied Mary.

'Then come, leave your table, and I will take you tae my da's bedchamber.'

A small man, seeing Mary leave her table, sidled up to her and grabbed her around the waist, and Jock laid a fist hard on his face, knocking him to the floor.

Jock spat on the man lying on the ground, and said, 'Go find your wife, *Spiteful Sparra*, if you fancy a hump.'

The man raised himself off the floor, and sitting, he drew his dagger, feeling the side of his head where Jock's blow had landed. 'Ye would nae be so free wi' yer fists if my brother was standing by!' He tried to stand.

Jock put a boot on Sparra's groin, to keep him down. 'I doubt your fetid kin could raise an eyelid, never mind a fist in your defence. He's a quart drunker than he needed tae be tae find senseless sleep. I'm surprised you cannae smell him in the corner, sleeping in his own piss 'n' shite.' Jock spat again on the man. 'All you *Littles* are spiteful sully-men.'

Sparra tried to raise himself up, but Jock moved his boot to his chest to keep him pinned, and pushed him down flat to the floor.

Sparra tried again, but Jock's boot was firm. 'Ye Halls think ye better than yer neighbour,' hissed Sparra, 'Ye gi' yerself graces… The great clan… Ye think yerself as Scotsmen, proud dae have an English bounty on yer heids. But now yer name is a much English as it is Scots… ye've sullied yer bloodline… yer kin are nowt but mongrel bred.'

'Ye spit yer words, Sparra. But a dog needs tae ken its place.' Jock removed his boot, and Sparra sat up. 'Now go, get out of my sight.'

Sparra sprang to his feet and sheathed his dagger. His eyes showed nothing but hate, Fear and caution was about his movement, and he kept his distance from Jock Hall. His parting words to Mary were broken, as if he wanted to cry. 'Ye'll get nae pleasure from that creature, *lassie*, his dissolute lusts lies elsewhere.' Sparra spat at Jock, his mucus bullet falling far short of its target.

Jock walked Mary to his father's rooms within the complex, which was not a tower or a single house, but a series of buildings connected by long and short wooden galleries. On her route, for there was no direct passage to James Hall's first floor apartments, Mary could see, amongst the domestic buildings, there were more buildings that were ecclesiastical in origin, possibly leased out by the Franciscan monastery.

Jock eventually brought Mary to the first floor, the one that lay over the large refectory hall, to stand outside his father's apartments; two rooms; one for his father, and one for the four boys who tended the crippled man.

A latticed metal grilled yett stood over the stout oak door, and Jock banged hard the oak. The door opened, and a boy of thirteen or fourteen stood on the other side of the yett.

'The lass to see the Headman.' Jock took out his sword and dagger and laid them on a nearby table.

The boy, seeing Jock lay out his weapons, took a key from a hook inside the room and opened the padlock, which held the yett locked.

'Does your father fear?' asked Mary.

'No one gets past these boys wi' a blade. No one feeds my da but these boys. These boys wipe my da's mouth and his arse. They wash his balls. They dress him. They sing him songs. They read him stories.'

Once inside the first room, the boy ran his hands over Jock, looking for hidden blades. Jock raised his arms and stood, legs apart. He closed his eyes, and held a half-smile, as the boy ran his hands over all; examining cap and hair, collar, shirt and leather vest. Checking the folds of his breeches, his hose and his boots. He found nothing, but a comb, which the boy laid on a table. Then he moved to Mary.

'Let him search you, lass.'

Mary stood back. She recoiled, as the boy approached.

'Stand still, lass. Let him search you. He will cause no harm tae you. He'll just bruise your dignity… *a wee bit*.'

The boy's hands searched under Mary's skirts, in her bodice. He checked each stay and each hard edge carefully. And for all Mary was embarrassed to be invaded so, the boy seemed to take no pleasure from his fumbling, and so Mary felt her modesty was maintained… *a wee bit.*

After he was satisfied all was well, the boy retired and nodded his head.

Another boy knocked on another door, and a small hatch opened. A boy's face appeared, and the door opened.

Inside the room, James Hall was sitting up in a bed of simple construction, propped against large plain linen-covered pillows, which were arranged to cradle him.

In the corner of the room, sat another boy looking out from within an iron cage. And within the iron cage was an iron screen, behind which the boy could take shelter. He sat with a brace of pistols on a table next to him, all short-chained to his wrist.

Jock Hall looked to the boy in the cage, as a gesture to direct Mary's attention. 'He ensures you don't touch the auld man.'

Mary looked bemused. 'I do not understand. In matters of your father's care, what keeps these boys safer than his sons?'

'Kin-blood is nae guarantee of safety in this land, and *Da*, here, has three ambitious sons. These boys have their parents held hostage tae guarantee their loyalty and their good conduct.' Jock pointed to a white-painted circle on the wooden floor. 'Go stand on it, lass. Do not move from it, unless it is tae move away.'

Mary walked slowly to the circle, watching all the while the boy in the cage, who raised a pistol against her, cocked and ready to fire.

James Hall spoke, 'I… I see ye… only as courtesy tae Lord Maxwell… He is… is a man who owes my clan nae favour.' His words were measured, a struggle to release. 'I… I see ye… tae learn Maxwell's game… He plays poor… He hopes we hurt ye, I suspect. He hopes we give yer father-in-law… and… and yer husband cause tae find greater feud with the Hall name…' He became increasingly breathless. '…Another ally tae his cause.'

James Hall beckoned the boy, standing with Jock, over with his eyes, and he came forward with a filled beaker with a length of reed. The boy placed the reed into James Hall's mouth and the man sucked the liquid deep into his throat. When the man had finished, the boy carefully removed the straw from James Hall's mouth and mopped the spillage from his chin with a cloth.

'I come to ask you to intercede in the raiding on the Solway coast.' Mary's voice was weak, as she was humbled in the presence of this crippled man. 'Reivers attack peaceful peoples on the English side, for no reason other than greed. There is no honour for Scotland in what they do. Their motives are not feud, or country's call, or even faith's fight, but simple profit and evil's deed.' Mary stepped forward, but remained in the circle. 'I implore you, Master of Hall, to use your influence over the lawless in your land to stop it. Lord Maxwell says you are the man to do it.'

'You…' For all he started, James Hall seemed to lose his words. His eyes appeared pained. He found the exertion to speak too difficult.

Mary stepped forward. 'Er… can I help you?' Her concern real in her voice.

The boy pointed pistol.

Jock called out. 'Stand lass!'

James Hall shook his head gently, his face flushed about the cheeks, and he looked at the boy, and his pistol dropped. The other boy came forward and he leant into his master. Quiet words were exchanged. The boy beckoned the other boy from the other room, and both lifted John Hall's head and they placed another pillow beneath it.

The fragility of the man gave Mary the confidence to speak out boldly. 'Will you intercede?'

'Ye… have wasted yer time.' James Hall blinked his eyes, and the boy leaned in again for his instructions. The boy then left the room. 'I have… three sons in my care and bastards by the score, born in lust.'

'I think I have met only two,' said Mary.

'No… I suspect you have met all three.' James Hall wanted to laugh, but only a tortured groan was heard, followed by a terrible and lasting cough. The remaining boy sprang forward with a cloth to catch the discharge from James' mouth.

'I do not understand,' said Mary. She was confused, and she

wondered if he was speaking only addled-thought. 'I only ask that you use your position to intercede with whoever is behind the raids.'

'I have… three sons… no daughters… a half-brother and a nephew. None are fit tae steer the Hall name tae glory… None are fit tae serve the name and my clan… None who will, in time, be Wardens themselves and greater than the Maxwell… None, because they dae all fer themselves… and not fer their name. Ye… Ye have met my brother… ye have met my nephew… and ye have met my other son.'

'I have not been introduced to your brother. And only your sons Jock and David, have revealed themselves to me.'

James Hall shifted his eyes to the window. The black night made it a mirror and he saw Mary's reflection there—and shadows in the doorway. 'I… I have given instruction fer ye and yer escort tae be safely returned tae Maxwell lands… Dinnae come back… Dinnae trust Lord Maxwell… I suspect he sent ye here tae be harmed, or ransomed… I have nae doubt my sons and my half-brother would prefer it.'

Mary was still confused, and then she reasoned, and remembered. She recalled the men she saw at the refectory tables with smiles on their faces. She replaced the smiles. She painted the sallow faces of the men who committed such cruelty on Allonby onto the drinking men. And then she saw familiar faces—*the reivers*.

'Ah lass… we meet again'

Mary turned to see the old-grey reiver at the door.

'Ma brother once was the better man. A son born in wedlock. I stood in his shadow, him been bold and brave and righteous, and me being a bastard-born. I did all the stealin' and he did all the soldierin' fer king 'n' country. All still know him as head of this clan, and we stand protected behind his reputation and his good standing in Kirkcudbright.' The old-grey reiver smiled. 'Aye, he's head of this clan alreet, fer his head is all that works. His body nowt, but a withered leaf.

'Let the lass go…' pleaded James Hall.

'I am not sure it is good policy, brother. To let a bag of gold walk oot of oor grasp.'

'You'll bring ruin on this house… if ye... harm her.'

The old-grey reiver walked to a table and took up a cloth. He walked to the bed and the cage-boy raised two pistols against him. The old-grey reiver looked at the boy and then to his brother, and James Hall blinked twice. Pistols were lowered, but Jock signalled the boy to hold the pistols ready. The old-grey reiver took up a cloth to mop the man's mouth, the saliva running down his cheek.

'Calm yerself, brother.'

Mary did not know what to do. To run. To stay, or to stand on her circle close to James Hall. But another man stood at the door, one with prurient eyes and a smile on his face.

The old-grey reiver retreated to stand next to Jock. 'Now you've met the headman…' he looked at Jock, '…and the lady of the house. Now reacquaint yourself with my brother's other son, my second-in-command, Richie Hall. I'm afraid he likes the lasses, even when they don't like him.' He walked up to Richie, standing at the doorway. 'Keep it sheathed, Richie boy. *Dae ye understand?*'

Richie looked beyond the old-grey reiver, to Mary standing stolid. He smiled. He licked his lips.

Chapter XV

The pain was more than Mary could bear. More than her pride could keep quiet.

'Sir… *ahh… please stop, stop, you're hurting me!'*

Sparra Little held Mary down to the floor, on her knees, her arm-twisted so she could barely move, but she still resisted.

'That's the idea… pain before oor pleasure,' offered Richie Hall, licking his lips. He laughed at his companion's efforts to keep Mary restrained, and stood back while he enjoyed the sight of Mary on all fours, while he loosened the cords tying his hose.

Mary was moving, pulling away from Sparra. She fought the pain and pulled against restraint.

Richie shook his head. 'Sparra, ma lad, have ye ever took a lass against her will?'

Sparra looked up, struggling to hold onto a fractious Mary. *'Eh?'*

'Hold her tighter man!'

Sparra renewed his grip on Mary's arm and twisted more.

Mary screamed.

'If the lass promises tae be quiet, Sparra will let her arm loose.' Richie bent down to bring his face level to Mary's. 'Well lass, will she be quiet? Or should Sparra break her arm?'

The pain was unbearable and Mary agreed. '*Yes… Yes!*'

Sparra seem to relax his grip, but Mary was still held, helpless.

'Before ye tak a lady, Sparra, pull free yer pyntle. Work it in yer hand a little. After all, a pyntle, a little self-pleasured will be better swollen wi' pride, and so be a better weapon tae drive yer *point* home.' Richie looked earnest in his foul tutelage. 'That way it'll give a lady greater delight as it finds entry.'

'What if she is nae greased tae receive, Richie?'

'If one finds the lady unwilling, it is too late fer soft entry. Yer thrust is committed. Dae not falter, thrust hard. Ye may smart a little… *at first…* but the lady may find pain is her pleasure. If not. Her pain will be yer pleasure.'

Their words ringing in Mary's ear, disgusted… and terrified her.

Richie Hall was not for holding back. His stiffened prick was in hand, and his hand was moving towards Mary's head.

'Forgive me, lass, I needed tae find my bed, and find a wench tae fill it. And fill the wench ma pyntle's depth. My lassies are all hidin' from me… So ye'll be ma pleasure tonight.'

'*Leave me!*' cried Mary.

'My da thought he could hide ye from me… Told me tae stay away. Auld Kerr thought he could lock ye away from me, but he picked a poor guard tonight, in this sorry wretch holdin' ye now.' Richie's mouth ran wet, and he approached within an inch of Mary. He looked at Sparra Little. 'Hold her fast ye little tick.' Then back to Mary. 'Bite ye bitch, and Sparra will break yer arm.'

Mary's mind found horror. It found disgust. She could not bear to think what was going to pass. She held herself tight, and twisted her head to the side as if she could resist the man's depravity. She did care about the pain and the pain to come, but her revulsion was absolute. She would not comply, but resist.

She made a plea, no pride had she, not a prayer in her mind, but a call she made.

'Jack!'

'A man bleeds bad from a cut pyntle, Richie.'

Richie span round, his free hand pulling at his dagger. Behind stood his brother, sword drawn against him.

'On yer way, or ye'll bleed,' grunted Richie.

'But you are in my way, brother. I am here tae see the good lady, so put away your *blade*… the dagger too.'

'I'll have my pleasure with the lass first.'

Jock looked at his brother's member, flaccid in his hand. 'I fear that sorry weapon will offer nae delight tae you. And that lass is nae for your pleasure… She is tae be put back tae the road… *carefully*… Da's and Auld Kerr's orders.'

Richie adjusted himself in his hose, and then pulled a wheel-lock pistol from the table next to him.

Jock looked at the pistol held against him. 'It's a gun, brother. You need to pull back the dog, or have ye not even sprung it?'

'I'll shoot ye… I will.'

'Shoot me, brother. But your problem is, pistols are often fickle. Sometimes they forget tae work—badly loaded—damp powder.'

'Na, mine's good, as ye shall see.'

Richie pulled back the dog and pointed the pistol at his brother's face. He pulled the trigger and Jock flinched as the hammer came down.

There was no shot.

'Is it even loaded, brother?' asked Jock.

Richie snarled. He put down the pistol. 'I did not know.'

At sword point, Jock retrieved Mary from Sparra Little's grasp, and he ushered him to stand next to Richie. He then ordered them both from Mary's room.

He watched his retreating brother. 'Some poor lass will be sore in the morn.'

Mary was in tears. 'Thank you for rescuing me.'

'You are tae be on your way. But we will keep your brother-in-law and his men for a while, see if they fetch a fair price.'

Mary protested, 'Your father promised us safe conduct.'

'No, Maxwell's letter requested safe conduct for you, and we have honoured that. It says nothin' about your brother-in-law and your guard.'

'But if you hold Will, his father will come for him.'

'No, he will pay. It is the way of it. He will try tae recoup his loss by theft from our land… We will be waiting.'

'But I cannot travel alone. Let Will and his men be my escort.'

'What happens tae you on the road and out of our keeping will be of nae concern tae us.'

8003

Mary was set to the road on her horse, thankful she was clutching Ruff, unharmed, both pleased to be reunited. She was lost for how to proceed. She did not want to leave Will, and so she stood her ground thinking what to do.

Should she ride home as fast as she could? Raise a force to set Will free?

But her father-in-law would still be in Edinburgh, and Jack was in England. Who could she turn to? Jack's men were gone, and the followers of her father-in-law's clan would not move against the Halls without direction from Jack's father, or Will, who was now interned.

She felt powerless. She felt alone. She was not even sure how to get home.

A woman of strong resolve, she thought herself. A woman with the heart of a man, that's what others thought of her. But as she looked up to the stars, then to the pitch black of the road ahead, she knew she was lost. *Not strong at all.*

She looked back to the road on which six Hall men had brought her, and she could still see the light from their flaming torches in the distance. She thought to ride back, on the path most known to her; the one from which she came, the one back to the Hall's compound. She thought again to see James Hall; a man to perhaps undo his sons' misdoing. But then she thought, how could she penetrate their walls, steal into their home, and stand over their leader like an assassin to ask for help? She shook her head and brought Ruff close to her face, to rub her tears into his soft fur. His eyes sought an understanding from his mistress, a task or trick for him to do to make her glad. But he could not charm away her sadness. His tail could not wag away the hurt.

'What am I to do, Ruff?'

And for all the times she had felt alone in a strange land, not of her choosing, in a marriage not of her design, she realised what depth loneliness could actually be. This time she was truly alone. She missed Will. She missed Jack.

Even in the dark, with nothing but eerie shadow and blackened view, Mary felt she had been left on a different road, and not the one she had earlier travelled with Will. She had little sense of the sea; she was too far from it. The Solway's whisper was too quiet, its smell too muted. The sea was always with them on their journey into Kirkcudbright; it was a longer road perhaps, but it held a sweeter view.

She thought the road she presently travelled, likely see her in trouble—peril from the menace that stalked the night-ways of Dumfriesshire. She thought the Halls wished her hurt, to blame other miscreants for the foul act that would befall her.

She did not know the Halls had put her on the road north, following the course of the River Dee to Castle Douglas and

Threave Castle, watchtower of the Maxwells, and likely safety for her. The Halls had their profit. Will's father would pay the ransom, his son was worth more than the gold he possessed, and retribution was not worth the men he might lose. It was good business. Maxwell would not have his ally against the Halls, and the Halls would have more gold. Will would be safe, as there was little profit, or pleasure, in killing him—nothing to gain in harming him at all.

Mary thought to return to Kirkcudbright, to seek help there. To the Kirkmaster or the burgh council, surely someone would give charity to a dispossessed traveller, lost. And in the dark, and in her reasoning, she thought the known road travelled, better than the unknown road to come, so she turned her horse around and travelled back to Kirkcudbright.

She knew she was right about the road when the sea came into view, but she found armed men on the road further down, and thinking them to be Hall's men, she was forced to turn back from the town, heading east, riding off the road keeping the Solway sea on her right hand. Although Mary was fretful, she felt she had taken a better way. She felt security in seeing the sea, guiding her east. She felt safer off the well-travelled way. She felt saved from her poor design to enter the town to seek help from likely suborned men.

Off the road for three hours, picking her way inch by careful inch, letting her horse walk its way, guiding her over the land, hill and moss, she did not think to stop and wait till dawn's light. She was too frightened to stop. Everything was strange. Everything was ugly. In her trepidation, all waited to assail her in the dark. But some comfort was given while Ruff stayed his growl and bark, and while her horse maintained his calm. Their noses and ears were her guardians. Harm was asleep in its cave, burrow and hut.

On the way to Kirkcudbright, Will had took her past *Dundrennan Abbey*, so she thought to find it, to seek comfort from the monks, but she missed it by a stretch. But fortune smiled, and she had found the road again. She maintained it until she reached *Auchencairn*, but there no one would help, they told her to travel back to the Abbey and seek charity from the monks, for they would not do anything without their instruction.

Then near *Palnackie*, she came upon a round tower, standing strange. And the three good ladies within, sisters by the name of Cairns, only saw Mary as another lady in distress, not of their land, but a lady of breeding. The sisters were no friends of the Halls, having their stock thieved by them in the past, and saw to it she was assisted and fed. Mary took great comfort by the Cairn's fire and enjoyed pleasant and good-humoured discourse with three women of fine border character. They gave her watered spirit to relight her resolve, and well made potage to feed her soul. Ruff too, engaged well with the three ladies, and by the end of their brief repose, he counted them as friends, to sit and perform tricks on request for scraps of lamb and pork.

The ladies made arrangements with their steward to have Mary escorted home at first light. The payment of some coin to two village men, would see her guided safely, and Mary, in turn, promised the men they would be reimbursed for coin again more, when they reached Mary's home.

All in all, Mary had much to thank the Sisters Cairns for.

Before Mary left the kindness of the ladies, she had opportunity, before the sun rose in the east to paint the hills, to walk to the shore at low tide. The round tower was a good walk and half from the best of the coast, from the rock and seaweed strewn beach that had Mary sighing at its sight, and Ruff chasing sleeping sea bird and rolling wave. A place made entirely better by the path to the shore, and early blooming blue tufted vetch that smothered marsh thistle, still yet to bloom. It was a perfect sky, with a light wind that gifted her the scent of the sea. She loved it there. But still, in her distress, Mary sought a better thought, and strangely to her, it was Jack that came to her mind.

There were many times Mary had a thought for Jack that was without censure. A thought born of fond memory, and not foul anger or foolish pride; memory rooted in times when she was with him, and standing in a calmer place with a kinder view. Good places, where remembrances of better times visit freely, and nothing exists to sour one's reverie.

And as she thought of her pride bitterly, and her man kindly, her feelings began to grow into love once more, as times past remembered added the toll of affections, joys and dreams, so much so as to outweigh the bad of him. Times, when she saw the best of him. When he smiled softly and spoke sweetly.

And as her heart warmed to Jack, it began to throb at the thought of him, and then it cracked at the thought of him gone from her. So she looked over the Solway, to see England's shore, hill and mountain, to where she thought Allonby lay. Where Jack might be. And she said an earnest prayer of thanks, and then another of petition.

'Please keep him safe, Father. Keep him safe for me.'

Solway Sand

'Seven reasons they have for risking life… not fealty, faith, nor fee, but reasons of their own and cause enough to die for.'

Chapter XVI

On Solway Sand, April 1554, day 15

Each day, Jack would walk the beach. Walk the sandy plain. Follow the seashore north, for north was the draw. He would put his mind to dilemma, to the imagined thought of reivers riding the shore, and the village of Allonby meeting them in fight. He feared their losses. He feared dire retribution on their families and homes. His mind thought the worst of it, and doubt and disquiet was his reward.

But as he walked, he met drawings in the sand; a horse; a fish; a mountain stag, all signs that the Girl had travelled that same way, that same day. All within the time of the tide, travelling fast on legs gifted to run. His mind ran on too, to thoughts of Mary and discourse with himself on dilemma of a different sort. No death and destruction there, but suffering nevertheless—dolour of a different sort.

Along the beach, a while more, Jack came upon another drawing of the Girl's. A work of some skill, for the Virgin Mother was clearly seen, holding the infant Jesus in her arms. Jack took comfort from it. And as he looked over the Solway to Scotland, a wind washed over him—a strong wind's blow from nowhere, to stop him in his tracks, to disappear in a moment more. And then fresh thoughts pierced his woe.

There are times thoughts come without invite. Thoughts of events thought long forgotten, of times past of little consequence. But for some reason they come loud and bright into one's remembrance. Sometimes the thought of a person walks in, to embrace kind thought, and one cannot help but live a past time real in one's mind.

And so it was, Jack thought of Mary as he looked over the Solway to Scotland, as the sun rose behind him to paint the hills. He thought of a time when he found Mary bundled in the grass, hurt from a mantrap, then another; Mary sitting in her bed with Ruff at her side enjoying her affections, then another; Mary riding hard to escape his authority. And his thoughts were only good, and his remembrances fond. He wondered why he fretted so over his union with her.

He did not know why the notion of her should, this morning, form a kinder affection in his mind. There was no reason for it. No one around to prompt his thought of her, or focus his attention away from his watch on the village.

So again he looked over the Solway to Scotland, to think on his duty that morning as watch, and he tried to dismiss his thoughts as fancy brought on by the splendour of the dawn.

But the moment of the day had him tight in its grasp, and the thought of Mary would not leave him, and instead Jack chastised himself for his pride and his anger. He only thought better of Mary, because Mary was the best for him. He was a fool not to see it. And then a pang of hurt filled his heart, his head with sorrowed thought for all his unkind words offered to her. And Jack lowered his head in atonement for a good wife, badly regarded. And his anger abated. His disquiet soothed.

On his return to the village muster, Jack was met by Francis marching towards him, flint formed face, scowl formed jowls. A jewel in hand, colours bright, lustrous, feathers proud, bright green dyed, freshly plucked and seated in the crown; his steel peaked burgonet, brighter than his blade, stains and tarnished removed, dents diminished.

'Captain Jack, yer washer woman has polished my armour.'

'What's wrong with that, Francis?'

'I like my poor armour to keep me quiet on the battlefield.'

Jack formed a teasing smile. 'What do you mean, Francis?'

'The rogue with his arrow. Is he going to put it into a man with dung on his back or gleaming silver about his chest?'

'Don't fret Francis, you deserve to look good in your armour.'

'Let those shiny captains and their velvets and gold draw the first fire.'

Jack looked about himself, at his finer attire, better armour and jacket stitched and edged with gold thread. His armour, not border fashion, but a gift from Henri Hueçon to set him apart from his Border brethren. Half-armour in articulated polished steel, in the Nuremberg fashion. His sword arm protected by steel from shoulder to hand; *pauldrons, rerebraces,* and *vambraces.* A peascod formed steel breast replacing his leather waistcoat. Armour fit for the show of grand battle, and not mere border skirmish.

Jack looked back at Francis. 'Never mind, *laal* Francis. Your shiny armour will make you seem splendid in your enemy's eyes. Blind them to your bullet fired.'

Francis simply spat on the sand and brought Jack to the muster.

Jack studied the men, Thomas had taken two weeks to assemble. Forty stood before him, but there was barely thirty, for twenty of them were either boys yet to shave, or old men too feeble to lift a razor; these he each counted as half-men, and to make one whole he married the vigour of youth to older reasoning.

Thomas stood behind him with the *Steward of the Manor's ledger*, the steward the appointed person of the Crown to manage the Manor's affairs, the ledger, his record. Jack wanted to know the nature of the men before him. In terms of their holdings and commitment to the parish.

Jack walked the line with Thomas. Farm boys and fishermen, but sons of Cumberland men, so not puny bred. At the sixth man, Jack stopped.

'What are you?'

'I'm a fisherman.'

'With your own boat?'

'Nah, I share with three others. Our homes are at sand's edge. Our boat tied up half a mile over the sand, well beyond the foreshore.' He pointed out over the coast. 'If the sea's kind and the fish friendly, I'll land a couple of skeps of herrings. We fish fer crab and lobster too… The sea is gud to us.'

'What do you lose when the reivers call, outside a few baskets of fish?'

'Nothing, They never bother our catch, only our lives. My brother was killed proper the last time they called. My father two years back was cut bad. He was a good-looking man. My ma did not appreciate the scars they left behind.'

Jack nodded in recognition of both the man's loss and his reasons. He stepped to the seventh man. 'What are you?'

'A farmer.'

'What's your name, *farmer?*'

'William Dover.'

'Are you tenant?'

'Aye, I hold my land by customary tenantright.'

'How many households are in your care?'

'There are four families workin' the land, all kin, bar one.'

'Do you know why you should fight?'

'Aye. I toil. The Church takes its rightful toll fer my soul's condition, so does the Manor for the land, my home. But when the reiver comes to call, he has no right to profit from my toil... So I will fight.'

'How much land do you and your kindred farm?'

Thomas interjected, 'They farm ten acres at West Newton.'

William Dover shook his head. 'Barely eight, a good deal of it is marsh.'

'*William!*' Thomas knew the truth of ten good acres, and the marsh drained by the enterprise of monks twenty years before.

William corrected himself. 'Ten acres; half to barley, one to oats, one to grain... ninety bushels of meal and oats produced, and twenty-five bushel's measure kept back for re-planting.' William Dover brought his hand up, and his other tugged at his fingers in turn, counting the distribution of his labours. 'Six bushels for the church and two more bushels for the Manor in lieu of rent and fines... and two for the thievin' reiver when he calls.'

'And how much left for your purse's profit?'

'After feedin' ourselves, I'll be lucky to see a bushel and a peck or two of meal and oats to sell on.'

Jack looked deep into the man's eyes, and held a silence that saw William Dover squirm. 'Ninety bushels seems a poor yield, especially in this good soil, free from clay, and in fairer climate.'

Thomas looked down the Manor Steward's ledger. 'Ninety bushels, two pecks. That is what is written for last season.' Thomas stared at the man. 'But what is farmed, William Dover? *On your oath now!*'

'Hear the priest, for your soul is resting on your answer,' added Jack, 'Don't see yourself in Hell for a lie.'

William Dover paused awhile, thinking on the truth and

separating the lie from it. 'If God is good, and the seasons kind, twenty more bushels of whatever we grow.'

Thomas shook his head. 'William, remember your soul.'

With eyes cast down, *forty* was the reply.

Jack nodded gratitude for an honest answer and studied the man. 'God is good to give you such fine soil, and such kind seasons. Your belly is big. Your shirt is not too worn, and your shoes are not too old. So your yield sees you in ale and food, new shoes each year and a new shirt on your back. Are ye a greedy man? Is your life worth the two bushels stolen by the reivers?'

'No… but my pride is.'

Down the muster Jack went. From the land, more farming men, shepherds, peat cutters. From the sand, boat breakers and builders, sea-salt makers. From the sea, fishermen and ferrymen, and from the forest, charcoal burners and basket makers.

At the end of the line stood a lad of ten or eleven years. Jack's men dubbed him, *the Boy*. He was a familiar sight to Jack and the other men, as he had shadowed them closely since their arrival in Allonby. Not a view was without his presence. He stayed close to the men to be seen and be judged.

Jack took another look along the line of men and boys, and then looked to Soldier next to him for his approval; a sign that the men were worth the training.

Soldier walked the line, and when he reached the end, he took from the Boy an oak stave he carried. The Boy was the only one in the line armed. Soldier felt the stave's weight, and he checked the grain.

'This yours, Boy?' asked Soldier.

'It is, sir. I made it.'

Soldier estimated the staff at around seven feet, the boy barely five. It was good wood, a short-staff, cut from the quarter of a split tree, not from a branch, as often was the case with poorer staves.

It was straight and true, good weight. Signs of practice were evident.

He passed the stave back to the Boy. 'Can you handle a long-staff?'

'I've never tried one, sir.'

'A man that can handle a pike well, is a man worth his pay… Can you handle your short-staff, Boy?'

The Boy presented his stave in the low guard position. Back hand on the end of the quarterstaff, his leading hand eighteen inches higher. He faced Soldier, leading hand and foot presented forward, as a fencer would stand. Stave well positioned to parry.

Soldier turned to Jack and nodded.

Behind both men stood Francis, Slack 'o' Jack and Geordie. Francis added his own thoughts. He shook his head.

Jack looked to his new company and counted the assembly. One was missing—Bendback. Only one knew where he was, and she was missing too.

Chapter XVII

On Solway Sand, May 1554, day 16

It was no mistake she fell on the resting place of Bendback. A man taking rest from the open mockery of his friends and the hidden disdain of those he had chosen to help. She knew the place he had found to call his own, amongst the trees, near a stream.

'What's yer name?'

'My friends call me Bendback Bob.'

The Girl smiled at the back of Bendback's head, and the cruel name, obviously given by others in mocking recognition of his deformity.

'What did yer ma call ye?' she asked.

'My mother… I cannot remember.'

'Then what's yer God given name?

Bendback smiled at the thought of his *God given name.* A name he rarely heard these past years.

He shifted on his rock to face the Girl, and said, 'It is Henry Musgrave. A good enough name for a man, but a poor name for a monster. So Bendback Bob suits me well, or Big Bob if it sounds better to your ears.'

'Then Henry, my name is Melissa, and now we're properly

introduced.'

'And now we are introduced, it would be more proper if you were to move on about your business.'

'Do ye not want company?'

'My thoughts need no more company than me, lass. So you'd better be away, so I can get back to them.'

The Girl looked to the bank of the stream and turned her head left and right to see if they were alone. They were. She then moved closer to Bendback, to sit before him, folding her legs beneath neatly arranged skirts.

'Why are ye sad?'

'I'm not sad, lass.'

The Girl shook her head in soft rebuke.

'My name is Melissa, but my friends call me *Lissy*. Ye should call me Lissy, I think.'

Bendback turned away to look onto the stream once more, heavy with water from recent rains filtering from its source, eager to join the sea and salt.

Melissa crept on her knees to sit next to Bendback, to see the stream and its ribbon of water flapping over the rocks.

'What's in the stream that's more interesting than me?'

Bendback turned his head, lost for words, lost for an explanation as to why a pretty young girl would be talking to him. Mockery was thought as reason, and he turned to scan their surroundings to catch sight of her friends, perhaps hiding, playing a dare or a tease at his expense. But she seemed alone.

'How old are ye?' she asked, as she foraged around her seat for sticks and stones to throw into the swift waters.

'Too old to play childish games, but not too old that you should be talking to me without permissions from your ma and pa.'

But the Girl ignored Bendback's reproach, and continued in conversation. 'Do ye think I'm pretty?'

'Has anyone said you are not pretty?

'No.'

'Then I will not be the one to disagree with them.'

'Ye're different to the rest of the soldiers. I've watched ye.'

'And what do you observe, pretty Lissy?'

'Ye seem to be deep in thought, but yer friends never ask ye what ye're thinking… What do ye think about?'

'Nothing important. Thoughts not for young girls. Thoughts the pleasure of the stream softens. No… they are thoughts without importance.'

'I think they must be very important, because I think ye're important, ye being a fine knight in a poor village.'

A knight, thought Bendback, how the cruelty of pretty girls cuts deep. Mockery. Bendback felt uncomfortable. Flattery was not known to him, unless it was a feign to hide mischief and ridicule at his expense, and he again scanned his surroundings to look for giggling girls, but they were alone.

'Have you not chores to do, girl?'

'All done. I rise early to do them. So when the day is at its best. When the land is warmed. I can take my time to see all that is pretty.'

Bendback looked to the trees; old oak, new birch. He looked to the lay of the stream and how it cut deep into fresh green grass. He looked to the horizon, to the undulation of the forest clad hills far in the distance, and how the land fell away towards to sea, towards the clearings, well farmed, and the woods well left to shelter the plantings from the salted air and harsh winds of the sea and hills. Bendback looked once more to the Girl. He caught her eye and fixed a gaze, and then in a low measured tone said, 'There is much beauty here.'

The Girl blushed and jumped up. She ran towards the Plain, away from the village. But she turned a head to Bendback, not breaking her stride.

'Thank ye, kind knight… I've never been called beautiful afore.'

ഇരു

God's gifts were as surprising as the weather gifted in the spring, for one could not foresee if God would lay rain, or wind, or drought, or cold—or even snow over the land. God's plan for man's year on the Earth was a mystery to unfold, for God's plan was not for mere man's interpretation, even if Thomas tried to put his thought to the conundrum of his flock's complaint of dry spring and raging sea.

And it was no wonder the good people of her village thought the Girl's gifts were surprising too, considering they thought her a marvellous gift from God; born premature to a woman thought barren, without the signs of carriage. The Girl should have died a few breaths from birth, or not be born at all.

But for the many who thought her a gift, many more thought her a curse, because although her gift of life was surprising, she had no benefit to her father or mother. No seamstress skill, no help in the kitchen, not a talent with the broom, or a mothering nature, or even an eye for a mate. For she liked to run, and there would be days she would run out the house at dawn to return at dusk, to talk all the next day of her family's news.

The Girl's family reached out along the northern Solway coast; an uncle in *Silloth Grange*, an aunt in Parton, and four score more in between; cousins in Mawbray, nephews in *Ellenborough*.

Those she could not call family, she would call friend, and friends she had, for she would not pass a stranger without a greeting, or use a single word in hello when a dozen more would do. And so it was, that the traveller, peddler and beggar that journeyed the road with the Solway sea on one side and Cumbrian mountain on the other, would wave a cheer as she ran her miles from there to here.

All were pleased to see the Girl as she ran into their days, and many owed her favours. The lady of *Flimby Hall* had reason to thank her, for the Girl discretely ran her letters of love to her suitor in *Camerton.* The suitor had reason to thank her, for she would carry carefully his richly made gifts to a lady in Ellenborough. That lady too, had reason to thank her, for the honest girl carried money safely to Parton, to see the lady's mother protected from her creditors, and the old mother had reason to thank her, for the Girl would run a basket of food to the old mother's widowed sister in *Distington.* The widow had reason to thank her most of all, for she was forever lonely, and would welcome the Girl's visits, and news she would bring of the widow's misbegotten son, a gentleman of Flimby Hall, who often fretted on the chastity of his wife, the condition of debtors in Parton, and of his spendthrift brother, a gentleman of Camerton and his dalliance with a lady of ill-repute in Ellenborough.

She would run. She hoped to find her place at breath's end... But her breath took her to the limit of her world, and still she did not feel whole.

Some days, at the mouth of the *Eln*, she would run to the hill, to the point at which a castle once stood. She would climb the steep slopes of the ramparts, down ditch to climb again the summit of the inner motte, to stand in her imagination, to be a princess on her keep. She would listen to the music of her moment. Hear the sandpiper and curlew picking in the marsh below, then to the sea. She would look northwards to the Solway, to the lower slopes of Dumfriesshire across the water, then scan eastwards to the rise of *Criffel.* She wondered of the world across the sea. The Scottish man. The beast. An easy face she gave them. Demon men. And then, when the beast had formed large and threatening in her mind, she dreamed of a good English knight to save her from her woe. A man in good armour, with a good heart to see her safe. She would see herself in fresh white linen, running alongside a noble horse; hand on mane, her heart in his hands.

Oh how it is, the beauty of naivety, the simplicity of dreams. She had no knowledge of the good and bad that dwelled in all men, either Scottish or English, and the hurt they could bring.

Chapter XVIII

On Solway Sand, May 1554, day 17

At Elnborough, a little way down the coast from Allonby, Jack, Francis, Slack 'o' Jack and Geordie called on William Waite. His name was given by Thomas as a man worth the visit, someone who knew all things concerning the pains and pleasures of the Solway folk about; a possible recruiter for Jack's army and a sage to proffer suggestion to problems nagging Jack's rest—*why Allonby? How could they see at night to land on a speck on a limitless shore? Why risk a crossing over an inimical sea for a poor prize. If indeed the prize was poor?*

'Do the local landowners not mobilise? Is it all left to the March Warden to provide security in these parts?' Jack's question was well made, and William nodded his understanding, shifted on his bench and sank his ale completely.

William Waite, old, grey beard in hand, wrinkles worn by smile rather than frown, settled his mind to Jack's question. But the children around him took away his attention with their games, observations, and endless questions.

'Are all these yours?' asked Jack, his voice touched with appreciation of the old man's procurement.

'Sometimes I think they are, for they inhabit my house like the brown, spotted butterflies that dance on the bog grass. Two flit away and another four we find. But the village children always know a good story is to be told here, and good food to be had.'

Then his wife entered the room, as if she heard his silent call, and removed the children with promises of pie and honey on bread.

'There's always plenty of honey to be had. The Blacksmith brings his bounty, his surplus. His bees work hard. Well loved those bees are, and therefore liberal with their labours—honey to give.'

Jack turned to Slack 'o' Jack. He winked at him. 'Yes, William, there's plenty a soul grateful to the bee for their salvation.'

It took William a while, after quiet had found a room not usually quiet, to rethink a worthy response for his welcome guest.

'In truth, this area does not suffer the raids and privation of the land to the north of Carlisle or to the east along the *Picts' Wall.* The families here are, in the most, at peace with each other. Even if some disharmony exists, village with village. I cannot say we have been free from raid, or that we still are not governed by the need to defend from it. But the Lords of Holm and Allerdale do not provide routine strength to defend. Their knights move their castles to pretty places, and farm rather than fight.

Yes, we provide men to the muster; *March Days*, as dictated by our rights of tenure, but the war is quiet, and it has been some time since I saw men walk from the Solway coast with spears on their shoulders and flags to the fore.

The reiver from the north usually strikes across the shifting sands at high tide, at Bowness, and is governed by the time of the tide returned. He never strays far south. I do not say the reiver is not likely to knock on our door, bloody our nape and steal our silver, but we have tinkers, Cumberland born, who do no less a harm. The thief is the itinerant man from the south, and not the Scot-man from the North.'

Jack asked, 'But the raids on Allonby. Who takes it upon themselves to defend the land?'

'Village and village. Do not think we are community whole. Each village is to its own ends. Folk from Flimby keep to Flimby, and so on. So the poor souls from Allonby are alone in their woe.'

Jack nodded his understanding. 'I will see the Master of Ellenborough and talk to his good nature.'

'Indeed he is a man of good nature, married into a house not of his ancestry. But his sons are not fighting men, but a preacher, a collector of antiquity, a man of singularly peculiar habits, and another son with habits best kept hidden.'

William refilled everyone's cups before refilling his own. He broke bread and past the larger pieces to his guests, before dipping the remaining crust into his ale. 'This land breeds industry and craftsman. Men linked to the sea and the land by the bounty it holds. They are not soldiers. They will fight if need be and be canny about it. They are good at ball and drink well enough, but they do not seek other men's troubles. They keep themselves to themselves.' William stood up and opened his arms. 'Now come to the hall. It is an hour before dusk. The work is done. The stock is fed, and the people come to taste my pottage, bread and beer. All is good, because my good friends in Ellenborough have gifted their surplus, and I, through the Lord, have turned waste into wine.'

William Waite was a man possessed. Possessed of the spirits of faith, hope, and charity. His house and hall were forever open to the people that lived around the area, from the village on the banks of the river, to the fishermen's homes at the mouth of the Eln. People called it a hall, a meeting place, but it was nothing but a clay and timber built long-house, put to better use in the wake of the theft of its animals, and a man too tired to procure new life for it. Instead he set it with tables and benches, places for all to sit, and kept a good fire to warm all those who could not afford a fire of their own.

William was married to a Jewess called Miriam. She was late of Lancashire, born in the growing and populous town of Manchester. Daughter of a merchant of wool and linen, a man who found an early grave before he could find a better placed Judaic husband—better placed for wealth and prosperity. But she had converted a score of years past to the Christian belief, for which she held dear and close to her heart. As close as her husband, whom she took great comfort from, for he was the embodiment of a goodly man, free from pride, words free from scorn, contentment in his heart, diligence with regards to his duties, devout, generous and chaste.

Gawyn Borrowdale sometime ago in a mass, praised the good of William and Miriam's home and hall, and the good work within it. He spoke of the love and care that came from it. He said they kept a home there for all, and no child was ever hungry, no traveller was without rest, and no ancient soul was without family or someone to care. He said William spoke fervently on behalf of the peoples about, and was always the first and last to speak at the manor courts.

In the hall, a Cumbric minstrel recited lyric, and a piper played to his prosody. The hall was full of noise and people, good humour and cheer. All came to the gathering.

The call of the hall was always charity. Donations meant the pot was well filled with meat, and bread always aplenty.

'Food and shelter are always free here, friend. We only ask for good company do you bring, and a song or sonnet in return for your supper, or a gift to be given for the benefit of all in the hall.'

Jack drew out his purse to find a few coins and placed them in William's hand, and he gestured to his men to do the same. Geordie's donation was poorly offered; not in terms of coin, matched with Jack's, but in terms of paired reciprocity—*he hated parting with money.*

William made sure they had space to talk, free from interruption. But, just as Jack thought he had the old man's attention, he looked away to far end of the hall. All fell quiet as a man stood on a bench. It was plain the guests knew the man; that they knew what was coming. They held their breath and held their tongues in readiness to hear his offering. A lyric accompanied by the piper, now playing a lute instead;

'See not the hills, the lakes, and Solway sand,
But instead the stone on which Cumberland stands.
Not the land that God created,
But the industry that man do maketh.
For the spirit of the Cum-ri,
Is not the green in which they dwell,
But the vigour o' the folk that live on coast 'n' fell.'

The refrain continued after the man finished his lyric, the sweet sound of the lute filling the hall. Peoples smiled. Nods were exchanged between neighbour and glances of friendship and contentment were about. The tune was unknown to Jack, and it was a sound to melt the hardest heart and to soften the harshest thought. Even Francis held tight his eyes in quiet enjoyment of the sound and the good thoughts it gave.

When it was finished and raucous noise filled the hall once more, William turned to Jack.

'I've been thinking on your raiders. It's not an easy crossing from Scottish shore to English sand. The current runs strong in the Solway. Sand banks shift, and it takes a good pilot to know where the boulder-strewn *scaurs* lie. Even in day, it takes a good sailor, good weather and kind providence to see a boat land where he intends it. At night it is almost impossible.

'Almost?' asked Jack.

With a strong light on the shore, a full moon perhaps, and a sailor born of these coasts, landing is possible. Without it, only God's hand could direct the tiller to see a boat land with such correctness.'

'A beacon lit?'

'Yes, there are beacons all along the coast. There have been such for over a thousand years, but they are only lit to shout raid in time of war.'

Francis offered, 'Perhaps lights from the houses, or the after-burning of rotten timbers from salvage works.'

William answered, 'The people of Allonby are gainful, but miserly… a single candle lit will hardly be seen across the sea. And no one burns a bonfire after dark unless it is a feast day.'

'Are there sailors from this coast working the Scottish side too?' asked Jack.

'There are a few,' answered William, 'And some who know both coasts well.'

'Will you point me to them, so I can understand the route that brings the reivers to Allonby? Perhaps I will learn the name of the eyes of the reivers, so they may be plucked?'

'I will.'

Francis took Jack to one side, while Slack 'o' Jack was kept in good company by William.

'Jack, without a sea crossing the reivers would be hard pressed to make a raid worth the while along this coast.'

'Perhaps. The reivers strike only for the bounty of this land and sea—meat and salt, and whatever else falls their way by chance.

They use ship because this cannot be driven away like stock on the hoof.'

Francis pressed his point, to have Jack see he was the one to resolve the problem. 'Exactly. A raid on horseback would be foolhardy this far along the coast, for the March Warden could easily strike out from Carlisle and shut the gate on the raiders as they try to return to the crossing on the sands at the mouth of the Solway.'

Jack stifled his smirk, but his words released were full of scorn. 'So Francis, do you think we should hunt down and *kill* every good Solway sailor? Or perhaps we should burn every boat?'

Francis was irked by Jack's contempt for his *solution*. 'No, Jack. Kill only the sailors in the reivers' employ, send the message to them all. There is no profit piloting these robbers.'

'Francis, we shall put our blades to the stealers and not to the necks of the sailors.'

'So why do you need to know the pilots, if not to kill them?'

'I do not think to remove the reivers' pilots, only to understand their crossing.'

Francis turned away, resentful, bitter. 'Then when the reivers land on the shore, and we six stand alone with cowards at our backs…'

Jack put his hand firmly on Francis to stop him finishing. 'Then when we meet God, it will be journeying from an honest fight and not soaked in the blood of murdered men.'

'These pilots are not innocent.'

'They only serve their masters, no doubt to save their lives and families.' Jack saw continuance, a route to see Francis' discontent turn to anger. And his anger usually travelled with a blade.

'Come, Francis, join Slack 'o' Jack, for he has the right solution. See he dances with William's good lady.'

Francis was not for dancing, and instead he took his ale to sit by himself and sulk.

Jack stood up with William to set about a jig with the crowd, and Geordie, unsettled by the two pennies lost to Jack's charity, sought all night to recoup his losses and add to his profit. He weighed the pewter drinking vessels in his hand, plates too, and a cup (a gift to William from a Lady of Flimby Hall) found his bag. He looked to people lost in revelry and picked their pockets and cut their purses, he even stole a dull knife or two even though he had three keener knives more.

Chapter XIX

On Solway Sand, May 1554, day 18

The day after heavy drinking, all of the men had sallow faces and sore heads. Even Soldier looked poorly, even though he had escaped the other men's drowning in ale and beer, music and jig, by the duty of his watch held over the coast. He had sat at the highest point, at a signal beacon at *Crosscanoby*, at a place a mile or two between Allonby and Ellenborough. It offered the best vantage over the sea, although it was barely a hill, just a rise on the plain.

He had spent the night, sitting damp within the foundations of an ancient fort. Sitting and watching the sea, with a mind to light the beacon fire and sound church bell, if reivers came calling from the across the water.

Jack, Francis and Geordie had come from Ellenborough, Geordie to relieve Soldier's watch, Slack 'o' Jack to remain at Ellenborough, still abed on the reed and sacking in front of William's fire.

Leaving Geordie to his watch, the three men walked the beach back to Allonby.

All three showed poorly. Wit was absent. Sleep desired. The

three trod the sand. Walked not rode. Strolled not stepped. Jack, Soldier, and Francis. The sky was black over Criffel, a hill of heather and bog-cotton sitting high over the Scottish coast, and blue sitting over the Solway Plain running the land to the mountains of Cumberland.

It became usual that the men's eyes kept vigil on the sea, even though it was expected that the reivers would come at night across the water.

Francis kicked a hole in the sand, urinated long, and then dragged the sand with his boot to cover the puddle.

'I say it's not good to defend,' muttered Francis, 'The houses too far spread. The site too open on all sides.'

Jack turned from the waters to scan the landward horizon; the long stretch of flat plain running along the head of a beach, that in turn ran half a mile or more to the Solway. He knew it ran flat as far as the eye could see in both directions. He had seen it so every day since his arrival. Some would sigh deeply with its endless sight, but a crapulent man has a poor view, so he returned his reddened eyes to study the scattering of clay-daubed cottages; mostly single storey, thatch topped, sited at the edge of the beach. Some stood on the beach, some stepped back on the Plain. Some had floors built higher on a few course more of stone to escape flooding from spring tides. Some even had two storeys, with storerooms to stay dry and byres below. The blacksmith's stood proud this way. It stood singly to the north. It stood tall with forge above and stables below. Few other buildings showed different, and none showed wealth.

Jack turned to Soldier, standing by. 'What do you think?'

The Soldier pointed to the carcasses and skeletons of boats strewn along the beach. 'The hulks will give good cover for musket and bow to fire on the reivers as they disembark their boats. New walls, fixed tall, will direct attackers towards enclosed firing points in the village. We will have good cover, if we make it so.'

'The reivers will be poor targets in the night, or the half-light of dawn,' growled Francis, irked that his opinions were not sought above a man unfamiliar to Jack. 'They'll ride in hard to rout... We'll not be ready. These farmers will run at first sight.'

'Then Francis, my little man, it is up to us to make sure we cull five times our own number, and earn five times the bounty,' returned Soldier, 'Besides, they may come by day, or even land somewhere other than this beach.'

Francis growled again. 'They may even be on their way right now... to catch us ill-prepared,' Francis turned his back on the men to mutter beneath his breath, 'Ill-prepared and badly led.'

Geordie had stood sentinel at Crosscanoby for an hour. His gaze constantly shifting from the sea, from the sight of Scotland over the water to the land behind the expansive beach, and the village standing naked on the Plain in the distance. He had stood long enough to raise a shouted mock-complaint from men working hard under his watch post, at a saltern at the head of the beach. Long enough for his mind to play out the arrival of the reivers and all the possible scenarios to come. None were a kind outcome for the people of Allonby.

But as he thought, he reasoned the reivers must hold the key to the treasure his comrades were keeping from him. He concluded there was no treasure in amongst the penury within his sight. The people here worked the land only for their daily bread and for the profit of absent, richer men.

'Allonby has no gold, or hidden riches,' he said to himself, 'It is only an assembly point for the reivers, attacking the Plain. Yes... only an assembly place before the crossing back to Scotland.' Geordie looked back to the Scottish coast and in his mind's eye he saw three, four, perhaps five ships sailing across. 'Their ships will come from across the water to be filled with gold collected from their raids into Cumberland', he whispered, 'Yes, heavy loot from raids, too much to risk a land crossing at Bowness. Ships to carry the gold back, whilst the reivers ride on faster for the lack of load to bear.'

Geordie looked towards the men puddling clay to line the sleech-pits. They would lay the straw to filter the salted-sand, piled high nearby.

'Yes, work, *poor fellows*. Brownfield aims to steal the ships and leave you to your fate… Yes of course… Steal their ships while fight occupies the reivers on the land. A good plan. Wait till the ships are loaded. Then attack on land… a diversion… *A very good plan indeed.*'

He convinced himself of the amount of stolen booty. Cattle, goods and chattels became chests of gold and buckets of rubies. Fishing boats became caravels, and then galleons in his fevered thought, so big was his dreamed treasure, and then he worried. He was not convinced by his comrades' efforts. Reivers would not let their prize go easily. And he worried his share of the prize may be at risk. Farmers with sharpened tools and a fighting stance did not qualify them as men-at-arms. But he was not blind to the mettle of men. He had seen the fervour of peaceable peoples driven to fight, blood burning and their anger alight. He had seen untrained men overwhelm knights and seasoned fighters. He had seen the peasant mob tear into soldiers and render them naught but butchered meat. But the odds this time were not favourable… The odds were not kind at all. Then he concerned himself with how many of the men would be left standing. The fewer remaining meant his share of the spoils may be so much greater… but still there was risk.

Below, the *Salty-man* watched Geordie. He wondered how he liked his perch. How the view suited him. The Salty-man's home-hut once lay within the foundations of that ancient fort, so he knew the view was fine. He sniffed and blew out the congestion in his old nose. He looked to his work, and the other men working. Then he thought again, shouting more mocking words at Geordie—him standing proud, with nothing to do but stand and stare at Solway sand.

The old salt-maker took his rest, because puddling clay was hard work. And even though he worked hard, and all was heavy toil, his old bones and tired muscles meant rest was needed more often than the work allowed. So he took a few minutes to look up at Geordie again, and studied his man. He wondered about his honour, his belief and his journeys.

The Girl was close by, to bring her Salty-man a drink to quench a thirst ever present. She loved her Salty-man. Salty to the kiss he was, working the salterns. He was always salty to her kiss, and he always offered her a smile and a hug for the love she gave and the ale she brought him.

She sat on a barrel and stroked a fat grey cat. A cat, smug with the attention she lavished on it. Hers was the only hand it would have on its back—cruel history taught it well. Only the hand with food to give was a hand worthy of tolerance. It had learned never to bite the hand that feeds it, or scratch out the eye of a friend. It had learned the old salt-maker's and the blacksmith's fires were the places to sit and stare, to sleep, and the Girl to find when hunger was his call, and warm languor was preferred to hunting.

A few miles along the beach, Jack, Soldier and Francis reached the point where the last building stood overlooking the sea. All looked to the leaden sky. Violent it was. Day turned dark. Calm. Then wind, suddenly in anger, and the men were caught in a storm of sand. It stung their faces. Removed all thought. Gave discomfort. But pride was showing, and all stood their ground against the blow. Then the wind retreated and all stood still.

Darker and darker, and then the rain. The world became wet. And such a downpour it was. Heavy and hard on heads, soaking their leather and wool, soaking the sand beneath their feet. Then came the blow again. Furious.

The men were forced to retreat, run, put aside manly ego and seek shelter—the nearest house—the blacksmith's.

In the blacksmith's were the Boy and two men; one man as old as the Plain, his face wearing forty and more wrinkles, and another man as dirty as the earth, his face wearing the soot of forty fires.

Soldier smiled at the Boy. He saw a face lost in time. His son's face, long lost to his eyes, but forever kept in his memory.

'You boys wet then?' The old man, raised a smile. 'Ye don't read the sky d'ya… Could you no see the rain comin'.' He nodded to the Blacksmith. 'At least ye've found the right place to dry. My brother smithy burns the only fire that keeps the cold from my bones. I'm sure he'll share it wi' ye.'

Jack, Soldier and Francis, came to the fire, and the Blacksmith grudgingly stoked it into flame. The heat was welcome.

The old man spat to the earth. 'Take off yer jacks and coats, *soldier men.* Sit and be warmed. Me and my man here, are sharing tales.'

'You got ale, *Blacksmith*?' asked Francis, curtly.

A gruff voice replied, 'You got coin, *Mercenary*?'

Soldier, his hair dripping on the hearth, picked up a cloth from the floor. 'Watch yourself, *Brother Smithy*.' Soldier ran the rag over his long mane. 'A niggardly man with a sour head has never a kind temper.'

The Blacksmith glared at Soldier. 'In my house, hospitality is free only to those invited to it.'

'Seems yer ire burns as bright as your fire, Blacksmith,' replied Soldier.

'Don't be like that, my man...' The old man cast an uneasy smile at the Blacksmith, shifted on his seat and broke wind, '...show the boys some comfort.'

Soldier grinned at the old man. 'Seems the storm blows as hard inside, as it does without.'

The old man appreciated Soldier's keen wit, and nodded his approval.

But the storm still blew, even if the old man's arse was no longer doing the blowing.

Francis spat on the Blacksmith's floor. 'While we sit in your village, *Smithy man*, your house is our house. Best you think on it... keep it in your mind... that's if you wish us to stop the reivers burning you out.'

'We don't need you, *soldier man*.' He spat his return into the fire, for the pearl of spittle to hiss on the coals.

The old man, stood up to walk to the stool where a jug sat. He struggled to find three cups. He found only one. But had the sense to pour a drink, at least for Francis and refill the Blacksmith's cup. Spirit to calm the churlish man. He apologised to Jack and Soldier, handing Jack the jug to sup from, and to share with Soldier.

'So, Blacksmith, how do the reivers hurt you?' asked Jack.

'They force iron-fixin' from me... Broken bridles and dull weapons.'

'Force?' said Francis.

'Aye, *force*.' The Blacksmith looked up, scowled and spat again into his fire. 'Do you wish to see the burns applied to my hands, arms, body 'n' legs. All to see my labour given without fee?'

Jack shook his head, not in disagreement, but in condemnation of the reivers cruelty.

Francis, however, challenged. 'But there again, show me a blacksmith in all the World who does not have such burns... It comes with the craft.'

The Blacksmith spat into his fire again. The hiss lost amongst the rattle of the wind's hold on the smithy. 'Believe what you wish, *little man.*'

Jack oft tired of Francis' rankle and malice, and rebuke was forever issued instead of order. At times, Jack thought diversion a better policy. He knew constant rebuke poked at Francis instead of praise would not make him a less contrite subordinate, but a more spiteful man. But praise was hard to find, unless it was in regards to his war-craft, which he was much lauded for.

So ignorance to his spite was found, and Jack asked the Blacksmith, loud. 'Do many monks still live amongst you?'

But it was the old man that replied. He quickly interceded. 'A few... Pensions took... They are all good farmers.'

The Boy, sitting in the corner of the blacksmith's, on a coffer of plain design and poor build, studied the three soldiers for a long while. He admired the men's armour, battle bruised and tarnished, swords and hangers, daggers, leather jacks and felt jackets torn and patched from a score of cuts.

But he studied Soldier, more than the others. He watched Soldier's hands, callused, moving from his beard to add gesture as he talked, as he confirmed a soldier's thought with his captain.

So his study complete, the Boy settled on Soldier, him being older and bigger and more impressive in both his build and his face, which was not fine featured like his captain's, but hard-worked like the Blacksmith's. He re-examined his armour and weapons, his sword and daggers—one to use with his long steel to parry, and one, a ballock dagger like his father carried. The Boy was happy his father owned a similar weapon, a weapon belonging to a soldier. So in his mind his father was a soldier too, and thus he, a soldier's son.

'Have you seen fight, old man?' asked Francis.

'Many times I have fought in rank 'n' file as militia, called by my master's muster.'

Francis poured scorn on the old man. 'Miltia, pah! Serfs with staves. Sheep to herd in front of the enemy, only to break at first shot. Pity you have not been a soldier. We need good example to set before these farm and fisher boys.'

'How many battles does a militiaman need to fight to call himself a soldier? I have a soldier's sin, in the tally of dead and bloodied men to weigh heavy my journey to Heaven's gate.'

Francis shook his head to mock the old man's worth.

Jack nodded to acknowledge an old man's sufferance, and Soldier seemed to lower his eyes slightly in faint contrition. The Boy simply sighed in great admiration of his newfound hero—Soldier.

The wind's blow grew louder, so quiet discourse between men was difficult, and the old man was forced to raise his voice.

'God throws the sand at the land to build more land for us to graze, such is His grace.'

'The dunes?' asked Jack.

'Aye, the dunes. *Laal* stones and beach blossom will be covered by sand on the blow and built into hill and green.' The old man picked his teeth, and shifted on his stool.

Jack opened a shuttered window facing the lee of the wind, to see the storm at its worse. He saw a shadow in the hail, running the beach, not to shelter, but to the sea. He squinted, to focus his eyes to be sure of what he saw. A slight figure running the surf, hands to the sky, clapping. The figure span around and kicked as if doing a jig, then leapt to the sky. Jack rubbed his face, to clear eyes sullied from a night of toping on a jug and two of best-brewed ale, and looked again.

His eyes did not lie.

Chapter XX

On Solway Sand, May 1554, day 19

The Boy's father was an able man. Well, all around him declared it so. It was what former Abbot, Gawyn Borrowdale declared at the manorial court baron, when customary tenantright was transferred to him from his grandfather's holding for a whole two year's saving of entry fines and fees. It's what Thomas said too, as he gathered the other children at his feet, to fill their ears with stories of heroes, both from the Bible and more often than not from Greek antiquity.

But the Boy thought different.

He thought his father a cruel and spiteful man, angry with the toil of life. He thought him a sheep, following his neighbours into a life on the land. A life without glory or honour… There was no bravery there. No cheers shouted as there was in war's song. He was a coward. A coward because he chose to sweat his days out, digging dirt and felling tree, rather than raising a spear to the enemy and earning a name to wear with pride, like the Boy's heroes; *Hercules and Odysseus.*

The Boy's father was called James—*James the 'Less'*, after the Lord's blessed disciple of that name. He was born to a father called James, and so the babe was called, in affection, James the Little, and so he was baptized as such.

And like his father before him, the Boy was also called James.

Thomas could not offer a worthy description of the nature of James, the Lord's Disciple. So he seemed less in the Boy's mind, no hero. So instead, the Boy fashioned his own name, in secret, as *Achilles*, and he carved a wooden sword in the fashion of that great warrior, its design taken from an illustration Thomas had shared with him from one of his books.

'The men with guns are getting better, *da*. Firin' straight and true… well some of them.'

'Humph!'

'Soldier let me fire his pistol yesterday… I nearly hit the target.'

'Humph! It's only been five days, lad. It'll take five months to have all our boys shoot straight. Besides, where do they get guns from?'

'Old Meg found them.'

'Humph, Meg? Where does that old crow find guns?'

'I don't know… I'm spending the day wi' the soldiers, training our neighbours on the beach.'

'You done your chores?'

'I was up two hours early to do them.'

'They'll be badly done, I suspect.'

'Why aren't you training with the men?'

'I've work to do here… Just like you.'

His father sat astride his *horse*. Wood it was, not flesh, nor fast. It was his father's and his grandfather's horse before it was his. And it would become the Boy's when he learned to ride it well enough.

His father worked his two-handled knife over the oak 'smarts', shaving the pieces of wood, ready to be formed into a swill basket.

'It's bad enough I have my home littered with a soldier-man

and all his doin's. It's bad enough yer ma has to pick more spring greens from her tired garden and find more meat to feed that bloated belly of his.' He looked up from his swiller's horse to see the Boy. 'But it's ignominy to have him corrupt my son with more thoughts of war and battlin'.'

The Boy's father applied his knife too hard to a smart he had gripped in his horse. His knife cut all the way through the wood with his error.

'Curse ye for a son!'

The Boy ran out the house, leaving his father to throw the ruined wood to the ground—*kindling for the fire.*

A father looked to the door, and remembered a time when he had ran out that same door to find his own father. How his own small arms and tired legs brought him ale and beer as he worked his grandfather's workshop deep in the forest—*a thought for the better.*

He looked to the Boy, outside, fretting, and remembered a time when he had also ran in anger from that same door, as his grandfather carried in his father's swill-horse—*a bequest for a son.*

He mourned his father's death. His grandfather was proud. He said he should be proud too. He died on a foreign field—*fighting for his king.*

He was six years old when he heard the news of his father killed in France. Three days off the boat. Twenty years dreaming of war. All for three days campaigning and an hour's fighting. Eternal rest for a lost father, they said. A wasted life of dreaming, he thought.

The Boy ran into Soldier waiting on the track.

Thomas had billeted Soldier with the Boy's family, against reason, as their house was nearly a league away from the coast and Allonby, and Soldier would have half the hour to respond to alarm's call. Jack questioned the merit of it, but bowed to Thomas' reasoning. For good reason, Thomas had to put a fanciful boy with a tried, and perhaps tired, veteran soldier. He perhaps thought time with tales and truth of the hardship of war might dispel the fancy of it. But Thomas did not know Soldier.

'My da doesn't approve of you.'

Soldier put a hand on the Boy's shoulder. 'Your pa resents fighters amongst the village?'

'He does. He says, you disrupt the work of the village. He says, you bring only greater harm.'

'Does he not lose to the reivers?'

'No more than to the poor seasons, the Crown and the Church, he says.'

'And what's your ma say as she tucks you in your cot, little warrior?'

'She isn't allowed to speak about it.'

'It's a rare woman who keeps a tongue from shouting its mind.'

'She's from across the border.'

Soldier laughed loud. *'A Scots lass!* What's he done? *Cut her tongue out!'* Soldier's laugh abated, but left the smile on his golden face. 'A Scottish ma on English soil. It's not unusual I suppose, even though it is against Border Law for English to wed Scot.' Soldier looked at the Boy, listening intently. 'It's a pity too. I often find a Scots wench a fine shag… But all pale away against French women. A finer shag they are, believe me, but they are harridan wives much like the Irish. All pretty women are. Tender obedience is not their way.' Soldier squeezed tight the Boy's shoulder. 'I say, wed yourself an ugly English lass, boy. They'll tend to you well, keep your home, keep faithful whilst you adventure and whore away on foreign soil. And if you find yourself fighting the Muslim man; have one of his women, for you will find no better delight on this earth.' Soldier checked the Boy's understanding. The Boy was smiling. 'No better delight I say, except of course bleeding your enemy.'

'My ma is pretty,' said the Boy.

'Hence why your pa stays at home, to watch over your ma, lest she wanders, *eh boy*?'

The Boy was sheepish.

'So where does your ma hail from? The Highlands and Islands, the Lowlands? Or does she hail from the far north, a feral female, half woman—half goat.'

'She's from Kirkcudbright.'

'Ah, a siren from across the sea.'

The Boy took a look over his shoulder to see if his father or mother was watching from his home. He could hear the steady rhythmic sounds of steel drawing on wood.

'Never mind him, boy,' said Soldier, looking back to the open door of the cottage.

He gathered up the Boy and led him away down the path to the sea. 'In the past, your pa will have been on the bad end of a burnin'. Perhaps he saw his church destroyed, his home looted.' He looked to the Boy, and drawing his sword, he raised the hilt to his eye. Then pointing the blade to the sea, his eye looking down the steel, to see the edge on it was keen and true, he said, 'It's better to have yer hands on the torch that sets the flame than be the one who feels its heat.'

'Have you fought many wars and battles?' asked the Boy.

'Wars, no, not many, for our realm is always in war, and so war is continuous and not spats to fight and forget. I cannot remember a time we shouted peace. Battles, yes. I have seen many actions. Mostly against the French, the Muslim, and of course the Scot.'

'Do you ever think on the next battle to fight, or ones already fought?'

Soldier turned his head to the Boy. He held his tongue for a few moments to clear his mind of his appetite for war and to find the truth of it. 'A general once told me, a true warrior wins or loses his battle before he's even fought it.' He raised a finger to his temple. 'He wins or loses it in his mind.' His finger dropped and his hand clamped on the Boy's shoulder. 'I have stood the battleground and seen many battles, and in truth, boy, I have fought less than a handful. For it is the way of some battles that they are lost or won quickly on another part of the battlefield, or away from it entirely.'

The Boy frowned.

'But it matters not, boy. So long as you are paid for your attendance and given opportunity to test your craft.' Soldier winked. 'But beware, boy. Repairs to armour, arms, flesh and cut-jacket often cost, so keep your enemy from landing his blows.'

'Can you see the coming battle?' asked the Boy, 'Do we win or lose?'

In Soldier's mind he was only a winner. 'If the reivers expect resistance, I can see them riding in hard. They will be ready, and will be riding to scatter us.' Soldier flicked his eyes towards a man carrying his heavy burden from the fields. 'Poor souls like he, will raise his cleaver to the riders, but will be ridden down before he can bloody his tool's blade. Many will stand bravely, and some will even dismount a reiver or two, even put a blow or two on their man. Men will even hesitate, because of their fear, or their uncertainty, but the reivers will not hesitate. They will ride in support of each other, and all who fight against them, unless they stand firm, will be ultimately overwhelmed.'

'You talk a poor outcome.'

'For all I love the fight, you have to see it real, and not as well-wished glory, honeyed by fervent tongues. In war, do not have faith in your neighbour, but in your own skill. Remember that.'

The two walked into the training area, and the Boy was excited to see men being drilled with stave and sword, bow and matchlock. Francis held one group around him. Slack 'o' Jack another.

'You're a bunch o' ragged arse loons.' Francis was fierce in his delivery. 'Soldiers you are not… not until I tell you, that is.'

Slack 'o' Jack sat easier amongst his group. Men and boys about him like friends sharing a yarn. 'Ye men with guns, take down their nags, an easier target on the move. Ye men with spears run in tae blood the fallen afore they can recover. Me and the boys with guns will reload and cover those who remain mounted, those who pose a threat to ye ones exposed as ye cut yer enemy. Mind ye boys wi' spears, dinnae think on them boys that are mounted, ye only think on cutting them ones in the dirt afore they recover.' Slack 'o' Jack studied the faces about him. He counted fear and fortitude on faces in equal measure. 'Remember dae not give yer enemy a moment… Thrust yer blade in his flesh quickly and hard, and thrust again, and again, until yer blade goes in easy… because then ye've destroyed his flesh and likely killed yer man. Take nae pity on him, be deaf tae his screams, fer he'll give ye nae quarter… Give him the opportunity, and he'll cut ye… and these reivers are fightin' men. Their cuttin' will be well laid on ye… laid tae kill.'

'Will that be enough?' came a voice from Slack 'o' Jack's group.

'Ye will surprise them on the first pass, as they ride in. Make it count, kill as many as ye can… dae not let them turn and run… dinnae let them run tae return.' He looked around. He took pity on the faces. 'The ones that are left alive tae run or ride, will retire to think on the blood ye spill. Perhaps they leave ye alone, perhaps they'll be back, mair careful. Perhaps even they'll be back in greater numbers… It depends how much ye hurt them, or hurt their pride. But these are likely clanless loons, nae kin nor clan name tae uphold… They may hold together fer profit and fer protection. Take that away and they may leave ye be.'

'How many will we take down on the first pass?'

'Perhaps a quarter number... Enough tae make them think.'

Jack was about, with a group of five. Sword drill. Soldier picked up a sword and handed it to the Boy and stood in line. Jack's men were chopping at broad wooden pales driven into the ground. Soldier stood in place of a post and invited the Boy to strike and chop at him, as the men about did on their sham reivers.

The Boy was hesitant. He was frightened to harm Soldier, but Soldier goaded and encouraged the Boy to strike hard.

Still the Boy resisted.

Soldier glared and again told the Boy to strike.

But he could not.

Soldier spat to the ground. 'You feckless youth. Dig the dirt, boy, clean out the latrine. All you'll ever be fit for is shovelling shite.'

The Boy's anger grew, but still he didn't strike.

Soldier smirked. 'Perhaps I waste my time with you, boy. Perhaps that Scotch bitch you call a ma be better use of my time.' He looked away to the direction of the Boy's home. ' I'll have her shagged hard and cruel for my pleasure.'

The Boy found his anger, and brought across his sword to chop at Soldier's left arm. But Soldier quickly returned his attention to the Boy, and raised his hand to hold off the blow and deflect the blade. In turn, Soldier brought his own sword to bear down on the Boy. He stopped short, the blade to rest on the youth's shoulder.

The Boy looked at Soldier's sword on his shoulder. An unstopped blow would have cleaved him in two. Then he looked to Soldier's other hand; the one that had made contact with his own blade. He had made a fist. It was bleeding badly. Cut by his sword. The blood poured from it.

'I hurt you.'

'At times, boy, it is better to sustain a lesser wound to inflict greater harm. Use your hand to parry the blow if need be. But be a blade of grass and not a tree. Travel with the blade to remove its temper. Do not hold the blade, for your enemy will be able to withdraw it sharply causing a deeper cut.'

Soldier opened his palm to the boy. The cut was bloody.

'My hand bears many scars. Let me see yours.'

The Boy held out his hand to Soldier.

Soldier studied his hand, callused with toil, but free from cut. He held the boy's hand and brought over his sword. The Boy knew what was coming. He tried to withdraw his hand, but Soldier's grip was resolute, and he drew his sword blade over the Boy's hand.

The Boy screamed.

Soldier covered the Boy's wound with his own cut hand and gripped tight.

Blood on blood.

'Now, boy, ye have a soldier's blood running into yours. Let it see if it does not infect your own blood with my courage.'

The Boy held his hand, trying not to show his discomfort.

'This is my advice, boy. Find your anger. Use your sergeant's goad to find it. Find your skill. Buy the best armour you can afford. Assign yourself to only those generals with a name earned in victory, and fight. Draw blood whenever you can, because at times your sword and spirit will be idle… don't let battle see it. Make sure your skill, resolve and blade are keen from constant trial and test.' Soldier paused. 'But most of all, God requires good Christian soldiers. Remember that. He's the root of your talent, boy. Remember that also. So when you've found your anger to fight. Kill it. Fill instead your heart with the joy of it, the joy of God, not anger or hate. Enjoy the killing, boy. There's glory to be found in it.' Soldier smiled at the Boy. 'Now forgive me for the slight I inflict on you and your ma, and go polish my weapons like I showed you. Let me talk to our captain here.'

Chapter XXI

On Solway Sand, May 1554, day 22

With it being early May, the Solway weather was at its best, with sun, clear skies, and a warmth that allowed cloaks and mantles to be left inside, but not too warm that work gave a heavy lather on toiling man and beast.

Good weather however, was not a welcome gift for some. Some men disliked its calm and clear evenings, because they brought the threat of the reivers near. Some men of war, however, looked kindly on the still evenings and cloudless nights.

Soldier wanted and waited for the fight.

But Jack was not ready. The Allonby men were not ready. There would be no reinforcements from Robert so soon, and so Jack breathed easier when dawns came after calm nights, and rested easier when nights were with heavy cloud and strong blow.

Labour to prepare the defences was continual, with new wall and ditch, firing stations built and sentinel posts established. The men trained well. The Blacksmith worked hard, and was never to be seen without a blackened face or a sweated brow. He made caltrops to Soldier's design and put a keener edge on the men's cutting tools. Meg found old weapons; pikes, halberds, spears and even bows and matchlocks. She would not reveal her source; a secret cache, held quiet by Gawyn Borrowdale.

But there were days when all training and work was abated—Sundays.

After a thanksgiving, held in the Abbey church at Holm Cultram, Thomas and Jack gathered the children, both boys and girls belonging Allonby, to walk them the miles back along the coast to their homes.

As Thomas had offered his home to Jack—that is, offered a good bed in Borrowdale's home; a clergyman owing Thomas favour, Jack was requested to offer his time to the children.

Gawyn Borrowdale had gladly given up his home and his bed for Jack's comfort, for he was uncomfortable with the world and the world around him. With soldiers and raid on his doorstep, it was a place not to better his rest. So he travelled to Liverpool to seek respite from his ills.

It was Thomas' idea to share the men's gift of knowledge and the world around them with the young as they walked, for the gift of knowledge was with both men, and both men shared it freely.

At a point along the walk, Thomas and Jack sat on a large and long oak bench that fronted the sea. It was carved with fish and flowers, marked with *1502* and initials *MH* and *CH*. It was a league from Holm Cultram and half a league from the nearest house. The seat offered good rest and was large enough for both men and half the children to sit. Thomas told Jack the history of the bench, made in love by a husband for his wife to sit on at the end of each day, in order to watch the sun go down over the Solway.

'They are both long gone, but their seat lives on for all to enjoy repose,' declared Thomas.

'It is a good view,' replied Jack, and as his eyes scanned the horizon before him, his hand ran over the carving, tracing his fingers over the lettering and the numbers. He imagined the man who had carved it. A man in love enough with a woman to fashion the seat so. He admired the seat, far older than he, that had stood its place for all to enjoy its rest and its lookout. A gift for all from a selfless act.

'It is a large bench for two, Thomas?'

'I suspect it was made by a man who had large dreams, and wished to fill it with a large family.'

'And did he?' asked Jack.

'No, his dreams of family came to naught.'

'Still, it's a good view, Thomas.' Jack looked ahead to the sight of the Solway. 'A very good view indeed.'

Thomas and Jack sat, while the children ran off to play games of ball and catch. And Thomas could see Jack was lost to the view before him, and had fallen into reverie.

'What are you thinking, John Brownfield?'

'I am wondering why I am here, defending an English village against the Scot, my brethren.'

'Brethren, John? Are not these good folk your brethren, Border born?'

'My father would not approve of my actions here.'

'But I expect Mary would.'

'Mary?'

'Yes, John, Mary. I see you think on her more these days.' Thomas smiled and put a hand on Jack's back. 'I thank God daily for the gift he gives me. Because for all my sin, for all my pleasure taken.' Thomas patted his belly, 'I have one treasure to give, that what God has given to me—*my discernment.* I know when a man is lost in the thought of God, or in the worship of sin. I know when he thinks of his work, and of his children. I know the quiet man who hides a hate, and the husband who hides a love for his wife, and even the husband who covets the other man's wife over his own. I know proper action, and the men who hide a hurt, or embrace a love.

So I know it is Mary's approval you seek, not your father's. You show this by taking up arms in her regard, although you do not admit to it. You think you do it in spite of your father, or anger. Yet those are stimulus that last but a moment. Yet you have been here three weeks. You could have left at any time. Yet you stay and fight for the good people here.

'There is something about this place.'

'Yes… It is said, Alan, the second Lord of Allerdale took a liking to the place. It suited his melancholic spirit, it being lonely. He is the one who rebuilt the Abbey of Holm Cultram. Just as he saw the pleasure in Allonby and gave it his name, just as the Vikings who settled here, I think you see it too, and you seek to remove the harm from it, and of course seek the approval of Mary.'

'Mary and I do not sit well together in the same house.'

'Then find another house.'

'You counsel that I should leave her?'

'I did not say that.' Thomas wagged a finger and pointed it to the sky, 'I say find another house, together. I know Mary to be a wondrous woman, full of compassion and a learning of such depth. Any man would find her a blessing, but challenging if he were not learned too.'

'Yes, she is exceptional.'

'Then why are you here and not with her?'

'To prove I am better than the men who hurt this land.'

'Yes, I think you wish to prove this to Mary. You wish her to regard you, respect you.' Thomas laughed. 'That troublesome coo you profess her to be.' Thomas calmed and he took Jack's hand. 'Do you love her, John?'

Jack looked away to find a half-truth, a refusal of the heart, a qualification to allow him to say no. But he said, 'Yes.'

'Mary and I have talked long about life for her. She is not happy living in your father's realm, and neither are you.... You are both internees of sorts, both educated beyond your peers. Both are dreamers of the wider world. Mary is right to wish escape... But she stays at your side. Have you thought why?'

'Because she has nowhere else to go.'

'She would find welcome anywhere in this land. She may be southern born, but she loves the Cumberland, and knows well its people and respects their way. I could list you a dozen worldly men of this land who would give all to her.'

'So what do I do?'

'Do what a man must do. Fight your righteous fight... Then go be a husband, and together see the world together, until you both find a place to suit. All need salvation, John. She is yours.'

'And what is yours, Thomas?'

'Mine, is all what I must do and tend the good flock here. The Church must deliver God to the people in all its guises.'

It can be said that man is on a journey, from the origins of his birth to his final resting. It can also be said that man, because he is never satisfied with his place on Earth, will consider his journey never completed. For he thinks he is greater than God, so he seeks to create better than God created. So his search and journey goes on. This will be his downfall, for man was created by God, and God is greater than man. So it is a wise man that knows his place before God, seeking to humble himself before a greater good, for no good can become of his conceit and his own ambition when it seeks to belittle God and His own.

Amongst the folly of man is John Brownfield, who is not wise, as he sets himself and his intellect above God's word, and he questions all that is put before him in God's name, and so he journeys without finding rest. But I know God smiles kindly on John, for he must know John's heart is pure and his final place is before him in humble reverence and unquestionable love. But I think God will put John's journey to the test, but knowing he is his own, and despite the trials along the way, I suspect John will not share the fate of other men; those who would journey on to their own demise, and perhaps to madness, or even to burn in Hell.

Thomas Smith of Holm Cultram, MDLIV (1554)

Chapter XXII

On Solway Sand, May 1554, day 25

'Take me riding… I have never ridden on a horse.'

The noise of the rain entered the Blacksmith's stable with the door opened, and Bendback looked to the stand of wet rags with suspicion. Waiting for a pun or a jibe at his expense. But the Girl just stood and stared, wet running off her auburn hair. Her smile was constant, not cruel. And Bendback felt unease. He turned away to grab new straw, and again rub his horse's chest, looking up to catch his horse's approval of his effort, to which *Mars* nodded appreciatively.

'Will you take me riding?'

Bendback stared deep into his horse's eyes, to seek an understanding his friend may have regarding girls and their ways, but his horse was no help. So, perhaps, he thought mockery of his horse was meant, or cruel comparison of himself to his friend, Mars; his bay Flemish horse; sixteen hands high; sixteen years old.

'He *is* a fine horse. Can I help ye groom him?'

Bendback weighed up the request in his mind, and thought to keep his horse safe from the wicked attentions of the Girl; Bendback only knowing the revilement of womankind and the cruelty of their words.

But as the Girl approached without fear, not hesitant, his horse marked his approval, by offering only a calm demeanour and a willing sound. And as she picked up straw to rub flank and thigh, Mars marked his approval with his 'tail' leaving its sheath.

'He likes you, lass.'

'Does he?'

'Aye, can you no see… He likes your touch.' Bendback's eyes directed the Girl to Mars' belly.

The Girl giggled.

'Mars gives his approval, and he's a discriminating beast.'

'He's a beautiful horse. I have not seen taller.'

'He's sixteen hands tall, according to my last master's roll, but some say he's more like seventeen.'

The Girl took great care rubbing Mars' flanks, her eyes full of regard for Bendback's mount. 'He's a knight's horse.'

'Aye, he comes from good stock. Good mounts that served my ancestors well.'

'Are ye a knight?' The Girl's voice was excited.

Bendback smiled at thought of such a thing. 'No, lass, I'm no knight.'

'Was yer father a knight?'

'He was born of a knight.'

The Girl's eyes widened at the thought of standing in knightly company. 'Then you are a knight.'

'No, lass, knights are not born, but he *was* a gentleman. Mars his gift.'

'Ye have a good father, to gi' ye such a gift.'

Bendback nodded in acceptance of the Girl's observation, well meant, but poorly made, Bendback knowing the truth of it.

'Will you take me riding, *Sir Knight*. I have never ridden a horse afore.'

'Then how do you travel? Ox cart?'

'My legs take me as far as I can go.'

'And how far have you been, lass?'

'I have run as far as *Egremont*, to the autumn crab fair. I heard boys would run for a prize. It took me a morning to run there. But the men would not let me enter the running-race. But I ran anyway,' she giggled, 'The men tried to stop me on the path, but they could not catch me. I can run faster than the wind. I chase the ponies in our fields... No one can catch me. If the Egremont men had not chased me off, I would have run the race and beat those boys,' The Girl twirled, 'I was back home in time for supper. Mind ye, my da scolded me bad, and I've never stayed away again.'

The Girl looked to the open door. The rain had stopped, and the sun found the world around them. She looked wistfully to the land over the Solway.

'I have never seen the world outside a few miles of our coast. What's it like, Sir Knight?'

Bendback continued to groom Mars, but he did turn his head to the Girl, silhouetted in the doorway, her still wet woollen kirtle moulded to her body. She wore little else except a pair of shoes. She dressed lightly so she could run free and fast. And for all she was slight in shape, she had curves. Bendback looked. Mars nodded his approval, and Bendback felt his own approval grow.

Bendback took his gaze off the Girl and back to his friend. 'My world is the Marches, I have not seen the green of England, or the high mountains of Scotland, or travelled the seas to Ireland, or to the lands to the East.'

'I would like to see it all...wouldn't ye?'

'Can the grass be different? Can the water flow dissimilar?'

'Thomas talks of endless seas of sand. Lands that live in snow and night. Cities in water, and cities of marble from where our Church sprang from.'

Bendback put down his straw. He looked at the Girl. He smiled. He was not anxious, or afraid of cruel words.

'You talk of lands where nothing grows, where thirst and cold are man's reward. Cities… *pah!* Can man make better than God's own green?'

The Girl returned Bendback's smile. She sighed at his wisdom and his countenance. And she moved forward, hands held out to touch her knight, and gave him her heart.

Chapter XXIII

On Solway Sand, May 1554, day 33

The spring tides always brought the sea into Meg's home, and she would need to chase the salt water from her floor. Her broom turned into brush.

She would often brush Francis from it too, he being billeted in her home in lieu of her family killed by reivers. He would lie too long in his bed, longer than she thought convenient. So a harsh word or three would be cast at him to rise and rout, and leave her to her cleaning and her cooking.

'Ye're a bitter wee man, Francis Bell.'

'Better be bitter, than be an old badger, Meg Hayton.'

'Ye must carry many a sore to make yer face so sour?'

'The only sore I endure is your face, Meg.'

'Get yer arse from ma bed, and put yer legs to good use… and get out of my home.'

Francis thought to defy Meg, but he had his fill of his bed. He threw back his cover, and in hose and shirt, he placed his feet on a wet floor and cursed.

And through the damp and sodden reeds, he walked out of Meg's house.

The village had been washed with a spring tide, now receding. Francis began to walk his route to the sea to piss and defecate, as he had done every morning since he arrived in Allonby. But the beach had gone. Sea was all around. But still he walked through the water towards where he thought the beach stood.

But then he stopped, while grass still stood under his feet. He had his fill of this *seaside idyll*, as Jack had named it. All Francis could see were the pigs in the lane, splashing about, and sheep on the grass on the higher plain. He saw their beasts too. He hated it all; the wet at his feet, the sight of the sea, the cold wind and the chatter of life in his ear. So he dropped his hose where he stood and let go his foul stench.

Meg shook her head at Francis, cursed him for being a man, and closed her door. Sweeping done, she returned to her cooking. Men to feed.

Her commitment to care of the men was absolute, as was her hate for the reivers that killed her reason to be. Although a new reason she found in the form of six new children she had procured, although she counted Bendback as three more for the food he had consumed. But she fretted a little. Peeved her skill was in decline and her taste had muted with age. She had noticed Bendback, lately, had left a plate or two of hers not consumed, preferring to share it with the dogs in the lane.

So with her hand firm on the bowl, she dug her spoon into the mix and tasted again. She added a little more salt.

All seemed well.

Her clap bread was a favourite amongst the men of her charge, and they were never without a large cake or two in their bags.

So she turned her hands to mix flour with water, to roll it her hands, to throw the ball of dough onto a round board deformed into a very shallow bowl, to clap it round, to drive the dough to the edge of the board. The cake was thin. Her job was done. But then, to relieve stiffness in her shoulders, she stretched her neck and back. Her eyes lifted to the ceiling, to the room beam.

Thoughts of her family hanging filled her head.

Anger swept her mind, not sorrow. She gathered the thin dough and rolled it into a ball again, to drive it to the edge of the board, her hate beating the dough as thin as paper.

Another cake to be transferred to the iron plate; a girdle, a bow handle to hang it over the coals. Another cake to be baked. Baked with hate.

Chapter XXIV

On Solway Sand, April 1554, day 35

Nights arrived and nights passed by into day, as the watchers waited for the reivers to come. Their homes barricaded, the women and children would travel to nearby farms, where more isolated, hidden bastle house and fortified barn would provide better protection to wait out the night.

Whilst the armed men waited out the dark, some ready to fight, some ready to run, they would congregate around a fire kept bright in the middle of the village. Some other men, without sentry assignment, when sleep eluded, would join the watch-men for company.

To ease their discomfort, Thomas would lead in prayer during the night and keep spirits cheered by stories, or readings from the Bible. Jack too, would sit by the fire most nights, his mind full of disquiet and restless thoughts; angst fuelled by the confusion that tossed his mind's thought into a raging sea and not the calm that begets restful sleep.

Some evenings when the weather was foul, and crossing the Solway unthinkable, Jack would spend it with Thomas at Holm

Cultram. And on an evening, with Jack as his guest, with supper eaten, all the wine drank, and cheese passed between the men, Thomas sat in silence for a time.

The silence was too long to suit Jack's comfort. It nagged him as he tried to rethink his words into ones better to apply to the page. But unease pricked him, and he looked up from his journal to see Thomas, a man in careful study staring into space. Jack now studied the man whom had, all evening, listened to Jack's empty words and careful chatter; comments on the weather and the state of policies applied to the Marches. He had revealed nothing of himself, his woes or the fight to come.

Jack could not help but wonder Thomas' thoughts. And because his own thought was, that evening, poor in nature, he felt Thomas was, perhaps, judging him unfavourably too.

Thomas felt Jack's eyes upon him, but did not raise his eyes to greet him. Instead he maintained his thoughts on his guest and the nature of the man beneath good clothes and a fine deportment. He contrasted the emptiness of their conversation that night with earlier thoughtful discourse. He thought on Jack's own confusion of feeling. He compared Jack's sharing to the stark contrast of the declarations of frustration, loneliness and distress made to him by Jack's wife, Mary, during her visits to Holm Cultram, where theology and suppers shared within his meagre rooms given over to him by Gawyn Borrowdale, softened a proud woman's resolve into revealing the wounded soul beneath.

But in all their discussion, Mary had not proclaimed her husband to be a poor man, only a poor husband, shaped by his own discomfort, dwelling in a household not of his desire. In this respect, Thomas was glad, because he liked Jack. He had spent some better time observing the man, beneath the show. He could sense a man of value, of learning, and discernment like himself; a man of deep worth, but lost to his heart-felt desire to find his proper place, to find his spirit content in its finding.

Jack had applied his thoughts back to his writing, but with the thought that a scholarly inspection might be offered on his prose, Jack was having difficulty applying his pen. It hovered over the page, too frightened to commit to his words thought. Words he felt were formed in a mind clouded by the worry of his task ahead, and the deception of his selfish aim. He was fearful his mind's intention would be discovered, so he closed his journal to save it from other eyes.

'What do you write?' asked Thomas.

'Nothing. My mind is too tired.'

'Then what would you have written, if your mind was afresh?'

'My thoughts, as they are. So that in days to come I can remember the truth of my time and not see it better, or worse than it was.'

'Do you share your thoughts with others?'

'Not freely. But there are others I confide in, when confession is required.'

'Your priest?'

Jack thought to soften his reply with a lie, but thought again. 'No.'

Thomas smiled, for he already knew, from Mary, the truth and shortcoming of Jack's piety. He smiled because Jack chose to tell the truth in the face of a servant of God, not fearing judgement or scorn.

'You write your thoughts. Are you ashamed of your feelings?'

'At times.'

'Do you write your sadness down?'

'If it is sadness I feel… I write it down.'

'If I were to read your journal, would more pages be formed by sadness, or by joy?'

'I have never counted the pages, or assigned their sentiment with a heading to each entry. I do not write as a study of my own psyche, only as a record of my time on earth, while I have time to be.'

'Would you allow me to read your journal?'

'Not now, but perhaps in the future, when time and age balances my view on the world.'

'Are you ashamed of the now?'

'N…' Jack hesitated, '…No.'

Thomas felt for him, and pondered his journals. But he did not need to pore over his words. His face told his story. 'Do you think your writings weak?'

'No, my rhetoric has been tutored by a scholarly man of great eloquence.'

'Ah, *Edward Hendon.* Your wife, Mary, speaks in great regard of Mr Hendon. You are fortunate to be spoiled. To have such a tutor within your household is a rare thing.'

'He teaches Mary and I without favour, or bias. Indeed Mary is better schooled than I. Her sciences better understood and her writings better formed.'

'I suppose she has had the benefit of more time in Mr Hendon's care. She with little to do, and you absent with responsibility to protect your father's lands. Yes, she speaks most highly of him.'

Jack felt uncomfortable, hearing hidden slur within Thomas' words, even though none was meant.

Thomas still reading Jack's face, perhaps misunderstood his chagrin, and therefore perhaps misread Jack's heart and head.

'I have studied the science of melancholia. It is the Devil's fume; vapour to befog the virtuous man. It is an insidious assault.' Thomas looked to the Heavens and closed his eyes. 'It is God's will that man will encounter trails and torments. It is the way of man on earth since Adam met Eve. And so long as this is understood, and man is humble before it, God will give him the strength to thrive.' Thomas brought his head back to earth and opened his eyes to Jack. 'Beware pride, *John Brownfield.* For the man who thinks he is worth more than his station, who is dissatisfied with his place, will be in poor defence against the trials. For the weight of your pride will be too hard to bear. Then when you are weak, the Devil will strip your assiduous armour from your will and replace it with sloth. Then, his corruption will place envy and wrath where kindness and patience once stood. It will have no reason. Your anger will make no sense. It will come without warning and cause great hurt. He will replace contented endeavour and satisfaction with gluttony and greed. Love will be cast aside and lust will find the melancholic man wanting.' Thomas paused, indication that Jack should perhaps reply. He looked at Jack, he was listening, but no utterance did he make. 'Beware it, John Brownfield. Know what causes your anger. Is it just? Know it, and then remove it from you heart. Anger without reason is one of the fumes of the Devil—spiritual sin. Where it exists without proper cause, other sins wait to see you damned.'

Jack was lost to Thomas' sermon and aggrieved at his assertions, if assertion was made.

He did not suffer melancholia.

'Thou shalt not covet thy neighbour's house:
neither shalt covet thy neighbour's wife,
his manservant, his maid,
his ox, his ass or anything that is his.'
Exodus 20:17

Yesterday a good friend, a one not seen for many years, took his pleasure reading my journals. I was pleased to see him read my words, for he was a man I held in high regard for his wisdom and his wit. He read my life led to that point; a history of trial and adventure, and he said to me, that it was a good tale, and correcting himself for his modest words, he said, 'No... it was a wonderful tale', and in his newfound understanding of my time on earth, he declared to me that he was envious of my life.

His words were a revelation, because in all my years of disquiet and search for a quiet mind and rested heart, it had never occurred to me that another might find my life preferred to their own; their life I thought already moulded more wisely.

In truth, I have never wished to be another man, to breathe his air and to wear his shoes. I admit, in my shame, I have taken his life, stolen his gold, and borrowed his wife, but I never wanted to live another's life in fair exchange for my own.

The thought of it sorrowed me, for in my own malaise I have oft disregarded those things of my belonging which another may find valuable, and so in turn I may have encouraged envy amongst others, who seeing my possessions not valued, would grow a greater want for themselves, for they may value it more in turn.

I pray to God that his wisdom continues to instruct me better through his servants, and that future foul consequence will never be the result of my ungratefulness.

John Brownfield, MDLXXXIV (1584)

Chapter XXV

On Solway Sand, May 1554, day 36

Slack 'o' Jack spent days with William Waite more than he could afford. His tasks, given by Jack, suffered and the Watch over Allonby was lacking a man.

Jack did not fret, he knew Slack 'o' Jack's worth; his value only to a brother, whose duty to kin kept him in mind, and as a newfound uncle of little real consequence. So command issued to Slack 'o' Jack by his captain was work to be done, but work of a kind not needed so much that the defence of Allonby would be weakened by its absence.

'I have simply ridden on the wave o' life. Never swimmin' against the current. It was always the easy path fer me.' Slack 'o' Jack shifted his arse on the damp ground, and chewed a stalk of grass between his teeth. 'I cannot even say, with the time, with the years given back tae me, I would have done things different—worked harder, tried harder.' He looked to the sun and closed his eyes to the glare. 'No, I could never say, *I did my best*, because in truth I never have. And my discomfort of mind now is the price of wastin' a life, and robbing men and women of theirs.'

Slack 'o' Jack pulled another shoot of long grass and discarded the one already in his mouth, well chewed. 'No, I think I would be as lazy again. I have nae been a gud man, William. I dae not blame anyone, or point tae the accountability of others for their failure of my care. It is my waste, fer a man cannot step outside his nature.'

William worked his scythe, cutting the grass from the field behind his hall. The children used the field for games, and he seemed forever in that field mowing the grass, clearing the way for others to enjoy. His few small black-faced sheep did a poor job, and there was always much tall grass left by animals, already well fed on better feed, provided by a kindly and generous man.

He did not break the flow of his cutting. 'You think sin a nature?'

'Nae a natural one, I accept,' Slack 'o' Jack stood up to peel his wet hose from his arse, 'But one bred from circumstance, of family origin, or a born fever of the head.'

'Then you do not think the Devil puts in our hearts such sin to make our Lord weep?'

'I think man places sin upon himself fer his weakness, William. And weakness is the measure fer those who walk in the shadows of heroes.'

William put down his scythe, and walked to Slack 'o' Jack in order to retrieve his ale jug and take a drink. Only a sip was left.

'The man who understands his own nature and the sin he carries because of it, is already halfway to heaven. And the man who acts for good, against his own nature and his mortal sin, will see him lauded in heaven for he works far harder for his place at God's hand than any hero, whose unthinking nature is to be brave and foolhardy.' William gripped his back and stretched out his fatigue.

'Pah!' Slack 'o' Jack smiled. 'I'll have my praise on earth, William.'

William walked back to retrieve his scythe and beckoned Slack 'o' Jack to follow him. When Slack 'o' Jack hesitated, William gathered him in, with an arm around his shoulder.

'Praise, Slack 'o' Jack, is a peril to those who do good work. For immoderate praise heaped on the head is an easy route to pride. But surely, *fine man* is a far better salute than *feckless man*?'

William stood Slack 'o' Jack in front of his scythe, lying in the grass.

'Now my feckless friend, an hour with the scythe is a step closer to redemption for your sin. A penny given in alms for my ale you quaff, another. Think yourself another good and selfless act, and I can say you are on your way to Heaven.'

ꟾ

In William's hall, children gathered around Thomas. He was in discussion about spiritual and corporal sin, the topic of Thomas' lesson for that day. William asked for permission for himself and Slack 'o' Jack to stay, and with it given, they sat with the children. Geordie sat too.

Geordie had been placed at William's convenience, and tasked to make repairs to the hall's roof. A charitable gift, William thought. But Geordie's labour was simply offered as concealed restitution; a punishment meted out by Jack for a wrong, without cost to Geordie's pride. For Jack had discovered William's losses during the hall's gathering, twelve days back, concealed within Geordie's pack.

One of Thomas' students, a boy, had the gift of sagacity and so sat closest to Thomas. Thomas was always keen to foster good gifts in the young. He was not lost to the influence the young have on the young, and he knew a discriminating child could only do good amongst his peers.

The boy, keen to impress upon his friends, his boldness and his age over them, said to Thomas, cheekily, 'Good lesson, *Thomas*, I enjoyed it.'

'I'm glad it met your favour, *Mr Beeby*,' replied Thomas, his voice heavy with sarcasm; poor wit offered instead of rebuke for the boy's impertinent lapse in courtesy to his elder and better. The child was lost to Thomas' satire, and so bolstered with pride, he puffed up his chest and presented himself to his friends as a man to be addressed as so.

William smiled at the boy's confidence in the way he addressed Thomas and reached down a hand to ruffle his hair.

The boy's brother, who was not as old or as bold as Samuel, sneered his envy at his brother's acclamation. 'Our da thinks our Sam is arrogant, and that will see him lashed and beaten by our betters.'

Thomas sighed and smiled at the younger boy, putting his own hand on him to reassure him that he held no favourites amongst the children. 'Your brother is not arrogant, just self assured, rare in someone so young, but it may see him well when he is old enough to make his own life.' *Or see him suffer for it*, thought Thomas.

'Da says he's too proud.'

Sam hurt by his brother's chide, looked to Thomas for more support. 'When does self-assuredness become arrogance, *Father*?'

Thomas replied quickly to reassure Samuel. 'The self-assured man knows the outcome of his actions, but remains silent. The arrogant man declares the result to all before he acts, and boasts to all when he succeeds.'

Sam nodded his understanding, and Thomas smiled, because he could see on Sam's penitent face, that he understood.

'What is charity, Father?' asked a small girl, keen to have Thomas' attention.

'*Caritas* is the love of all humankind, my child. And if all humankind embraced it, there would be no want, no war, and no wasted lives in this world… Caritas is the way taught to us by our Lord, because our Father wants us to live well on this earth as we would in Heaven.'

Thomas turned to Geordie, sitting uncomfortably with the children. 'Charity is often absent in the young, for they are often too busy grasping life to understand it.'

Another small girl walked up to Thomas and tugged at his gown to attract his attention away from Geordie. 'If there was no want, *Father*, would there be no beggars?'

'No, my child, for beggary comes from want, and there would be no want, for all the wealth would be shared by those who have, with those that have not.'

'But how would they make a penny, without beggary?'

'Because they would earn a pound more, because honest work would exist for all, for all on the Earth would see to it. But until the World wakes up to God's word…' Thomas turned his attention back to Geordie, and addressed the children in a raised voice, 'Children, what do we do if a beggar asks for a penny?'

'Give him two,' came back the children's voices.

'And if he asks for two pennies?'

'Give him four.'

'And if you do not have four to give?'

'Give him your cloak.'

'And if you do not possess a cloak?'

'Give him your home.'

'And if you do not have a home to call your own?'

'Then give him your life.'

'And if your life is spent?'

'Then we are at God's feet, and have all the riches in Heaven.'

Thomas looked to Geordie. 'If all the World would be like children, there would be no want. For it is the avarice of men that brings poverty.'

As Thomas' lesson was ending, Slack 'o' Jack and Geordie were listening to the children's chatter, and their own notion of sin. Talk that belied Thomas' belief in the innocence of youth. Both men smiled at each other, their smug faces confirming the wicked ways of the world are with all mankind, young and old, and only those who embraced sin, would rise to the top, even though their souls would see damnation.

'The time to repent is on our death beds, *eh, Slack'o' Jack?'*

Slack 'o' Jack remained silent.

One child talked that he would covet all the gold in the world. Another said she would rather have all the food. Another said, he would be the greatest warrior and would not suffer another man to say otherwise. It was clear the children did not understand lust, but all agreed sloth was the most desirable sin to possess, for all agreed they could forgo their chores and while away their days on the beach, playing games or fishing in the river. They all agreed it could not be called sin to please oneself, and besides—*what harm could it do?*

Thomas heard the chatter, and he sighed at the children's reasoning. He was disappointed his lesson was lost on young minds, and so he gathered them about him with promises of another story, and when they were seated and quieted, he began…

The King of the Forest

(as told by Sir Thomas Smith)

'In northern lands, there was a great forest, called *Inglewood.* It was a vast wood that covered Cumberland from mountain to sea. In the winter it was a sea of green, and in the winter it was a harsh place of bare branch and empty glade.

The forest was so vast, not one king could rule it all. So the forest had many rulers, lords and chieftains.

In Inglewood, there once were seven animals that met regularly. They were the King's Council for the part of the forest where they lived, and in summer they met where the trees parted and the sun shone, where the water sparkled and the grass was taller. Taller, for the trees did not shade the sun or drink the water from the pond that sat in the clearance where they met.

This day they met, was a sad day, and therefore it was a sad meeting, for their king was dying. The Council met to both praise a good king and also to mourn his demise. The old Badger King had been a good provider and ensured the forest had food aplenty to feed the beasts that dwelled in the green; bird and beetle, leaf and shoot, and in the winter there was root and fruit aplenty to see them through. But the Badger King had not sired a successor with his Badger Queen, and so all debated who should rule in his place.

The Badger King looked to his Council, and then looked to his queen, for he was unsure who was best fit to rule in his place. The badger's queen gave him a knowing look and the King, being a wise old badger, and knowing his Queen and her thoughts, suggested a competition to decide who should succeed as King of the Forest after he died.

He proposed that the one from the Council who was best placed to rule was the one to feed his Queen and all the creatures of the forest when winters were harsh and spring's bounty was poor. So he proposed the one to rule was the one to provide him with his last meal, and his Queen the best meal to eat when the sun went down and the day was nearly dead.

On the Council sat a bear, an owl, a jackal, a fox, a dog, a weasel and a snake.

The Bear thought he would win, because of his size and skill, and because he knew where the salmon swam in great numbers. He was always better fed than his neighbour, so he thought he would be the one to bring the best meal of fish to the old Badger King and his Queen.

The Owl thought, as he was a bird of prey, he was easily the best hunter, so he would be the one to bring the best meal of small meats to the Badger King and Queen.

The Jackal had a pack of jackals at his call to find and bring food. With such resource he thought he must surely become king, and he smiled as only a jackal could smile, mean and spiteful.

The Fox thought, I am always chasing off rivals for the prey in my territory. My endeavours in fright and fight ensure I have first call on the food in my part of the forest. I am the best to ensure there is plenty of food available.

The Dog knew where the food ran thick in the woods. I'm on the Council, because I am the best fed, he thought. I am certain to win.

The Weasel thought, he was too small to bring food, and he wished he was as big as the Bear, a hunter like the Owl, as cunning as the Jackal, had a pack like the Dog, or was as war-like as the Fox, or as sly as the Snake. But still, he would do his best.

But the Snake just opened an eye, barely bothered to think of the challenge to come. He closed his eye again, with only a passing thought.

Something will come along. What will be will be.

As the animals readied to journey into the forest, thinking of their catch for the day and dreaming of the golden crown on their head, they passed the Snake, still curled on the ground, basking in the sun, where he had laid all day.

The other animals mocked him. 'Look at that idle snake. He has not moved at all. No kill will he find. No food will he provide.' They all jeered as they travelled on, expecting the Snake to follow. But the Snake barely opened an eye to his dissenters, happier to be lying in the warm sun that filled the clearing where the Council met.

The Bear soon found the part of river where the salmon jumped. And so a feast was ready for him to catch. He was pleased. The crown was his. He was certain.

The Bear worked hard, and landed large salmon upon larger salmon. No salmon that jumped escaped his reach, and soon the pile of fish on the riverbank was vast. It wriggled and writhed. It glistened in the sun.

He thought to sample a salmon, to ensure its flavour was as it was the day before, good and tasty. So he bit into one, and finding the salmon to his liking, began to eat all the salmon he caught. He ate and ate, and ate and enjoyed eating the salmon so much he forgot to return any fish to the clearing.

The Owl was too proud to hunt by day, so he waited until nightfall. His prowess was better demonstrated at night, when all the small creatures fell under his spell. He thought his catch be far better caught when he was at his best, and his best was all that was good enough for the Owl. So proud was he, that he forgot the King and Queen's supper was always taken at dusk, so in fact the owl would be too late with his catch, although his catch would be considerable.

The Jackal reached that part of the forest where food was in abundance. Where the deer, rabbit and the red squirrel played and played, and so was easy prey for a sly old hunter.

Jackals hunt in packs, and the jackal of the Council was the lord of his kind, made a lord by the tally of his kills kept for himself. He was by far the greatest of all jackals, measured by the number of kills he made. But, because he was Lord, his authority was always tasked by other jackals, and so he feared his kills being taken from him, and so lowering his tally.

The Jackal went about his business, and soon he had amassed a huge tally of kills. But this being a day like all others in his kingdom of the jackal, all his vassals about him went about trying to dispose him and take his bounty. So in order to protect his wealth and his lordship, he closely guarded all of his kills fervently, and so never brought any of it to the clearing to share.

The Fox had his dominion in the forest, and *beware* was always shouted to any other fox that strayed into his territory. The bounty of his land was immense, more than enough for a hundred foxes to share, but still, any other fox that dared show his brush within his realm, would incur his wrath and he would go to war. That day he was too busy to hunt, as he busied himself fighting other foxes that strayed into his part of the forest. Yet still he was happy enough that his vixen, an able hunter, was there to provide the meal for the King and Queen. However, so busy was he with the business of war, he did not know his vixen was poorly, and therefore did not hunt at all that day.

The Dog counted his fold by the puppies he sired, and puppies he had by the dozen. His strength was in his pack, or so he told himself, as he covered all the bitches he could find.

The Dog felt with his numbers increased, he would easily have an army to feed the forest. So he went about that day covering his bitches and finding new bitches to sire more puppies. The dog liked his work, but so busy was he enjoying his work, he forgot to hunt food for his sovereigns' supper.

The Weasel, in his weasel's lair, paced the ground. He whiled away the day, too busy wishing he was something he was not. He wished he were something grander, big enough to bring down a deer, or boar or even a bear. And even though he was a skilled and able hunter, easily able to fill his quota by speed and endeavour, he paced the ground and sat by the river muttering to himself, kicking his heels, and pacing some more, berating himself for being so small and scolding those he thought larger than he.

The Snake simply lay curled in the clearing, waiting for the day to end and to see who would bring back the best meal. He had no ambition to be king.

At the end of the day, the King and Queen were hungry for their meal and eagerly anticipated a feast, because they both knew of the prowess of the hunters in the Council.

The animals came back with their stories and excuses. The

Bear talked of a vast pile of giant salmon that wriggled and writhed in the sun. The Owl promised his king and queen, the best of meals from his hunt as soon as the sun went down. The Jackal was missing, as he had stayed with his kill so the other jackals would leave it alone. The Fox, in his anger with his vixen, blamed his poor wife for her failing. The Dog promised more puppies to bolster his hunting pack, even though he only procured more mouths to feed. The Weasel simply fretted to the King and Queen he was not as good as other hunters on the Council, even though the smallest beetle brought would have seen him be hailed as the best hunter on the day.

The King and Queen chastised the Council severely for failing to provide them supper, and in an attempt to divert their sovereigns' displeasure, the Council all mocked the Snake who they had seen had not even tried to provide food for their ruler's table.

'Look he has not moved. No kill has he,' they all scoffed.

At that moment, the Snake sicked up a mouse, bald and half-digested. A mouse he had caught the day before.

The Badger King ruled the Snake had won, even though his quota and the supper he provided was poor, as he was the only one to bring food.

All the forest rejoiced at the coronation of their new king. But in the following winter, many forest creatures perished in the cold for lack of care and preparation, even the Snake King, because there were no voles or mice for him to eat.

No good can come from sin, sloth most of all.'

Chapter XXVI

On Solway Sand, May 1554, day 39

His purse loved him, because he was a niggardly man. However, his purse wept, because his game was cards and his skill at cards was lacking. He played it not for good camaraderie, or for the sport of it, he played it only for a win. For a win would bring him delight to his purse. A purse in mourning, for it grew ever lighter from the money he would lose. So for all his purse's love, it also despaired, because he was not a prudent man.

For most of the men, games of cards and dice often filled the evenings as they waited out their time in Allonby. Days too, as thoughts of reivers attacking the shore dropped from men's minds and boredom sank in as replacement.

Endless sea, endless sand, endless sky… Endless hours, endless days—tedium.

Their views became plain. There were no women of easy virtue to satisfy idle hands and needy lusts. Inns were too far away to sit out poorer weather, and when the villagers were not training for fight and sharing a joke and jabber, they were working…

working… working. So when Jack, their paymaster, was not present, the men under his watch would find themselves soft labour, instead of training for an attack they were beginning to think would never come. The men would find the Blacksmith's as a good place to sit and wait out the day and night, for his fire was always burning with the plentiful supply of charcoal from the forest.

'There is always smithy work to do,' claimed the Blacksmith. 'These *Culdee* bastards forever break their tools… Better they break their backs.'

The Blacksmith had a monopoly on charcoal. He paid the charcoal burners the best price for it. They were happy men. Not so happy were the men boiling the brine at the salterns. They complained bitter. Peat and sea-coal burning poor on their fires.

So in the blacksmith's, Francis, Soldier, Slack 'o' Jack and Geordie would game and gamble. Bendback would abstain, he not preferring the company of men to mock and tease him.

Games of *Maw* were played more often than not, although rules were often in dispute (depending on who lost the greater purse). Arguments would often grow between men, not already fond of each other, and general discord would lead to *Piquet* being played instead; a game for twos and not more.

But Maw was the game (although some called it *Mack*) that played out more days and evening hours.

'You held *the Ace of Hearts*. You kept it from the pack,' growled Francis.

'You lose poorly, little cur,' replied Geordie, not concerned with Francis' pettish rant.

'No, *Mr Cozener*,' snarled Francis, 'you win badly, because you cheat. You dare sit and cozen a profit from your friends at this game.'

'I am no cheat,' replied Geordie, 'and I see no friends.'

'And I am no gull, sir. You have held the Ace of Hearts too often to be dealt it fairly.'

'Let go, man,' pleaded Slack 'o' Jack, 'I've held the Ace as much.'

'No, *Slacky*, let him yap,' added Soldier. 'Little curs like to yap and nip.'

Francis spat on the floor, which raised an angry yell from the Blacksmith.

'This dog bites hard,' barked Francis, 'if you care to tease him further.'

'Should a bear fear a cur?' said Soldier, rising to the bait.

Slack 'o' Jack shook his head at Soldier. 'I would not lay odds on the bear. The dog is faster.' And sensing men's blood boiling, he sought to put out the fire of fight. 'I advise ye tae wrestle, Mr Bear… because I've seen the cur fire a pistol and wield a blade. He'll put a long knife in yer heart and lead in yer eye, afore ye find yer footin'.'

'I'll take the bet.' Geordie sensed his coin increasing. 'Fight with fist, Mr Bear and earn me coin,' He looked to Slack 'o' Jack, 'A shilling, eh?'

Francis and Soldier rose and squared up to each other, Francis raising his eyes a good foot and more to meet Soldier's bellicose stare. Both stepped back. Hands rested on sword hilts. Fingers to curl around leather, thumbs to caress cross-guards.

Jack stepped through the blacksmith's door with Thomas.

'There's been a raid… on Bowness.'

The men's ears pricked to the news.

Jack continued, 'Runners from Bowness, talk of riders from across the sands, spoiling the church. The villagers are in pursuit… *of their church bells!* Thomas frets for Holm Cultram, he needs to see if it fares well.'

'Our reivers,' asked Soldier.

'We don't know,' answered Jack, 'and we need to know… so a man to travel to Holm Cultram with Thomas to see to his safety, then ride on to Bowness… A man with a keen eye and nose to the situation about him.'

With a few hours past since the raid, early reconnaissance was important, especially if Allonby needed to prepare. And whereas a raid striking over the sands between Scottish Annan and English Bowness by horseback was not uncommon, any reiver strike on the Solway coast was enough to raise Jack's alarm and his enquiry, *have the reivers turned away from Allonby?*

Jack looked at the four, seated on the floor, cards and coins scattered.

Soldier was too valuable to let free of the village defence, Francis' irksome face told Jack not to ask, Slack 'o' Jack was too feckless to trust, so only Geordie remained.

'Where's Bob?' asked Jack.

Francis replied, 'Look for the Girl. He's never too far away, sniffing the trail the bitch leaves behind.'

Jack looked to Geordie. 'Ride with Thomas, Geordie. Best not make a show of it. Leave your armour and keep your weapons hidden. Look to your route. See everything. Listen to Thomas… And mind the Warden's Watch., they'll be jittery.

Thomas and Geordie were galloping the road out of Allonby within quarter-of-the-hour, and within the half-hour the two were at the canter, making short the distance to Holm Cultram.

'Your church at Holm Cultram has wealth enough to steal?' asked Geordie.

'No, Mr Reed. The wealth is in the land.'

'Is there much at Bowness to steal?' asked Geordie.

'On a market day it has wealth on its stalls, but overall it is simply another village.'

'Just on the route to better pickings, eh?'

'There is no direct route along the coast south from Bowness. Roads take the rider close to Carlisle and the Warden's muster. Holm Manor lies between Bowness and the port at Skinburness. And Skinburness is guarded by a strong watch.'

'Therefore reivers would surely find strong resistance and the beacons lit if they struck and stayed long past Bowness. Easily cut off from their return over the sands, *eh Priest man*?'

'Yes.'

'So why do we ride so fast? The reivers will be long gone. Back over the sands to Scotland.'

Thomas kicked his nag from the canter to the gallop. 'I go to tend to harm inflicted on my Abbey Church.'

At Holm Cultram, all was well. No signs of raid. Thomas then rode on with Geordie to see to the harm inflicted on St Michael's church at Bowness.

With danger to Holm Cultram rested in Thomas' mind, the ride to Bowness was taken easier, with the morning now well lit.

Along the road, the two men came upon a wagon, pulled by two oxen, a wagoner walking it, a rider alongside it, and a girl and a cat aloft the barrels upon its oak deck. All were familiar.

Bendback, aloft Mars was a sight to widen any man's eyes, and with his twelve-foot over-sized border lance, more pike than spear, carried upright in his hand, he stood as a tower.

Geordie looked to his own meagre shirt, waistcoat, woollen cap, and dagger tucked into his breeches, then at Bendback; steel breast, metal plate around his arms, chain mail draped like a shawl over broad shoulders, axe tied about his great back. But about his steel bonnet, he wore a crown—a ring of flowers. Sea—Pink, Campion, Bindweed, and Kale, Silverweed and Yellow-Horned

Poppy. More flowers adorned his lance. *Gifts from the Girl, perhaps? She had been busy amongst the dunes this morning,* he thought. And as he looked again on Bendback, he said quietly, '*So much for a quiet show.*'

United with the old salt-maker, taking his salt to Carlisle, the fat grey cat and the Girl as his companions (she riding aloft the wagon, not running, so as to be close to giant Bendback) and Bendback riding escort as good will for the Girl's Salty-man, Thomas and Geordie joined the group. Thomas hoped such a motley band would not raise alarm amongst the Warden's Watch riding in chase or travelling to bolster defence, especially with Bendback's steel-clad monstrous form shouting loud on the exposed lanes of the Solway Plain.

With the ox cart, progress was slow. But the news of Bowness being attacked was well travelled. Bendback had already heard it, and with all Bowness village on the chase, there seemed little reason to hurry their travel, even when they were stopped by English soldiers on the road. Soldiers who only raised a smile and a cry, '*Peculiar!*'

The brilliant red sky of the evening before, foretold the brilliance of the day ahead. A haze covered a clear-view over the waters, and the sun lit their way. And with the calm, Geordie once more was lost in his dream of gold and riches. But as new miles were added to miles already travelled, he began to see the world around him—a realm of country penury, with field and forest, sand and sea, hovels of daub and thatch. No halls, or dwellings of wealth. No palaces or castles, or even tower houses. Instead, there were barns and cow-byres—kingdoms of dung and drudgery. He had watched men sweat at the salterns, and poor-dressed labourers collecting beach cobble, stripping hulks and building sea walls. He saw labour, but no reward amongst the dunes, and now as he rode the green plain to Bowness, he saw naught but sheep, beasts and herding men.

He looked to the old salt-maker for a reason for this place.

'I ask you, is this land worth the fight?'

The salt-maker, walking close by, leading ox that already knew the way, looked up and said, 'Nay, there's better land. Land that offers more shelter from the winter sea. Land that does not flood.'

'So is it worth it, to stay in the face of threat from Scot and Borderer. Worth it to see your family suffer?'

'There's sufferin' at the start of life, at the birth of it.' The Salty-man rubbed his ox's nose. 'More sufferin' at the end of it. No time on God's Earth is free from it. Life is to live, and live here we choose.'

'Why do you stay, *salt-maker?* If I was you, I would go to the city and live in jug of ale, till either the ale or the city killed me off.'

'Nay, my place is here.'

'Why… have you family that needs you?'

'I stay not for the livin', but for the dead.'

'For the dead?'

'My ma and da are buried here. Their da's and ma's too, four generations of them. My first wife and three wee'uns lie under a tree. My brother and his wife lie close by. I stay to keep their bones safe, so that they will rise safely come resurrection.'

Geordie pondered the salt-maker's loss. It recalled to his memory, his own dire losses. 'I'm ignorant of the resting place of many I've called kin, and those worthy of heart's thought.'

The salt-maker looked up at Geordie with incredulous eyes. 'How can you live without an easy mind, not knowin' where ye'll be restin'? The pains of this life are easier to bear on the shoulders with the thought of life everlastin'.'

'Do you think it important to know where your bones rest after death?'

'Aye. It is clear to see your faith is errant,' said the salt-maker,

'I've spent my life on another man's land, never owning the soil and sand I till. I've spent thirty years forced by plague, or cruel lord, from a dozen places I would call home. To know where I rest is the only comfort I can take in this world.'

Geordie thought on the salt-maker's words. He thought of the man's buried treasure, not gold or rubies, but bones. Geordie always thought he would eventually buy his way into heaven, with a church built in his name, built on the gold of his profitable endeavours. *But what if he was to die today?*

Geordie relaxed his shoulders and took another long look around, and saw what he saw—*nothing of value.* And as he scanned his surroundings, he caught the fat grey cat's irascible stare, as it sat aloft the barrels of salt on the salt-maker's wagon. He raised a smile to the little warrior, and smiled again to himself at the thought of a cat so fat—then he was lost. No thought had he. No thought of who he was, or what his purpose was about.

He sat aloft his horse and let go the reins. He let her take him on. And he looked around him—to the sea, the trees, the green, the sky, the life amongst the dunes, rich with bird and butterfly. He raised his face to the sun, and a wave of euphoria washed over him, greater than the thought of a mountain of gold and jewels. He raised his hands before him, as if he could embrace the day. He closed his eyes and felt his heart fill. He had only a sense of a greater reality than the one his self-serving mind had invented, and for the first time he saw the grace of his surroundings.

He had dreamed of a mountain of gold tomorrow, *but what if he were to die today? Where were his riches? Where was his church built to see him to heaven? Who would watch over his body?*

Geordie looked at the salt-maker, walking the lane, his hand still on his ox as if it were family, and he said, 'Promise me, *old man*, if I fall in defence of your village, lay me nearby. Take my armour, my horse and all that I have as my bequest to you, and watch over my bones until you die.'

'You strike a poor bargain, *warrior*, for I have only a few years of breathin' left.'

Geordie removed his purse and emptied the contents into the salt-maker's old hand. 'It is I who have secured a better deal, and a better place to rest, better than my eyes have seen. Now take this coin, all I have today. Keep yourself well so you may live a little longer. And, *old man*, for my guarantee, make sure you take yourself off to the trees when trouble comes, so your bones are not interred afore mine.'

The salt-maker counted the coin in his hand. 'This is good coin.'

'Aye, today I am richer for having my soul saved. For finding my church to see me to heaven… My church on Solway Sand.' Geordie smile broadened. 'Besides, *old man*, the cards offer poor salvation… and my purse will be happier to see its children go to worthy ends.' He winked. 'Besides, earthly riches may come tomorrow.'

A while to go before Bowness was reached, the group came upon more wagons and carts on the road. Thomas questioned the wagoners as men in the know. The first wagon was with goods for the port at Skinburness. The wagoners talked of the raid at Bowness and the price of bread and salted herrings at its market. The second wagon was empty, its wagoner known to the old salt-maker. Known because he was a cousin and collected goods from the coast to market in Carlisle. He talked of the Scots invading. The third wagon, had three men who only talked of the fine weather and their reclaimed timber for the sea wall at Skinburness, bought from Carlisle.

The Girl, now on foot, patted the lead horse on this third wagon, one of two yoked in tandem, its *pair* being much larger.

She was concerned to see the bigger horse well sweated, and so moved her loving hands from the smaller horse to the big horse's muzzle. She worried for its wellbeing and so called Bendback over.

'Is she sick?' the Girl asked.

'No, just well-worked, lass.' Bendback surveyed the bulk on the wagon, covered by sailcloth. The load was large, and the wagon wheels sunk as far into the ground as the salt-maker's wagon with all its salt. 'It's a heavy load, Melissa.'

The salt-maker pulled on his ox, and moved on his cart, and the wagoners urged their own team on as well, but not before they cast their eyes over Thomas and Bendback.

One shouted, 'I see your salt has both the Church and the Devil to protect it?'

The salt-maker looked towards the Girl, sitting back with the cat on his salt, and replied, 'With the fairies and the cat of Hades guardin' ma white-gold, I need no other protection... *believe me.*'

At Bowness, the village was empty. Thomas arrived at the red-stone church of St Michaels. Built four hundred years prior from stone from the *Picts Wall*, it stood proud, with two score of daub and thatch buildings between it and the sweeping sands of the Solway.

Thomas was saddened to see the church spoiled. Its call plucked out from its tower. Inside, through a twisted yett and a broken door, the stone floor showed drag marks, caused by the great bells being wrenched from their holy place. Nothing was left. The alter had been taken, the lectern, all coffers and cabinetry, candelabrum and candle boxes. Damage was all around.

'The Devil's work.'

Thomas stood with Geordie, and he turned to see a man in a sodden nightshirt, hose and boots. Not dressed for the day, but dressed as a man roused from his bed in haste.

'They took it all, Thomas… every stick of it.'

Thomas nodded his head in sympathy with the loss, and turned to Geordie.

'Geordie Reed, this is the rector's verger, John Barton.'

Geordie nodded in recognition of the dishevelled man. 'Does it rain?'

The verger looked down at his dripping clothes. 'The Solway waters come in. The curs left the bells on the sands. The Rector directs the villagers to keep ropes on them to save them from the tide. They hold the bells fast, until they can restore them to our church.'

Thomas thought on the bells. 'It's foolish men, who think they could drag such great bells with success over soft and wetted sands.'

'How big are they?' asked Geordie.

The verger replied, 'Each one possibly has the weight of two or three men. They are a great prize. They do the church much honour, and the village's honour stands greater still, for their presence.'

Thomas shook his head, and muttered under his breath, 'Pride goes before destruction, and an haughty spirit before a fall.' He walked into the bell tower to see the damage caused by the bells brought down with poor care. There was bruised stone, much splintered wood and cut rope. He looked up to the roof, to the belfry, where the bells and their frames once were held, now void.

'Sometimes the fall is greater than the pride that hoists it high,' he said to himself.

Thomas came out of the bell tower to question the verger more.

'Have they caught the reivers?'

'No,' replied the verger.

'What of the contents of your church?'

'We presume they brought a wagon to carry it away.'

Thomas, led Geordie and the rector to walk the drag marks on the ground from the bell tower along the stone floor to the open door, over the grass and onto the road leading to the sands.

'Deep are the welts,' Thomas said, 'the bells dig deep.'

'They are great bells. The largest for miles around,' replied the verger, his hands open in praise.

Thomas stood closer to Geordie to share a confidence from the verger.

'The bells here are much finer than what was originally procured.'

'Stolen bells?' asked Geordie.

'Yes, Geordie, perhaps they originally came from a now reformed protestant church—a Scottish church. And perhaps Scottish gentlemen of the protestant faith try to reclaim them from a country newly restored to a Catholic faith.' Thomas led Geordie further away from the verger. 'But they did not spoil the church of its holy utensil and its furnishing.' Thomas directed Geordie to look at the drag marks on the grass. 'The bells were dragged clear, out of the church and over the grass to the sands. No attempt was made to place them on a wagon, which surely would be a better carriage for such a weighty prize.'

'Perhaps they planned to lose them in the Solway. To rob us of our pride,' replied the verger, eavesdropping.

'Where's the profit in that?' asked Geordie.

'In matters of pride, profit is a poor cousin,' replied Thomas. 'Why bother stripping a church and carrying it away, and then drag the greater prize, its bells? In terms of profit, they are worth ten times over the fittings and fixings of this…' Thomas cast a withering eye towards the verger, '…*modest* church.' Thomas looked to the direction of the bells' travel. 'No, the theft of the bells was religious fervour and not one of profit.'

'But they stole all,' pleaded the verger.

Thomas looked back at the church. 'If it was their intention to ruin the church, why not burn it to the ground? If their raid was profit, there are beasts aplenty in the fields to drive over the sands; a far greater profit than the furnishings of a church.' Thomas turned to address the two men. 'Besides, my rule of guilt is not satisfied.'

'Sorry?' asked the verger.

'Six rules I apply to determine guilt. *Instrument, intention* and *instance. Avoidance, fiction,* and *aberration.* Six rules that are not satisfied by the reivers' raid.

Firstly, *instrument.* A wagon was needed to carry away the spoil. I doubt reivers, riding hard for a fast foray would risk a wagon, but if they did, surely the bells would be the prize they intended to carry away.

Secondly, *intention.* If it was their intention to raid for profit, surely the bells are far too difficult to simply carry away. Beasts on the hoof are far better. If they intended to spoil the church, why not burn it to the ground?

Thirdly, *instance.* I grant you they had opportunity to steal all... Yet how comes their wagon, fully loaded, escaped over soft sands. Yet they leave the bells stuck in the same sand?

And the rest; *avoidance, fiction* and *aberration.* Well you would need to question the reivers to ascertain their guilt, as it should be, for no man should be judged guilty in his absence.'

Thomas put his arm around the verger. 'I suggest the robbers of your bells are safe in Annan now, sharing a consoling ale. But you should muster what men you can to reclaim the rest of what is lost to you. I suggest you travel on the Skinburness road, or more likely the *Wigton* road from Holm Cultram, and stop a two-horse wagon. Perhaps they have your church.

Geordie asked, 'Why do you accuse the wagoners?'

'Because they satisfy my six rules.'

The verger was lost to the reasoning, and he poked a sorry finger into a wet ear to remove any blockage that may have perverted Thomas' words.

Thomas addressed the verger. 'Firstly, *instrument.* They have a wagon. Secondly, *intention.* Simple opportunity. Theft for profit. Thirdly, *instance.* An empty village and an unguarded church.' Thomas cast his eye to Geordie. 'Temptation, *eh, Mr Reed.*'

Geordie, shamed, nodded his head in contrite acceptance of his thieving ways.

'Fourthly, *avoidance.* The wagoners did not talk of raid, only of weather, yet they ride through a village raided. Weather is only talk for people with nothing interesting to say.'

'Is that proof of a lie?' asked Geordie.

'No,' replied Thomas, 'only proof of avoidance. It is easy to hide a lie from your lips if you avoid a lie being said.'

'Fiction?' asked Geordie.

'Holm Manor supplies all the timber for the coastal sea walls from Skinburness to Workington. It has been that way since the Abbey once held and managed all the industry on the coast. It would not rob good local folks of trade. No, all the timber comes from hulks broken on Solway sands… and not from Carlisle, as it would irk coast-peoples to put coin into city merchants' pockets or the Warden's pursc.'

'Aberration?'

'The wagoners claimed to carry timber for a sea wall. Why would one cover such seasoned timber against the elements, especially on a fine day like today? The wagon had two horses, yet when we came upon it, the smaller horse had only been put to the yoke recently, because only the large horse was sweated. I suggest the wagon started out empty, pulled by only the large horse, the smaller horse pulled behind the wagon, because it was not needed.

Not needed until, of course, the wagon was loaded and the large horse unable to pull solo. The only village or farm close to where we passed the wagon is Bowness, which brings us back to the fiction. Surely a stop over in Bowness, to pick up honest goods, would have come with discussion of a reiver raid?' Thomas rested, and he waited on his audience to applaud or act.

Geordie smiled at Thomas' acuity, and the verger ran to raise men for a chase.

Thomas watched the verger running and shouting in the distance, drawing men and women to his call. '*Seven rules met,*' uttered Thomas, slightly smiling, half-holding down conceit, half smiling his self-regard.

'Seven?' Geordie was confused.

'The wagoners felt foul… *My seventh rule.* A rule of my heart, not of my head… my perspicacity if you please. A rule of my own, to dictate if I should apply the other six rules to my thinking.'

Chapter XXVII

On Solway Sand, May 1554, day 41

The riders' heads bobbed. They seemed to jounce the same dance. Comical it was. Their nags at the trot, short in leg, made it so. *Bob—bob—bob.* She smiled at the sight—frightened she should have been, but she held no fear of men on the road. She counted two, then two more. *Bob—bob—bob.* Then the four riders broke their rhythm. They had seen her, and at the canter thought to make sport of a pretty girl watching from her rise.

The Girl watched the riders, not thinking their reason. But then in a moment she knew she should fear, and her amusement gave way to urgent retreat.

She ran from her rise to the tree line, away from the sight of the riders, but the sound of riders on her rise behind her forced her to turn. She held a hand to her mouth to catch her scream, they were chasing. Pursuing. She ran hard and fast. Ran her race to the trees, better than any boy at contest. Ran to the cover of the bracken—to gorse and green ways, difficult on foot, harder for horse. She ran, and ran, and all the time she could hear the jeers of the riders behind—lust and laughing—the sound of savage Scots. The sound of hooves, close. Closer. Closer still. But she reached the sharp gorse and ran through narrow ways, piercing dress and tearing flesh. But the horses did not stop, and she did not dare to turn and count them.

The way was not as hard as she thought, and the gorse was a poor defence. The riders pressed their nags on through the hurt, with shout and kick, to see their mounts progress through the thorns.

She turned to see the way, to look for denser cover. But she had entered the trees at the wrong place, and instead of tight cover, the paths opened up and she did not know where to go. Only two riders had cleared the gorse, no more. And they were close. Determination was with them, and their bloody screams shouted their intent. She ran down a green lane. Trees formed its walls, their canopies the ceiling. She hopped through the brambles, and pushed passed the tall green that grew in the clearings and light. But the horses came on.

She knew her race was lost. The sounds of the men were there with her. She could hear their beasts and the men's own breath. The sound of metal on metal, flesh and leather on flesh.

Then from the clearing beyond came a shape. Human dressed, monstrous in its form, red face, snorting spit and fire. And she froze and screamed.

The riders pushed passed the Girl to ride down the monster, but it raised its steel, and stood firm against the two.

It was her knight.

The knight screamed murder, but the horses came on. He brought his axe hard down on the first horse's head and it fell, throwing its rider. The second horseman corralled the knight and raised his sword.

The Girl screamed to see the steel brought down on her paladin warrior.

But the rider's blade sparked on the steel shaft of the knight's tall axe, and the cut was blocked.

The knight ran at the second horse, throwing his weight at it, and the horse unsettled and galloped on, the rider fighting to control him. But further on in the thicket he lost his seat and tumbled to the earth. The first rider, had by now, found his feet, and approached the knight carrying his ballock dagger before him, but his resolve was poor and he hesitated. The knight did not delay. He was on him. His axe swung in plane caught the man hard in the shoulder, almost splitting his arm. He dropped his dagger and clutched tight the wound, as if to hold his arm firm. The knight then span a full turn in reverse, to bring the spike: the pick-head of his axe, hard into the man's neck—a fatal wound.

The knight ran into thicket to find the fallen second rider barely recovered, still on the ground. Seeing the malformed knight upon him, he presented his sword in defence, but his blade was poorly applied. Not so the knight, who swung his axe's pick into the man's thigh, and ripped a broad hole in sinew and flesh. The man cried loud, and retreated along the ground, crawling and dragging himself over the earth.

The knight looked behind. He checked the way was clear. The Girl was not in sight. He walked over to the stricken man and put his big hand to his throat, pinning him to the earth. The man recovered his wits, ignored his wound, and lashed out at the knight with desperate fist. The knight took the strike, hard hit, and smiled. The man then with both fists beat wildly against the knight's body and face. Lashed out with all the fury he could find, and yet despite hard blows, the knight still smiled. And as each fist found its mark on the knight's skin, as each strike stung his face, the knight closed his hand, and squeezed a throat a little harder, until the poor man's fists abated and life was wrung out of him.

When the man was dead and the knight again joined the world to locate the Girl, he said aloud for the man's soul to hear, as it departed the green for the fires of Hell, 'Little man, I've spent my life in pain. Hurting with bent back and crooked shape. Did you think you could hurt me any more?'

As Bendback re-entered the clearing, axe in hand, muscles sore, he saw the Girl pressed hard against a tree. Her clothes cut from her body and well bloodied by the gorse. She gripped tight the tree, as if the elm would protect her, clothe her. And as much as Bendback was a shaped deformed, the Girl was a shape in perfection, and Bendback dared not look upon it... For it was too beautiful for him to see.

But she saw only a knight, brave and valiant. Rescuer. Vanquisher. And in truth, as Bendback was begat of a knight's line; his ancestor, Musgrave, listed more than once in the tilting yards of Lancaster, perhaps you could forgive her for thinking so.

But work was to do and Bendback stood firm. He turned to inspect his butchery of the first man. The rider was dead, but his horse still breathed. Its wound terrible, and Bendback shook his head at his foul work. He crouched to place a hand on horse. To feel how much life remained in the beast.

'Is she dead?' called out the Girl.

'Soon,' replied Bendback softly, reaching to pick up the rider's fallen dagger close by. He held the blade, hidden from the Girl, gripping it hard.

The Girl looked on to the horse, sadness veiling her eyes, and she cried, 'Will you end her sufferin'? Her pain?'

'She sleeps, lass, there is no pain… only sleep.' Bendback held still his hand on the horse's neck, his eyes closed in contemplation of the horse's life ebbing away.

But the Girl cried, 'She lives—she suffers—end it please!'

'No lass. She sleeps. She dreams of running with her sisters in the hills. Her mate and her foals… She sleeps now… Let her have her last dream.'

Moments passed, and all around them was quiet as if the World held its breath in anticipation of its loss. Bendback removed his hand. 'There… she's gone.'

The Girl wept, and all her fear and anxiety poured out as hate directed at Bendback. No longer a knight did she see. 'You killed her… *Monster!*'

Bendback looked at the Girl, and then at the fallen rider, bloodied on the ground. He shook his head. 'She was a warrior's nag—a weapon of war. She died so I could live… and save yer sorry flesh from been ridden by her rider there, dead on the ground.' Bendback plunged the dagger into the earth, and picked up his axe. He stood up to face the Girl, still sobbing. 'Perhaps consequence will teach you to think twice afore you wander the hills, and flirt with danger.'

But the Girl did not answer. She just turned and ran.

The Girl ran the lane towards the blacksmith's. Her heart was bursting, but still she ran. Along the road she ran, sea to her right, fields to her left. And as she ran, she felt she was not alone, and looked behind to see if Bendback followed.

But Bendback was not there. They were a minute or two behind her. She could sense their breath on her back—the two that had broken off from the chase before.

Her mind fevered with the thought of the two horsemen riding her down, steel to the fore, murder in their mind. She did not think of the worse that could befall a pretty young girl.

She looked behind, but the horsemen were hidden by the bend in the road.

Perhaps they have not seen me? They are on foot, not giving chase. God is good. They have not seen me.

The Girl burst through the door of the blacksmith's, breathless, covered in snot.

'Fightin' men… Henry killed two… more follow me… *I think*.'

Soldier took the Girl by the shoulders. 'Catch your breath, lass.'

'Fightin' men… comin'… down the road… Bendback killed a horse.'

Soldier put an eye to the gap in the shutter that closed the window to the lane. 'A horse! Shame he didn't kill a man or two more… Are they close, lass?'

'They're only a step or two away, on foot, leadin' their horses,' replied the Girl, now squatting on her haunches, still breathing hard.

'How many?'

'Two.' The Girl stood up and moved to the window to share Soldier's view, but Soldier held the Girl back. 'I recognised one. He's a man from the reiver band.'

Soldier put his eye back to the hole in the window's shutter and bid the Blacksmith to do the same.

'Shall I run on to warn Captain Brownfield?' asked the Boy, standing in the shadows.

Soldier said nothing.

Two men, leading horses, walked into view of the blacksmith's and Soldier studied them.

Soldier beckoned the Blacksmith to take a look. 'Are they from the reiver band?'

The Blacksmith offered, 'The large man is Big Tom 'Langrake' Little.'

'Is he one from the raiding band?'

The Blacksmith sighed. 'Aye, a worse one ye'll no find. He hates everyone; Maxwell's, Scotts, Armstrongs. His reputation is well made both sides of the border and all over the Marches from sea to mountain. They say he killed his father for no reason than he slighted him. Quick to temper. A violent man. The other is

'Sparra' Little, a cowardly man made braver with his big brother by his side.'

'A scouting party,' announced Soldier.

'D'ya think so?' asked the Boy, now straining to see through any crack in a portal.

'Two, or four reivers only, south of their territory,' announced Soldier, 'yes, they're scouting.'

The Blacksmith nodded his head. 'Makes sense, Sparra's a man who knows well the shifting sands of the Solway crossing.'

Soldier thought aloud. 'But why would they be scouting?' They have not done so in the past. A boat trip over the Solway is their way. Raid and run on the tide.'

Soldier, pensive, turned from the window and primed his pistols.

The Blacksmith picked up a poker. 'Out of all the reivers, they say they are the worst and the best. Reputations for fightin' 'n' killin'. Some say each man has twenty kills to their name… But I think Sparra's tally is him dispatchin' his brother's wounded count.'

As the reivers approached it seemed they were passing by. No intention to enter the blacksmith's. And the Blacksmith seemed to let out a sigh, long held to himself.

'If we keep still and quiet. They'll pass by.' The Blacksmith took his eye from his watch and pushed himself hard into the wall next to the window as if to hide. 'Please God, let them pass by.'

Soldier nodded in recognition of the Blacksmith's fear and beckoned the Boy and the Girl to follow the older man and stay out of sight, passing on a primed and cocked pistol to the Boy and man in turn. The Blacksmith's hand shook, his face in fear. The Boy's face however was pure delight, grateful to have Soldier's trust with a primed pistol.

'Keep your fingers off the triggers. Use only in defence. Point them not in my direction. I'll not be happy if I have to pull my own lead out of my own flesh, because a friend fires foolishly.'

Soldier broke cover to leave the blacksmith's and walk slowly to the road to meet the two men leading their horses.

He stood in the middle of the track, his hand held against the two men. Eventually the two men stopped, eyes searching the area for others about, and saw no one.

'What's your business?' asked Soldier.

'And whit's yer name, tae be askin' us oor business?' replied the smaller man with scorn in his voice and a wry smile to his lips, 'Are ye the English March Warden perhaps?' He turned to his brother, but Big Tom was not for joining the joke, he simply stared at Soldier, carefully weighing him up in his mind.

'What's your business?' repeated Soldier.

'Knowledge fer my friends and nae a stranger on the road. A stranger oot of place in this peaceful spot. You look like an Armstrong tae me, or a Hodgson… Nah, ye have the stench of an Armstrong about ye.'

Soldier, stoic, with eye-contact affixed to the bigger man, repeated his question again. 'What's your business on this road?'

But the smaller man simply continued with his own discourse, smiling, and ignoring the threat Soldier posed. 'Has the Warden posted men tae guard his charge? Nah, we've seen nae armed men on oor way from Bowness, the small man looked down, 'or has the village hired the Armstrongs tae protect it? We've lost two of our friends. And I'm wonderin' if ye've seen them?'

Soldier, eyes still on Big Tom, replied to Sparra, 'I am no Armstrong, *little man*, and relieved to call myself stranger in these parts. A backward land that breeds runts and giants, as brother shags sister, and son shags mother.'

Big Tom took the offence. Sparra swallowed his spit and hid his growing anxiety behind his smile.

Soldier continued to insult. 'By your poor appearance, you

must be Maxwells, with crimes are aplenty and foul intent. I must inform you, *wretches*, there is a new law in Allonby. No beast is allowed to shit in the street… Which means no Scots are allowed on good English soil. So take off your armour and your weapons, and turn away back to your sty.'

Big Tom let go the reins, his hand dropping to his sword.

The smaller man, still smiling, kicked his heels in the dust. 'Ye insult us. We're nae Maxwells, we're Littles, and nae kin of yers tae accept insult. It is not wise tae have grievance with us, stranger. Yes, I think ye be a stranger. A fightin' man, and by yer dialect, stranger tae these parts. A stranger we should be killin', because a killin' ye will be easy without fear of reprisal from kin hereabouts. Now stranger, dae I gi' ye reason tae draw yer tool?'

'Give me a while to pray for your godless souls.' Soldier closed his eyes, as if in prayer. He thought on the assault and outcomes. Then he opened his eyes and studied the big man. He read his angry eyes. A moment's thought. A strategy considered. He part drew his sword. Hesitated. Then sank the blade back into its scabbard. 'You not be worth my sword, I'll get a butcher's knife, a fitting tool for carving. My sword is only for man-flesh.' And he turned away.

Hand on sword, hand on knife, Soldier closed his eyes. He kept his ears pressed to the sounds of movement—noises of a big man moving in steel and stiffened leather.

One came on fast, vicious. Sword drawn—hoisted high to strike down hard on Soldier's back.

Soldier's action was fluid—a play of many parts—seamless in its execution. From a feint of retreat; to a sword drawn; to a blade brought round in smooth arc—perfect momentum; to a deep cut made in flesh—a whisper below the man's stiffened leather jack.

The big man stopped short. Still. Shocked. Eyes wide. Sword dropped to his side.

Soldier now faced Sparra. He did not fear the counter from the wounded man. He knew his cut was deep enough—harsh enough to disable his will—temper his strength. The big man's gaze, distant, spoke of a man in realisation of his own death. There was no sign in his eyes, in a dying mind, of reprisal against Soldier. Soldier did not need a second cut, his eyes falling briefly on the big man's hose; showing dark and wet—the wound hidden beneath the lie of his jack. His blood loss grave, the man fell to his knees.

Sparra hesitated. He thought to run, but then came on. He thought he had no choice.

Soldier dropped his guard—an easy strike for Sparra.

The little man approached slowly, sword held ready to thrust at Soldier. And a sword's length away, he stopped.

Soldier stood still. The watchers from the blacksmith's could not see Soldier close his eyes. But Sparra, seeing his moment pulled back his sword to thrust.

Soldier opened his eyes quickly and raised his sword to parry the blade away, moving in quickly to walk past Sparra and grab him, with his arm enfolding his chest from behind. He pulled Sparra in and pulling back his own sword arm, thrust hard into Sparra's back, so his blade pushed through his belly. Soldier worked the blade in his man to make a greater cut and to rip the blade up into his chest.

Those in the blacksmith's could see the horror on Sparra's face, as he watched the steel saw up into his chest. All but the Girl, who hid her eyes in shame.

Soldier pulled clear his blade only when Sparra's breath left his body.

Two men lay dead, and the Blacksmith and the Boy came out of the door and gathered round in awe of Soldier's work. Two men stilled by the will of another, backed up with a killing craft none of them had seen before. Soldier raised his eyes to the sky, to mask a pain felt in his body from his exertions.

The Boy eyed up the reivers' weapons, wondering if he dared to take a sword, a knife, a piece of steel, and excited by it all, took to his heels to alert the other men in the village of the 'battle of Allonby'. The Blacksmith spat on the bodies, and the Girl slipped away to run the beach. She hoped to find her peace at breath's end... But her breath took her to the limit of her world, and still she could not lose the horror.

Geordie and Jack arrived at the scene and Geordie kicked at the foot of one of the reivers to be sure he was dead. 'What do we do with them? Perhaps there's a price on their heads… profit to be had.'

'Perhaps, but better they be buried and this forgotten,' said Jack, 'lest they attract kin with scores to settle.'

'But their horses, their chattels—a good price they'll fetch at Carlisle, and a likely bounty for each of the dead scum cannot be ignored.'

'No,' said Jack, 'bury them in a quiet grave, no marker… Dig it big enough for their horses, and forget what happened here today.'

Geordie thought to argue, but was not for changing a mind made in good sense.

Soldier took Jack to his side. 'Four men make a poor raiding party.'

'But a good scouting party,' replied Jack.

Before the sun had fallen, and the day was dead, the four reivers had been buried with all their belongings. No trace of them falling at the village was left.

Chapter XXVIII

On Solway Sand, May 1554, day 42

The Boy was a happy boy. Not only for his witness of Soldier's killing craft a day past, but pleased to have eaten well and to have passed firm stools. He had been poorly of late, and was glad to be feeling the pains in his stomach had abated, his appetite renewed, his pleasure of the food taken returned. His duties to the men seemed less onerous now he was feeling better, for there could be no respite from labour for reasons of discomfort. Indisposition because of malady was only for men with servants and subordinates to hand.

So he tended the men's horses (all but Bendback's that is, for he would allow no alien hands to rest upon his horse, such was their bond). He cleaned all what the men gave him. Mended all that the men told him to mend. He made sure victuals were at hand, and that the men's jugs were filled. He shaved their faces (those with a favour for clean chins), trimmed their beards (those with vanity enough to see well shaped hair upon their faces) and carried their burdens. All this he did, so he could be close to the men preparing for the fight to come. He worked hard, and courted the men's attention so that one-day they might call him a soldier.

But still, regardless of his growing familiarity with the men, none attracted his interest more than Soldier. For his battle experience was the greatest, and his countenance was the more soldiery, with seasoned armour and steel better tested.

This day, six weeks since the men arrived in Allonby, the Boy was working the Blacksmith's sharpening wheel-stone, turning the crank with all his strength could offer, watching carefully as Soldier honed his blade upon it.

With the appearance of scouts, Jack fretted. Because where scouts travel, a force was not far behind. But with the appearance of riders, Jack could only think the reivers no longer approached by sea, but by land. So Jack placed a good watch within the Blacksmith's—Soldier and Francis—a good sentinel over the northern approach to Allonby.

The Blacksmith was not happy, but since his forge had been occupied since the men arrived, he seemed resigned to having his work disrupted. So he continued to serve the industry that filled the lane with carts, and filled the hands of the people with tools of iron.

'Have you killed many men?' asked the Boy, cranking the wheel.

'Many?' answered Soldier hesitantly, as if he did not understand the question, clearly put by the Boy.

'Yes, killed. A hundred? Two?'

'Do you think I keep the tally of lives I have taken?'

'Yes... is it not what makes ye a better soldier? The number of enemies killed?'

Soldier took his blade from the wheel and ran his thumb down the edge, to ensure the edge angle was not too shallow. He looked at his thumb and smudged the blood away from the cut. 'When you kill a man, you kill more than a man. You kill his kin's joy, their livelihood. You take the coin from his wife's coffer and the food from his babes' mouths. You see others he tends, wither for his loss... So yes, I count the men I kill, women too, children as well, for when war visits a city, a town, or village it takes its toll in death of innocents as well as combatants.

So I have killed seventy-three men, fifteen women and six boys of an age that boys are able pick up the sword... but I think far, far more have died for the toll I've taken.' Soldier lifted his sword to look upon the blade, to see the straightness of the edge he placed upon it. 'The question is, *boy*, should I feel proud, or should I feel shame?'

The Boy was caught upset by the thought of women and children killed by Soldier. 'I'm sure you had good reason to kill the women and boys for war's purpose.'

'No… I place no noble reason upon the innocents I have killed. I am a soldier and my tally is my endorsement, the toll my damnation.'

The Boy was silent. His face pale.

Soldier looked upon the Boy, tainted by the truth of war. He returned his sword to the wheel and beckoned the Boy to turn the crank. 'Boy, there are men who lust for gold, or women's flesh, and there are men who lust for blood, not in anger or requital, but only for blood's sake and the quickening it brings to the heart and the dark satisfaction it breeds in the soul.

But… yes, I say, become a soldier. It is a good life. But it may be a short one too. So pray you keep whole, and not lose a limb, for the pension is poor and the beggar's badge a poor substitute for booty's share.'

The Boy was happier now he had Soldier's endorsement. For his lust for battle was a thought that filled his head from dawn to dusk. Glory was his desire, not gold or good family, but the blood of any enemy upon his face and his sword well tested and applauded in war. Yes, the Boy was a happy boy.

Chapter XXIX

The appointment

St Mary's in Carlisle rang the hour bell. A telling of the time. A reminder of the hour. A call to keep appointments.

The apartments were comfortable, and offered *him* a place to meet in better surroundings. Well, as good as *he* could find in a poor northern city. Richard Musgrave's own quarters had been poor to *his* eye; they were plain and functional, and so *he* politely refused the Justice of the Peace's offer of the hospitality of his rooms to have *his* private meeting. His ladies, however, had a better eye to comfort, the furniture in their apartments was well upholstered; covered in good cloth and skins. More candelabrums held more candles, and the wainscoting was better by design. The fire offered a bigger fire, and the paintings that hung the walls did not, on the whole, offer too much fright to *his* eyes.

So the ladies were displaced, and *he* was installed.

In his thanks, he had the good grace to offer improvements to the rooms he occupied. He repositioned chairs and cushions to better please the eye. He threw down skins and tapestries from stools and walls to the floor, to soften the oak and to protect the soles of his shoes. He even found a better setting to place a miniature of a dowager mother—in the darkest corner of the room, out of sight—and out of his mind. He even had the good grace to lose his memory of the secret room he had found, and the secrets found within; love letters and poems written to a wife by a devoted husband of another woman. Of course his memory returned a little while later, when he had left the hospitality of the Justice of the Peace, and he read the letter he forgot to replace.

His guest sat patiently as he satisfied himself all was well—while he repositioned the chair and skins upon it again. While he sat and straightened his suit and placed his limbs to enhance the elegance of arm and leg—a pose for his guest, as if his guest was an artist commissioned to paint a perfect picture.

'*Ahem*… Y-Your man stands against reivers.'

'And which reivers does he stand against?'

'The Halls of Kirkcudbright.'

He examined his sleeves. The threads were regular. No snags. No blemish could he see. The white satin, embroidered with gold thread to form the semblance of feathers, was perfect. He examined his cuffs. All was well. He examined his hands. They were clean. Fingers correctly adorned. Nails polished and cut-square as he preferred.

'How are his odds?'

'*Ahem*…T-They are, perhaps, seven riding against seven and seventy more, perhaps greater numbers, perhaps less. But the game, so far, is blind to me. He defends a paltry village, while the rest of his men muster in Scotland.'

He examined his white-satin feather-patterned breeches and his socks. The white of his socks were mis-matched by barely a shade.

He murmured, '*Un match mediocre*,' and thought to scold his tailor. But he adjusted the lie of his legs, as he sat, so shade would hide the flaw. He examined his shoes and bent down to remove a speck from the toe of his left foot. A linen cloth was applied to both. All was well again.

'*Ahem*…What do you want me to do? Do I speak to the Merchant, or alert the Warden of his presence in his charge, so he can put his men to halt the game?'

'*Non*… It matters not, fate will see them dead, or see them live. Let the game play... That is the sport of it.' He looked to the embellishment on his jacket. A gold thread thought to escape. He and his stiletto thought to remove the errant thread. Then a finger is raised. Wagged. The thread instead is tucked within jacket's seam to nestle with its brothers. A finger is raised again. 'Yet, it is a game I would hate to lose, and fate is such a poor ally.' He brought up a hand mirror to his face, to fill his view with pleasure, and he brought a comb to join it all, to attend to his hair, even though every hair on his face was in its place. 'I say, let the game play on. But deal out the Warden… but, *mon ami*, ensure my man remains in the game. For it is not my game to lose my man.'

'A word with the Merchant?'

He looks upon his own glass, still with its fill. The fill a poor match for his glass, because the Justice of the Peace keeps his spence stocked with wine not of his provision.

'A word or two, *oui*. Let us hope, *mon ami*, the Merchant's trade into Kirkcudbright comes with influence over its burghers and their charge over their citizens.'

Chapter XXX

On Solway Sand, June 1554, day 45

'Ye're loved, William. I envy ye. A tenth the love ye receive would be a hundred worth tae me.'

'Would I be so loved, if I were not diligent, *feckless man*?'

He looked to the hall's rafters. 'I suppose not.'

'Then I say, sweat only a little for your neighbours' benefit, and receive your tenth.'

Slack 'o' Jack had burst into flames. The fire that engulfed him was a sight to widen the narrowest eye. All who knew well the sluggard spoke of little else. It was if he was a lifetime's store of tinder waiting for a spark. And the spark had been set, and he burst into flames, and he did all he could to fuel the fire.

If there was a task to be done, it was done without a thought or direction. If there were walls to build, Slack 'o' Jack was there, lifting the stones. If an errand was to be run, he would run it, for there would be work waiting for him, and he would be wanting that work done that same day.

He moved as much as twenty men's fill of sand and pebble to fill the gabions the swillers made. He supervised and engineered the placing of the baskets of earth, providing defence from the sea and road attack. And when he was happy he smiled, and when he thought the gabions and their earth could be better placed, he directed that work aswell.

He rose at dawn and only rested at dusk. He did all, helped all, and completed all that was needed.

Francis cursed him for a fool. Bendback cursed him for the labours he directed. Soldier raised an eyebrow. Meg kept him fed and watered. Geordie questioned the profit in his industry, and Jack looked to the Heavens, wondering which angel had been sent down to save his soul.

Jack questioned Thomas. He did not know. He questioned Slack 'o' Jack. He would not take the time to say. So Jack looked to the Solway Plain, to the sea, to the sand, to wonder from where a miracle had sprouted.

But for all the questions raised in his head, he accepted his soul had been saved. Saved by the magic of Solway Sand.

How else could he explain it?

Chapter XXXI

On Solway Sand, June 1554, day 47

'I love Henry. I want to be with him… forever as his wife.'

'Abbot Borrowdale will not allow it.'

'Then Henry and I will run away.'

Thomas looked at the Girl and then at Bendback. 'Would you take Melissa from her home?'

'If it means I be with her… Aye.'

'And if your union is one not bound by the cords of virtue, but chained in sin, do you think you do her well?'

Bendback looked to his boots, as if the answer was written in the leather. '…Nah.' Then he raised his head to Thomas, and showed a bold countenance. 'I want to marry the lass. Make a proper union.'

'And Bendback, what if you fall when the reivers come? Do you wish to see Melissa a widow afore she's a wife? And I mean a wife in all the joys of home and children?'

Bendback nodded. 'Yes, the reivers will come. Their scouts proclaim it,' he looked once again to his boots, 'and I may fall.' And once again he raised his head proud. Even his crooked back seemed to straighten. 'And if I fall, and if I'm wedded, Melissa will inherit all I have.'

Thomas looked hard into Bendback's eyes. And then he thought on Melissa, a girl with a poor family name, no roof in her husband's title, no children to call her mother.

A sad affair; a girl without proper kin to see her safe.

Then he thought on her as a wife, glad, with a man-and-a-half to see her secure. And for all of Bendback's fearsome form, Thomas knew nothing cruel hid beneath his fright to hurt the Girl. But then he thought on a secret shared, and the scold *Abbot* Borrowdale would deliver.

But then he thought again.

'I will handfast you. Join you as a man joins with a woman in God's sight. Contracted and betrothed.' Thomas looked into the couple's faces. He saw nothing but delight in their eyes. 'Do you agree?'

Both agreed.

'Then I will swear you to each other' Thomas joined the Girl's hand with Bendback's. 'Are you both baptised to assure your salvation?'

Bendback's head dropped. 'I have never been baptised.'

Thomas shook his head. 'Did not your father and mother…'

'Nah, I was taken away as a new born babe never to see the faces of my kin and neighbour. I was hidden, as all monsters are, lest they frighten little children as they lie abed.'

Thomas screwed his mouth, and held his face away to hide his disappointment with mankind; the lack of charity, the sight of deformity as a slight to shut away.

The Girl took Bendback's hand, squeezed it, and Bendback read the solace on the Girl's face.

'Come Bendback… the river,' said Thomas, walking away.

The three walked a while, through the trees that bond Holm

Manor to the river. They walked a while more, the river's flow that sought final release into *Moricambe Bay*, inlet to the Solway Firth. They came upon a ford of sorts, for a crude stone causeway had been constructed, although barely discernible through the swollen waters from recent rain. Thomas waded to the deepest part, stumbling on the stones as he found firm footing in the fast waters, tumbling and breaking on the stones about. He beckoned Bendback to follow him. Bendback was hesitant at first, but Thomas' words were encouraging, kind.

'Trust me my son, your salvation will soon be assured. By this act, your sins will be cleansed and you can start anew… Let go your hate, Bendback Bob.' Bendback closed his eyes and let Thomas take his weight. And it was strange to Thomas that Bendback felt like a babe in his arms. 'You are a feather in my hands, *my son*.'

'Melissa has stolen the hunger from me… I have fasted for twenty days.'

And down he went, under the water, and Thomas said, 'Repent, and be baptized in the name of Jesus Christ for the remission of your sins, and you shall receive the gift of the Holy Spirit.' And up Bendback came, *a sinner saved*.

Thomas led Bendback, sodden, back to the riverbank, as a father might lead a young child, hand-in-hand.

'Come, Melissa, hold your love's hand.' And Thomas put the Girl's hand softly into Bendback's, with a smile gently offered. 'Bendback… what is your family given name?'

'Musgrave. I am Henry Musgrave.'

'Then say after me, Henry; I Henry Musgrave take thou, Melissa, of this parish, to my spouse wife as the law of the Holy Church, and thereto I pledge thou my troth.'

Bendback repeated Thomas' words, slowly.

'And you, Melissa.'

'And likewise, I the said Melissa, of this parish, will take thou, Henry Musgrave to my spouse husband as the law of the Holy Church, and thereto I pledge to thou my troth.'

Thomas completed. 'Then I declare you betrothed to one another, until such time you have union and so be married.'

And so Bendback for the first time in a life despised, found a hope. He could not believe it. He dared not think it… *and he smiled.* And for the first time too, he felt no pain. And as he looked over Solway Sand to see the blue, to feel the breeze softly on his skin, his crooked mind broke free his crooked form—the thought of love made it so.

And as the Girl sat her place to eat her supper, to share the bread and to hear the tales and gossip of the day from maid and man, servant and sinner, she held a thought, kept it close, held it tight. She had her knight. She found her man. Henry Musgrave, a man of rectitude and goodly valour, soul and spirit cleansed.

Bendback stood the sand and faced the sky. He saw the gulls. He raised his arm to touch their wings so he could fly amongst them. His arm found its limit, the restriction of a twisted back, or so he thought, for it reached higher than it ever had, and he shouted his delight. No, he roared it.

The Girl put down her spoon, smiled, then breathed, then sighed, and thought of her love found. She dared not tell it. She thought best not to share it—*better that way.*

Bendback turned his back to the sea, and scooped the sand. Held it in his hands. He looked to the land, scanned the sweep. 'Home, I have found it! Rest, I have found it! Love, it finds me! Oh what a wonder this place be! Oh what a sight to see! Endless land, boundless sea, Solway Sand. Oh God bless me!'

'God bless me!', said the Girl

Chapter XXXII

On Solway Sand, June 1554, day 49

In they came, thirty or forty horsemen, Francis could not confirm. All at the gallop, bunched tight. Francis was in the blacksmith's. He opened the shutters wide as they approached. And he pointed his first pistol. Right hand held firm, his shot rang out. A reiver fell, but still they came on. He levelled his second pistol, and fired, but it was simply aimed into the crowd of horsemen as they galloped past his position, too fast to pick a target. The shot hit. But he could not see what carried his lead into the village, horse or man. Twenty-nine or thirty-nine horsemen, Francis could not tally.

Francis, as the sentinel watch, was worth his praise. As he saw the riders in the distance, he had sent the Boy to shout the alarm loud to Jack, running the long stretch from the blacksmith's to the village. He gave Jack some time to prepare with the men he had at hand. The men he had at the ready—fewer, because the attack was unexpected in a daylight hour. More thought it would be in twilight.

He had just enough time.

In the village, where the concentration of huts and houses was greater, more gunfire rang out. The reivers recoiled at the shock of it, for there were a dozen shots. The old-grey reiver had to shout loud and cuss hard to urge his men on, to keep the charge's power and strength.

The old-grey reiver had not been surprised that a lone gunman in the blacksmith's had fired wildly at his charge, taking a man and wounding another. There was always a man, or even a lass, with mettle enough to have a go. Reason enough to throw their hate at good sense. They were simply fortunate with their aim. Unfortunate it was to have their shots placed in his men.

But then arrows flew from windows, doorways and from behind new walls, and the old-grey reiver knew this ambush was conducted by men of war and not by ploughmen.

'*On!*' shouted Kerr.

Kerr galloped on and brought his men with him, to gallop hard through the village and not to stop, for the welcome was more than a complaint; it was a fight more than the old-grey reiver had reckoned with.

And as he rode hard, he had his answer to why his scouts had not returned, to why his signal had not been sighted. He thought the Warden's men had caught his scouts. He had not thought the villagers had a new will to fight.

Riding through, the horses' hooves found the caltrops scattered on the ground. The small iron balls affixed with spikes, stuck into their feet unsettling their charge. Several horses stumbled. Then the village boys broke their cover and hurled their stones. The reivers' horses shied and whinnied as they felt the stones stinging. The reivers grimaced as stones struck and horses bucked.

Kerr knew the truth of it, and cursed it all.

The old-grey reiver felt a strike, hard to his back. Through gritted teeth and clenched eyes, he felt the pain of it. But it would take more than a stone to unhorse the old bitter reiver, and he rode on through, cheering his men as he spurred them on to ride clear of the village.

One rider, delayed by his horse, untrained, faltering in its run through the village, brought up the rear, delayed further by its rider stopping to tend to his fallen friend.

His friend was dead.

The rider did not fear the arrows or stones thrown by the boys. He simply re-mounted and kicked hard his stubborn nag to take him through the village in pursuit of his comrades.

But a lone figure had broken his cover and stood in his way.

The rider came on, and Soldier stood his ground. He did not flinch. He did not flee from horse and man. He raised his arm and pointed pistol, braced and steadied it with his left hand.

Jack feared for him. Jack drew a breath.

The rider was low in the saddle, in good steel and a poor target, galloping in to tilt. But Soldier waited, still and calm, and the rider came on, into range, past the point of pistol's limit, and the rider's lance was couched and pointed. The rider was on Soldier, a moment away.

Jack cried out, *'Curse you. Fire!'*

But Soldier held his ground, uncaring of death a moment away. Then a blink from Soldier, a sigh, and the wheel-lock span and flashed, the pistol recoiling in Soldier's hand, and he allowed it to swing to the sky triumphant. The horse fell, its rider thrown face down and helpless on the ground.

Soldier walked over and drew his sword. He put it to the fallen man's neck. The rider began to recover, but it was too late for him, and Soldier jabbed the sword into the man's soft flesh and pushed hard in the blade, until the blade escaped his throat to meet the earth beneath him.

Two pools of rich red stained the ground, two under horse and man… both dead. Soldier did not examine his work, well done. He simply walked away without regard.

Geordie had joined others in the road to see the fleeing reivers, and was first to comment, as he kicked the body of the fallen rider to make sure he was breathless. 'Nice work. Shame about the beast. She had good form, in poor hands.'

A half a mile ahead, Kerr had halted his ride, and turned his men to face the village once more. 'We've seen the strength of them,' shouted the old-grey reiver to his men, 'now we ride on through again.'

But his men were slow to answer his call, fearing a fight more than they imagined. But Kerr had counted their guns and marked their positions. He had lost only three men, and so he knew, with another thirty of his men in reserve, he could overwhelm the village with his numbers alone, never mind the better skill of his men with musket and bow.

'Come on lads, they've made their mind tae shout at us, so let us yell back and cut some bastards down… We'll make 'em pay for *Sweet Bob, Auld Nixon* and *Baby Trotty*.'

'Ye'll be wantin' the arrow removed first,' replied Davy Hall, still breathless from the charge.

'Arra'? Whit arra'?' asked the old-grey reiver.

'The one stickin' oot yer back.'

Kerr reached to the point of discomfort, and felt an arrow's shaft.

'Well stop gawkin' ye bastard and yank it oot!' His horse reacted to his twisting, and span on the spot. 'Better still, leave it there.'

Sensing his men were not game for a second rush, and knowing his need for attention would be better served in quiet, he led his men off to find safer a site to rally.

Chapter XXXIII

[Silence]

Shadows, barely discernible, formed abstracts in the dark. Deep greys framing ridged the blacks. Shades of dark and gloom. The world before them was fixed still, immobile, stiff, an unnatural picture. Night's view, a transformation of a landscape of colour, form and beauty, into a dark-scape of hidden sight and fearful thought.

[Silence]

Even the breeze held its breath. Nature was in fear. It joined with the men, but not Meg. Meg was not frightened. She held no subconscious fear of the dark. No fright at what it hid, just anticipation of what it may bring; work for her broom and bad men to sweep onto her knife. More flesh to carve. More of her anger to sweep away.

[Silence]

All eyes scanned the night, not looking for the badger and the fox, but looking for the wolf and wild dog—the reivers. They stood behind their barricades and waited. All watched the night.

[Silence]

Then a shift in the shadows. A whisper heard? A whisper more? Men on the move? Slack 'o' Jack raised an eye to the parapet, and Francis cast his eyes over the beach to make certain the shadows were still in their place.

[Silence]

But silence was restored and imaginations calmed, and the world before them was fixed still again. Those on the watch on the northern wall began to breathe once more. And the sounds of a familiar voice ringing in their ears, bringing them respite in the form of a basket of ale and bread was a welcome tune.

ᛜ

There was little point to resistance. The reivers were amongst them. The sentries overpowered. Jack and his men held at weapons' point. Even Bendback, never a man to be bested by puny souls, was held by three lances, and only submitted to his captors' will on Jack's pleas for him to yield.

All were brought from their watch. All were brought out from their billets. All were made to stand. All looked to their fate in the dark before dawn.

And as they stood, it was clear to Jack that the full weight of the reivers was amongst them, perhaps seventy and more. All about. All had the villagers guarded. All Jack's men were taken without a fight.

'How did they pass the watch without alarm,' asked Jack.

Geordie, who stood nearest to Jack only raised his hands in mock surrender.

Jack looked to Francis. 'You and Slack 'o' Jack were on watch, how did they steal their way in?'

'They were on us in a moment… No alarm, no fight. Someone asleep methinks.'

But Jack was not convinced a single sentry asleep would cause a breach made in such silence.

Jack looked around to count his men, to see them all, and between the stand of villagers on the road he spied the bodies of two men, faces to the dirt, blood to their backs. *Treachery*, he thought.

Dawn turned to day, and such a dawn it was, made so by the Solway coast. Made so by those who saw it as their last. Still and calm, blues of different hue, shadows of a ghostly kind. And from the still came a wind from the west. Strong it was. Sand to sting the face and a blow to send a shiver. And then it was gone, and in its place a devil walked the shore.

The old-grey reiver walked from the sea to stand amongst his men, a dog amongst his pack, the worst of spirits even amongst the heinous sinners and evildoers in his keep. He gave his orders and the defenders of Allonby were corralled and set in a line for a devil's pleasure.

Kerr walked the line of men; villagers turned soldiers and soldiers too. He studied their faces, and judged contrition from defiance. At the sight of Bendback his eyes widened, and from Bendback's crown, his eyes dropped to Francis and his sneer broadened with the presence of *'Laal'* Francis in Bendback's shadow.

'It seems God brings afore me the mountain and the mole hill... *So good is he.'*

Next in the line was Geordie, and Kerr stopped to face him. 'It's gud seein' auld friends, eh?'

Geordie smiled back at the old-grey reiver. 'Aye, and some friends are best not forgotten, *eh*.' He thought an acquaintance, once held, might find his treatment kinder at the hands of this cacodemon.

Kerr fired a mucus bullet at Geordie's foot. It missed by a hair's breadth. 'I see ye're still fightin' on the wrang side. They must be payin' ye well fer ye tae be sittin' poor on the English coast, fer there's nae rich churches, abbeys or merchants tae spoil here. Nae wars and nae foreign princes hirin' surly men with purses too large tae fill.'

Geordie shook his head. 'It's been five years since I thieved from God's house. And lootin' was always three-fifths my pay… sanctioned and agreed under commission. I will not work for less than my worth.'

'Aye, and I wager ye would take home mair than ye deserve, for ye always were a greedy man.'

Geordie ignored the insult, partly because it was true, chiefly because he was in no place to argue, Kerr with the power over life and death.

Kerr threw a look towards Jack, standing next to Geordie, and a nod was given to indicate he knew who he was. Kerr spat again, but this time Geordie moved his foot so his bullet hit wide of his boot. Kerr then walked past Jack, to study the line some more. He reached Slack 'o' Jack.

'I see ye're still livin', Slack 'o' Jack.'

'Aye, It's gud work, livin' is.'

'The last time I saw ye, Slack 'o' Jack, gaol was yer bed and the gallows waited tae see ye sleep.'

'Aye, that was a long time past. The Sheriff was a kind man. So it was my thought, tae gi' him some gold fer his kindness.'

'The law is strangely accommodatin'. Especially tae those with gold tae grease the gaoler's grasp.' Kerr put a hand on Slack 'o'

Jack's shoulder, his right hand, for his left remained on his sword's hilt. 'And whose gold was it that reprieved ye, for ye never had any earned through deed of yer own.'

Kerr looked back at Jack, as if he had a conundrum to solve, then he searched out a face in the crowd as if it would give him an answer. He saw Thomas standing with the village men, held under armed guard, and he shouted to him, 'Gold can see ye out of gaol and even into Heaven... *eh, priest?*'

'You will never see Heaven... *murderer!*' shouted Thomas in reply, and he moved forward only to be restrained by a reiver guard.

Kerr grinned at Thomas' outburst. 'Ah... how the priest forgets... He forgets ma generosity tae his church in days gone. My donations in time 'n' skill tae his abbeys, Holm Cultram, St Bees and Furness. Payment of grace in lieu of my smugglin' services. My mischief given in return fer absolution and of course sanctuary, should I ever need it.'

'Your time here is over,' shouted Thomas, 'No abbeys to protect you. No wealth to need protecting. Move on reiver... and don't ever come back!'

'Your priest-man has fire in his belly,' Kerr turned back to Jack, 'Brave even with a blade in his sides.' He then walked a circle so all could see him, and he returned to Jack, voice raised so all could hear. 'I should hang ye all. I've lost seven gud men. Seven widows tae compensate. Seven less in my line. I should hang ye all.' Kerr looked to his boots. He wanted to murder every man before him, but good prudence tempered his anger, his sponsor's words still ringing in his ears.

'A man named, Jack Brownfield may stand against you. Him and his are not to be harmed for they have work to do for a good friend of ours.'

Kerr stood and looked to the sea, to his crippled brother and to his sponsor. He thought on his position. Then he turned to the land and the danger upon him as he stood still on English soil, for no doubt by now the English Warden was alerted to his presence.

'I'm a God fearin' man and it's nae my measure tae be cruel.' Kerr looked to his assembly to detect the dissent in the crowd. 'But fer all my kindness, three will be dragged and hanged, as a warning tae the peoples about that I'm nae a man tae be crossed. This village and all in it are mine. My subjects tae rule.' Kerr turned to face the crowd, he shouted, 'Consider me yer Laird, and ye will be only fer my will.' He then walked to Jack, with quiet words. 'I will let ye and yer men, nae of this village go. Be sure ye never return, fer if ye dae, I will kill every second person here today.'

Kerr walked the line of captive men, and he stopped at two with defiance on their faces and put his finger on them, and they were led away. He walked on and reached Soldier, and the Boy standing next to him. 'Yer name, *boy*.'

The Boy, looked down to his toes. He did not answer.

Kerr grinned. 'Such a young-un, full o' fear.'

Then the Boy looked up, no fear on his face. 'My name is James Moss, son of James Moss, and if I had my knife I'd prick out yer eyes.'

The old-grey reiver smiled. 'Bold words, *boy*. Let us see if ye're so bold when ye're dragged village tae village. Skin taken from yer flesh and then hung like butchered meat on a tree. Ye'll make a fine example.' Kerr looked to Richie Hall, pointing to the Boy. 'Him.'

Soldier stepped in front of the Boy, pulling him behind himself. 'Take me, *you sorry bastard*.'

Kerr shouted, 'A volunteer, lads.' He laughed. He looked into Soldier's eyes. He puzzled over the whites, for they were not white. 'Na, I like my dragged souls tae howl and wail, fer what's the message, if it's nae screamed tae the good folks about?' Kerr looked over Soldier from head to toe. '…and ye are nae screamer.'

Then another man ran forward with his lament. 'The boy is young, take me in his stead, I'm his *da… take me, take me, I beg you!*' The man fell to his knees, sobbing. *'Take me, I beg you!*'

Kerr looked to the Boy and to his father grovelling in the dirt, crawling towards the old-grey reiver, so as to kiss his boot.

All watched as the man crawled the few yards to Kerr, to reverently caress the top of his boot, take it in his hands and kiss it as a man may kiss a prince's foot.

'This man is the example ye all shall follow… Ye shall all kiss my boot afore the day is done.' Kerr put his hands softly on the man at his feet. 'I'm a man tae understand a father's sacrifice fer his children.' He then raised the man up gently, and offered him to his men. 'Take him.'

Two reivers stepped forward and dragged the man away.

The Boy tried to run to his father, but Soldier held him back. 'Stay, lad.'

'Let me go ye bastard.' The Boy tore at Soldier's grasp, tears running down his face.

The Soldier spat to the earth to mark his anger and the Boy spat at him, his only weapon against Soldier's unrelenting hold.

'See what your war brings… *my daddy to die… Bastard soldier men!*'

Kerr looked back to the Boy and Soldier, happy with his work, and he looked to the line left standing, his eyes running the whole length of men and boys. He took his time to see them all, to mark the horror on their faces. He then took Richie Hall to one side.

'Richie, drag them well. Make sure a little life lives in them long enough tae see them gurgle on the tree and nae bleed all on the road.'

Richie nodded his understanding. 'Dragged not t' death.'

'And…'

'Yes?'

The old-grey reiver thought again on his sponsor's words, '*Him and his are not to be harmed.*' He considered them carefully. Then Kerr pointed to Geordie. 'Drag him too.'

'T'death?'

'Aye.'

Richie smiled, now a little happier. He did not approve of letting Jack's men go. He fancied cutting throats and hanging necks. 'If we're sparin' men, is it nae better tae spare yer friend and hang their leader?'

'Na, fer a friend less is one less tae call on my purse when he's wantin'.'

Kerr smiled at his own wit and looked to the Boy's father, kneeling, held firm by two of his men. 'And Richie…'

'Yes?'

'Drag the boy too.'

'T'death?'

Kerr shook his head. 'Nae the boy. Just till he bleeds a little. Till he wears scars all will see fer all his days and theirs too. So that the folks aboot see my cruelty, when it visits, is nae somethin' tae foster.'

Geordie swallowed his fear, and seeing his fate before him, grabbed Jack's arm. 'Jack, would you give a dying man his last request?

Jack replied, 'Yes.'

'Then tell me of the bounty we are here to take. Tell me the secret. You can trust me now. Dead men tell no tales.'

Jack pulled back, but Geordie's hold was tight.

'Tell me Jack… tell me of your plans… Your tale of treasure at the end of this sorry account.'

Jack thought to deny claims of gold and bounty, and looked to the barrels of salt and meat that stood stacked for loading by the reivers. But he looked into Geordie's eyes, pleading for a lie, so he could rest easy with his life forfeit for a cause to his sorry heart's liking. 'Yes, Geordie, there is coin, gold and silver hidden in the barrels. The reivers take it to their ships to join more coin collected… *A mountain of it.* We are here to take it all from them.'

'I knew it! And my share?'

'More than you could carry on two nags.'

Geordie's eyes shone bright, then wetted with tears. 'Then promise me, Jack. Cut the curs from their plunder and have my share made into a gold cross to lie over my bones.'

The five were dragged. Hands bound behind their backs. Each ankle tied to a separate rope. The ropes harnessed to a reiver's nag. Each pulled like a litter, lying to face the sun, their arms to tear and break. Skin to be pulled from flesh. Flesh ripped from bone.

Their screams were heard for no ones' pleasure but the reivers' own, for the people on the roads were few, and the few stayed away from the reivers' parade.

Along the lane, four bodies were left to hang, red, on the trees, a terrible tribute to the reiver man, and Richie Hall made poor his promise to the old-grey reiver; two died on the lane, only two on the trees, Geordie and James Moss (the elder). But even the hanging was a mercy, for the pain of their bloodied and broken bodies was more than they could endure. The Boy bore his pain well, but with terrible scar, a crippled body and blood shared with Soldier, his life would have been better rubbed out next to his father.

Jack, Francis, Bendback, Slack 'o' Jack and Soldier were all led from Allonby on horseback, hands tied, weapons withheld. They were escorted along the coast through Ellenborough and Flimby, and brought to Workington as a procession; a march to show all their contrition and defeat at the hands of Auld Kerr, the old-grey reiver. The militia did not come out to threaten the reivers, and the good gentlemen of the parish, including the knights in their towers, stayed their places for fear of fight.

The men were quiet when their hands were untied. No words were found amongst their weapons returned. And all took the road to *Cockermouth* for no other reason that it was the road in their way.

Chapter XXXIV

The riders rode the green lane. Jack was alert to the road ahead. He was the only one. The four that followed carried their heads low. Eyes to the dust. But even in Jack's mind, defeat dwelled. Jack's discomfort was his wounded pride—his absolute failure to protect the village and see his charge safe. Slack 'o' Jack cursed his poor endeavours. Bendback carried fear for his love left behind. Francis was bitter. Soldier held hard his shame; he felt that in his own lust for his cause—the fight, he had known the Boy's loss and his suffering. His conscience would not leave him alone.

Two of the men halted their horses.

'I'm going back,' said Soldier.

No one questioned him.

'I'm comin' wi' ye,' offered Slack 'o' Jack, pulling around his horse to point to the way already travelled.

Soldier turned his horse too.

Jack looked ahead and sighed. He knew this foul brew would spill out of the pot. No lid, no matter how good a fit, could keep this boil contained. So he halted his nag and turned his head to shout his counsel. 'If you go back they will kill you… and no doubt more besides.'

Soldier looked pained, as though he held a hidden injury to muscle or head. He turned back his horse to face Jack.

'That old reiver, that bastard Kerr, will kill more, regardless. You know this to be true, Brownfield.'

Jack turned back his head to the road ahead, to hide his face, for he wished to deny Soldier's words, but he could not.

Soldier pressed his point, as the remaining men halted their travel. 'More will die, young Brownfield, and more and more, while bastards such as he take as much pleasure in death as they do in war's profit.' Soldier rubbed his horse's neck, and patted him tenderly in lieu of the Boy, now lost to him, but still deep within his mind. 'And more and more will die, until the word is shouted to all such devils, that this place is not for them.'

Jack looked hard at Soldier. Through steel-grey eyes he glared at the man; a soldier at odds with who he was. A man seeking to strike, in hate, a man not unlike himself. A man who lusted after the fight and the cruelty it brings. Jack held hard his stare. But Soldier was a man lost to his decision. He would do, what he would do.

Then Slack 'o' Jack rode onto Jack. His face, sombre. His horse's gait, laboured.

'Nephew, fer me, a rope always lies around the corner, and one day the noose will find me. And I suspect the World will applaud it, as I have given nothin' much of myself in life.' He turned again to join Soldier, turning his head back to Jack. 'I would like tae see my death be better used.'

Jack sought Francis for support, because of any, he would be the one to put his life and good sense above other routes, and self-seek safety for himself.

'Well, Francis, what have you to say?'

'The odds are against them. Return will mean their deaths.' Francis filled his mouth with sputum and launched the product to the ground.

Jack nodded his agreement with Francis, an ally to good sense.

But the Francis added, 'But if all here choose to take the fight to them, then the odds are better.' Francis issued a rare smile. 'So long as we roll sixes, *eh Jack*?'

Jack sighed for his own route was being recast, man-by-man. He looked to Bendback. He did not have to ask the question, because Bendback offered his reply.

'You know me, Master Jack. I go where you go. But with my Melissa in peril, my heart remains with her.'

Jack turned his horse and rode towards Soldier. And as he passed him on the road, travelling back the way he came, he winked at the big man. 'Then I will go with you. For could I ride on with the thought that better men return to fight and die? Return for no other reason than it is right to do so?'

As the five rode the lane, back the way they came, a girl was seen running up the road. Bendback cheered, kicked Mars and galloped the distance to meet her, dismounting at the trot.

'*Oh, lass, lass!*' cried Bendback, and embracing her tightly, he swept her onto Mars. All smiled at the sight of Bendback, a mountain-bear, big and mighty, tenderly holding his spindle-shanked filly, and hoisting his girl like she was gossamer.

'I ran the course, Henry. I knew I would catch ye.'

Jack was touched by their reunion, and he shouted, 'Come lovers, we have a road to ride, and a mile or three to cover.'

All galloped the green lane. Six heads held high.

The Girl told the men that the reivers had made plans to stay the night, bolstering Jack's already made defences. She heard talk of them signalling their ships to come in during the dark to take all Allonby had, and to supplement their efforts and losses with quiet raids into the Plain, to rob all they could. Many more Allonby men were to face dragging, and Kerr had threatened to hang ten more men before they left. But Meg had cut their guards' throats with her broom as she swept the ground at their feet, and released the ten onto the Plain. But now twenty more were held in lieu of the ten that escaped. Not just men, but women and children too—those who had remained with their husbands and fathers, and not sought the sanctuary of the hiding places as was directed by Thomas and Jack.

The six camped along the Derwent river, near Workington, a poor strand of houses that ran its course from Curwen's tower to the sea at *Derwentfoot Haven* and the church that stood sentinel over Solway waters. They kept hidden from the tower's watch, for only hindrance lay in its walls, not help.

They fished a salmon or two to make a good meal. Broke bread and drank wine, brought out from Bendback's pack.

Francis thought, *a fitting last supper.*

Throughout the early evening, Jack held a council of war, but only four participated, Bendback spending an hour alone with the Girl, as it should be between a wedded man and his newly wedded woman.

All agreed five were a poor counter to the reivers, and it was decided that they should seek to cut the head from the wolf. Kill Kerr and his captains, Richie and Davy Hall.

'They'll not stand alone,' argued Francis, 'Headmen always have their dogs when travelling.'

'Well let's hope Richie and Davy Hall are Kerr's dogs, and loiter at his feet,' said Soldier, stabbing his knife deep into the ground, twisting the blade sharply, 'so we can cut them all at once.'

'They'll avoid a counter to their raiding,' explained Jack, 'they'll be raiding late and early in the morn, so they can load all immediately onto their boats and retreat across the sands.'

'How many do you think will raid?' asked Francis.

'Probably more than half, perhaps in two or three parties… Fifty, perhaps, with the remaining to keep Allonby and their ships' landing safe,' offered Soldier.

'There will be more men on the ships,' complained Francis.

'Perhaps… but perhaps not so many. Men, horses and spoils take up a lot of room,' said Jack, 'There'll only be sailors, I suspect. A guard or two, perhaps to keep the sailors compliant.'

Jack waited for his men to speak; further counsel, chagrin or complaint. None came.

'So it's settled.' announced Jack. 'We strike quietly whilst they raid. Kill off any headman that remains in Allonby. Release the villagers. Take their ships. Wait for the raiders to return. And ambush.'

'The odds are still against us,' offered Francis. 'They'll be on their mettle. None will have a lazy eye to the world around them.'

Soldier brought out his knife from the ground. A worm, impaled on knife's point, wriggled and twisted. 'None will have an eye at all, after I've pricked them out… *for the Boy's promise.*'

When it came time to steal along to Allonby, two were missing. The Girl and Slack 'o' Jack. There was no clue to their retreat, and Bendback was silent to the Girl's absence.

Francis bleated bitter that Slack 'o' Jack had turned tail and turned coward. 'Does a sleeping dog become a bear as it grows older?'

Jack was sad, but not surprised at Slack 'o' Jack's absence, and his silence confirmed all to Francis.

Jack's mood was sombre on the final ride in, and his men being men, facing peril, thought to make light of the danger to come.

'I hope Meg's been baking more bread,' offered Bendback,

'I'm regaining my appetite. It comes with the thought of butchering.'

'Knowing Meg, she'll have poisoned all the reivers by now,' added Francis, 'and be butchering them as we ride… She'll bake them in hundred pies for her pantry. Yes, I guarantee that ugly bitch will do us out of the pleasure of bleeding the scum ourselves,' Francis grinned a little, 'yes… I, Francis Bell, *of Cumberland*, warrants it.'

Soldier, roused by the men, smiled. 'We ride on to Allonby as four. Yes, four feels fair, for five feels foul.'

ᘛᘚ

On their silent approach to Allonby, Jack could not observe much. They had no cover, and so had to keep a good distance from the reivers' watch. In his mind, Jack could only place the guards where perhaps the torches burned. He hoped none lurked in the shadows. But without good reconnaissance, his estimate of the strength of enemy in Allonby was only his own supposition, and he doubted himself.

Torches and a signal fire lit the beach. A hulk had been packed with fuel and pitch, and set alight. And Jack could see at least four men at the fire, keeping warm on a cold night.

It was two hours before dawn.

'They need the signal fire to land their ships,' whispered Jack, 'hence why they attacked Allonby by land. Because our presence in the village prevented the signal being set.'

Soldier nodded. 'There be a traitor in the village.'

'A traitor who back-stabbed our watch,' added Jack.

The four kept to the tall grass of the dunes, as they moved forward, and found themselves with better view of the reivers' positions. Each torch seemed to have two men, and five torches were lit amongst the houses. One set of guards seemed to stand the door of a house, and Jack reasoned the Allonby men and women must be held captive there.

'We need to take at least two sentry positions to free the villagers quietly,' suggested Soldier.

With the night, came a wind from the sea, and so the noise of the men skulking in the shadows was hidden. The Solway chose to blow, and the waves, coming closer and closer with the tide, chose to crash loud, as breaker on breaker hit the shore—their shout to be carried on the wind into the reiver's ears.

Francis and Soldier worked well. Francis, with his bow, took down each sentry in turn and Soldier ran in to put a knife into the men. It took half-the-hour for Francis and Soldier to work men dead quietly, so Jack and Bendback could each tackle a guard on the house—a neck to the knife and a neck to be broken.

Inside the house the villagers were tightly crammed. Thomas stood over his flock. He stood between his children and the wolves at the door. Glad he was to see Jack and his mountain by his side, and Jack glad to see Thomas safe.

With all freed and Thomas leading off the women and children into the night to seek sanctuary well away from the battle to come, arms from the fallen reivers were distributed amongst the men, as well as iron bar and sharpened tool taken from the blacksmith's.

The guards on the beach and the remaining sentry positions were rushed. And within ten minutes, with Jack, Francis, Soldier and Bendback each leading companies of men, six reivers lay dead and eight more were captured. Jack saw three casualties amongst his own. Cuts bad enough to see all the wounded men retire. But Jack was relieved that no mortal wound was sustained.

Jack stripped the dead and captured reivers. He had them trussed tight and gagged. He dressed his own in the reivers garb. He armed them with their weapons and positioned them in the places vacated by men now held prisoner, naked, in the house that once held the villagers captive. Francis and Bendback broke two reivers who did not comply with capture. Men who thought escape a better option. Francis directed Bendback to wring the life from them, and he left the bodies to lie amongst the living as a warning not to flee.

ꕥ

The ships arrived as daylight came, and Jack fretted. He fretted because the dark had been his ally, and his ally was now retreating. It had been five hours since Jack and his men had retook Allonby. Time enough to prepare, but with the light, the reivers arriving from both the sea and the land would perhaps see strangers waiting to greet them, and not friends and allies.

The two ships lay off the coast. A mile or so from the shore. And all waited to see. Jock '*Ladyman*' Hall was too far away to see a foul reception on Solway sand, so to him all seemed fair. But as he waited, Jock was wary of the delay. He waited for his kin to strike out from the beach in boats to greet him and set up embarkation protocols. But no boats came, so his concern grew.

So Jock Hall set out on a boat with four men to scout the way, and espy any threat that waited on the shore.

It was a long time to row, and Jock worried more that the vessels were too far anchored out to make rapid transfer of spoils from sand to ship. It took his thought off possible danger ahead.

On the shore, he hailed his comrades, but none came, and he drew his pistol to lead the way, with two men following, swords drawn and shields forward. He instructed the remaining oarsmen to prepare the boat, in case a hasty retreat was needed.

As he walked the beach, he felt unease. It was quarter the mile to the nearest man on the sand, and all *seemed* fair. Even auld Kerr's flag flew over the village. He studied carefully the hulks that stood around. All was quiet.

But as he walked the sand, nearing the village, still no greeting was made, and he thought the worst of it. It seemed foul not fair, so he turned to retreat to the boat, to the safety of the ships.

Francis appeared from behind the timbers. Hidden in a boat, he fired a matchlock, and a sailor following Jock, dropped to the sand. Jock let loose his pistol at the hulk, but Francis had taken cover, and the shot buried itself into the timber. Francis re-appeared in a moment with his own pistol. The second sailor dropped, a wound to the knee.

Jock Hall ran, shouting to his men to get ready the boat. Leaving the wounded sailor to his fate at the hands of men now running in, eager to engage the retreating reiver.

The sailors at the boat did not wait.

Jock ran the beach, into the surf, into the sea. He tried to catch the men, rowing away. But Francis had also ran the beach, and with a newly primed matchlock, he let loose a shot which caught Jock in the shoulder.

Wounded, Jock turned and drew his sword and dagger and charged back through the surf to tackle Francis, but he was a distance away, and Jock's progress through the sea and surf was impaired. Francis had time to reload and prime. He let loose a second shot which caught Jock full in the chest.

Jock fell to his knees, gasping for air.

Five men ran past Francis, to find Jock in the surf on all fours. All rained down their swords and iron on the back of the reiver. Again and again they hit and stabbed, until Jock gave way and lay face down in the surf.

The sea ran red about him.

Just as dawn had brought the ships, it brought back the mounted reivers too, fresh from raid.

Jack had hoped to tackle the groups returning separately in ambush. But the two parties had regrouped on the Plain, from their raids on the Manor of Aspatria and the market town of Wigton.

They rode in hard, alerted by the noise of gunfire, the sight of a fight on the beach, and their ships at sea waiting for their cargo.

Jack rallied his men from their cover on the beach and shouted them to relocate to points amongst the houses, but the reivers were close and threatening Jack's muster.

Then from the dunes in the north came Meg, her broom in the air, men by her side; the men she had released, bolstered by a few more she found in hiding.

The old-grey reiver screamed bloody murder, as he willed his boys on. Jack's men were still scattered, and Meg's small group were too far to immediately bolster Jack's numbers.

'Cut all ye dinnae ken,' shouted Kerr as he led the charge.

Richie Hall cheered, and he clenched the reins between his teeth. He bit down hard. He drew two pistols, and peeled off the charge to quench his own thirst for glory.

Davy Hall yelled, 'Kill the bastard curs… *Kill'em all!'* And he led off twenty reivers to encircle the houses.

Against Jack's fears, his scattered men found purpose, not panic. They formed to fight in pairs and threes as they were instructed, and took good cover to allow the reivers to run out their charge.

Fight was amongst Jack's men, and as the horsemen past, an ordered array of two or three men would inflict wound on their horses. Another group would rush out of cover to tackle the riders to the ground, whilst another group with bow and latch, would keep other reivers from supporting their fallen comrades.

Soldier worked as one, and he ran amongst the horsemen, dodging blade and wounding horses and men alike. He ran like a demon man with no fear, or regard for good sense. Not killing, but wounding all in his reach. He sought not a tally of kills, but to reduce the number of able fighting men at the old-grey reiver's command.

Francis, with a bow, found his place on a roof, and with a quiver full, he emptied it within a minute. Six reivers hit. Six reivers fallen.

Bendback stood an island in the storm, his knight's axe in his hand. A bolt hit, sinking deep into his arm, but it did not stop him, and he grabbed the bridle of a reiver's nag in canter, to halt it. The rider rained down a sword, but Bendback's axe parried it, to snare it between his own axe blade and steel shaft. He twisted his axe to snap the reiver's blade. The reiver struck his half-sword at Bendback and it drew blood on Bendback's face, but Bendback's axe did more in return, and it cleaved the man's leg. He screamed. Bendback let go the bridle and grabbed the man. He pulled him off his horse. The man struggled against Bendback's single-hand hold. But he was stilled when the hunchback brought down his axe to split the man's skull. Then Bendback ran amongst the reivers, to distract their fight from the villagers.

The reivers, with many of their number still mounted, had the best of it. And as villagers retired from the fight with wounds, or ran away in fright, more Scotsmen came in from boats, put down by the ships. More than Jack had thought.

Meg's men had reached the fray, but they were not enough, and they quickly ran into the houses and into fields for escape.

Jack's sword was well tested, and he kept on the move, slashing and cutting. Two reivers lost feature and face as he lunged at head and neck looking for fatal wounding. Another two retired with deep and mortal cuts. And when fight was not with him, Jack was constantly looking around, to see to his own force, and where weakness lay. But all seemed lost.

Jack thought to sound retreat and send all running for cover, respite and safety. He thought the reivers would need to retreat urgently to their ships and to the sand crossing at Bowness, and so would not have time for bloody reprisal against the village. But with the hulk still in flame, he knew there was time to fire the village and cut to death those who couldn't run.

A call was made, loud and triumphant, and Jack looked to its origins. He feared the worst, and thought the reivers had won the day. The call was made again, and Jack saw Francis standing on a roof, bow in the air, voice in cheer. He looked again to confirm what he saw, what he heard. It *was* Francis, and he was cheering.

Slack 'o' Jack came like a general ahead an army. He ran with a flag held high and a hundred behind, in his call-to-arms. Militiamen mustered by good William Waite and his neighbours' plea. Men seeking revenge for the ill the reivers did the Solway coast, for the men they strung on good Ellenborough trees. Good Englishmen laid waste by the Scot.

And then from the Plain, the Girl came ahead another group of men and women, all with staves and tools aloft. Friends, who had listened to her entreaty, and thought better of leaving Allonby to its own fate.

The reivers scattered.

Richie Hall rode a narrow gap between two houses to escape. No mounted men to guard his back. Ahead, four village men with staves blocked his way, behind him, three more with spears running in. Any fear was absent in the village men; their courage found in numbers—murder in their shouts.

Richie Hall cursed, and turned his nag to face the three, but he had lost momentum. His mount spooked by battle. He had little control. His balance on the twisting horse was poor. His vigour lost in a night of persecution and rape.

Out of a doorway, in reach of Richie, stepped Meg, broom raised high to the horse's head. It reared and the reiver fell.

Richie knew he must recover quickly. They would be on him in a moment. There would be no quarter given, and death would be painful and prolonged. It was time for those to soften his flesh and crush his bones with all the hate he had himself delivered.

He tried to move, but he could not.

The mob was on him, but Meg waved the men away. The reiver was her prize. And the mob complied. Meg would have her own way with Richie Hall, and none dare argue with her broom. She pushed hard the broom into the face of the fallen reiver, forcing his head to the side, to escape the discomfort of the bristles.

She cursed. 'I am a fool, *wrong end*.' Then spinning her broom around quickly, she thrust her knife's blade hard into the cheek of the reiver, before removing it to run the blade onto the man's throat.

Richie held his head rigid, away from the woman's knife. He tried to move his legs. He could not, and thought them broken. But there was no pain.

His back was broken.

Meg held hard her broom to the reiver's throat, and the reiver stared at death's instrument and smiled.

'Aye, revenge is fittin' purpose for a gud fightin' tool… But ye should stick tae yer sweepin' with yer pokey stick.'

But Meg stood her ground, knifepoint held on the reiver's throat.

She spat her words. 'Revenge is a man's sin, born of his pride.' She forced words through gritted teeth, worn and blackened with age. 'I'm no killin' ye for revenge. I would not stain my family's place in Heaven for so foul an act.'

The reiver took a breath, carefully, lest his throat was pricked. 'Then why am I under yer cookin' knife?'

The reiver found life in his arms and moved, and Meg reacted instantly by pushing the blade into the reiver's neck, enough to break the skin and draw his blood.

'Hold yerself, reiver!'

'Hold yer knife, woman!' The reiver stretched his head away from the blade, stinging his neck. He thought of a strategy to remove it––perhaps to grab the blade and force it aside. Sacrifice his hands to counter the thrust. But with his back broken he would not be able to parry the woman, and while she held him to surrender, his fate was bettered. Better than a fate at the hand of a dozen men, baying for gore and bloody reprisal.

'So ye no threatnin' me because I killed yer kin?'

'Not because ye killed them. Fate decreed their death. Their passin' was written at their birth. Ye simply the instrument of their earthly demise.'

'Ye nae angry, woman?'

'Only with ma loss of my place, carin' for a family.'

The reiver narrowed his eyes. There was little sense in his situation, and he thought again to raise his hands to remove Meg's blade, but as he shifted, Meg pushed in the blade harder, cutting more. Blood pumped freely from his wound.

'Do ye walk on God's path?' asked Meg.

'I'm afraid it's many years since I gazed upon the Virgin Mother.' He swallowed carefully. 'The last priest's sermon I received was less than upliftin' as I stole his purse and burnt his church.'

'Then is there something else I can do for ye in lieu of confession?'

Richie sighed. His pain gone. His certainty that his back was broken, evident. He thought on his life and smiled at it. He thought on his future and grimaced. He saw himself crippled, helpless, wheeled to the gallows to be hoisted high.

He thought and said, 'Nae lass. My back is broken. I cannae feel ma legs. Ye'll be doin' me a kindness, lass, if ye kill me. I wish I was sorry fer killin' yer kin, but they meant nowt tae me… If I said anything else I would be lyin', and I dinnae want tae go tae God wi' a lie on ma lips… tae add tae a wicked life already past atonement… Push home yer blade, ye ugly coo… Send me tae Hell.'

'Then I kill you now, and I'll be givin' ye somethin' ye did not gi' ma kin.'

'What's that, woman?'

'Dignity in fated death.'

Her blade sunk deep into Richie's neck, and she twisted. Her face showing all the effort of her butchery. His eyes rolled. He gasped. He gurgled. He took a while to die. His death drowned in a flood of blood about his neck.

Francis was now on the ground, cutting at any man who was unhorsed. And as with the Soldier, his sword strikes were well placed. The reivers were in complete disarray, their lust for the fight missing. Some asked for quarter, but Francis and Soldier offered none. Reivers who dropped their blades were cut down. Reivers who turned and ran, were chased.

Francis chased such a reiver, who though better of fighting. Francis did not think to let him go, and he chased him between two houses. Meg still stood there. Francis cried out a warning, but the reiver surprised Meg still studying her kill, offering a prayer for both their souls. She blocked the reiver's retreat, and so he ran her through with his sword. She fell.

And Francis fell to his knees to cradle his washerwoman.

Jack, meanwhile, rallied the men still caught in fight. He found Davy Hall lying down in the sand; eyes open, facing the sun. He seemed dead. Still. No breath. No movement. His fat body bloodied, cut and pierced. His head blackened and bleeding. But as Jack kicked hard his head, the reiver groaned and his eyes blinked as he found consciousness, and with it, he found pain.

'Ahh... I'm cut bad...ye...ye bastard.'

Jack stood over the reiver, looking down at the sorry mess of a man, well bled. 'Yes you are. Hell awaits you, *fat reiver man.* Should I find the priest to save your soul?'

Davy's head was still, his eyes staring, trying to focus. His words came with blood from his mouth. 'Na, it's too late fer me... my blood is all but gone.'

Jack looked about the red pool that spread out from underneath the reiver, deep and dark, sinking into the sand. 'Yes, your sorry life flows into good sand.'

But the reiver seemed not to hear, as he was lost in his final thoughts. His next words started strongly, pushed out on a deep exhale, but they finished on a whisper. 'Shame ma brother didnae... *shag her.'*

Davy Hall seemed to smile at Jack. Smile, like a joke was shared, before his expression finally relaxed in death. But Jack made sure, and drove his sword into his heart.

A group of reivers, no longer led, retreated over the fields. They thought to flee towards Bowness, to escape over the sands, hoping tide would be with them. But they ran straight into more men running in from Wigton, chasing down the original reiver raiding party.

The reivers, seeing the men running towards them, halted for a moment. They thought to turn and disperse. But seeing other reivers gathering, they took courage and ran at their attackers, their weapons aloft. But the supporting reivers scattered, and without any great concentration of number to counter the attacking Wigton men, the reivers in the fields only found the anger of many axes, cudgels, staff and spear about them.

Kerr, well protected by half-a-dozen men with sole intent to see him safe, seeing all was lost to greater numbers coming in from all sides, sought escape from the melee around him. Villagers, too numerous, streamed like flood tides around the houses. His men were lost, so Kerr left his own guard to fend off the flood, and turned his nag and kicked it hard.

He took to the beach, and a good clear ride he had, no one would catch him. He spurred his lady on, and she kicked up the sand and took him to flight amongst the sound and sight of missiles filling the air, directed by Francis to bring him down, but he remained untouched.

Blood boiled in his veins, and he kicked harder still, rallied his nag and cheered her on. He scattered sea birds by the flock. He kicked up the sand by the load. He splashed across waters running the sand from land to sea. But his horse stumbled on soft sand, a hidden rock perhaps, and it took him an age to recover.

A musket shot found his horse and she bled. He rode her on. But lame and shot, her heart would burst. She fell. The old-grey reiver was caught beneath her. Leg pinned.

The villagers approached, running; a mob with murder on their minds. He strained his neck to see them coming. They were screaming, and he tried desperately to release his leg, but it was stuck fast. They were closing, and he tried again, and again, but he could not pull away his leg. He clawed desperately at the sand to dig free his leg, but the mob were moments from him.

Seeing his time was at an end. A life spent in greed and envy to be foreshortened, he ran a kindly hand over his nag, lying still, her life ebbing away.

'Ah old nag, ye're nae friend tae me today. Ye're goin' tae see me killed.'

The old-grey reiver looked to the sky, clear and blue. Sun warm on his face. A smile replaced effort, and quiet replaced the sounds of the mob in his ears.

He looked into the blue. 'Still… it's a bonny day tae die.'

Chapter XXXV

The villagers counted their kill and moved their dead. Thirty reivers killed or captured, and only six villagers had lost their lives, although many more bore terrible wound. The bodies of the reiver men were placed on the sand. Side-by-side, feet to the Plain, heads towards their own shore across the Solway, to see it no more. No shrouds for them, only the sun to cover their corpses. Wind to dry their bodies. Blown sand to cake on wound and blood.

Some declared it a miracle and sank to their knees on Solway sand to pray. Some marched on the Abbey church to offer up more prayers, carrying the bodies of the fallen, including poor Meg.

Jack was left to scan the area to locate all those he knew, and make good wounds and spirits bruised by the fight. Slack 'o' Jack and Francis marched with the pallbearers to the Abbey church. The Girl tended Bendback's wounds, that to him were a mere scratch and a bruise or two, no more—he would live. To others they would see deep gash and terrible welt, and marvel at his stance. Soldier, he found searching the houses.

'Where's the Boy?' he shouted.

No one seemed to care.

Soldier stopped a man in his tracks. Held him hard by his shoulders. *'Where's the Boy, where's the Boy?'* he bellowed, the force of his words making the man pull back.

The man tried to shrug his shoulders, but Soldier gripped them hard.

But Soldier could see the ignorance in the man's eyes and said, 'the Boy, the Boy… The lad that was dragged.'

Another villager intervened to save the poor man a shaking.

'He is cared for in Ellenborough. William Waite's wife took the poor lad in, to tend to his wounds… His mother sits with him.'

Soldier did not pay heed to Jack as he tried to hold him steady. To be counted and put to task that comes with clearing the ground of battle. Instead, Soldier found a reiver's horse, mounted and beat it hard into the gallop for Ellenborough.

At William Waite's house he found the Boy, but the Boy was lost to the world around him. Given Miriam's bed by she wishing to see a broken lad in what comfort he could find, his smashed arms had been set in splints, and wrappings had been applied to wounds that bled on both his limbs and body.

William's wife tendered her care, washing the Boy's remaining skin as if it was gossamer silk beneath her fingers. She used milky liquids and clean woollen swabs, and applied ointments and poultices to areas of broken skin already cleansed.

Soldier looked to the raven-haired woman sitting at the Boy's side. Her stare not moving away from Miriam's charge, her soft brown eyes, wetted.

'Are you his mother?' he asked quietly, so as not to wake the Boy.

'Aye,' she said softly with warmth in her voice for her true love.

'Will he live?'

'He is a strong boy,' she put her hand to his hair, gently, to tidy the wayward tresses, 'although he has been sick of late.'

'He is good lad,' he said.

'He will live,' she said, her mouth trying to smile. 'Crippled he'll be… Scars to wear… My sins to carry.'

Soldier looked on the woman, so beautiful even in her sorrow. No running tears, or wails, or whispers of woe. Nothing but a calm and a gentle spirit.

'Your sins?' he asked.

'Aye.'

'I am sorry for your pain, and I am sorry for your loss, madam. Your husband will be missed. And I am sorry for my part in bringing this pain and loss to your door.'

'Did you drag them both? Did you seek to hurt my angel? Did you hang my man?'

Soldier dipped his head.

'The Halls lie bloodied,' he said, 'their men lie killed or captured. Some to face the Warden's rope, no doubt. Justice to be served. So I apologise if any may be your kin, for I understand you hail from Kirkcudbright… and so it stands that men of that parish may lie on the earth with my cut to their bodies.'

'Aye, there is kin of mine on the sand.'

Soldier dipped his head lower at the cruelty of war that sees family put against family.

'Then I have reason more to be sorry.' Soldier grimaced.

'Why?' said the Boy's mother, 'Did you have me christened, *Hall*, a daughter of James Hall? A lass born proper, in wedlock, shunned and wiped from the family's record. Disregarded because she bruises her name.' She looked up for the first time at Soldier's face. 'Such is the pride of men for their name. My husband—a good man of an English forest. My son—a good son of a good man. They wore their name, James Moss, with kindness, not as pride's foul badge.'

Soldier stepped close to the Boy. He wanted to lay his hands on him. He moved them so. His mother did not complain, and Miriam retreated, her work done, and now a place to find and prayers to offer for his recovery.

But Soldier felt unworthy to lay his war-soiled hands on something more precious than all he held dear. He rubbed his hands down his sides. He brought them to his face. He looked deep into the callouses and cuts. No action would remove the blood from them. He cried.

The Boy did not wake.

Soldier looked on at the Boy's mother, holding her vigil. His eyes were dim, poorly—yellow. He reached deep into his shirt to pull out a small bag attached to a long cord tied about his neck, to which was tied a silver cross. He kissed the cross and pulled at the leather cords that held the bag closed. He emptied the contents into his hand. Six large gold coins of foreign design.

He placed them quietly at the side of the bed and walked away.

Soldier returned to Allonby, to be where he was expected to be. He rode to where the grass ended and the sand began, dismounted, unbuckled his weapons and steel, and walked awhile, looking out to the sea.

Jack looked on and saw Soldier; a man at odds with the scene around him; jubilant villagers, still filled with their victory, all smiles and bluster, and others still counting the cost of their loss. He thought to leave Soldier to his own company, and then he thought again, and he began to walk over to see what had removed him from the crowd.

As he walked the grass, and before he reached Soldier, Jack shouted, 'Come on, Soldier. Good work we have done today.'

But Soldier stood still and maintained his gaze over the sea.

Jack came alongside to share his view. Not the view of boats and men, but of sand, sea, hills beyond and sky above. Soldier's weapons were not about him. His armour removed. His helmet discarded. But he held tight his knife, pointed to the ground.

Soldier did not look at Jack, but announced, 'I came here to fight, because fight is always the hunger I have to feed. Then, with this place, and in all its… *serenity*, I came upon a rested mind…' He turned his head to scan the horizon. 'And placid thought is the physic that calms ardour, because it brings reason and consequence instead of a fever of need and the urgency of want,' Soldier seemed to fade, 'Fever… Fever which drives desperate and unquenchable appetites,' Soldier sighed deeply, 'I came to think this fight, a fight against all the odds, a fight to see me killed.' Soldier turned his head to look at Jack. He laughed a little. He hid a pain. He looked to the sky to feel a light breeze on his neck, then back to the sea. 'Mmm… a noble end to a soldier's life.'

Jack thought the declaration strange, and cheerily offered, 'You are a good man, and we've fought a good fight. People would miss you if you were laid out bloody. Come on, let's find some company and some ale. The ripple on the sea is a kind sight, but the ripple on a jug of ale is far kinder.'

Soldier turned again from the sea and faced Jack. He smiled. 'Yes, a soldier does as he is told… In all things… He does not have to make the difficult choices these folk here have to make each poor season, with the courage to care for the young and look after the pains of their parents.'

Soldier's response bewildered Jack, as he tried to understand Soldier's poor humour and what specifically, in the face of such a victory, had brought such melancholia to his words. 'Do not lay your curse on a soldier's life, my friend. It is their choice to work the land, as it is our choice to fight over it. Come, we've fought and now we should drink… our work here is done.'

Soldier nodded, and added a wry smile. 'Yes, for every day we fight, we sleep and drink ourselves happy a dozen more. Our bed is given. Our food provided. Gold fills our purse from the vanquished and occasionally from our employers. Fighting is our pleasure, and the rest of it… The hardships of a soldier's life, well, they are easily endured.'

Jack's impatience was showing. 'Then be a good soldier, and do as you are told… Come, ale to make you happy.'

But Soldier did not respond. He stood stolid. Deaf to Jack's words.

'I should have died today.' He turned away from Jack, back to face the sea.

'Come. Take comfort. Rest awhile,' said a terse Jack, irritated by Soldier's gloomy oration, 'the good people here will be glad if you decide to take off your boots in their village. For a little while longer, *at least*.'

But still he stood, unrelenting, and Jack thought to leave him to his thoughts.

Then Soldier said, 'The Boy suffers for the lust of men warring on men. Now I promise God, my blade to innocence. And in truth, the spirit of this place has whispered to me for weeks, *secure your blade in a coffer and not in your hand*.'

'All men must retire from their craft eventually,' replied Jack.

'I do not retire from it, but renounce it…' Soldier suddenly clutched his belly as if wounded, and Jack moved forward, but Soldier waved him away.

Soldier cried out in pain. He held firm his stomach. He bent double and fell to his knees, his face contorted in agony.

Jack rushed forward and knelt with him, looking to see his wound, but again Soldier waved him away.

He found some composure, but remained on his knees holding his belly. 'I prayed to die a hundred times.' His words were forced out between gritted teeth. 'I thought fight would take my life… *[ahhh]*… Often I would close my eyes before an enemy strike, to say a prayer… to guide his blade, to meet my death…' Soldier fell on all fours. 'But it seems God spares it… to make me suffer for my sin.'

Jack did not know what to say.

'I have a rot within me… The pain of it grows stronger each day… *[ahhh]*… My father died of it… *Tumour*. They say the canker in his body distorted his skin… and he screamed for months before he died.' Soldier screamed out again, but he turned the scream within itself and yelled his anger at it, through clenched teeth. '*[Ahhh]*… He was a bold man… my father… Not so bold was he when he screamed out for the pain to stop.'

'I am sorry, Soldier.'

For the first time, Soldier seemed to truly acknowledge Jack, and still kneeling, he lifted his hands from the ground. He looked up at Jack, his eyes yellow. 'Sorry? Did you give me the canker?' He drew himself back up, still kneeling and gritted his teeth against another unbearable hurt. 'I wanted to die today, sword in hand. I wanted to say goodbye to the waking day and seek eternal rest, now I have found good earth to cover me… *[ahhh]*… But I live. I do not die. But I will not fight again. Never again lust for it… *[ahhh]*… My blade will never again know *another* man's blood,' Soldier forced his words, 'And if God chooses to punish me, then it is all I deserve for a life spent in lust for war.'

'Come on Soldier, we'll talk on it more with a drink. An ale will ease your burden, and we will see you have a surgeon from Carlisle for your discomfort.'

With pain abated, Soldier bid Jack to help him stand. Jack hoped to return him to the world and seek comfort for his pain. But Soldier turned to the sea, walking on instead, leaving Jack at grass' edge.

Jack did not think to accompany him. It seemed as if his pains had ceased. So Jack left Soldier to himself, because it seemed his own company was what he wanted to keep. Instead, Jack turned away to walk towards the village.

He did not see Soldier walk the sand to the sea. Nor did he see the Soldier fall into the surf—never to rise again.

He died from his wounds, they said.

ജ്ഞ

Gatherings from Holm Cultram, and all the way along the coast, south to Workington and north to Bowness, celebrated that night and for another night after that. All brought ale and beer, food aplenty, and every musician or man with a whistle played a tune to set feet a-dancing and voices a-singing. William Waite opened his house once more, and other people did too. Neighbour met with neighbour and all were kindred. Peoples from Flimby embraced the people from Mawbray and the people from Ellenborough embraced the niggardly souls from Skinburness, for they were seen as niggardly no longer.

Many in Allonby were sorry to think on Jack's men gone, especially William Waite, saying his goodbyes to Slack 'o' Jack. Many offered keen thanks for a new story to be told around the fireside, and proud declarations were made to all Jack's men, and remembrances were promised for those who had fallen in their cause.

More good news that night came in to bolster the villagers' celebrations, by way of the Warden's troopers responding to the raids by the reivers on the market town of Wigton.

All the retreating reivers were caught on the sands of the Solway, swept by the tide. All drowned, but one.

They said and they sang, *he would have a tale to tell.*

The Warden's men ordered the bodies of the reivers loaded on carts and taken to Carlisle to be tagged, to be hung from the city's gates. Even the four already buried were exhumed, so their numbers could swell the tally of Scots overcome, as they would laud, *by the mettle of simple English hearts armed with stout English stave.*

The old-grey reiver, Auld Kerr, would hang without the Hall name he envied. He would hang high on Carlisle's Rickard Gate next to his nephew, Richie Hall. Some women would perhaps mourn *his* loss, but only for a moment, no more, and many more would be glad to be spared his lust and beatings. His fat brother, Davy Hall, was hung with two ropes for the weight he bore. Big Tom Little was hung the highest for the number of crimes he held against his name, and the corpse of his brother, Sparra, was left in a ditch to rot, as the Warden's men, lazy, grew tired of hanging men. Only Jock Hall's body was returned unmolested to Kirkcudbright's walls. His body paid for by his father with a favourite to mourn.

James Hall's family would eventually wither for the lack of revenue brought in by Auld Kerr. The pride for his name could no longer be bought, and eventually the town of Kirkcudbright with new civic virtues discovered, saw the Halls from their walls.

Where be anger?

The Warden's man excused Jack's men of their involvement in the fight at Allonby, even Slack 'o' Jack's presence was given the blind eye by the Warden's captain. But no credit would they receive, no bounty, no reward, no acclamation.

Jack and his men were allowed to remain at Allonby to see to their arrangements, even to receive more Scotsmen from the north as Jack's retinue. The Warden's captain was not sorry to see more scots from the north to leave for France… away from his harm's way.

But Jack planned to leave for Liddesdale as soon as he could, as soon as Robert came with the muster. This he kept from the Warden's captain. Jack was keen to return home to Mary, and Bendback keen to see him safe, so he could return back to Holm Cultram to be with his wife.

As the celebrations continued, and talk was ebullient, one was missing. One Jack wanted to see, because his absence from the fight and the celebrations nagged at Jack's reasoning.

Was he a coward in hiding? Perhaps so? Or a man about his work?

But also within his reasoning was a reckoning required. Two men of Jack's watch were back-stabbed. The reivers were aided from within.

There was a traitor still in their midst.

It did not take long for Jack to find him. He was where he was always to be found, tending his fire, working some metal. Hammer in hand and sweat on his brow.

'Not celebrating?' asked Jack.

The Blacksmith drove a rod of iron into his fire. 'No, that job is done. New jobs to do.'

His twisted in the metal and stood to face Jack.

Jack studied the Blacksmith. He looked past the grime upon his face to see the man beneath, to ascertain if he was a man relieved to see the fight finished and the reivers vanquished. If he were a man to see his smithy work free from harm.

The Blacksmith held Jack's stare until he returned to his craft. He took his hammer to the rod of iron, white hot from the fire, to cool to yellow, and between his forge tongs, he began to work it with zeal and purpose.

But his skill-craft did not direct his blows, but something else–*–anger.*

'Not a happy man, are you?' said Jack.

'What do ye mean? The battle is over, *and won.*'

'For we, not thee, *Smithy man.*'

The Blacksmith remained silent as he beat the iron rod, as he beat the anvil hard as he lifted the rod away and thrust it back into the flame.

'Come,' said Jack, 'put down your work and join the celebrations.'

'Will it bring my child back, and my love?'

'It might, we've broken the back of the reivers. They may be able to return home.'

'They'll never come back, these bastards chased her out.'

It was dusk, and the light was dim in the smithy, dark so the Blacksmith could see the colour of his metal. He worked it again briefly with his hammer, and returned it back to the forge to heat again.

Jack noticed one door to the smithy could be opened to the sea, and he walked over to it. He pushed it open, and the forge burst into flame, bright.

'Hey, mind the door. Mind the draft,' shouted the Blacksmith.

Jack looked to the flame burning very large and bright. So bright he had to turn away to look through the door, open to the sea, and he saw Criffel in the distance.

The signal! Jack thought.

Jack thought to challenge, but then thought more caution and less accusation a better policy, with the Blacksmith armed with red hot metal and hammer.

The Blacksmith pulled out the iron and again began to work the metal. And Jack thought to leave, for he was tired, and he thought the villagers, not he, would perhaps better apply investigation and justice to the Blacksmith. And besides, he had sympathy with a man perhaps coerced to betray, in order to protect those interned.

But the Blacksmith was mumbling. 'They promised me to make them suffer… *Bastards all!*'

Confused at his words, Jack prepared to leave.

'Your daughter and wife will be safe.'

'My daughter! That girl! She is a slut, like her ma… I have nae more regard for those sorry harlots than that bastard cat they left behind. He pointed the orange metal to the fat grey cat, sitting supercilious on a sack. 'That bag of shite, that beast of Hades, has sat in judgement over me while I've worked my forge for these last three years.'

'Then chase it on,' offered Jack, without sympathy.

'They were supposed to make the village suffer. They took my child away, sent away my love, bastards all!'

Jack did not understand. 'What do you talk about, Blacksmith?'

'Now they farm and fish, those devils in robes… But I remember when they sat silent, in their prayers… their piety. Sat in their cloistered world, within stone and under tile, while we sat on the earth under thatch. They sat and judged my love, one of their sisters, their own, and sent her from her home… sent on my child, conceived in love. I never held my babe, or knew if it even lived.'

Without warning, caught in the gaze of the cat, the Blacksmith picked up the hot rod with his hand, its tip glowing bright and raised it to Jack. His hammer too. Jack drew his sword. The Blacksmith took one step, then two more. Jack presented his sword, and drew his dagger too.

A feint with the sword, and a rush with the knife, close, would see the Blacksmith dispatched.

But instead the Blacksmith, caught again in the gaze of the cat, hesitated. His eyes shone, and wetted. His blackface showed sad. He stopped. He dropped his hammer. Dropped his iron. He put his hand up to his eyes and wept. Remorse.

'I loved my girl of Christ… They sent her away.' He looked at

Jack, still with blades to the fore.

'Did you kill your neighbour, Blacksmith? Did you back-stab your friends? Has your treachery seen man as well as monk suffer for your anger?'

The Blacksmith broke into more sobs. *'Oh... oh... what have I done!'*

Then without warning the *blackened man* turned to his fire, drafted and burning bright, and plunged deep his hands into the furnace.

His screams ran Jack's blood cold. The Blacksmith pulled free his hands, red and smoldering. He stared in horror at his work. Eyes wide, Terrified.

He ran from his smithy howling pain and anguish.

He was never seen again.

ꕥ

The next day, they buried their dead. All was with quiet reverence, and even the Solway was without a stir. Sea of glass. Sky of calm.

Thomas, as part of the service, read the honour roll at the Abbey Church;

Geordie Reed, Soldier
A man, God's good servant, Brother Soldier
Cuthbert Fawsett, Allonby, Fisherman
Stephen Beeby, Allonby, Fisherman
Richard Pape, Mawbray, Fisherman
John Moss, Allonby, Swiller
Widow Penrise, Flimby, Seamstress
Meg Hayton, Allonby, Mother

Soldier was buried without his name in a quiet place, and Thomas prayed earnestly for his soul. Geordie Reed was buried with his cross of gold—a swill maker weaved it well from fine dry straw, and the Salty-man made sure he was laid close to his own kin, lost in life. Meg was laid to rest with her family, her cook's knife in her hand. Francis placed it that way, not for the anger she bore, but for the care she had offered, and now for the care she would give everlasting.

'She'll be washin' behind God's ears, and cookin' his dinner now,' announced Slack 'o' Jack to Francis with a kindly arm about his shoulders.

Francis was stolid. 'We won a good fight, eh, Slack 'o' Jack?'

Slack 'o' Jack looked around the crowd of people, three or four hundred strong, kneeling solemn before Thomas, leading in prayer. He looked to William Waite and his wife, the children all around him. He looked to the faces of family and their friends, and villages joined in union. All in prayer. All together.

'We won nothin', Francis.' And nodding his head to the crowd around them, he said, 'We won nothin'. They won it all.'

Chapter XXXVI

The Guest

The merchant in Annetwell Lane sponsored Mary and her tutor's visit. He paid, and as a guest of Lord Wharton, they lodged graciously within the walls of Carlisle Castle.

Mary was not for resting. Her resolve was strong. She would stand with her husband in life or death. Her fate would be decided with Jack's. Life lived long; love lasting, or death delivering two, hand-in-hand, into God's good care. But it was the Tutor's idea that Mary should rest a night in Carlisle before journeying on to Holm Cultram. He fretted over her decision for her safety's sake, but knowing Mary, he knew once her mind was decided all he could do was see her safe.

All was done to make Mary and the Tutor's stay a comfortable one; with fine beds provided, good food and pleasant company by way of the ladies of Lord Wharton's household. His ladies were more than pleased to occupy his guests, Mary being affable company and the Tutor being a very handsome and charming man. Even Lord Wharton greeted Mary like a long-lost daughter, and Mary in-turn was pleased to be greeted so.

Old friends make a good visit better, and another guest, a

familiar face atop brightly coloured clothes, reminded Mary of a time past with mother and sisters. She remembered pleasant company and engaging diversion. She remembered words the satin-clad gentleman offered to young girls, to her sisters, Edith and Eleanor, giggling and blushing at his assertion that they were women and should be treated so. Mary was ten-years old. Her tutor, twenty-five. And again, just as then, the Tutor seemed especially engaged with the gentleman, even more so than with Wharton's ladies, who fawned over the Tutor like he were a pile of pearls.

'It concerns me to hear *Jacques* faces such a trial… I will do all I can to help him.'

'Thank you. You were always his friend,' offered Mary, 'Could you not intercede with the Warden?'

'*Mais non*… The Warden is a man of singular determined thought… He would as readily punish *Jacques* as he would bear arms against these raiders… I fear Lord Wharton better ignorant than enlightened.'

Mary dropped her eyes to the floor then found a smile in a thought. 'Thank you, for your consideration. Jack has put much store in your wisdom of the world. I will do so also.'

'My consideration is such a small thing that it embarrasses me. So for your comfort and my embarrassment, I will ask you to remain here, *safe*, whilst my men go to furnish intelligences to better see you safe.'

'My safety is not my concern.'

'But it is my consideration, and in this I would make a larger contribution. My men are able, and I would see you safely delivered to your husband.' He straightened the rings on his hands, so each jewel on each finger lined up perfectly. 'Stay longer…. Let my men, send word to *Jacques* to have him greet you at Holm

Cultram, and let my men, able brawlers all, bolster his defence.'

Mary thought on the offer. And thought more men to Jack's cause be better assistance than his wife.

'I shall pray you get my message of love to him quickly.'

He removed a ring. It displeased him, for it shouted louder than the others on his perfectly manicured hands. He placed it on the table, discarding it.

A gift for he, or she, who should find it.

He looked at the Tutor sitting quietly at his place at the table, eyes to the oak. 'While I get a message to *Jacques*, would you, Edward, ensure Mary is comfortable here. And remains so until I say it is safe for her to travel?'

The Tutor kept his head down and sighed. He raised his head and smiled. 'I will.' nodding his agreement as a servant would acknowledge his master.

Mary smiled at the fine dressed gentleman's reddish-yellow suit, so well cut, so perfectly tailored. She admired his blue cloak, his feathered collar, his crested cap dyed to match his cloak. In this city he was like a prince in a pigsty. In this place she reminded him of a creature that sits aloft a riverbank perch to swoop and catch its prey. King of his domain, the perfect fisher—*the Kingfisher.*

Chapter XXXVII

As agreed, Robert Hardie, Jack's second, arrived in Holm Cultram ahead of the muster from Liddesdale and Annandale; only sixteen men in all. The men had missed the action at Allonby by four days, and Robert was happy to see Jack and the others safe.

Greetings between the men were warm and heartfelt, and Tom Kemp, riding with Robert, wasted no time in leaning out of his saddle to ruffle the hair of his captain.

'It's gud to see ye, Jack.'

'And you, Tom.

Jack's smile was not diminished by Tom's action. He was not belittled by it. Tom treated his captain as his captain when duty dictated, but often the affable Cumbrian still saw Jack as the young boy he had adopted into his generous heart, when he had reason to guard the callow youth interned within his previous master's keeping.

'How was Edinburgh?' asked Jack.

'The bitch, Marie of Guise is now Queen Regent. So yer da is convinced war is on its way.' Robert bid all the men behind him, men who had travelled far to avoid the Warden's watch, to dismount and seek comfort for themselves and their horses. Their clatter of steel and blatter of utensil rang around the ruined walls of the former Abbey house.

Jack knew all the fourteen men at Robert's command; all Border horse without exception. No boys. No greybeards. All keenly tested in skirmish and raid. All ideal for Jack's commission. But the numbers were light, and Jack initially sighed relief, for his commission was in doubt while he determined if his lady, Mary, would accompany him in his quest to France, or prefer to remain happy waiting for him to return. His commission relied on her will. Her wish was everything, even if he needed to turn away from Hueçon's assignment. But to do so would mean these men would need compensation. So fewer was better than more—*for the sake of Jack's purse.* But there again, France may be a place to suit Mary, and a commission in a French noble's keeping would see them both well. But in that case the numbers he had to call in times of war were lacking.

Jack counted again the men behind Tom and Robert.

'You seem to be travelling a little light.'

Tom smiled and then sighed. 'Aye, yer da got wind of the muster. He was none too fond of yer plans. Threatened any who joined us wi' eviction for their families… Still we have some good boys wi' us.' Tom handed Jack the muster roll, and Jack pushed it into his shirt without reading it.

'His blood was fair boilin' when we left,' added Robert, 'Ye be better of fightin' and diein' in France, cos yer da will be likely beatin' ye bloody if ye ever return.'

Jack smiled. 'Then I'll be facing his wrath sooner rather than later, as I'll be returning home now. I want to return to Mary, before anything else. I'm sorry for wasting your time and good nag-shoe-iron, but we'll be heading back.'

Robert looked at Tom, as if Tom would know better words

to say.

Jack did not see the look between the two men.

It was Robert who told Jack.

'Mary's nae at home waitin' fer ye. She left yer home seven days afore us, without announcing her journey or her reasons.'

'Where has she gone?' asked Jack, worried for his wife.

Again Robert looked to Tom for support. Tom simply shrugged his shoulders.

Robert hesitated, and then announced, 'I'm sorry, Jack, she's fled.'

'Fled?' Alarm coloured Jack's question.

'Aye, fled she has,' added Tom.

'Fled where too?'

Tom came in close to Jack, so that his words would be only shared between the two men. 'She had fallen foul of yer father. She had travelled with Will on a foolish errand to reason wi' the Warden and the Halls. Will was held for blackmail.' Tom put his hand on Jack's shoulder. 'Fortune smiles that gold was paid weeks back fer his release.'

'Aye, very fortunate, ' added Robert, 'especially when we learn of so many Hall kin bloodied by ye. Will's neck would have been stretched fer sure.'

Jack thought badly of Mary's vanity in thinking she could affect a solution, more so because Will's life was put at risk. 'Foolish lass,' he muttered.

Tom continued, 'Yer da took away Mary's privilege in his house, and cussed her badly fer her foolishness. Ye could not blame her fer running away.'

'I can, Tom,' replied Jack, 'her place is in my home. But I will find her.'

'There's mair,' announced Robert, 'She's ran away with the Tutor.'

Tom threw a look at Robert, to chastise words best left unsaid, but Robert simply shook his head at Tom.

Jack looked to the stone. To the Abbey Church. He looked anywhere that men's eyes could find his face. He hid his hurt with anger. He said nothing, but thought the worst of it. An unfaithful wife and betrayed by a friend. He was silent, and the other men waited on for Jack to speak. But Jack did not speak. He simply stood. The good of Mary did not find its way into Jack's reasoning, instead he covered his anger with his pride restored, and walked away.

An hour past, perhaps more, as Jack vented his hurt to the Plain. He did not seek out Thomas. He did not wish to hear good counsel, only his own words muttered to himself, as his wounded ego debated with his chilled empathy.

Without Mary to return to, France called Jack, and he was wanting. And so he turned out his men to seek the peoples about to join him in the adventure.

But none of the men of the Solway coast, who fought the fight, wished to travel on with Jack. They had their life well invested in their homes and families, and life would be better with a few less reivers to fear. Jack did not press any of the men to join him, for he understood.

There was much more the Solway men could lose than ever gain in war's bounty.

So that night, while the men rested, Jack took the muster roll given to him by Tom and wrote it out again, adding Bendback, Francis, Slack 'o' Jack and his own name to the roll.

And so Jack renewed his commission; a fight to find in France, set by Henri Hueçon.

<u>The Muster Role under John Brownfield, assigned troop captain</u>

Robert Hardie ~ Lanarkshire

Thomas Kemp ~ Cumberland

Ned Little {known as Tup Heid} ~ Dumfriesshire

James Nixon ~ Liddesdale

Henry Musgrave {known as Bendback Bob} ~ Cumberland

Edmund Turner ~ Liddesdale

James Clarey ~ Cumberland

Thomas Irvine {known as Pinchback} ~ Annandale

Stephen Howard ~ Carlisle

Henry Crosser {known as Digger Jack} ~ Liddesdale

Richard Hunter {known as Thumper} ~ Liddesdale

Francis Bell ~ Cumberland

Henry Gilchrist, {known as Windy Gilly} ~ Annandale

Robert Black {known as Slack o'Jack} ~ Annandale

Edward Irvine ~ Annandale

Finn McCuul ~ Carlow, Ireland

Henry Harden ~ Cumberland

Stephen Moffat ~ Dumfrieshire

Henry Nixon ~ Annandale

The next morning, in the half-light of dawn, after goodbyes were said and heart-felt partings offered, twenty men took to the path, that led to the road, that travelled South along the coast to Barrow and a boat to find, to take them to a better port for France.

The Girl ran with them for a league or more, her hand holding tight to Bendback's leg, her voice forever announcing plots and plans for Bendback's return, and where their home may be, and what they'd grow, and what they would sow for profit, and the names of their children, three. But they too parted and it was a sorrow to even wet Francis' eye.

'*Grit*, that's all,' he claimed.

There was discussion along the way, but Bendback was lost to it, and Jack too, abstained from contribution and questions. His eyes were closed, his mind walking the Solway sand and grassy Plain. His mind, cut by wounded pride, hoped to find peace again in the scent of the sea and sight of the sand. But hurt had its hold and he dismissed the thought of a better place for a bitter peace, and resignation to seek another place and forget Mary.

Then all discourse was gone, and all heads sank even though the sun shone and the wind was lazy.

Within a mile or two, or three more, they saw a shepherd amongst his flock, lying on a hillock, chewing a piece of bread and drinking his flask of beer. And as they filed by, they each had a thought to a shepherd's life. And in turn the shepherd had a thought for the procession that marred the Plain…

The Solway Plain was always a better place to be when the sun shone. Winter or summer, spring or autumn, there was very little sense of the discord that filled the world of man. There was only a sense of God's good work in his placing of his green, and tree, and sea.

All was perfectly set down for sheep, and the shepherding man loved the land and the bounty it provided. There was always good grass, with trees surrounding—filtering the wind that blew from the Solway Sea to the west, and from the Cumberland hills to the east.

The man on the plain was free of his troubles—nettling mother and quarrelsome wife. He could sing without censure, curse without rebuke, and scratch his nether places without scold. His sheep bleated a kindlier tune than his womenfolk. They caused him no pain, well not so much to cause him to cuss so bitter.

In all, the Plain held good things to quieten his mind, and to enrich the flavour of good bread made, and his beer to drink.

So with bread to scoff and beer to quaff, he lay on the grass, to look at his world, and to think on how to make it even better. He looked to the trees, the grass and the sky, and all was perfect, nothing he thought could make it finer. Then he looked to his shirt, patched and worn; his jerkin, cut and torn; and his hose, dirty, his codpiece stained; and then examined his poor brogues, rough and patched a dozen times more than his shirt. So he imagined himself in better boots, and then in hose of finer knit, a shirt of linen perhaps, and a doublet of better cut, and perhaps even a livery coat of fine colour—a soldier's coat. He thought some more on the soldier caste and the two-penny a week pay as a reward for wearing finer clothes, and polished steel to better see him safe, and so into reverie he went, marching proudly through his new imagined world, with strut and bluster.

Then perchance some horsemen came into view, carrying arms. *Soldiers in steel,* the man pondered. And he thought to hide, in case ill fortune was about to spoil his fine sunny day. But instead the shepherd stood his ground, and he counted, to be sure of their number. So when those who had a concern asked him, the information he gave would be true. He counted in shepherd tongue—shepherd count, *'Yan, t'yan, tethera, methera, pimp, sethera, lethera,* and even though more came into view he stopped at seven... and he thought to stop counting.

Men bearing arms on the road from the coast. From Allonby, perhaps, Flimby, Workington, or Mawbray, or Ellenborough even, all travelling to Barrow no doubt.

And as he studied the men further, he saw some had sad faces, drawn and grey, their jacks badly cut and their shields badly dented, and he thought, Glad I am to be a shepherd, free of troubles, with both a good mother and wife. I can sing without censure, curse without rebuke, and scratch my balls without scold. My sheep, my labour, bleat sweetly; they cause me no pain, well not so much to make me bitter.

[Jack and Mary's story continues under the title, ***Truth and Madness***.]

Epilogue

The breadcrumbs remained in her hand for only a moment. The wind made it so. She looked to their travel, as they found new ground to rest and birds to feed. And as she looked to the ground, another coin she found—a penny.

'God provides. A penny fer the poor. I shall buy more bread at Ellenborough. More food to see the hungry fed.'

The gentlemen waited on the answer to their question, but seeing their words may be lost on the old woman, they repeated them again. 'We are in search of a gentleman, a *Mr Senhouse.* We are told his hall is nearby. I'm afraid our escort boasts beyond his knowledge of the highways and byways in these parts, and has…' The older of the two gentlemen looked behind to see a sheepish man tending their horses, '…and has instead rendered us lost.'

The old woman smiled at the two men. 'Strangers to these parts are ye? Ye look like learned men.'

'We are scholars… of sorts,' offered the older man with a wry smile, 'We are seeking antiquities. My name is William Camden, and my young friend is Mr Robert Cotton. We survey the *Picts Wall* and the ruined and broken Roman walls running the Solway Coast. Do you know where Mr Senhouse keeps his hall? We understand him to be a fellow antiquarian.'

'Aye, I know it well. As I do all the homes and fields. All the hills and rivers.'

The younger of the two gentlemen turned to his companion to express his misgivings. 'I doubt, William, we'll find the proper way from this poor soul. Her wits are gone.'

The older gentleman, bore his frustration well, concern made it so. 'Do you need help, old woman? Can our horses carry your burden on? To your home, perhaps?'

'Kind sir. My bed is always the last house I find before dark finds me. I offer a penny or two for my lodging, but the folk about here never take it. I am never without food, or shelter. Never without a kind word given on the road, or a smile from the good folk who live in this land. I could find ye a bed nearby, but for well-dressed travellers such as ye… ye will find better cheer and comfort at John Senhouse's hall. He is a good man. Learned like you. A lover of all things old taken from the ground. His home has many such old stones, pagan altars and the like; all lifted from our earth. Artefacts found from the soil. I will show ye the way.'

The older gentleman smiled and gestured to his guide to bring up the horses, even though his companion looked warily.

'Do you trust this woman, William?' asked the younger gentleman.

'I do, Robert, I do.'

The woman smiled at the older gentleman, that earned a smile returned of both great warmth and comfort.

The party travelled down the lane towards the sea, to find the road that lead to Ellenborough, and the hall that stood nearby as the Senhouse seat.

As they walked, the younger gentleman felt sorry for the woman carrying her heavy burden, and offered to have her bundles carried on the horses. But she shook her head.

The bundles, fixed by ropes about her back, cut deep into the shoulders of the woman. Her load made worse, as her free arms clutched a small bundle as if she swaddled a baby to her breast.

'Please madam. Allow us to carry your bundle.'

'Please sir, I am strong enough… Once I used to run these lanes. Now I walk them instead. I carry clothes for the poor,' she hesitated, 'My love is coming back soon. Don't ye fret. He told me so.' She pushed her finger to her nose—a sign of a secret to keep. 'I have my white linen kept safe. I do not give that away. I keep that for myself and for my Henry, *my knight*.'

'What do you carry there?' said the young gentleman, pointing to her small bundle clutched tightly.

'It was my true ma's. She died ten, twenty…' the old woman pondered, 'What year is it?'

The young gentleman frowned at the old woman's frailty and her apparent senility. 'It is the sunset of the century, 1599.'

'Then she died twenty years back,' the old woman again pushed her finger to her nose. 'I thought I knew my ma. I did. But I learned she did not give me birth. She was only a kind, barren woman who kept me safe instead when my true ma could not.' She walked closer to the men, so only they could hear. 'She was a bride of Christ you know. She had her home in Holm Abbey. She had a vow of chastity to keep and a vow of charity to deliver. So now, I keep her baby safe and see to her good work in her stead.'

Author's Note

'Blending fact and fiction into a believable story is the joy. Separating fact and fiction within the historical fiction novel is the challenge.'

As introduced, this book is unashamedly a brief history-tour guide of only a small part of the Solway Coast, written by a writer with a selfish agenda. It perhaps, in terms of story, will neither be the most complex or perhaps most exciting tale of the Borderer Chronicles series, but in personal terms it will be the most important to me, as it embodies the prime reason for my work, that is, to promote the West Coast of Cumbria as a place to visit and its people to meet; a people most warm and engaging.

With three hundred years of border war, and dozens of well-documented reiver actions during the time of our fictional hero, it is perhaps perverse to write a totally fictional reiver action in an area of Cumberland that saw little of the privation and raid that blighted the Borders.

The story leans more towards the English side of the Solway, mainly because it's the ground I know well, and secondly, because I only wished to journey along the

Scottish coast to contrast the nature of the opposing sides of the Solway; one quarrelsome, the other better at peace with itself.

I have portrayed the nature, industry and circumstance of the Scottish and English sides of the Solway using contemporary reports of the period. Although I must admit that period extends at least fifty years both sides of our story's time, in order to glean records enough to paint a likeness of the time and include the local stories of the day. Perhaps it is a painting in abstract, because I can only imagine the colour and form of the time, and even through archaic writings, it is hard to sense the true atmosphere of the place, as record then, as now, is tainted by the author's skill and agenda.

Language used of course is modern in its creation, and I have blended dialect, terms and names from antiquity with modern understanding and tagging, simply to help the book become more accessible, as contemporary writings are often indecipherable without an academic understanding of regional dialect and spelling.

For this reason I have used modern place names, as the names written in the sixteenth century will be often found spelled as the author understands them. Local pronunciation will in turn lead the places to be spelled as they sound. Kirkcudbright is spelled in sixteenth century official council documents as *Kirkcudbryt*, but is also seen to be written as *Kirk-coo-bree*, which probably better reflects local pronunciation—border pronunciation that stands today. So to avoid confusion, I have used modern tags for all, much to my disappointment, as archaic place titles are often far more poetic in their archaic calling.

Research for the story was a challenge, as often there are significant gaps in sixteenth century local record, especially with perpetually occurring raids and war. These frays tended to leave behind a scorched earth policy, and so more local and personal records tended to be burnt. But where record exists, it has inspired the elements of the story; including the theft of the bells of Bowness; pirates raiding a ship bound for Workington, supplying the ore mines of the Cumberland mountains; letters appertaining to the burning of a church by a careless worker, who in turn tried to malign another; household accounts of a sixteenth century Border lord, showing five thousand fir saplings ordered for planting; a sixteenth century Korean mummy discovered to have Hepatitis B (Soldier's ailment); Manor records from Holm Cultram, and Kirkcudbright's own town council minutes.

I often read such antiquarian official records with a cautious eye. After spending most my working life in Public service, and with a million words written by myself as record, and making decision over a million more read, could I say every record was true and factual, not tainted with bias, and self-agenda?

I was particularly intrigued to read Kirkcudbright's own council records. And in a time when it was the way to use ten words where one would do (and perhaps still is, especially within pubic record, written by bureaucrats without an economy of language, or clarity), it sits strange in amongst the lines upon lines dedicated to seemingly trivial matters, that where a seemingly important issue is recorded (one involving a substantial sum of money, or transference of land), there exists the merest acknowledgment of the decision and agreement. Perhaps one with a conspirator's mind may read more into what's unwritten rather than what's written. And so reading archaic record, one must be aware what is written is rarely full fact, but occurrence tainted perhaps with a bias view.

I ask forgiveness from the Hall's of Kirkcudbright for using them in such a nefarious way. Hall's did live in Kirkcudbright at the time of our story, as they did both sides of the border, some as reivers, but I have no knowledge that the Hall's of Kirkcudbright were either pirates or reivers. Hall is simply a local 'reiver' name plucked for reasons of fiction.

There is no record of Allonby ever been attacked in the sixteenth century, although the Abbey at Holm Cultram was a significant target in medieval times. It seems that Allonby has lived in peace all of its life. Peace and quiet *on Solway sand.*

Mark Montgomery, Author, MMXIV (2014)

THERE *was a time when Solway sand was golden, when man had not coloured it dark with spoil from the earth; debris from the spoils of wealth; from coal, iron, and sulphates. When man's wealth was formed by faith and the toil of his labours. When the Church had industry, wealth and charity given over three hundred years in wool and trade.*

There was a time the Solway was rich and not poor, when the land was not conquered by government or greed.

There was a time when to think of a Cumbrian, was not a paint a pretty picture, not to think of shepherds and sheep, mountain and lake, but to think of greatness bound in history, by the tribe who resisted Celtish ways, and Roman *and* Norman *subjugation. When to be Cumbri born was to be proud, and only the Vikings, they akin to a canny trader and canny thinker, could call them friend.*

There was a time justice was poorly applied, when men were not equal. There was a time…

Historical Note

For much of the thirteenth century, there was peaceful coexistence between Anglo-Scottish Borderers. Conflict in the borders was first truly nurtured with Edward 1 in 1296, and the English monarch's policy of aggression towards Scotland, as he sought to annexe it into is own kingdom. And from then on, for the next three hundred years in fact, while separate monarchs ruled the two realms, the Borders were racked by bouts of raiding and war.

Both sides plundered the other mercilessly. Border life, once prosperous, became hard and many were reduced to poverty as the people, both sides of the border, found subsistence farming impossible to maintain in a war-zone. It was no wonder the peoples of the Borders took to robbery to survive.

But it is clear the Marches were not all victim to the times. There is little evidence of raid deep into the Solway Plain on the English side, and whereas Northumberland and the lands North of Carlisle bore raid and rapine, most of the West Coast of Cumberland saw a relative peace, and its industry, once greater under the management of the great abbey houses, still thrived in the shadows of the turmoil of the Borderlands.

This can be seen by the stark contrast and power of the defensive towers of the Borders, particularly in Northumberland and Scotland, and the 'softer' homes of those on the Solway Plain. Curwen's Hall in Workington and Netherhall, near Ellenborough, saw little or no action and attack. And so in these places, the once defensive pele towers developed into more comfortable homes for gentlemen and their families. Medieval castles and towers, built at more defensive sites were abandoned, as homes for the knights of the day were built in more pleasant locations. Even Wolsty Castle, supposedly built to defend the Abbey of Holm Cultram (but perhaps built better to suit its first occupant rather than as a defensive keep for the Abbey), was left to decay.

Today there is little evidence of the great towers of the English West Marches, and the once Tudor power-house of industry, Cumberland and the Solway coast, with its mining, salt production, fishing, coal and its once reputation as the second largest wool-producer in England, is but a faint shadow of its former self.

Journeying down the Solway coast today, one can still get the sense of the beauty of the coastline. Indeed, an area from Rockcliffe, near Carlisle, to Maryport is designated as an area of outstanding natural beauty, one of only 49 in England, Wales and Northern Ireland. Travelling the whole coast, however, it's sometimes hard to see, as hundreds of years of industry as marred some of its beauty. The condition of the whole Solway coast per-industrial age was, as put by John Cunningham, a sixteenth century traveller of the day, *'A beauty to widen the eyes and fill the spirit and cause a smile, all the way from Carlisle to Barrow.'*

Travelling the coast today, one can still see there must have been more than economic and defensive reasons why the great abbey houses were established and thrived on the Solway Plain. More than good land and fishing that saw the Vikings establish themselves on the Cumberland coast. It was perhaps what Alan, the twelfth century Anglo Saxon Lord of Allerdale saw, as he gave his name to Allonby, after finding comfort in his melancholia. Something greater than man… perhaps a greater sense of God.

Reference Works and Places to Visit

References Works.

- The Steel Bonnets, The Story of the Anglo-Scottish Border Reivers, George MacDonald Fraser (1971)
- The Solway Firth, Brian Blake (1955)
- The Border Reivers, Godfrey Watson (1974)
- Life and Tradition in the Lake District, William Rollinson (1981)
- The Reivers, Alistair Moffat (2007)

Places to Visit

- Tullie House Museum, Carlisle City, CA3 8TP
- Holm Cultram Abbey, Abbeytown, CA7 4SP
- Senhouse Museum, Maryport, CA15 6JD
- Carlisle Castle, Carlisle City, CA3 8UR
- The Citadel, Carlisle City, CA3 8NA
- Curwen Castle, Workington, nr CA14 4AS
- Milecastle 51, Saltpans, Maryport
- The Stewartry Museum, Kirkcudbright, DG6 4AQ
- Caerlaverock Castle, Dumfries and Galloway, DG1 4RU
- The Solway Coast Discovery Centre, Silloth, CA7 4DD

Websites

- Solway Plain - past and present – Holme St Cuthbert History Group.

Made in the USA
Lexington, KY
09 August 2019